HARLEM BLUES

Harlem Blues

ISBN: 978-1482359336

Me, Malcolm and Langston

I've been here in the Mecca of Black America for close to fifty years. That's right I've lived most of my day's right here on these dirty, grimy, streets of Harlem and loved every single, solitary minute of it. And during this time, I've had the rather unique opportunity of seeing a little bit of everything when it comes to Black folks. In a way, I guess I've been blessed to have the chance to observe, analyze, and evaluate Black folks as well as anyone since Malcolm and Langston took up the task some years back.

Similar to Langston, who lived only a few short blocks away, I studied Black folks right here in the Harlem community. Yet, unlike Langston who observed solely for the purpose of his journalistic pursuits; I chose to study Black folks around me to not only get a better understanding but also to enlighten the rest of the nation about a group of people disenfranchised and who, for all intensive purposes, were thrown away and all too often forgotten by the larger community.

Still, what makes this study so doggone interesting is that despite Black folks being left out in the cold and all the hardships that have befallen them, they've not only managed to survive they've actually thrived under these very adverse conditions. Not only that, they've evolved into an integral, and influential part of the larger community that was and still is so intent on destroying them. Now, that's really something if you stop to think about it.

Langston drew upon his observations and experiences and documented his findings in a daily column, behind the guise of a rather simple minded fellow aptly named Simple. Simple's depiction of Harlem was if nothing else colorful and I credit Langston with being our first true Harlem anthropologist. Langston was the first person I ever encountered to observe, analyze and document at least a segment of the rich culture that was and is Harlem and its populace.

In my lifetime, and because of my own research I made it a point to read every one of Langston's or better yet Simple's portrayal of life up here in Harlem and found much of it to be required reading if you were going to study Harlem Negroes and were intent on living here, working here and maintaining your sanity. But Langston's, Simple was written close to fifty years ago and many of his findings haven't stood the test of time although his writing is still eloquent. His Simple portrayal was, at best, just what it was intended to be; simple, if not trendy. Problem is, we've evolved as a people and simple was just that. Simple.

3

He was too simple to be representative of the evolution and makeup of such a complex group of people.

In my tenure as an anthropologist, I've found that we are, too wide, too diverse a group for any one man to draw a complete, meaningful study in an attempt to analyze and draw a composite of us as a people. Perhaps a committee of well known anthropologists, such as myself, familiar with the subject would be better in attempting to gain these ends. There may even be a need for some discussion to plot a suitable course of action should we attempt doing so. This after all is no easy undertaking but a Herculean task that I have attempted.

The only other person that I would credit with even attempting to get a handle on the dynamics of Harlem and its' inhabitants is Malcolm who compiled a fairly comprehensive study of the inner workings of the community and its people during his brief time on 125th Street and while ministering at Temple #9 during the late Fifties and early Sixties prior to his assassination.

Malcolm's findings are pretty comprehensive though not quite as in depth as I would like for them to be because his concentration was not concerned with just Harlem and her inhabitants but with Black folks in general and the nation as a whole. That being as it may, Malcolm did us a great service by just bringing the plight of Harlemites and Black folks as a whole to the forefront.

However, if we consider the task to be Herculean in attempting to cover Harlem's inhabitants then think of the task at hand when attempting to cover and analyze the Negro population as a whole. Still, he produced a body of work, second to none and had a firm grasp on the heartbeat of Negro sentiment and conveyed it with eloquence to the nation at large.

If I have one complaint, one beef, with Malcolm's work as an anthropologist in the true sense of the discipline it's that Malcolm could not separate himself from the control group he was studying. Malcolm loved Black folks so much that he could not separate himself and thus could not produce an unbiased study. That is not to say that he did not embody all that we are as a people but his love was so that he could see no negatives in our culture as a whole. Or if he did – and I'm sure he was aware of the fact that we have one or two minor deficiencies—his intentions were to unite us, to build our pride and self-esteem as a people and therefore it would have been self-defeating to dwell on or to portray us in a negative sense.

After all, in Malcolm's eyes we were already beaten down enough by sufficient forces that I'm sure that he saw no point in beating a dead horse. And by the time Elijah called Malcolm from the temple in Harlem to lead the Nation of Islam nationally Malcolm had traveled enough recognize that Black folks problems in Harlem were neither unique nor innate to Harlem but were common in Black folks in America as a whole. And so he began to generalize and Harlem lost its' own rather unique uniqueness and became simply a microcosm of the Negro problem at large as far as Malcolm was concerned.

Understand, however, that I still consider Malcolm to be one of our greatest and perhaps one of the greatest Negro anthropologists that has ever lived, and that includes yours truly. I must also say this on Malcolm's behalf. The fact that Malcolm suffered so and gave his life for the portrayal of his subjects has to put him at the head of his class. I'm not sure that I would do the same even as impassioned as I am about my work.

The only other flaw I find with Malcolm's study is his technique. The minute he became involved and impassioned surrounding the plight of his people was the same day he lost the ability to view them objectively. He became so intertwined with their predicament that he became bitter for a time and this more than anything may have led him to such an untimely demise.

That's why I make sure that I keep a bottle of Richard's Wild Irish Rose with me at all times. A lot of people are unaware that I am an anthropologist, a scientist by nature. Most people only see

an old man with a bottle of cheap wine at his disposal and want to refer to me as a lush or a wino. I find this extremely offensive but feel there is no need for a response.

What they don't realize is that the Rose is there purely for the purpose of me pursuing my studies with an air of objectivity. It is an instrument essential in my work. It is no more than a tool of research that refuses to allow me to become too involved and often times gives me an air of ambiguity allowing me to remain aloof.

Just as a biologist must use a microscope to view his specimens more clearly and an astronomer a telescope to view distant constellations. It is also imperative that I have Richards to gain a clear view of my subject without being jaded in my analysis and evaluation.

The Richards is also there as a buffer, so that I'm not caught up in my surroundings as was Malcolm and like I said is no more than a tool that I use so I don't become affected and infected by whatever it is that ails those around me.

Just as a surgeon uses gloves and a surgical mask to keep germs and infection at bay so do I use Richards. That way I can remain aloof and objective. If I didn't, chances are I would fall prey to everything that affects my people. I first learned this during the war when the Gerry's were shelling us with everything they had at their disposal when we first hit the beaches of Normandy. I was just a kid then and had a hard time trying to understand why someone was trying to kill me that I'd never said as much as hello to. Yet, here they were trying to kill me.

When I started to see my buddies dyin' around me I really had difficulty comprehending and began having terrible nightmares at which time I was told that I was taking this whole war thing way too seriously and what I needed was a buffer to keep some of the shit that was going through my mind at bay so it didn't consume me.

It was at this time that I was introduced to the grape and as it worked well at the time as a shield against the war and what I termed man's inhumanity to man, it has since then allowed me to view things from afar with a certain degree of aloofness and objectivity without getting caught up in the fray. It also eases the pain caused from a terminal case of racism which I contracted upon my birth.

Aside from that though, I have used it solely for utilitarian and scientific purposes ever since. Most people are not aware of this but that's another story entirely. Of course, there are side effects. The most obvious side effect is that I often tend to ramble, digress and be somewhat repetitive at times, although this may also be caused by age and the fact that I have a slight case of Alzheimer's.

Being that as it may, I hope that you will bear with me as I embark on my journey. On my journey I will present a few of the case studies I've compiled of Harlem Negroes over the years and perhaps you'll be able to better understand the beauty of such a rich cultural heritage. At other times, I will address some of the seamier sides of life as we know it and perhaps then you'll truly be able to better understand my affinity for the grape. This study which I present to you now is incomplete and involves just a few of the participants which accounted for my control

group. Some are involved in simple scenarios I've observed from afar with, as yet, no logical conclusion. They are still considered works in progress. Others are mere glimpses of lives which I've encountered in my seventy odd years that stood out in my mind for one reason or another.

The honorable Reverend Barnes, a local minister, has approached me on several occasions surrounding the documentation of my life and my case studies and although I hardly feel compelled, he insists that my studies be documented if for no more than—as he puts it—posterities sake.

I am, therefore, with the help of Sister Gerty putting my research studies on paper, beginning with an introduction of myself and how I come to get my name. If at any time you find that I lose you or happen to digress I apologize and hope that you bear with me and realize that at the time that I am writing this I am an old man with a certain affinity for the grape and perhaps a mild case of Alzheimer's. But let me not digress any further. Let me begin by introducing myself and explain to you how I come to get my name.

How I Come To Get My Name

Most people who know me call me William. Other people call me 'Willie'. A lot of people out here in these streets, who see me every day but don't really know me from Adam, call me 'Willie the Wino'. When I first heard that it used to really bother me but I don't really pay it no mind, no more. It's mostly the younguns' what calls me that anyway but like I said I don't pay 'em much mind for the most part.

Half of these younguns' that's runnin' around here callin' people names and actin' half crazy ain't got the sense they was born with no how. They're a lost generation if you ask me. Most of 'em don't know where they come from or where they're going. Hell, I've forgotten more in my lifetime than most of 'em will ever come to know.

And I'll tell you what, at first it really used to bother me. It really used to tug at my crotch hairs but like I've said I've gotten to the point where it really doesn't bother me all that much anymore. After all, you gotta look at the source. Most of there momma's and daddy's is ignorant as well and like my old grand pappy use to say the fruit never falls far from the tree so I don't pay 'em much mind. Now, whenever I hear somethin' I consider disrespectful from 'em, I just look 'em square in the eye and tell 'em to have respect for their elders. But I'm starting to realize that in order to have any respect for their elders they have to have some respect for themselves and most of 'em don't have any respect for themselves so I just leave 'em alone. But I still watch 'em. And I don't just watch 'em I watch 'em closely. But then I watch everybody. You see that's what I do. I study people. I observe 'em the same way a scientist observes rats in

a lab although I must admit that that is a very poor analogy except when referrin' to these younguns that is. In their case there are some definite similarities. Most of the time they just go scurrying around here with no rhyme or reason, almost aimlessly.

For better comparison I would have to liken myself to that there white woman, who spent a lifetime travelin' around the world to study the different varieties of Black folks. Do you remember when she over to Australia to study them Negroes over there in the Outback. That's the name they give it over there in

Australia when you ain't in a house but prefer to live out back in the woods somewheres. Anyway, she studied every aspect of those Black folks lives then documented it and brought it back to share with the rest of the world most of whom didn't know Black folks existed in that part of the world. I'm referring to Margaret Meade in case you didn't know. She was like the Jacques Cousteau of indigenous people.

After she got finished over there in the Australian Outback she went south to find some new Negroes. And I don't mean down to Alabama or Mississippi somewhere. I mean she went all the way south to where she could find some altogether new Negroes. And that took her to the rainforests of South America. Yeah, you didn't know they had Negroes there too, now did you? Anyway, her travels took her all the way down to the rainforests of the Amazon River Basin.

Of course, she could have probably found the same thing right here somewhere off the coast of South Carolina or even up here in Harlem where you've got more Negroes per square mile than anywhere else in the world but for some reason she decided to go traipsing down to South America. And from what I understand she lived with 'em for quite a spell too. From what I've

read and I've read somewhat extensively on the subject she ate with 'em, slept with 'em and everything. Anything they did, she did right with 'em in attempt to learn about them and their culture. Well, almost everything. I really don't think she actually slept with 'em. I think she slept among them, if you get my drift. Her sleepin' with Black folks wasn't what you would call real popular back in them days. If she had slept with them she would have not only have lost her job but her credibility as well. Now that's not to say that she didn't. But if she did there wasn't a word written about that.

In any case, that's neither here nor there. In fact, going off on that tangent only goes to show that only shows that I tend to drink a little too much and sometimes have a tendency to digress a bit too much. Anyway, I read a good deal about her and her work back in the fifties and early sixties when I was studying up at Columbia University.

Yeah, I spent quite a deal of time up at Columbia taking classes when it got too cold to panhandle outside. You see, I did a little panhandlin' up there to augment my income after the war 'cause the little bit of benefits the army bestowed on me couldn't feed me, let alone pay my rent. Anyway, while I was up there, I became increasingly interested in the field of anthropology and Miss Meade's work in particular. Yet, I had a most difficult time trying to understand why with close to two and a half million Negroes right here in Harlem she felt so compelled to go traipsing all over the world to study them when here they were right here in her own backyard. I never did quite figure that one out although I certainly had my suspicions.

Still, I knew what a gold mine I had at my disposal even if she didn't and I was hell bent on studying these Black folk right here to see exactly what it was that made them tick. So, with that in mind, I decided to carry on her work and went about setting up shop right here on the corner of 135th and Lenox. And here is where I began my own in-depth study. Now in my fifty some odd years of bein' out here I've compiled a body of work that would rival anything Miss Meade has done and leave her gasping for air.

A good deal of my work is anecdotal, a hodgepodge of character sketches which will require me to categorize and analyze them at a later date. But for the time bein', they are what they are, a kaleidoscope of glimpses, a collage of lives that blended together in a sweet cacophony of sounds and rhythms and heartbeats pulsating individually and collectively make up Harlem. They are twisted and funny and heart rendering depictions of people that I've come to know over the years and the first one I'd like to share with you is the story of my friend Sweet and the time he came home from work and found his no-good wife, Wilomena cheating on him. This was, oh, I'd say close to ten or twelve years ago. But before I begin I have to tell you that I'm damn near eighty years of age and all too often tend to have a hard time staying on-topic so please bear with me.

In any case, ol' Sweet and I have been friends since I first arrived in Harlem some sixty some odd years ago and he's always been one of the warmest, friendliest guys you'd ever wanna know. Now, I guess ol' sweet stood somewhere in the neighborhood of six-four or six-five and weighed close to two hundred and fifty pounds and posed quite an imposing figure. And yet, he was one of the sweetest, gentlest guys you'd ever wanna know. Well, that was until he got mad.

10

But in all the time I knowed him I ain't seen him get upset but once. But I heared him tell of how he got more than a little upset when he was livin' in Decatur, Georgia when some ol' red-necked farmer accused Sweet of stealin' some of his precious peaches and from what I heared Sweet all but dismembered that cracker.

A day or so later he arrived in Harlem. Still, I can't really say that I witnessed him getting' angry with anyone. To tell the God's honest truth, I can't even recall Sweet saying a harsh or a derogatory word about anyone in the entire time I've knowed him. And by the same token, I've never heard anyone say a bad word to him although bein' the size he is I don't think that would have been too wise a move. Now that I'm thinkin' about it, not only didn't he say a harsh word, I hardly ever heard him say a word, period. Of course everyone that knew Sweet attributed that to the fact that Wilomena, that was his wife, talked enough for both of them.

Ol' Sweet didn't seem to much mind though and when I'd see him down there at Small's Paradise on the weekends, Wilomena would be there in all her finery just a rantin' and a ravin' and goin' on and on about nothin'. Either that or she'd get to ramblin' on about whatever happened to enter that little mind of hers after a couple of drinks. And Sweet would just sit there and grin, almost like he was just glad to be going along for the ride. Boy, talk about undying love and devotion. Sweet really loved that woman.

Sometimes he'd invite me over and I'd join them. I always had an open invitation anyway, but most of the time I'd just sit back and take it all in from a distance. You see that's what a good anthropologist does. He sits back and listens and observes. You see a good anthropologist must

be most careful not to disturb the dynamics of the group that he's observing. Then when he's finished he can document his observations from an unbiased standpoint and can make a true and unbiased judgment since he in no way altered the control group. That's why I kept my distance. Well, that and the fact that I couldn't stand sweet's wife, Wilomena.

Anyway, to make a long story short, I'm sittin' back jotting down a mental note or two. You see, I've never been one to use pencil and paper. That's not to say that I don't have the ability, per se. It's just that I was taught early on in my career about the old African rote tradition that was used throughout history and has been lost for the most part. And when I first arrived in New York my first job was working for a Jamaican numbers runner one generation removed from West Africa, and with him came the old ways. One of the first things he instilled in me was that we had the capacity for memorization and that for centuries, our history was told to him only from memory. That was the Africans passed down traditions and as well as our history orally.

They would have considered it an insult to have depended on pen and paper to memorize anything. And if I considered running numbers for him I'd better not think about writing anything down. I didn't understand at the time and didn't think much about it but every year around election time when the police would get to harassin' us to let the good citizens know that they were out there, on top of things and doing their job I realized the importance of the rote tradition. And while all the other numbers runners were bein' hauled downtown to be made an example of we were still out there hustlin' and getting paid. And not a single solitary one of us ever spent a day in the pokey. No sir. And do you know why? No physical evidence, that's why.

Anyway, getting back to my boy Sweet. That wasn't his real name as you've probably figured, just like mine ain't Willie. In fact before I even get started talkin' about Sweet and the situation he found himself in let me introduce myself properly.

My real name is Henry Wadsworth Longfellow III. My mother named me right before she passed away right after giving birth to me, her only son. My daddy used to tell me that my mother was a very well- educated woman and was real fond of the written word and especially English Literature. I believe that's where I got my proclivity for reading and knowledge so she named me after William Wordsworth and Henry Wadsworth Longfellow.

Well, that's what my daddy told me and that may have been true except for a couple of things. First of all, I'm not the first, but the third, following in a long tradition of at least three generations of family members with the same name. Besides, my grandfather who was the son of a slave and who raised me down in

12

Natchez, Mississippi, among other places, after my dear mother passed away tells me a completely different story on how I come to get my name and be known as William Longfellow III. And I think he would probably know best since we share the same name. Besides, the way he explained it to me makes a whole lot more sense than what my father tol' me. And since it was a well-known fact that my daddy had an affinity for fabricatin', it was just hard to believe that that's how I come to get my name. My grandfather, on the other hand, had no reason to lie to me.

Like I was sayin, my grandfather was the son of a slave and the way he tells it seems a might more believable. Seems that when his daddy, my great grand pappy arrive here in America, the

overseer had a particularly hard time pronouncin' his African name, like he did most of the African's names so he waited until he could get a firm grip on a particular slave's attributes and then just like that he'd hang a moniker on him. Well, it seems that the overseer got around to naming all the slaves that worked for him except for my great grand pappy who was a pretty quiet fellow. You know the kind that you wouldn't notice if he was standing in a crowd or standing by himself.

Now the way the story that my great grand pappy was not a particularly large man, nor a particular hard worker, but was never really a problem for the overseer. He put in his hours, giving the absolute minimum effort required as he went about is daily tasks but since there were so many other Negroes on the plantation and since he hardly ever gave the overseer a lick of trouble he was for the most part overlooked.

In fact, the other slaves used to tease him about never having to run away since no one knew he was there anyway. That's how inconspicuous my great grand pappy was. In fact, if it weren't for the night time and for the other slaves complaining about the noise coming from his quarters he may have kept his African name and identity for his entire lifetime.

But those silly-assed Uncle Tom slaves, always trying to get a leg up and score points with the master went to see the overseer on more than one occasion to complain about the hoopin' and hollerin' comin' from my great grand pappy's shack each and every night. Well, being that the master was havin' a bumper

13

crop that year and cotton sales were good he and his overseer were quite willing to overlook a few complaints from a few sorry, shiftless ass, lyin' Negroes who

were always looking for any excuse to escape the stifling summer heat which greeted them without fail each sunrise in the fields of Natchez, Mississippi.

Now, from what my grand pappy tells me, there were close to a thousand slaves on this here plantation which ran close to ten thousand acres. And so you can see from the sheer magnitude that keepin' tabs on each and every slave was no small task. And from what I hear the numbers were increasing daily. You see back then, there wasn't no TV and therefore there wasn't much for a Negro to do but increase in numbers.

In fact, they said one ol' Negro slave named Mandy had somewheres around forty-seven children between there and the neighboring plantations. Forty-seven children...I have a hard time just imagin' that, even though, I wouldn't have much minded the practice.

In any case, the master and his overseer had their hands full as you can much imagine, but things ran pretty smoothly just the same. Everyone stayed pretty busy with pickin' cotton and croppin' tobacco and makin' sure that everything was done to the master's specification. (That was the overseer's job making sure everything was done right.)

So, a few niggras grumbling and complainin' about some niggra they couldn't even identify by name went virtually unnoticed and pretty much fell on deaf ears. You see they couldn't identify my great grand pappy because in all the hullabaloo surrounding the running of a plantation that size the overseer had completely forgotten about giving him a name. So, when his neighbors from the quarters went up to the big house to see the overseer and file their complaints about all

the commotion comin' from his one cabin every night all they could say was, 'Uhh, master, you know the niggra we're talkin' about' or 'you know the one, suh, the one you always be callin'   boy'.

14

Well, with close to a thousand hands on deck and 'boy' and 'niggra' bein'
common phraseology for the overseer he knew no more when the complaint was
filed than he did when they left. Still, as anyone familiar with the techniques of
good management knows, the overseer promised to look into it.

When another slave approached him a few days later with the same complaints
of screaming and yelling in the middle of the night the overseer thinking that
there might just be some credibility to the reports decided that he better check it
out before word got back to the master. But when the slave could not identify
the culprit any better than the others that preceded him the overseer became
quite cross.

"Well, boy what's the niggra's name causin' all this ruckus down in the
quarters?" he asked.

"Why, suh, the way I hear it told me, you ain't never git aroun' to namin' him,
suh," the slave replied.

"Well can you tell me what the niggra looks like?"

"Gee, massa that's hard to say bein' that we all looks alike," the slave replied.

"Well, where does the niggra live then? Can you at least tell me that there,
boy?"

Being that all of the slave quarters were lined up side by side in rows much like
the row houses found in Philadelphia and Chicago and New York nowadays the
slave could hardly distinguish between them.

"Tell me boy, is it in the third or fourth row of shacks?" the overseer asked his
patience wearing thin.

The slave noticing his master's disgust dropped his head and was soon sorry
he'd burdened the poor master with so little to go on.

"Why, massa, suh you know a niggra can't read or write and Lord knows I can't
count no rows," he replied, ashamed that he had once again been a
disappointment to the overseer he tried   so hard to impress.

15

"But if you like, suh, I can show you exactly where that fool niggra lives. I'd be much obliged if you'd follow me, suh," the slave continued knowing all the while he was treading on thin ice now. But he was at his wit's end; a good night's rest had become an anomaly and always a dependable field hand his work had slipped noticeably in recent weeks. By this time the overseer was fit to be tied and not overly impressed by the slaves' tale especially since he could tell him almost nothin' of this phantom of the night.

In his nightshirt when the slave arrived, he was not moved by the tale and chalked the whole affair up to a few connivin' niggras getting together to lessen their workload the following day

by attributing their overall sluggishness and lack of productivity in the fields to some mystical niggra that screamed and hollered the whole night through.

By this time the overseer was quite agitated and having lost all interest turned his thoughts to ol' Belle's daughter, who had grown into a rather attractive wench over the last year or so. She had to be damn close to fourteen or fifteen years of age. He wondered why he hadn't noticed her sooner. But now that he had and he summoned her to his quarters to break her in before one of them young bucks got a hold to her pretty little ass or the master himself caught sight of her.

She was after all Belle's daughter and it hadn't been that long ago that Belle had been the apple of his eye. And even though it had been some time ago, he still remembered Belle as if it were yesterday. Oh, he'd had the occasion to sleep with many a comely wench since Belle but hadn't met a one yet, young or old that could a candle to Belle in the bedroom.

The fact that Belle's daughter may very well have been his daughter mattered little to the overseer. He only hoped that she had inherited her mother's prowess in the bedroom. Besides that there was no way he was gonna ride all the way down to the quarters searchin' for some no name niggra havin' nightmares. What he wanted more than anything, right then and there, was for that simple spook who stood before him to go back down to the quarters so he could relax and enjoy what was left of his night in   peace.

16

Truth be told, he really didn't care how loud the niggas screamed as long as he was up at sunrise and gave a hundred and ten percent in the field the followin' day. In his eyes, all they were was animals anyway, no more and no more less than the oxen that pulled the plow or the team of

horses that pulled the mistress in her carriage. Each of them had a job to do and by God as long he was runnin' the show they were damn well gonna do it.

The overseer viewed himself as a fair man. He didn't whip the horses when they whinnied. And he didn't cuss the cock when it crowed at the crack of dawn and he sure wasn't gonna say nothin' to a screamin', howlin', cussin' niggra as long as he did what he was s'pozed to do in the fields. What he did on his own time was that niggra's business. Why he couldn't even contemplate chastisin' a niggra for screamin' at the nightmare that was his very existence. That's how fair-minded the overseer was.

Peering over the head of the slave still standing before him in search of Belle's daughter he wondered where in the hell she could possibly be. When he saw that she was nowhere in sight he became enraged at the thought of this little wench even considerin' standin' him up and was just about to lash out at the slave who still stood in front of him when somethin' the niggra said caught his attention.

"Massa suh, you don't understand. It's like they holdin' some kinda church revival or secret prayer meetin' up there. I ain't rightly sure if it ain't one of them voodoo rit'chals them heathen Africans is so fond of. All I know is it be different voices every night screamin' stuff like, 'Praise the Lord' and 'thank you, Jesus'. Or, 'thank you Jesus for the gifts you done bestowed on me tonight'. That's what they be sayin'. And, 'the Lord sure is good to me'. Sometimes I even hear them say, 'I knows I done found heaven'. Now I ask you massa, what slave workin' in the fields from can't see in the mornin' 'til can't see at night in this here Mississippi sun can

rightfully say he done found heaven? Anyway, then the hollerin' stops for a few minutes before the screamin' commences again. Now, I asks you suh, how's a niggra s'pozed ta get some shut-eye and commence to laborin' hard for you in the field, with all that nonsense goin' on every night?"

Belle's daughter's arrival was soon a distant thought. Hell, maybe there was something to these niggra's claims. It wasn't too long ago that some uppity niggra from North Carolina claimin' to be a preacher had the niggras risin' up and attackin' every god fearin' white folk they could lay their dirty Black hands on. By the time the whole upspring had been quelled, close to sixty innocent law abidin' White folks had been murdered in their beds while they slept.

The same thing would've happened in Charleston, South Carolina if it hadn't been for the good sense of a few good, responsible niggras warning their masters about the impending uprising. That's why the owners amended the slave codes forbidding niggras to congregate even when it came to worshippin' the Lord.

Well, it wasn't going to happen here thought the overseer sending the slave on his way and awakening the plantation owner. But as it was still early and all the reports claimed that the screams came in the middle of the night the two men decided to bide their time. At somewhere around one a.m. the two men, the mass and the overseer harnessed one of the mules to the buggy and headed down past the lower forty acres to the ragged rows of slaves shacks known as the quarters. No sooner had they arrived, a Colt forty-five revolver in one hand and a carbine in the other, they were met with the shrillest of screams. Not long before one spine-chilling scream

commenced then another would begin and in between some mention of the Lord. It was just as the ol' niggra slave had recounted it.

"Lord, God help me," came the scream followed by, "' Jesus sure is good to me!"

Convinced, they were in the midst of some voodoo ritual the two men made their way to the edge of the tiny, one-room, log cabin and peered through the slats in the wooden door only to find my great grand pappy lyin' on the bed of straw, smiling and staring at the moon through the ceiling which gave way to both rain and moonlight while Belle's daughter bounced up and down on my great grand pappy thankin' the Lord for all the wonderful gifts and endowments now bestowed upon her.

Seeing this, the plantation owner burst out in laughter at the utter foolishness of the whole situation. Hearing his laughter my great grand pappy jumped up in alarm at which time both owner and overseer were awestruck by the sheer magnitude of the situation. To say my great grand pappy was rather well-endowed would have been an understatement.

When the overseer finally gathered his wits about him he became infuriated.

"Is this your, man gal?" he asked.

"Why no, suh. Mohammed Abdul don't belong to no one gal, suh. Him belongs to us all, suh. Gals come from three plantations over and more miles than that to share Mohammed's palette, suh. I was just fortunate enough to get the call tonight, suh, but I ain't forgot you Master Orin, suh, she said lowering her eyes.

"I was still savin' the best for you, suh," she said with a smile she hoped would keep the sting of the whip at bay.

The owner turned to his overseer and smiled as he glanced back at my great grand pappy.

"Well, Orin, I've never seen a man that size. Say what's your Christian name, boy?" the owner queried.

"Master ain't given me no Christian name yet, suh", my great grand pappy replied.

"Well, from this day forth," the owner chuckled, "you shall be known as Longfellow." the master said, and lo and behold that's how I come to be called William Longfellow the III.

GQ

" A lot of people refer to me as a pimp so I guess that's how people perceive me. The little one's want to glorify me and a lot of the older cats out there bustin' their asses out there everyday want to vilify me. But you know. I don't really care what people think. Still, I prefer to think of myself as a self-made man a sort of poor man's Don King with a better barber.

I don't know whether you know it or not but by the time I was twenty-seven I was the owner and proprietor of three strip joints, two barbershops, a restaurant, a club right here in Harlem and a motel out in Queens. I guess if I was white I'd be called an entrepreneur but entrepreneur don't mean a whole lot to poor black folks up here in Harlem, strugglin' and tryin' to make it. They like seein' the flashy clothes, the big cars and the expensive jewelry. That's basically all you need to make you a ghetto superstar up here in Harlem.

You see you gotta understand Black folks. Gotta understand where they're comin' from. You see poor Black folks out here slavin' for the man from can't see in the mornin' 'til can't see at night on some low payin' gig and they still can't seem to get enough change together to put food on the table. So, when they see me out here runnin' around, makin' a fistful of dollars with no help from the man but in spite of the man you automatically become someone to look up to. I guess you could say I was Harlem's equivalent to the American Idol. We both came out of nowhere to ascend to the top of the dung heap. Both of us are overnight sensations. And like that sista that won the American Idol championship from some small town in North Carolina somewhere, neither one of us has very much in the way of talent. And you know what's funny about the

whole thing? The funny thing is that nobody cares about what you had to go through to get there. They just like the fact that you made it. Let's 'em know there's hope for them too. Then hey, after you get to the top of the heap it's all about marketing, baby. It's knowing how to sell yourself and how to work the crowd. When a hometown girl like Fantasia makes good, with little or no talent, it gives everyone hope that they can do the same thing. And all she's really doing if you watch closely is just working the crowd better than her counterparts.

When people see you every week and you looking good and you rising fast in the game and changing cars, clothes and women with the drop of a hat, they say damn look at that nigga. That niggas livin' good. That nigga ain't worried about shit. He ain't worried about the water or the gas gettin' turned off or whose name he can put the phone in next month. Nah, that nigga ain't worried 'bout none of that. He probably got an accountant to handle all that shit for him. And then they get to thinkin' and aspiring to be just as successful because after all we're coming from the same place. And I don't mean like Harlem or South Central, I mean we all comin' from the same experience—you know—being Black and poor in America. So they can relate. Sometimes when I'm walkin' down Lenox I hear some of the younger brothers say things like, "Shit, I'm not far off that nigga's ass. As soon as I get my income tax back this year I'm gonna be livin' large, just like that nigga, Q."

That's what I hear some of the younger cats sayin'. A lot of 'em don't necessarily like what I'm doing but all they see is it being a way out of the madness that's poverty.

You know ninety-percent of the time they can't see the forest for the trees. Ain't too many trees left in Harlem but it's still a jungle and shit can get pretty thick up here sometimes. Sometimes, it almost seems like there's no way out and your choices are so limited that even the most desperate situations begin to look good after awhile.

But going back to what I was saying initially. In all honesty, I don't care what people say or what they think they see. If they want to call me a pimp, then fine. Shit, they talked about Jesus Christ. Still, that's not how I see myself. And that's not what defines me as a man. Pimpin's just what I do to make a living. But if that's how people want to define me then I guess I'm cool with that. I only wish they were smart enough to look past the clothes, the cars, and the women. I wish they could see past the sensationalism and read the real story.

Look. If your president and the politicians would be honest with the American people, they'd tell you that we're all in the same business essentially. We both exploit those considered less fortunate for money. Isn't that it in the nutshell? We both exploit poor people for profit. You call the ones' the government exploits taxpayers and consumers when they're spending, military when they're killing, and patriotic citizens if they don't complain about being exploited.

Long as you getting' robbed quietly without makin' too much of a fuss you're in the runnin' for the good citizenship award but I ain't tryin' ta get into politics right now although I very well could. I don't know if you're aware of the fact but I was a political science major at John Jay before I dropped out to pursue more lucrative interests.

But since you're here to interview me around the pimping game let me get back to what first drew me into this particular line of work. As you can imagine, when I first started out I gotta admit I had some qualms with the whole thing because of ethical reasons you might say. But after giving it considerable thought and looking at pimpin' in the whole scheme of things it seemed like I was the only one out there that wasn't pimpin' or taking advantage of somebody. To me, it just seemed like everybody was pimping or taking advantage of yours truly so I just logically took my place in the whole scheme of things.

Besides prostitution has been around since the beginning of time and I figured if I ain't out there doing it somebody else would be. That was my rationale. In fact, prostitution is legal in some states. Right outside of Las Vegas they have dude ranches which are nothing more than legal brothels. So, tell me if it's not morally wrong there then why the hell is it a crime here? You don't have to answer. Just think about it. What's more there is nothing wrong with sex. Not a damn thing. There are too many people on this earth for there to be anything wrong with sex. But this country's got so many hang-ups when it comes to sex and most of 'em are based on some ol' crazy Puritanical bullshit that makes no sense to most people 'cept those who ain't getting' it right and on the regular. It's just another means of controlling the masses with the Catholic Church in charge of monitoring things and keeping everything in check.

Ain't that a joke? Right now the Catholic Church is the biggest transgressor of sexual norms and the biggest offender in the country. And do you know why? Let me tell you why, Clooney. Because the sexual repression the Catholic Church imposes on those men, those   priests is unnatural to say the least.

22

You see, man by his very nature is a sexual being which makes the abstinence imposed on them in their vows unnatural. Abstinence is unnatural and an unreasonable request to ask of any man. Ain't nothin' wrong or unnatural about sex. Not a damn thing. Like I said there's far too many people on God's green earth for there to be something wrong with it.

And all I am is a service provider of sorts. And I don't see any disgrace at doing something as long as it doesn't harm anyone and you're doing your best at it. And I've always done my best in providing the best. Ask anyone from midtown to Montauk Point or anyone from do-or-die Bed Stuy to Fire Island and they will tell you who GQ is. And you know why? 'Cause I've always taken pride in being the best and providing the best. And that's why I'm a goddamn Harlem legend.

When niggas mention Harlem legends, chances are you're gonna hear my name spoken in the same breath as Earl 'the Goat' Manigault and Nicky Barnes. And you know why? 'Cause despite the rumors, I've carved out a place in history with nothing more than hard work, street savvy, determination and perseverance.

Hell, when I started out I didn't have anything more than a desire to make it. Shit! I was flat broke and didn't have enough change to buy a Black and Mild. All I knew was that I was tired of scraping and clawing and scufflin' and hustlin' tryna turn a dime into fifteen cents. I'm telling you shit was hard out there. Not that it's changed much now and anybody out there on these streets that's hustlin' and tryna' eat will tell you that shit ain't easy on these here Harlem streets.

I can't stress that enough. But I took what the streets gave me and I not only made it but I rose to the top against all the odds.

Think about that, Clooney. I mean just stop and think about that for a minute then ask yourself this. How many of the people that you know and come into

23

contact with everyday can honestly attest to the fact that they are the best at whatever it is that they do?

With over eight million people in this city how many of them can actually say that they stand at the head of the class in their particular area of expertise. How many do you know that can say that? Well, I can say that.

Chapter 2

My real name is Gary Ellis Quinton and as I've alluded to me being the number one pimp in Harlem and the Bronx. A lot of people wanna say that I'm the number one pimp in all of New York but there's a lot of brotha's out there on top of their game and I'd hate to take anything away from them by proclaiming to be the best so I'll just be content to be Numero Uno in Harlem.

Still, a lot of people say that if you're the best in Harlem then that makes you the best in New York. Now if you follow that reasoning and agree that New York is the number one city in the world and if you're the tops in New York then it just follows that that would make you the best in the world. That's what my fans argue but I ain't gonna go that far although the idea does excite me some. But I'll leave that one for y'all to debate. I will tell you this though. I've got some of the finest Black and Latino ho's in the city at my beck and call and for the right price they can be at yours too.

Every day that I look in the mirror, I look at one wealthy young Black brother and I'll tell you, I don't fell one iota of guilt about anything I'm doing. And let me tell you why. It's because I've come to terms with who I am and what it is that I do. I am Gary Quinton or GQ, the earth shaker, the dream maker, the lady taker, the back breaker and the moneymaker. That's me, baby.

Now tell me about yourself, Mr. Clooney. No, don't tell me. Let me tell you. You are a left wing liberal or at least you used to like to think you were when you were banging that little Black chick in college.

But as time went on and you made that leap from college to the real world, you became a beat writer and were forced to cover some of the grimier aspects of New York City and found to your utter distaste that you were becoming more and more like your ultra-conservative, right-wing father.

How am I doing so far, Clooney?

After almost starving, trying to make it as an independent journalist, covering stories no one else wanted to cover you came to the realization that starving in isolation is not quite as romantic as Thoreau made it appear.

Still, you've got too much pride to let go of your dream of becoming a Peabody Award Winner and you're confident enough that you possess the journalistic skills to make you a top flight reporter. But Lord knows things can't get much tougher for you right through here. And what really disturbs the hell out of you is to see how far you've fallen from the dreams of groundbreaking stories and being one of the top notch reporters on one of Gotham's dailies.

It's a long way from those pristine ideals that interrupted your sophomore year in college to join the Peace Corp and go traipsing around Central America to aid some poor undernourished Latinos. It's a long way from graduating Magna Cum Laude at Columbia.

And then there's your father, who runs one of the largest investment firms downtown. He's always been proud of you. He's always dreamed of bringing you on board to help him in the

day-to-day operations of the company despite your liberal politics. 'Til this day, he still holds fast to that dream of making you a top level exec, working side by side with you and he's sure that it's only a matter of time before you come to your senses and forget all that humanitarian bullshit and groveling in the stench that is New York with no money. He still holds fast to the dream that you two will one day work together. He respects the fact that you feel compelled, almost driven to make it on your own but is growing increasingly, impatient with your quest for independence and the way you live.

How am I doing so far, Clooney?"

I had to smile. It was quickly obvious that GQ had done as much if not more of a background search on me as I'd done on him before deciding to cover the story. I had to admit I was impressed, if not feeling somewhat vulnerable though to a degree violated.

As deeply entrenched as he was in New York's underworld there was little doubt that his influence ran well beyond Harlem.

I should have realized this when he addressed me prior to the interview and brought up the article and the question of his own anonymity. There was no way he was going to let some little sniveling, gold digging, liberal, white reporter gain access to an empire it had taken him decades to build. I was impressed by both his fortitude and his candor without knowing who I was or how I was going to portray him.

"Shall I continue," he asked me, realizing that I was stunned by the proficiency in which he assembled the pieces of the puzzle that was my life.

"By all means," I replied, anxious to know how much he really knew and how much was pure conjecture.

"Okay, let's see… You've always championed the plight of the disenfranchised and the downtrodden. And you don't see me as any better than the crooked politicians who have been making billions off the backs of Black folks since they landed on Plymouth Rock? And no matter how hard you tried to understand this Black man and the hand that society has dealt him in your attempts to rationalize what it is that I do, you just can't. To your way of thinking I'm as much of a scourge, and a plague, as crack cocaine and Republican politics. And the more stories you're forced to do like this one so you can put food on the table the better your daddy's offer sounds. But your pride just won't allow you to now will it?

You look surprised, Clooney. You didn't actually think that someone with a realm and reputation as far reaching as you claimed mine to be when you gave your reasons for wanting to do this interview could get to this point without doing his homework, did you?"

I couldn't answer, at least honestly. He knew the deal but...

"You just can't see yourself doing a story on some low-life parasite who makes his money off the backs of women. But you know something, Clooney. You're the real pimp. You're the one

who makes money off of other people's stories, off of other people's successes or failures but mostly off of other people's tragedies.

What you don't understand, Clooney is that I don't go chasin' these bitches down. These ho's come to me. Most of the time they're just like everyone else who sees all of the flash and trash that goes along with it. They see a Black man out there that's respected throughout the community and then they see themselves. They know that no matter how hard they try they can't seem to scrape two pennies together to pay their bills and take care of their families at the end of each week.

Most of these women just want to see their money working for them the way they see mine working for me. But what they really want to see is some hope. They want to know, want me to assure them that there's a way out of all this gloom and doom that comes along with growing up poor in the richest city in the world.

Hard as they work, they hardly ever see anything for their labors. After they run out and get high trying to come to grips with what it is they're doing, the real pimps take their thirty-five percent, and when the bail bondsmen and the system gets finished with them, ninety-nine percent of the time they ain't got a pot to piss in or a window to throw it out of.

That's where I step in. All I'm here to do is manage their finances so that should something happen to them they have a little something to fall back on. Ain't no difference between me and Merrill Lynch. I take their money and invest it for 'em and of course I get a commission.

Every now and then I have to step in and provide protection from some silly-ass cracker from downtown that don't know or don't wanna play by the rules of the game, but for the most part I'm just here as a deterrent and to manage their funds. But like I said, you're the real pimp, Clooney. You're the one that had to put your little lily-white values on the back burner and come uptown to my hood to see me you so you could shop my story around and get paid off my labor.

"Now I want you tell me something. Why are you here, anyway, Clooney? Tell the truth. What are you doing up here in Harlem? I read the papers I even read your articles from time to time though I haven't read any lately. What's up? Why you slummin' nigga?

This ain't even your type of story, yo. I figure you to be more of the scandal breakin' type of reporter. I expect to see you Big Pimpin'—you know all suited up uncovering another Enron scandal with the big boys. But coverin' a Harlem pimp. What's up? This just ain't you Clooney!

What's wrong Clooney? Is the Bush backlash hittin' you too? Come to think of it, you should be rollin' in high cotton since the new administration took over. Ain't been nothin' but scandal after scandal since that mothafucka came into office. Hell, even his getting into office was a scandal. What's wrong? Afraid of being blackballed from the writer's guild?

C'mon, fess up Clooney. What's the real deal? Shit, you and I both know I ain't no real news in the overall scheme of things. So fess up, nigga, what's the real deal? Somebody send you up here to bring me down?

Hell, everybody knows that when a nigga starts to make some real chedda' he becomes a threat even if he's up in Harlem wit' his own kind. So, tell me? Who sent you? Everybody in Harlem knows somebody's pimpin' somebody. I'm just small potatoes baby, just another pawn in the game if you look at me in the overall scheme of things. Hell, a million five, a million six, a year ain't no money baby.

You wanna talk about real dough, though then look at your president. The nigga requisitions eighty-seven billion from Congress one week and the next week the check's in his hand. Not eighty-seven million—mind you—but eighty-seven billion. Now that's some real cheddar.

That ain't no Velveeta, baby.

Eighty-seven billion... I can't even imagine that kind of loot. And for what? What the fuck does a nigga need eighty-seven billion for when he controlling the world's oil supply and the price of gas is goin' through the mothafuckin' roof. He tellin' y'all he needs it for humanitarian purposes so he can help rebuild Iraq and ain't a mothafucka but James Carville askin' why.

You know what I really can't understand though is why? Why the fuck is he trying to rebuild somethin' he was so intent on destroyin' just a few months back? What sense does that make? But I don't hear no cries of outrage, no mention of the misappropriation of funds concerning taxpayer's dollars, nothin'. Ain't no outcry, no nothin'.

Shit, if a bitch asks me for twenty-five dollars to go to the goddamn supermarket, and I know the refrigerator is empty I still wanna know why, what she bought, how much it cost, with and

without her VIC card and then I'm gonna count my change. And here they are givin' this fool eighty-seven billion like its chump change. I'll be damned.

If it were money I'd wanna know where it went and what it was being spent on down to the penny. But not the American people. These fools are too damn trusting. You best believe if I was a taxpayer, ol' George W. would be held accountable. He'd be hearing from me.

He's out there right now, right this instant runnin' the biggest con, the biggest flim-flam in the history of this country and nobody's even questioning his motives. He and his daddy, already done made billions off the American people in the oil business. Now they're invadin' other countries just so they can take over OPEC and control the rest of the world's oil supply.

Shit, I go to fill up my ol' ladies Escalade and gas done jumped to three dollars and fifty cents a fuckin' gallon and that's after we invaded Iraq and took over the world's richest oil supply. One thing's for damn sure, I sure ain't benefitin' from the take-over. Gas prices are higher than they've ever been before. Now tell me whose pimpin' who?

Maybe white people didn't know but Black folks sure as hell knew there wasn't no weapons of mass destruction over there in Iraq. Hell, that man, "what's his name" Saddam Hussein was so damn busy building palaces—they say that nigga had forty-one palaces—for his women friends, he didn't have time to build no damn weapons of mass destruction.

Black folks knew that. Shit. That nigga Saddam's over there, in Iraq sittin' on billions and billions of dollars. Hell, everybody knows that you give niggas money like that and they ain't

thinking about fighting shit. Why in hell would he be thinkin' about some fuckin' weapons of mass destruction? Saddam was over there havin' a ball. Nigga was happy. Enjoyin' the good life. He thankin' Allah everyday for the oil, women and the money. And just like any otha rich nigga, he just glad to be alive. But because he's dark complexioned, too proud to bow down and because he's filthy rich your man says he got to be removed. When he was playin' ball with Cheney a few years back he wasn't no threat then. He was just another sand nigga doin' the U.S. government's bidding. So, why the fuck is he a threat now? Why? All of a sudden he gotta be a threat? Tell me that, Clooney.

I live in New York where they done bombed the World Trade Center not once but twice. Most Americans don't know that they bombed it twice but I'm right here in New York and I still don't feel like he's a threat to me.

The nigga ain't got no war machines. Hell, they had to steal the damn planes to bomb our ass. So, how in the world could he possibly be a threat? What makes him a serious threat to national security? I'll tell you why. He got tired of being a pawn in their bullshit games and refused to play anymore. Hell, he wasn't benefittin' from a few McDonald's chains being thrown up in Baghdad. But if you don't play ball that's what they do. Remember Noriega? Where's that nigga now? Ill tell you where he is. They got him locked down in some Florida jail if he ain't over there in Guantanamo. He used to be an ally, when George Sr. was in the oval office. But I bet you won't see or hear from his ass again."

Clooney laughed.

"But all that's beside the point. I believe the question you asked me was about pimpin' and my moral obligation to society or some bullshit along those lines."

Q picked up the bottle of Hennessy and finished off the last few drops before summoning the tiny waitress with the huge hips and hellacious booty over to the table with a wave of his hand and a nod of his head.

She nodded slowly letting him know he had gotten her attention and would be right over. When she arrived, he let his hand play with the tiny drawstring dangling from her g-string without ever making actual contact with her body. I smiled to myself as I watched the gesture then watched closely as he deftly pushed the twenty into the front of her panties. He was in his element now; working with the shrewd cunning and expertise of a hunter moving swiftly, silently as he stalked his prey. He was a Wall Street broker waiting for the Dow to open, surveying the landscape, placing his bid slowly, cautiously....

"More where that came from baby."

All you got to do is say the word. With an ass like yours and your personality, I'd have you bringin' home eighty g's easy, in less than a year. You still got my card? He was placing his bid now.

The tiny waitress nodded then glanced over at me wonderin' if I were john, a business partner or 5-0. It was obvious that she couldn't understand the relationship. Here I was in my five year old Brooks Brothers suit, with my attaché case, torn and weather-beaten from too many days on the

subways of Gotham in search of a good story. Here, I was a white boy in the middle of Harlem sitting across from Gary Quinton, better known as GQ, in his

31

tailor-made Versace suit and Italian loafers, easily costing more than my entire wardrobe.

Q was right. I could certainly attest to the fact that it was anything but easy being a free-lance journalist in this day and age and it almost seemed easier that first summer following my graduation from Columbia when I was a young, naïve intern with the Times than it did now. Even though as a free lance I at least had the freedom of coming and going at my own leisure without having the burden of having some cranky, white middle-aged editor one feature story shy of a Peabody handing me deadlines like some master handing out orders on a now defunct, post Civil War plantation.

Despite the hard times and an occasional bad assignment, like now, when I felt like I was totally out of my element, my passion for journalism remained steadfast and I often found myself driven. I loved the freedom of following a hot lead even if nine times out of ten there was no real story and my lead turned out to be no more than an effort in futility.

Still, I loved chasing those stories that my ultra-conservative white colleagues had little if no access to and even less interest in, like the one I was on now with Q. Although as I sit here at this particular moment I see no special or exclusive angle that would induce, my readers to embrace this morally degenerate egomaniac.

As far as I was concerned pimps had no endearing qualities that I could see but with his political views he could easily be the feature article that would entice Middle America to go on hating a

lifestyle they would never actually come into contact with or understand beyond what I exposed to them. The article written correctly, with some precision and with just the right gene se qua could be just what I needed to jumpstart my career and get it back on track and push those bleeding liberal and middle of the road Democrats permanently to the right.

As I alluded to before, GQ had absolutely no redeeming qualities that I could see and my article would probably do little more than perpetuate the hatred and the myth. But at the very least it would arouse curiosity, sell some papers and allow them to get up close and personal with the bad guy.

To tell you the truth, I'm not exactly sure what inspired me to do the story on Q. He was right. I like most of my class of liberal do-gooders with empathy for the poor and disenfranchised still had no particular affinity for his sordid lifestyle. Whether he recognized it or not I was just a stones throw from Middle America as far as he was concerned. And as everyone knows, yet no one is willing to admit, Middle America was more apt to order and watch the Playboy channel and masturbate behind closed doors on Saturday afternoons while Mary and the kids were at soccer practice than to go about procuring the real thing for twenty dollars. (Which if I must say so myself is a fairly reasonable price considering the state of today's economy.)

After all, Americans are for the most part a refined people. And no matter what happens behind closed doors everyone knows it's more politically correct to masturbate than to comb the streets of some seedy urban ghetto in search of a pimp to procure a prostitute.

Meanwhile, my rent was overdue again and I was being threatened with eviction for the third time in the past three months and my prospects for a feature article appeared dim at best. My novel now three years old sat dormant and collecting dust and cobwebs in the corner of my tiny bedroom, which also served as my living room and kitchen. I'd sold everything else of value as I waited for some publisher, any publisher to recognize the innate value of my story but as of yet I'd experienced nothing—not even a phone call.

My agent had long ago flown the coop. And that block buster story every reporter dreams of was no longer just around the corner or the bend or even over the next horizon. I'd lost my press pass for not being able to keep up with my union dues and good ol' AOL Time Warner had turned off both my internet and cable services on the same day.

I'd long ago grown tired of chicken and the thirty-nine varieties of Hamburger Helper with no hamburger to help it and drawn a blank as far as what readers my readers really wanted.

The new administration made scandal commonplace, the war in Iraq had grown old and was rather a touchy subject as the November elections grew closer.

There weren't any humanitarian of two headed siblings joined at the hip, John Malvo the D.C. sniper had been apprehended years ago, and the movie had already debuted and bombed. So, as much as I detested doing the story on Q, I had little choice. Time was running out.

At the time of Q's interview, I'd exhausted all of my sources for money. My checking account was overdrawn and my savings had a balance of five dollars and ten cents that I really could

have used right through here but I was too embarrassed to make a withdrawal and the ATM refused to relinquish any denomination lower than a twenty.

By this time, I was thoroughly convinced that all of my friends and colleagues' voicemails and answering machines had a chip in them designed to detect my voice when I called. So, here I was sitting in a sleazy rundown strip joint with GQ, the self-proclaimed Harlem legend who loomed larger than basketball great, Earl 'the Goat' Manigault and renowned Harlem gangster, Nicky Barnes combined—have him tell it. Yes, here I was allowing him to do what pimps do best—embellish himself.

Chapter 3

A few minutes later the very young, very attractive waitress returned to our table and I wondered if she'd graduated high school as she appeared no more than sixteen or seventeen at best. Stealing a closer look at the rather shapely young woman with the tray full of Heinekens and a bottle of Hennessey I wondered what could make so attractive a child throw her youth away to wait on the likes of those around me in this sleazy excuse for a club. Not seeming to notice my concern, she smiled one of those stewardess' smiles that say I'm only doing this because it's my job smiles.

Q, not noticing or not caring slipped another five dollars in her g-string along with another business card before making the same proposition as before. She thanked him as graciously as she could without showing the utter contempt that was so obviously there and moved on. I watched Q's reaction but he was on to other things and seemed not dissuaded by the brush-off.

"Stupid bitch…" I heard him mutter under his breath.

So, he had picked up on her cold indifference. And for some reason the girl's dismissal made me feel good even if disgusted Q and I hoped that maybe this might serve to bring him down a peg or two but he continued and it was soon evident that rejection was more of a pimp's life than I could possibly imagine. Thick-skinned motherfuckers, I thought to myself and wondered if I had the tenacity to do it.

Pouring his shot and then mine, Q turned and beckoned to the women on the stage that aside from the tiny thong, which separated her butt cheeks and the dozens of dollar bills that hung from it, wore nothing at all. Bare-chested and as I mentioned before, practically naked she approached the table. I suddenly felt very uncomfortable in her presence and didn't know whether I should avert my eyes from the heavenly body before me or offer her my suit jacket. Since I hardly knew the proper protocol, I did nothing.

"Candy this is Mr. Clooney. He's a free-lance reporter doing a feature story on yours truly and the game."

"Well there's no one who knows more about the pimp game than m'baby right here," the young woman said proudly.

Q smiled as well and continued.

"Want you to take him upstairs to the V.I.P. Lounge when you get finished your shift. No better yet take him to my suite and give him the V.I.P. treatment. You can bring one of the other girls with you too. Just make sure it ain't Diamond. She needs to be out here. She ain't pulled her weight in weeks and I'm tired of her bullshit. Tell her that when she gets off she needs to come and see me. I think it's time she and I had a heart-to- heart talk. I've been too damn nice to that bitch and she may be thinking that Q's getting a little soft.

Shit. I don't know what's on her mind but ain't no bitch in the world got my nose open or me pussy-whipped. Never has and never will. Too much goddamn pussy out there for that to ever

happen. Ain't no pussy in the world worth shit come the first of the month when the car people want their money and the landlord wants his rent. Know what I'm sayin'? Pussy don't pay bills."

The pimp dropped his head lifting his drink as he did so.

"Sorry. Didn't mean to come off like that, Clooney. Go ahead Candy, get out of here."

The woman bent over and kissed Q on the side of the face as she pulled on a sheer top then whispered, so there would be no mistake or misconceptions about what would transpire later that evening.

"Am I going to see you later on tonight, daddy?"

Q patted on her firm buttocks then pushed her away gently without replying, concentrating instead on me who sat mesmerized by Candy's perfectly shaped ass.

Q smiled at me making me self-conscious but I still had difficulty averting my gaze from the woman now walking away.

"It's all just an act, Clooney," he said apropos of nothing. "The name-calling, the fighting, the total disregard for the woman as a person is all just an act. And I'll tell you something else you may not be aware of but this has got to be off the record. Strictly off the record, is that understood?"

"Strictly off the record," I repeated tuning my tiny portable tape recorder off.

"Here's something you'll never find in the pimpin' handbook. And do you what that is, Clooney?"

"No, I can't say that I've ever read the handbook of pimpin'" I smiled, at once realizing how condescending I must have sounded and then doing my best to make light of the remark. But Q was a student of people in the same way that Plato and Socrates were and he was immediately aware of my patronization though he said nothing.

And for the first time in my life I was truly aware of my pretentious, middle class values and the unprofessional manner that I had taken going into this interview. I knew that I'd committed the cardinal sin by allowing my values to color the story. As every good journalist knows this is one of the first things that you're taught not to do. Every freshman journalism major at City College knows that one of the keys to being a responsible reporter is maintaining objectivity. At least it's supposed to be. That's Journalism 101. And though we often sit at home and have difficulty divorcing ourselves from a hot topic such as the war or the right to free speech we are all aware and realize the repercussions of infusing our views when covering a story. And I'd done just that.

Now my only concern was whether Q was so distracted by the young woman on stage that there was a chance he hadn't noticed. Grabbing my drink I took a long swig of the brandy, which since I was pretty much a teetotaler I felt almost immediately. I felt the warm rush and watched Q, who was now totally absorbed in the woman dancing on stage.

Perfectly proportioned and close to six feet, I immediately understood his fascination. Unlike the other women who preceded her onstage her breasts were neither too large nor too small. Her butt neither protruded grotesquely nor seemed to hibernate before my eyes. Watching her now, I could hardly remember ever seeing a woman so well endowed or so well proportioned. To say she was attractive would be a misnomer and take away from her greatly. So, I will no longer try to describe the woman that adorned the stage that evening but will only report that a hush fell over the crowd when she took the stage and I watched as patron after patron moved their chairs up so as to be closer to the stage. Those that had been somewhat reluctant about shelling out the cash for the other girls suddenly became philanthropists.

The woman's g-string soon filled with tens and twenties, not the singles the other girls had garnered while putting forth twice the effort. In fact, she hardly moved. Appearing distant and resolute, her distaste for her occupation obvious, it soon became apparent to everyone that her heart wasn't in it but it hardly stopped the eager young men from tossing dollar bills in her direction hoping to elicit more. Still, she eased up and down the firemen's pole with a nonchalance that said she'd grown weary of the whole affair and then made her exit to the sound of R. Kelly's, Step in the Name of Love.

Funny thing though, Q, whose whole being revolved around the bartering in women's flesh, who gave no never mind to them in general seemed more mesmerized by the woman leaving the stage than even his customers did. It appeared amusing to me that moment his eyes told a very different and I knew right away that this woman was somewhat different from the others.

In any case, I was certainly glad he'd been distracted enough or perhaps just chosen to ignore the sarcastic remark I'd made earlier. Turning to face me, I knew that he was now ready to continue our interview.

"That's Diamond. That's my number one girl. At least, she should be but she has no heart, no drive, no desire. Talk about all the potential in the world and you're talkin' about Diamond. She's got more potential than all the rest of my girls combined but she's not focused. You know, Clooney, there is nothing worse or that aggravates me more than wasted potential.

You look at Candy. She realizes that she's not the most beautiful girl in the world but she takes what she's got and gets the most out of it. I not only admire that, I respect that. I'm not talkin' about just admirin' that in Candy. I admire that in anyone who strives to get the most out of their capabilities. Look at me. I grew up right here in these same dirty, grimy streets as the rest of these good for nothing fools. I saw the same negative shit that everyone else saw but I made a conscious choice not to get caught up in it. I saw my mother out there workin', scufflin', tryin' to make ends meet. I watched my daddy runnin' round out there in those same streets always hustlin', always schemin', always tryin' his damndest to make a dollar out of fifteen cents and kick a drug habit that had his

38

name etched all over it while at the same time tryin' to make sure that we had everything that we could possibly want. I watched all of this. That's when I made a vow that I would never go through that. I said to myself, Q there's got to be somethin' better than this shit. There just has to be.

So I took a long look at myself and asked myself what is it that I do better than most of these cats out here? And since I knew I wasn't no balla and didn't know how to fit in or play the game down on Wall Street, I had no clue. But I was dating this female about ten or twelve years older than I was at the time and she kept tellin' me that I had hidden talents and that it was only a matter of time before they'd come to the forefront.

Well, I listened to her because she was basically taking care of me but she was also one of the brightest women I'd ever met. Aside from that, she treated me real good and didn't ask anything of me except that I realize my potential and be there for her. She wanted me to be true to her but she never really expressed that to me but then again she didn't have to. I knew. I guess she figured that if she brought it up, you know, made demands on me that I might leave her. Still, I knew she wanted more from me and wanted me to want more for myself. But I was young. I wasn't even considering settling down let alone getting married. Shit, I was having fun. I ain't gonna lie.

Like I said she was much older than I was. She had a pretty good gig working for the city and was the type that was happy just doing her nine to five, grabbing a bite to eat and crawling into bed next to me, throwing a movie on and waiting for me to rock her ass to sleep. That was the routine. And it was fine in the beginning but after awhile it began to bore me to tears. But I loved her. I loved her to death. I knew deep down in my heart that the only thing she really wanted from me was for me to be true to her but as much as I loved her that was the only thing that I just couldn't seem to do.

At first, I tried. I mean, I really, really tried but it just wasn't in my makeup. I began to feel duty bound, almost obligated and I saw no way out. I wasn't contributing anything to the household or the relationship and the more I thought about it the guiltier I felt. And the guiltier I felt, the more I ran the streets and chased women and smoked dope to forget the fact that I wasn't half the man my daddy was and he had a substance abuse problem.

Working was out. Bad as things were, I wasn't havin' none of that nine to five shit for minimum. Just wasn't me. Never has been, never will be. Like I told her on more than one occasion. I'd rather starve in Harlem than go downtown and push clothing racks for the man all day so he can get rich off of my labor. And if I didn't know anything else, there was one thing I did know. There was too much money to be made right here in Harlem for me to be commutin' all the way downtown and slavin' for the man and making no money.

Still, I got tired of continually takin' and feelin' dependent, which I was. My self-esteem really took a nosedive. I didn't know precisely what was happenin' but I felt low. The only thing that made me feel like half a man was when I was around a chick and she was praying to my ego. So, I really started messin' around in earnest just tryin' to raise my self-esteem back to where it was before I moved in with ol' girl. It wasn't intentional and to tell the truth I've never really looked at the whole situation 'til now but a male ego can wreak havoc on you.

Anyway, before I knew it, it seemed like I had a female in every borough, another one out on Long Island, one up in Connecticut and a second cousin over in Jersey that I used to just get high with. Every now and then when her drummer boyfriend was on the road we'd get down but we

were friends for the most part. I don't think ol' girl had a clue as to what was going on or maybe she just chose to ignore it. I don't know. Even when one of those little fast heifers got the number and decided to call the house I just explained to her that it was some far off distant cousin callin' about the upcoming family reunion.

After awhile the calls become commonplace which meant that either I had the world's largest extended family or the woman was just plain stupid. Deep down, inside I knew better. Still, if she chose to ignore everything that was right there in front of her, then hell, what would it look like for me to bring it up? Lord knows, I spent a lot of time away from home during that time away workin' on the planning committee for that family reunion,"Q laughed as he took another swallow of the brandy.

"You know, I don't know what attracted me to her, or her to me but one thing I knew. That woman loved some Q.

Let me tell you how she dealt with the whole charade. Instead of confronting me around my infidelity head on, she did something your people do, Clooney. She rationalized the shit.

What I'm sayin' my brotha, is ol' girl wasn't able to accept the fact that I was cheating on her and had grown tired. But, instead of facing rejection and another failed attempt at a successful relationship she simply chose to ignore it. If you weren't aware of it, let me tell you, there's nothin' worse than a woman approaching middle age without a man than rejection.

Women always got this thing working about their biological clock ticking and time runnin' out. Now you and I don't think about such shit but a woman does. And trust me; they think about it a lot. The only time a man will even entertain some shit like a biological clock ticking is when his shit stops tickin' altogether. But not a woman. She can hear that shit tickin' in her sleep.

Let me tell you what she told me. She told me that the only reason that I was out there runnin' the streets was that there was a void inside of me. I didn't know it but I was searching. Inside of me, I was lacking something. What I needed to do was find some way of filling that void with something productive, something positive. What I needed was to find out exactly what I wanted for myself. I needed to find out what I had an aptitude for and once I did that I could pursue it and I would undoubtedly be successful because as ol' girl put it, she had never, in her life, seen anyone as driven as I was. Never.

I must admit she was a great motivator and I was so damn tired of the way I was living that it didn't take much to make a change. I was tired of hangin' out with the fellas, shootin' dice everyday and sellin' just enough weed to keep me smokin' for one more day. I got tired of the life, tired of looking over my shoulder, tired of cheatin' on ol' girl, tired of feelin' guilty but most of all I was

41

tired of being broke with no hope of makin' my life any better. When she suggested that I take a couple of courses at City College, I literally jumped at the chance.

I'll never forget the first course I took was one entitled, America's Ever Changing Political Landscape, which I enjoyed thoroughly because I have a particular affinity for anything that has to do with politics or the political arena. In any case, my advisor was also the proctor of that

class and he used to applaud my enthusiasm. He was a rather unique kind of fella in his own right. I guess you could call him a maverick of sorts. He wasn't particularly interested in your political views although I'd venture to say that he was probably a moderate leaning a little more to the left than was popular at the time but he enjoyed the fact that I was young, inquisitive and somewhat of a free-thinker. Most of my comrades were just there for a grade and it was obvious they were just going through the motions. Whereas, I was there to find out how the system worked and how I could use it to my advantage or better yet exploit it the way it exploited everything it came into contact with.

Anyway, I'm enjoying the hell out of the class. I'm participating in every discussion and reading everything I can get my hands on trying to make up for lost time so I could hold my own.

Well, by the time midterms roll around, I'm flying high. I know I'm one of the top students in the class if not the top but I still don't know how to channel the knowledge and apply it to anything outside of the classroom. What I'm sayin' is that I didn't know how to make it relative to my world. But ol' girl tells me to just hang in there and have some patience and in time it will all come to me. Well, I knew she had my interests at heart and she hadn't steered me wrong so far and I figured that if worse came to worse I could at least pick up my degree and stay right there and teach.

I have to admit that a couple of times, I grew a tad bit disenchanted until I thought of my young brother Julius who despite my parent's protests, signed up for the Marines, the day he graduated high school. Now Julius has never been one to plan or to think an idea completely through and when the Marines came on television brandishing that sword and that bright blue uniform promising Julius a chance to be all he could be as well as a chance to travel and a career to boot, I knew they had him.

Julius had always been a funny kind of kid growing up, always making decisions recklessly and spontaneously without giving most things a second thought until it was too late. The decision to join the Marines wasn't much different.

Three months later, there he was, down there in the swamps of South Carolina in his bright blue suit wondering what the hell had just happened. Here he was graduating from boot camp, waiting to be assigned a duty station where he would receive specialized training in his career field. Julius, now retired, after twenty years, explained to me how the whole thing went down.

"Private Julius Quinton," the white First Sergeant bellowed.

"Yes sir," my brother replied. "You've been assigned to Camp LeJeune, North Carolina to complete your training."

"Yes sir."

"Your M.O.S. is 0330, Private Quinton. Did you get that Private Quinton? 0330!"

"Sir?"

"Yes, Private Quinton?"

"What is an 0330, sir?"

"Why an 0330 is a machine gunner, Private Quinton," the First Sergeant responded.

"Thank you sir," my brother replied before he turned to one of his boys, commented, and said, "They guaranteed me a career. Where the hell am I going to find a job as a machine gunner in Harlem?"

'That was my problem too. I had nowhere to apply what I'd learned but I loved the fact that I was doing something positive, something other than sellin' and smokin' weed everyday. Besides that, I was good at it and enjoying every minute. Like I said, I figured if worse came to worse I could always teach. That was the plan until I met with my advisor who told me that both my test scores and class participation were exemplary but that I needed to work on my writing skills, which I believed he called 'pedestrian'. Didn't know what pedestrian meant at the time but it didn't matter. Anyway, he suggested a tutor and I gladly accepted.

The tutor he recommended just happened to be a very attractive little Italian girl named Lisa something another, who'd grown up in Bensonhurst or one of those little Italian neighborhoods where they useta' like to beat on niggas when they got bored and although they didn't she didn't live there anymore you could tell she still had contempt for Blacks.

The other thing that was obvious from our first meeting was the fact that she didn't like me personally. In fact she couldn't stand me, and wasn't crazy about the idea of having to tutor my

black ass either. But her little funky attitude didn't bother me in the least. All I was interested in was improving my writing skills so I could show the world that there were some niggas out there that were goin' to make it despite the odds.

Are you getting all of this, Clooney?

Anyway, she must have made it known to my advisor that she had no interest in tutoring me. I think she told him something about it being too far to travel to tutor me as her reason for not wanting to tutor me but her financial aid was contingent on her completing her work-study and I was her work-study so she really didn't have a choice in the matter. It made her angry. And Lord knows she was giving me hell so she could get out of tutoring me. I could have let her off the hook and requested another tutor but she was supposed to be one of the top students in the English department and a pretty prolific writer to boot and I only wanted the best so like it or not she was stuck with me.

Some time later when she realized that I wasn't going to let her out of her obligation she began to open up. To her surprise she found out that we had quite a bit in common and she became fascinated with my depiction of Harlem and used to beg me to take her uptown so she could place the names with the faces. But to me that was like taking a Jewish family on a Sunday stroll down the Gaza Strip. Just wasn't happenin'. I was no more going to bring her to Harlem than I

44

was going to go clubbin' in Bensonhurst or Howard Beach on a Saturday night. There were some things you just didn't do.

Not long after that she admitted going to see Dr. Eugene concerning the long commute she had to make to tutor me. Seems the ride all the way up to the 42nd Street Library and then all the way back downtown everyday along with school and a grueling work schedule was taking its toll. Said it had nothing to do with me being Black and after getting to know her better, I believed her. And then there was the fact that she absolutely despised taking the subway after dark because people stared. Listening to her now there was little doubt that she was telling the truth.

You see Clooney I'd seen an awful lot in my twenty some odd years living in the city but up until that time, I swear to you that I'd never seen a body like Lisa's in all my born days. She had a pretty face, nothing special but she had the longest most curvaceous legs and the tightest little round ass you'd ever want to see. She definitely was not sufferin' from what Black folks refer to as white girl's disease. What, however, attracted all the attention were her breasts. The girl had the largest pair of ta ta's I've ever seen on anyone that small. I don't know how she couldn't possibly understand what all the fuss was about. I had to empathize with her though. So, when she suggested that I meet her at place down in Soho from that point on I agreed even though now I was the one forced to make that grueling commute.

Now I've lived in New York damn near my whole life but I had no idea that a place like Soho or the Village existed and was so damn close. When I got there I fell in love with Soho, the freedom, and that lil' girl with the big knockers. 'Course it wasn't nothin' like what she felt for me. She was by no means the finest girl I'd ever been with. I've been with some Latino women

and a bunch of sistas that she couldn't hold a candle to but she certainly opened my eyes to a whole new world.

This little Italian girl from Bensonhurst turned me on to Langston Hughes, Hemingway and a whole lotta brothas I would have never known about if I hadn't met her. And what it made it even better was the fact that I was killin'

45

the pussy at the same time. Bitch useta just bust out cryin' every time I tapped the shit. I kid you not, Clooney. I'm talkin' real tears. I'm not sure but I think she was a virgin before I met her. I can remember her telling me that she'd never experienced anything that good in her entire life. Then she made the fatal mistake of turning me on to The Prince by Machiavelli.

Clooney, I'm telling you, it was like a day of reckoning. It was like a revelation. I saw everything so clearly after I read Machiavelli. Machiavelli symbolized America. After I read that, all of this shit finally started making sense to me. He made me understand my plight in life. He made me understand politics and why there was no understanding politics if you feel what ah'm sayin'. Have you read it? What? Nigga, please tell me you're lyin'…You got the nerve to call yourself a journalist, a learned man. Brotha read Machiavelli! Before you do anything else… Read Machiavelli!

Trust me if you'd read Machiavelli you wouldn't be here doing this interview. You'd understand the nature of the game. Machiavelli is nothing more than political Darwinism. It's survival of the fuckin' fittest baby.

As far as that little gal down in the village, I'm not sure what happened to her. I know I rocked he world so well she dropped out of school and started giving me her financial aid, social security checks, everything. She was like Langston's patrons who used to pay him to write… Only I didn't make my mark on paper. But that shit got old quick. After awhile, we just stopped growing. I mean the relationship. Every time I went down Soho to see her she was in some new outfit ready to get into bed, drop the drawers and do the wild thing. It got to the point where, after awhile, there was no conversation and she was turnin' into nothin' more than a Victoria's Secret ad campaign. Ain't sayin' I didn't like her dressin' up in heels and shit but that gets old after awhile, so I eventually made my way on back uptown to my ol' girl wit' my tail between my legs and I ain't gonna lie, I was glad to be back.

But anyway, getting back to what I was sayin' about Machiavelli, if you'd read Machiavelli you probably wouldn't be here actin' like a fuckin' Boy Scout tryin' to learn the pimpin' game", Q said pausing to take another sip of the Hennessy. "Don't feel bad though, I useta be   naive like you Clooney…

Ya know, when I was a little kid I used to get real confused. I'd be sittin' in school listenin' to my teacher tell me about Columbus and how he came over to America to bring religion to the Indians and make them Christians and what not. And for the most part I'd be eatin' that New World, discovery shit up. Then a little later on we'd get to the part about the Declaration of Independence, the idea of freedom and basic liberties for all men—you know—the Bill of Rights and all that other good shit and I was still grinnin' ear to ear, still eatin' that ship up. Then we got into the next couple of chapters and that's when I started getting real confused.

They started talkin' 'bout Black folks like they were nothin' but objects—you know—like they were video ho's—you know—background dancers in a rap video. And by the time we got back to the Indians they been pushed clear across the Mississippi and the government had made up some shit call Manifest Destiny.

In case you don't know what that means, that means that all the treaties and all laws are written in concrete by the government until the government decides to change the laws for its own benefit. What it happened to mean, at that particular time in history, was that according to prior treaties the Indians owned all the lands west of the Mississippi River. Well, at least that was up until the government decided that more land was needed and then it became a question of Manifest Destiny.

You know what Manifest Destiny was, Clooney? Manifest Destiny said that by divine law, by divine right, which has been bestowed on me, by me, that if I see something that I want I have the right to access it despite the human casualties or the pain and hardship associated with obtaining it. Do you understand what I'm sayin' Clooney?

That's the way this country was founded. Then once everything was set in stone and the New World Order was in place there was no room for change. No change whatsoever and no chance for upward mobility. Once the social order was created, that was it. There were only the haves and the have-nots. Oh, they may tell you that you can be all you wanna be like they told my brother Julius but the plain truth of the matter is that all chances for growth are pretty much passé. They allow a handful to slip through the cracks to keep the masses motivated and

47

believing they can get to the mountain top but when less than one percent owns ninety-nine percent of the wealth, who are they kidding?

And no matter how much Black folks tried to act like they were part of the program they weren't, never have been and never will be. For the most part, they're still backstage at the theater, waitin' for their part when they ain't even been written into the fuckin' script. And since slavery they ain't even needed us as extras. All they're really doing is sittin' here waitin' for our eventual eradication. And most of us are so ignorant and I don't mean just Black folks per-se but poor people in general that we don't know any more about Machiavelli or Manifest Destiny than a man on the moon.

This ain't off the record, Clooney but I'll tell you what, if you add this shit, I'm tellin' you right now that if your readerships' made up of middle class Black folks, you gonna shonuff lose 'em if you start callin' a spade a spade and burst them nigga's bubble. You had better stick to that ol' Omar Tyree, Zane, Terry McMillan, bullshit they used to reading if you tryna get paid.

Anyway, that little ol' white girl down in Soho also hipped me to the Holocaust, Dostoyevsky and a bunch of other shit before we parted ways. And for the first time I realized that Black folks didn't have a corner on the market when it came to suffering.

Still and all, I was tired of suffering, myself. Call it low self-esteem, the dehumanization of the Black man; whatever you like but the bottom line was I was tired of the feeling. And I tried like hell to figure out what it was that kept making me feel this way.

After all, I wasn't doin' nothin' but tryin' to enjoy life the same way I always had. All I wanted to do was smoke a little weed, throw on my best gear, step out with a beautiful bitch and wine and dine myself with the best grub and liquor available. That's what life was all about. The only problem was that it got to the point where it just wasn't fun to me anymore. Something had changed.

So, school was a welcome change although, like I said, I'm still at a loss as to how to apply what I'd been learning. And after being back home for awhile

48

everything began to revert back to what was going on before I started classes. That is with the exception of my boys. I saw less and less of them, which was fine but it wasn't long before the women were back and the phone was ringing off the hook.

Not long afterwards, the guilt returned about me not being able to contribute to the household and what not and before I knew it I was sellin' nickel bags of weed again and I could feel myself slowly falling back into the same ol' hopeless charade I'd been in before college. I was in the second semester of my sophomore year now and my grades were still good but I was losing interest and I saw no tangible reward but I kept telling myself that I'd come too far to let it all just slip away.

Every now and then, I'd see Lisa on campus and we'd stop at some little coffee shop down around the college or hit some jazz club down in the village. Most of the time we ended up at her place afterwards, where we'd argue about racism or some other bullshit like Republican politics until the wee hours of the morning. I think her condescending attitude when it came to

race relations was one of the primary reasons I stayed in school as long as I did. I was so interested in showin' little Miss Polly Purebred that she wasn't any better than I was that I kept pushin' on even when my other world told me I didn't belong there.

By this time, I'm seein' about six or seven women on the regular and screwin' another one or two on the side. You think I'm jokin' don't you? You probably can't even imagine no shit like that, can you Clooney? But it's true. One day I slept with three different women all in the same day. I'm telling you the God's honest truth Clooney. I know damn well that that has got to be some of kind of Guinness World Record. But it didn't mean shit to me at the time. I was just tryin' to find some inner peace and the best way I knew how was between some woman's thighs.

One thing that I was sure of and that was the fact that since I wasn't happy with myself I couldn't be happy with no one woman either. I was searchin' for somethin' and still didn't know what it was. But if there was one person I could confide in it was my cousin, Torrie over in Jersey. And right through here everything seemed to be closing in on me. It got to the point where I couldn't even let myself go in the bedroom I was afraid that if I closed my eyes and let go I might call the wrong name.

After awhile, I couldn't even sell enough reefer to wine and dine all these bitches and couldn't smoke enough to forget that I couldn't afford to wine and dine them. And I couldn't let any of them go because by now I was either convinced that I loved them all or needed them all. It was a Catch-22 situation and it wasn't long before all I heard was how I wasn't spending enough time

with them or how the honeymoon must be over. Or what happened to the times when we used to go out and do things, Q?

After awhile it all got to be a bit too much. I got so tired of the bullshit that I got up one day and just left. I had to get away, so I just dropped out of sight for a while. I went over to Jersey and stayed with Torrie. Torrie was different. She was just cool. There were no strings, no pressure. All we did was smoke and talk and fuck. Being that we were second cousins and all we both knew that there was no chance to take it any further and we were cool with that. When I told her about them bitches sweatin' me all he time, she sat me down and took my head in her hands, looked me in the eye and said, "Daddy, don't you ever let no ho's sweat you. You're in demand. You've got what they want. And it's good too. Let them ho's work for you. You're sitting on a goddamn gold mine and don't even know it. Then she put on the Mel Gibson movie, What a Woman Wants, and told me to watch.

Have you seen it, Clooney?"

"No, I don't believe I have." I replied. Q looked at me with a curious glint and grinned mischievously.

"You don't get out much, do ya boy? Anyway, in the movie a bolt of lightning or some shit strikes Mel Gibson and it releases him from all that macho bullshit associated with being a man. Anyway, that bolt of lightning allows him to see what a woman really wants and needs, you know, her innermost desires. Well, that's me. That's what I do in the nutshell. I have been given the unique God-given talent of seeing and feeling and   empathizing. Not that I give a fuck

50

how these bitches really feel or what they want but I can, how do the faggots say? Yeah, yeah, I can read a woman and that's what it takes. Once you can read 'em you've got 'em. Then you can manipulate the mothafuckas. You can have these bitches eating out of the palm of your hand within a matter of only a few short days. You gotta appeal to their weaknesses and inadequacies and a woman in this society has got a hell of a lot of weaknesses and inadequacies.

For one, it's a male oriented society. Know what ah'm sayin'? A woman is powerless unless someone bestows some power on her. Then within her powerlessness there are some dynamics at work on the subconscious level that affects her that half the time she doesn't even realize exists. Everything in our society says that a woman is supposed to grow up subservient to the man. She's taught to play with dolls and be material since birth, which in itself make her dependent on a man. Are you feelin' me Clooney? From the very start, she needs a man to be successful. Her primary function, is to procreate, therefore, she needs a man.

Outside of public office, a man does not need to take a wife. A woman's life on the other hand is geared to growing up, finding a man and marrying that man. Don't believe me? Peep this, Clooney, I'm gonna lay some science on ya that you've probably never really thought about, s forget them bitches on stage and pay attention. When a man turns thirty with good looks and a smattering of charm and dates on the regular, he's referred to in glowing terms as a ladies man. Uptown we refer to them as playas. You feel me? By the same token if a woman reaches thirty or thirty-five and is still single, she becomes a social outcast. It's time for her to begin to hide her age. The connotations become negative. They useta refer to them as spinsters or old hags. We've moved away from that some. Just like the man don't call us niggas to our face anymore,

but the damage has already been done. The shits ingrained so deep, he don't have to call us niggas anymore. It's the same thing with women. Know what ah'm saying?

With all of the soap operas catering to women, they don't have to say anything anymore. Not outright at least. It's woven into the American tapestry that defines where we stand in correlation with each other in the hierarchy, in the overall scheme of things. And being that the Black man serves even less purpose than a woman and hasn't been needed since the days of slavery we're lookin' at the subtle genocide which leads to a very lop-sided ratio of men to women. They say the ratio of Black women to Black men in D.C. alone is eight-to-one. Where are the Black men you may ask? They're either married, living respectable lives or they're drug addicts, or incarcerated. It's a shame, but then again it's not.

You see that's where Adam Smith's Theory of Supply and Demand comes in. You are familiar with Adam Smith aren't you Clooney?

Anyway, that's where yours truly is allowed to come in and profit. I sell each woman a bill of goods. Each of these bitches is beautiful and unique in their own right, but they're all the same. They all want the same thing. They want companionship, an end to loneliness and someone they can depend on. They want someone to love and they want to be financially stable. And after I read them and assess their individual concerns then I fill their needs. But you've got to be careful. You can't let 'em suspect that you're reading them. And ya gotta maintain a cold, controlled indifference towards them at all times. Never let them bitches get close to you. 'Cause I'm tellin' you a woman is in more cases than not smarter than a man will ever be. She's

goin' to try and run the same game on you that you're tryna' run on her to satisfy her needs. If you get too close, too wrapped up in a bitch she'll pull it off too. All a man's got workin' for him is the power societies bestowed on his ass. A woman's got the power the good Lord's bestowed on her. If you ask me it ain't no contest so you can't go in there deaf, dumb and stupid. I seen too many half-assed plain Jane, Jennifer Anniston lookin' bitches wit' handsome, too die for brothas.

Know why a nigga ends up drivin' a Volvo station wagon, shuttlin' the neighborhood brat's back and forth to soccer practice and wonderin' what the fuck happened to his life? It ain't because they in love. It's because they're pussy whipped. Ya gotta forget that shit and realize that every woman has one and all of 'em use it to get paid. All of 'em.... Think about it. One way or another they use it to get paid.

52

Tell the truth, Clooney. When you see a woman walkin' down the street, are you looking at her mind or her ass? If you're the average full-blooded American male then you're looking at her ass. That's just human nature. And she knows it. That's when she throws that extra little jiggle in her walk. Right then and there, right at that very moment that she knows she has your full attention she decides whether or not she wants to reel you in or not. Yes sir, the first time you do a double take and she knows she's got you; hook, line and sinker. What I had to do, personally, was forget the societal thang that says a man must be subservient to a woman. Let the bitch support me, dammit. Its simple Darwinism, baby.

It's in the pimpin' handbook, baby.

Yes sir, here I was walking around head down, sulkin', thinkin' 'bout how times was harder now than back in '29 and feelin' like everything was about ta cave in. I'm up here strugglin' tryna make a dolla, so I can take these ho's out on the regular and they all hollerin' about how I never do nothin' for them or take them nowhere and I'm startin' to wonder if they might not be right.

I'm tryna keep up my profile and pretty soon I feel like the whole damn thing's about to come crashin' down when Torrie hipped me. Yeah, it sho was Torrie who told me that I was playin' myself. She tol' me that with my talent in bed and my brains I needed ta slap the taste outta all them bitches mouths for worryin' me when they was getting' more than just a little dick, more than just a little happiness and more than any other nigga was gonna give 'em based on what they had to offer..

Here I was, givin' all of 'em time on the regular when all of 'em together didn't amount to half a 'ho' when it really came down to it. It was then that I paused for 'bout half a heartbeat to think about what Torrie was saying. And that's all it took to come to realization that she was right.

That my brotha, was the last day that I let a woman rule me or so much as look at me the wrong way. And God forbid they're no knowledge, no college asses get the idea that they want to disagree with somethin' Q has to say. If I even get an inklin' that they thinkin' some ol' off the wall crazy-assed whacked shit

53

when I'm around, heads'll be rollin'. Don't get me wrong,

though, I don't put my hands on 'em. This is the new millennium my brotha. O.J. put an end to all that. A domestic charge, today, can turn into a felony in a heartbeat. And time is money so I ain't got no time for that. I just fine the bitches. Hurts worse when ya hit 'em in the pocketbook, anyway. But let's forget that side of the pimpin' game for a minute. Let's talk about these dumbass Americans for a minute so I can show you a pretty fair correlation that should illuminate things a lil' better for you. Let's talk about your president for just a minute and you fill in the blanks.

Bush ain't hurtin'. He done sold these stupid mothafucka's a bill of sales about them being in imminent danger from weapons of mass destruction and they scared shitless. They so brainwashed runnin' around here thinkin' about Afghanis and Iraqi's that they can't even see the danger right here in their own backyards. They so busy lookin' at the Middle East they're overlooking what's happening right here at home.

From what I understand Hewlett Packard laid off fifteen thousand a few months ago. Now tell me what you consider more destructive those fools over there in the Middle East or this declining economy. Add the families to those that were laid off today and now you're looking at close to fifty thousand people affected by that layoff. And it's so common place now that we just accept it and think nothing of it unless we're the one's affected. Exxon made a profit of eleven billion the last quarter and gas prices are still going up. And meanwhile, he's got us so riled up and so

afraid by these so-called alerts that all we can think about is where the next missile's comin' from when like I said the real danger's right here.

54

Those that still find themselves employed are sitting around on their little fifteen minute coffee breaks wavin' the flag and hating every sand nigger they see walkin' the streets or drivin' a cab with no good reason why except that Mr. Bush old them that they're the enemy. And we're still blaming them for higher gas prices and ignoring the fact that the American owned oil companies are making billions.

In the meantime, Mr. Bush's cronies are orchestrating the whole affair so they can get a lock on the oil market and a strategic foothold over in the Middle East. But CNN ain't asking why and these fools ain't got the ability to question motives. They just sittin' around swallowing every tid bit the media tosses their way and accepting it as gospel.

Funny thing, Clooney but I was watching Al Sharpton the other day talkin' about racial profiling which ain't really no more prevalent now than it has been but more a means of keeping Sharpton's name out there in the spotlight. But you can't argue with brother. It's a problem that does exist and affects us all. Black people that is. In fact, I had to sell my Benz just last year cause I was being stopped so much. I'm talking on a weekly basis. Now I let my wife drive the Escalade while I push this ol' beat up Chevy Caprice with the dent in the front fender and sounds louder than a bomb. And I'll tell you what, Clooney. I ain't changed my driving habits one bit and I ain't been stopped in the last six or seven months. But before that it was once a week. I

kid you not. Most of the time they call it a routine traffic stop to check your license. But in the case of Black folks it's usually to see if there's any drugs in the car, if we have any outstanding warrants or if our papers are in order—that sort of thing. Least that's the bullshit they tell you when they stop you. Don't know nothin' about that do you, Clooney?" Q laughed.

"It's almost like Nazi Germany up here, Clooney. Hitler made the Jews wear red Star of David armbands to identify them in Nazi Germany. It's the same thing up here only thing is our Star of David is our skin color and it doesn't ever come off. Nazi Germany even restricted the Jews to the worse housing conditions in the worst parts of the city and called them ghettoes. Same here. Only thing different here is that their concentration camps and ghettoes were

55

separated. Ours are together and the genocide in Germany pales in comparison to the genocide in Harlem and other urban areas. Did you know that the word ghetto was coined in Nazi Germany during World War II? Only difference is there ghettoes were walled in. Ours dare too but not with physical walls. Hell, they don't even need those anymore. The wall that separates us now is economics my brother. That's the wall that keeps us separated.

But thanks in large part to my old lady my paperwork is always intact even though that don't mean shit if the Gestapo really want to haul my ass in and I guess I've been pretty fortunate so even though being stopped, harassed and inconvenience constantly I let that shit slide. That's the truth, Clooney.

In any case and to make a long story short, I am not faulting Al Sharpton for addressing the topic because I can attest to what the brotha's sayin' from my own experience. But there's a bigger question Sharpton and most Americans aren't even attempting to discuss. We're so preoccupied with the small shit that most of us aren't aware and those that are aware are so busy going about their daily routines that they're the ignoring the significance, and the ramifications and pretty soon they all going to be thinking that they're all the victims of racial profiling.

I'm referring to the Patriot Act and Homeland Security. Those two acts make racial profiling look like petty theft—a fuckin' misdemeanor. But nowadays because of this so-called imminent threat from countries with no planes to get here let alone air force these mothafuckas can log into your personal computer that all of a sudden ain't so personal anymore while you're sitting there searching for Girls Gone Wild or Big Black Bootys and gather all the information they want on your ass.

Because of the Patriot Act, these mothafuckas now have the right to see what books you've checked out of the library. They can tap your phone on suspicion and all with the perceived notion that you could be a terrorist and a threat to national security. Picture that. This shit may prove worse than McCarthyism ever was. So, you see why I'm dismissing Sharpton's claims about racial profilin'. Hell, racial profilin' ain't nothin' but a footnote, a subsection, and addendum in the Patriot Act and the infringement on people's rights.

So, if you were to ask me I would tell you that our fears are unfounded. Americans are finally beginning to see that the real terror for most of us comes from being out of work, and not being able to feed your kids. The real terror comes when one of your loved ones gets sick and you can't afford a doctor and if you can then you can't afford the medicine he prescribes. That's why Clinton and Obama are such a welcome relief. There a welcome relief because thanks to them Americans are finally beginning to wake up and understand that the real terror doesn't come from the outside but the inside. The real terror comes when you can't take your family to the movies on the weekend or stop off on your way home from work on payday and get a little trim—you know—a little strange on the side. You do know what trim and strange are don't cha Clooney?"

"No, I'm sorry to say that I'm not familiar with those terms Q," I said having grown a whole lot more respectful of the man who sat across from me now. His vast body of knowledge was far more than I expected and tore down most if not all of the preconceived notions I'd had coming into the interview.

"You can't be serious," he laughed. "You honestly mean to tell me that you don't know what trim is. Boy you have been sheltered haven't you? Anyway, like I was saying, that's the real terror if you ask me. And who's responsible for a man not being able to stop off and get him a lil' trim after working hard all week? Why none other than George W. If you ask me, he's the only real terrorist. Shit, Osama ain't in hiding. He's sittin' right here. He's in the White House.

He's coming to you live on CNN every night. That's who the Homeland Security Department needs to watch if you ask me. But who am I? I'm just an ignorant, low-life pimp shut off from the rest of the world up here in no-man's land—up here in a Harlem they don't want no more.

But ask yourself this, Clooney while you're riding back to your big plush office downtown. Ask yourself who the real pimp is. Ask yourself who is really and truly pimpin' America. It sure as hell ain't Gary Quinton better known as GQ. Shit, I'm only big time in a ghetto wasteland white folks know as Harlem. While y'all tryna find an evil villain and a scapegoat Bush gonna steal your nose right from under your face and y'all still gonna be blamin' me and Osama and Saddam for the problems of the world today. But like I said I'm only big time in Harlem and that ain't nowhere in the whole scheme of things. Y'all save the big pimpin' for Brother Bush. He pimpin' all y'all.

The Preacher and the Prostitute

Chapter 1

"What's up girl? I just saw your boy Q on the way in and man was he pissed. Thank God the police was about to give him a ticket and I got hold of him before he got to you or he might have stomped a mud hole in that pretty little ass of yours. I grabbed him and pushed him into the back room before he had a chance to really get stupid. And let me tell you, I had all I could do to convince him that it wouldn't look good for business if he was to make a scene and especially with the police bein' right outside. The way he was actin' though I don't really think he gives a fuck about the police or anybody else at this point.

What in the hell did you do? I cannot honestly remember ever seein' him that angry with you. I mean he's pissed to the highest pissivity and that's unusual for Q. He was tryin' to come and see you but I told him to calm his ass down and let me speak to you first and try to straighten this shit out and let me tell you what this fool gonna tell me. He gonna tell me that I better straighten shit out or he's gonna come fuck my ass up as well. Picture that. Here' I am tryin' to play peacemaker in some shit I ain't got nothin' at all to do with and he's gonna throw me in the mix and threaten me. The whole thing's crazy if you ask me."

"Sorry, didn't mean to get you involved, Carrie. It ain't nothin' really. Q's trippin' 'cause he let me walk and I came back is all, I suppose. He may pretend that I've been coming up short with his money but the bottom line is he's upset 'cause he thought that I had enough common sense to walk away from the game and stay away. But here I am. He can't figure the shit out and it's bothering him. And I haven't really had a chance to have a face-to-face with him and he thinks I owe him at least that."

"And you're sure it's got nothing to do with the money," the older woman asked.

"It could. I don't know and don't really care." I answered tired of the rigmarole, the bullshit, and pretty much life in general. It had been a rough week up to this point and I really didn't feel like going through any silly-assed bullshit over a couple of dollars.

"You don't know and you don't care? Do you understand how close you were to getting your ass kicked, Diamond? And because it hasn't happened yet doesn't mean it still can't. I'm tellin' you the only reason it didn't was because I intervened on your behalf, baby girl."

"And I thank you for that but like I said it's nothing to worry yourself over, Carrie." I knew Carrie was only looking out for my best interest and trying to keep me safe. She'd been doing it for years and though I'd looked up to her in the past and was grateful for all she'd done on my behalf, there was little she could do to remedy the situation now. The fact of the matter was that I was tired. Exhausted. Tired of men and the games they played.

"Nothin' to worry yo'self over... Is that what I heard you say? Girl, you didn't see the expression on that fool's face a few minutes ago. Look, maybe you're not aware of it but Q's not just any run of the mill pimp. Maybe you haven't recognized it yet, but he ain't what you might wanna call typical or ordinary. And long as you've been with him, you should know that. So, I'm askin' you to please tell me. What the hell are you doing, Diamond? Are you just fuckin' with him for the hell of it? If you are, I'm here to tell you it's one hell of a dangerous game you're playing. You know Q's crazy about you. Always has been always will be but you seem like you're intent on destroying any love he has for you. The real truth is any one of us would love to be in your spot. Just to get a portion of the respect that he gives you. And what do you do? Your silly ass takes it all for granted.

You probably feel like nothing's gonna happen to you because nothing ever has but let me tell you. You're taking advantage of the situation. You think he won't put his hands on you if you're short on his money. Well, I'm here to tell you that there's a very good chance you could be wrong in this instance. You keep bluffin' and bullshittin' and see what happens. I've seen it. Besides, nobody forced you into this arrangement and since you agreed to give him his cut in exchange for his services then the least you can do is honor your agreement with the man. You feel me?

Damn! While the rest of us are out here walkin' these streets wit' Q's boy Jay standin' over us, watching every lil' thing we do, you're walkin' around in high cotton like you're some goddamn

queen. And from what Chocolate be tellin' me, the motherfucka done set you up in a penthouse, in the high rent district, over on the East Side wit' nothin' but the best of everything. They tell me you ain't fuckin' wit' nothin' but high class johns that pay so well that yo' ass don't have to trick but once or twice a week and you're still tellin' Q to kiss yo' ass.

You know, if you had any kind of brains at all, you would use whatever kind of hold that you have over Q to wrap his ass around yo' little finger, get paid and make it easier on the rest of us instead of sittin' up here makin' waves for no reason other than to watch the ripples.

I just can't understand you, Diamond. Would you please tell me what in the hell is wrong with you? To me it seems like you're just up here for the hell of it, for the yell of it while the rest of us be doin' our best tryna sell it. Is it the thrill of livin' on the edge out here in these streets that turns you on?

I know as tight as yo' ass is and wit' your broker friends investing for you that you've probably got quite a little nest egg to fall back on so there's really no need for yo' ass to come up short wit' Q's money. Any way you roll the dice. It just don't make no sense. So, like I said before, please help me to understand 'cause none of what you're doing adds up. It just don't add up, sugar.

I know you probably ain't hearin' me or are probably wishing that I'd just shut the fuck up but I can't. I wish I could but I can't. See, I been out here too long and had my ass beat too many

times to see the same thing happen to you. You know me Diamond. If I can help you out in some way so you don't have to go through the same ol' unnecessary bullshit that I went through then I feel compelled to do just that. I guess it's just something in me. Kind of like a motherly instinct or something. I don't know. Maybe it comes from raisin' eight younger brothers and sisters. Like I said, I don't know but if I feel I can save a sista a ass whoopin' then I gotta try. 'Cause to me there ain't nothin' worser or more humiliatin' than bein' dragged down the middle of Lenox Avenue at five or six o'clock when everyone's getting off work with some nigga beatin' your ass for the whole world to see. When that does happen, it seems like every nigga that you ever grew up wit, every nigga you've ever slept wit' or sat down to have a drink wit' just happens to be standin' on Lenox Avenue that day watchin' some low-life, two-bit, no-good, thug nigga rob you of any pride and dignity that you may still have. Trust me. It's happened to me and it don't feel good at all. And at the risk of sounding like I'm meddling or being nosy it's just always easier to see someone else's mistakes than it is to see your own.

Now if you want me to back off Diamond I will 'cause sometimes I do have a way of talkin' too much," the older woman admitted.

"No, Carrie go ahead. I know you you're telling me because you care and are just trying to look out for me but right now I'm so twisted and confused that whatever you have to say can only help."

"Well, for one thing Diamond the years have been good to you. What are you thirty? Thirty-one?"

"I'm thirty-five, Carrie."

"Good Lord! Know you're not. You mean to tell me that we've been together close to twenty years. 'Cause when me and Q found you under the bridge, you couldn't have been no more than sixteen or seventeen at the most."

"I was sixteen when you guys found me. It's been almost twenty years," I replied hoping to speed the whole affair along without dismissing or hurting Carrie's feelings.

"Well, you can hardly tell. You don't look a day over twenty-one or twenty-two. You're still young and pretty and probably don't think you'll ever grow old. How did the old folks used to put it? Probably think yo' shit don't stank… But like I said, Diamond, I've been around the corner enough times that they can name the damn street after me. And I pray that you don't have to go where I've been 'cause where I've been ain't always been what you might call pretty. I know some shortcuts that can help you get by them dark alleyways filled with nothin' but trouble and I'd like to help you get around them if I can.

Right now the shit you gittin' ready to git into is all in the past as far as my life's concerned. And you know what's nice about that is the fact that I can walk away from all this bullshit tomorrow

if I want to, never look back and never have a worry in the world. You see, I done did my time and I don't owe nobody nothin'. Not a goddamn thing.

The onliest reason I stuck around this long was because I really and truly do love that nigga, Q. I mean I really does love that nigga. I know it's stupid and don't make an ounce a sense to anyone but me but that's just the way it is. I always has and I guess I always will. When he tol' me he was gonna leave his wife back in the day I never really believed him. I pretty much figured he was just telling me that to make it that much easier to keep me around. But I figured that if there was any possibility at all of me having any parts of his life then it was worth hanging around. I mean even if it meant me being no more than his mistress then I had to stick around. Do you understand what I'm sayin' girl? Any parts of Q was better than having nothing at all even if it meant me being nothing more than his bottom bitch.

But do you know what Q was to me? Q was my salvation, my piece of happiness; maybe the only happiness I've ever really known in my life. And besides that, I knew that the onliest reason his wife was in the picture at all was because of his sense of loyalty. She used to take care of his ass long before he got into the game. And from what I heard, he dogged her just like he dogs all women. I don't mean he had her out there stuntin' or trickin' but he was runnin' the streets sleepin' wit' every bitch he could lay down wit' and she was always there for him when he got put out or just needed some place to rest his head.

Now don't you go repeatin' that. That's just somethin' I heard and you know you can't go putting too much stock in shit you hear out here in these streets. But just think about it. How many pretty young niggas would still be wit' an ol' hag twenty years their senior when they got a stable full of pretty young bitches at their beck and call? And you know as well as I do that a lot of these young gals out here still find Q quite attractive even at forty-seven or forty-eight. Why else would that pretty nigga be wit' a woman damn near seventy that ain't got no money?"

"Did you ever think that the front Q puts on for us is only a front and maybe, just maybe, he really does love that woman?" I asked Carrie and sorry I had as soon as the words left my mouth.

"Thought about it but it doesn't make any sense if you ask me. First of all, Q's first love is money and he ain't never made no bones when it came to the fact that if you're coming to the table you'd better bring a something and ol' girl

63

ain't got no money or at least the kind of money Q's used to. She gets a little retirement check from the city but that ain't no money to speak of."

I couldn't count the times over the years that Carrie had me sit down for a heart-to-heart talk. The conversation would inevitably turn to her undying love and devotion for Q. And everyone knew that Q didn't care any more about her than a man in the moon. I wanted to tell her that I really was no more interested in this conversation than Q was in her old tired ass. But out of respect, she felt compelled to listen knowing that aside from her the woman had no one to listen and I may very well have been the closest thing to a friend that she had and so I did my best to listen to a story I'd heard a thousand times before.

"Diamond are you listening?"

Carrie must have noticed that the younger woman was in another world. Embarrassed by being caught daydreaming Diamond snapped back to attention.

"Yes Carrie, I'm listening," I said staring her straight in the eye.

"Anyway Q's wife has got to be close to seventy if she's a day and Q ain't nothin' but forty-seven or forty-eight. Bitch is old as dust but he's still with her. Have you had a chance to meet her?"

"No, can't say that I have."

"Well to tell you the truth, Diamond; I don't really believe that he's ever going to leave her. Even if he don't like something he's one that figures that if he commits to someone or something he has to stick with it and follow it through to the bitter end. That's the one thing I admire about him most and in this case the thing that I most detest. He'd rather suffer his entire life with a bad decision than to break his word. That's just the way he is. He's the same way in the game too. And I'll tell you what, Diamond, you ain't gonna find too many pimps runnin' the game the way Q do.

Shit, that nigga been to college and everything. That's why the nigga knows his way around a checkbook so good. Hell, when this nigga first pushed up on me back in '82 I ain't had a pot to

piss in or a window to throw it out of. I'm tellin' ya girl, times was hard. Now thanks to Q, I got a nice little nest egg and a cute little, three-bedroom crib out on the island that's six months from being paid for.

And you know what else? The nigga ain't never laid a hand on me unless it's been in a lovin' way. And Lord knows when he did I couldn't do nothin' but grin and bear it. I'm tellin' you the God's honest truth, girl when Q used to touch me I'd tingle straight down to my toes. Straight down to my toes. Afterwards, I wasn't good for shit. I could have been out there all night long with every john in Harlem. I could have been tired and sore as hell and all he had to do was touch me and I was too through. Has that ever happened to you, Diamond? I mean when the shit was so good that your shit would just start tingling all over? Ain't nothin' like it. I get chills just thinkin' about it. I'd wake up in the mornin', wore-out, sex-funky and still cravin' for more. Talk about a nigga that could work a pussy into a frenzy. Q used to do that for me, girl. There were other times I'd come in at five or six in the morning and I'd be so goddamned tired my shit would be deader than dead, and Q would give that mothafucka mouth-to-mouth resuscitation and shazam, the pussy would wake up jumpin' and twitchin'; durn near good as new. Talk about a revival. My shit felt just like it had been born again."

I couldn't help but laugh but I sure wished she'd get to the point. I was tired of the scene at the strip club and didn't want to do anything but go home and crawl under my covers and call it a day. Looking at Carrie I could still the youthful exuberance that at one time made her, the top dog in Q's stable.

Carrie was still a handsome woman despite the crescent-shaped scar that had been into her left cheek by some jealous fool. Carrie went on but her smile was all but gone replaced now with hurt and desperation, which slowly crept into her eyes as she spoke.

"You know Diamond, I've slept with a lot of men, even more than I care to remember but I ain't never been wit' no trick or linked wit' no man—you know romantically—that made me feel the way Q made me feel. Back then, I was infatuated. I useta think the nigga was off the hook in the bedroom but now looking back I'm not exactly sure those feelings was purely sexual. You know what I'm sayin'? You know a woman ain't like a man. A woman needs and wants to be loved by a man and that man is usually enough to fulfill her every need. But a man just ain't built that way. A man needs more than one woman and most of the time he still ain't satisfied. That's the way Q is. Enough is never enough. No matter how much money or how many women he has, it's just never enough."

By this time, I'd had quite enough of Carrie's little pity party and in my time away, it wasn't one of the things that I missed at all but here I was back in the groove though not according to Q and listening to her crying over a man. Well, Carrie was right about one thing. Enough was enough. Much as I knew it would hurt I couldn't sit by and listen to this shit again.

"Carrie wasn't it you who taught me that a man was nothing but a man," I asked trying not to sound truculent.

"Yeah, I guess I did," she lowering her eyes and picking up her drink.

"And weren't you the one that told me that a woman who falls in love is a fool?"

"Yeah, I suppose I did but…"

66

"Weren't you also the one that told me that a woman falls in love whereas a man only falls in love with sex? Weren't you also the one that told me that a man ain't interested in anything but the chase and the eventual conquest and warned me about ever falling in love with a man if I cared about myself and that if it did have the possibility of working then it was a gift from God but whatever I did never ever fall in love with a married man? Wasn't it you who told me those things over and over again," I asked.

"Yeah, I told you that so you could protect yourself and never have to go through this. I don't know why but I figured that in the end, Q would come to his senses but each day I'd pray a little more that he'd see the light. I hate to say it but I used to wish that that ol' bitch he married would just up and die so's I could have him but you know what I learned, girl? I learned that you can't possess no 'nother human bein'. I guess now the onliest reason I still stick around is that I don't know nothin' else. Guess Q was right 'bout one thing. I was so caught up in runnin' the streets behind him that I forget what it was that I wanted out of my own life. Nowadays, he

don't really concern hisself wit' me much unless it's pertaining to business but I still remember the good times like they was yesterday.

When he gits the notion to have sex with me now, he still makes me feel like I did when I was twenty and I'm damn near fo'ty now. Still, out of all the men we've come to know you've gotta admit that he's been more honest and down to earth than most. And in most cases he treated us like queens, like we was really something special. You've gotta admit that," she asked almost pleading.

"Yeah, I guess he did," I said seeing just how hurt she was and not trying to burst her bubble anymore than I already had.

"That's why I have such a hard time tryna understand you, Diamond. I can remember when me and Q first found you down under the bridge around Hunt's Point. You was all swoll up after Pee Wee beat yo' ass. When we found you, you was lyin' face down in the gutter all beat up and lookin' half-dead. You looked like holy hell. And I ain't gonna lie. I tol' Q to leave yo' ass right there.

Last thing I needed was another dumb, troublesome bitch to have to chase down. Do you remember that?"

'Remember? How could I forget? Every time we sat down to talk Carrie told me the same story of how she found me and saved me and then brought me up to know the streets and be a classy and proper whore. Still, I nodded and smiled out of respect as if this was my first time hearing

the story. I watched her, smiling, Newport dangling from her lips as puffs of smoke rose and curled away to join the other puffs of smoke in the dimly lit club and wondered if this was one of the highlights of her life.'

"Hell, when we found your ass, we was just getting started ourselves. Everyday me and Q would patrol the streets of Harlem and the Bronx lookin' for pretty young thangs just like yourself that had fallen on hard times so we could bring 'em in. At the time, I think Q must have had about twenty girls in his stable. That was back in '86 when crack cocaine first hit the streets. That's the reason most of them no-account bitches was out there anyway. Outta the twenty or so he started with, half of 'em was on that shit and that was on the onliest reason they was trickin' in the first place.

Trust me Di. Bein' Q's number wasn't hardly no picnic back then. Half of those gals are dead now. Hard as I tried to work to keep them in check, most of 'em didn't want shit outta they lives 'cept another hit off the pipe and you can see where that got 'em. You've been around for a minute Di, so you know I ain't lyin'. The night we picked you up I seriously thought you were like the rest of them triflin' heifers that's why I was so opposed to Q pickin' you up. But Q saw somethin' even then. Through the dirt and the swollen cut up face of yours, he saw something in you.

I remember your mouth bein' so swollen that you couldn't even tell us your name. I told him to call an ambulance but he acted like he didn't even hear me and told me to give him a hand getting you inside the car. Do you remember those first few weeks you was with us? I named you, 'Can't Get Right' 'cause you couldn't get a goddamn thing right when I asked you to do something. I mean you was forever fuckin' something up. If it wasn't pickin' up the vice squad then you'd let a john fuck you 'til you passed out and forget to get him to pay you. You sure was something back then Di. You used to keep us all in stitches. But you was one beautiful girl and niggas would come back to pay you after they'd gotten away scott-free just so they could sleep with you again.

I think you was the one that prompted Q to start that escort agency he had back in the early nineties. He had so many fellas that just wanted you to escort them to this event or that without even wanting to sleep with you and willing to pay crazy money just for you to make them look good when they had some type of formal event to attend that Q seriously considered stopping you from trickin' altogether. But there was no stopping you. You was so eager to get rich quick that you wanted to do it all. Trick, escort, everything. Damn near wore yourself out that first year 'til I made you stop trickin'.

You was one beautiful girl in those days and that's not to say that you're not beautiful now Diamond but you had that youthful innocence back then. The streets have a way of leaving your looks but taking the innocence from them. Shit, there was days that I thought about raping yo' ass and turning you out myself," Carrie laughed.

"You wasn't too bad yourself, lady," I joked wondering how we'd gotten on this subject. She was rambling now and I knew that the Hennessey was having its affect.

"I know you ain't trying to flirt with this ol' tired ass," Carrie shot back flashing a smile that let me know she appreciated the compliment. She was staring at me now trying to see if all that she'd said up to this point had broken down the barrier between us. And I knew that as much as she cared about me she was working on her own behalf as well. If she could get me to open up then she'd have something to take back to Q and maybe just maybe she could turn his head enough for him to see her.

I could feel her probing the deepest recesses of my mind as if she were tryin' to unearth my very soul and expose what it was that made me tick. I knew that it had always been important for her to get a feel for the girls around her, to know what they were thinking so she could eliminate problems before they became situations. But in the years since we'd first met she'd never gotten to know me the way she wanted to and I had as much to do with keeping her at bay as anyone. We might have been close and I may have turned to her in times of need but my life was my life and not an open book for Carrie or anyone else to read and decipher.

"Like I was saying," Carrie continued. "You was bright and good lookin' and it was pretty obvious right from jump that you was pretty well-educated but Lord knows you didn't have a lick of common sense. But the streets changed that in no time at all. Pretty soon you knew your

way around the streets and the game better than most of them gals who been wit' me for years. Still, I gotta say your saving grace was your beauty and I just hope it saves you tonight."

Chapter 2

Unlike most pimps, Carrie explained, Q was not a violent man but that wasn't to say that pushed far enough he couldn't lose it too. When he was up and coming and fighting for his piece of the Harlem landscape, he'd beat a bitch's ass in half a heartbeat and never think twice about it. But as he'd aged, he'd mellowed considerably; kind of like a vintage wine that grows stronger yet smoother with time.

Now in his late forties he was nowhere near the brash young playa he used to be but it was a well-known fact that that you still didn't mess with his money or his ho's. Yet, there always seemed to be some game young buck out to make a name for himself that just had to go and test Q to see what he was made of.

Only two weeks earlier, a small-time wanna be playa fresh out of Riker's Island who went by the name of Pretty Toney decided that he'd lost too much time and too much money locked away and he needed to make up for lost time at Q's expense.

According to Pretty Toney, it was time to replace the old with the new and the only way he could do this was by stepping up the game and letting all the ol' hustlas know there was a new sheriff in town. Now why Pretty decided to target Q first was a mystery to us all. But target Q he did even though everyone in Harlem told Pretty that he was making a grave mistake in doing so.

You see anyone who had spent some time on the streets of Harlem knew that Q was not to be taken lightly. Well, that is everyone except Pretty Toney.

In any case, Pretty must have gotten the notion that Q was getting soft since in the short time he'd been out of Riker's he'd been to all the clubs and after hour spots and not once in those first couple of weeks out had he seen Q around. To Pretty that meant that Q was no longer on the scene and was letting business slip. To test the waters, Pretty decided to hit on a couple of Q's girls letting them know that he was back, was about to open up shop and that they could join him at any time. Then he went about making the usual promises about what he could and would do for them if they were to jump ship.

Well, Q had feelers all over the place and it didn't take him long to get wind of Pretty's antics and bein' that Q is a fair man and lenient to a fault he let it slide but he did warn Pretty that pushing up on his girls was a no no. But I guess since Q didn't approach him screamin' and yellin' with a bazooka in one hand and a Beretta in the other Pretty must have thought Q was just bullshittin' or somethin'. He went right on talkin' shit and rollin' up on Chocolate, Paradise and some other gal. I can't recall who the other gal was since she didn't mention it but Chocolate and Paradise are good girls and have always been pretty loyal and one day both of 'em came in and told Q what had been going on after Q had warned him. Of course, Q already knew and was still trying hard to let it slide but when they came and told him, he didn't have much choice since that's his job to protect them from harassment and threats and shit along those lines. But he tried

to let it slide. I swear he did 'cause that's just the way he is. He's always sayin', give a nigga a lil' rope and he'll sho nuff hang himself but give a nigga give him too much rope and the nigga ends up thinkin' he's a cowboy. And that's just what Pretty must have been thinkin' when Q didn't jump on him the first time. I mean not only did he think he was a cowboy he really got to thinkin' he was the new sheriff in town. Not only that he started tellin' everybody that Q couldn't keep his women and pretty soon he'd have 'em all.

A couple of days later Q caught Pretty talkin' to Chocolate up on 145th and Lenox. And let me tell you, girl. In all my days, I ain't seen no shit like what I saw that day up on Lenox and 145th. It was just like something out of the Old Wild West. Q rolled up on that nigga and pulled him right outta that brand new silver and gray Hummer and got to pistol whippin' that pretty nigga right there in front of everybody. Started whippin' that nigga's ass right smack dab in the middle of Lenox Avenue. Now I'll tell you honestly, I've seen so much shit out there in those mean streets that hardly anything affects me nowadays but I really and truly felt for that pretty nigga. When he got finished that pretty nigga wasn't hardly pretty no more. I mean Q whipped that nigga's ass to where his momma wouldn't recognize him. Then when he got finished beatin' that boy's behind he turned to his boy 'J' and said, 'lullaby this bastard' And anybody that knows 'J' knows that 'J' don't play. 'J' said, 'rock-a-bye-baby', and emptied the whole clip from that big ol' nine millimeter into what was left of Pretty Toney's ass right there in front of everybody. And then as if that wasn't enough, Q walked over to that boy's body reached into his

pocket grabbed Pretty's keys and told that dead nigga's hoes to get in and drove the fuck away with four new bitches to add to his stable.

Do you remember that, Di?"

"Do I remember that? How could I forget. I was the one of the one's that Pretty was hittin' on. I just never said anything 'cause I didn't want anything like that to happen on my account," I replied. "I never did particularly care for Pretty but like I said, I'd never want anything to happen to anybody on my account. He was funny to me. I never took him seriously. He was just another low-life nigga tryin to come up in the game is all. Wasn't no need for no drama. Everybody knew Pretty Toney just liked to talk. He had some of the corniest lines of any mack I know. He was harmless."

"That's all true but I think you're missin' the point, sugar. This ain't about Pretty Toney. What I'm tryin' to tell you is that Q's a pretty good brother as far as pimps go. But what I betcha didn't know is that Q adopted Pretty when he was about fourteen and raised him like a son but one fuck up and he had him killed. Now I betcha didn't know that did you. He sent that boy away to prep school and everything after his mama died and did everything he could to keep him outta Harlem. And you saw the end result. I said all that to say that Q treats us better than any nigga out here. Hell, what ho you know that's got benefits from layin' on yo' ass all day? None! Now, I'm warning you 'cause that's what the fuck I'm supposed to do. That's my goddamn job but I'm also warning you because you and me goes a long way back. You more like a daughter

to me than my own kids and I done my best to keep yo' ass alive this long and I'll be damn if I let somethin' happen to yo' ass now. I've always had yo' best interest at heart and much as I love that nigga I don't know what I'd do if he put his hands on you so whatever beef you have between you two I suggest you fix it with the quickness 'cause Carrie's to old to go to jail over some dumb shit.

I don't want nobody comin' up to me tellin' me that they done found yo' body like they found Pretty Toney's over in them foul-ass smellin' swamps in Jersey. And Lord knows it's pretty damn hard for me to explain to Q how a bitch drops from twelve hundred a week to six or seven and I ain't even gonna try. It just ain't no accountin' for that. It's like Q be tellin' us all the time Di: if you don't need his services then just let him know and you on yo' own. It's as simple as that. It ain't that Q ain't appreciative of all you've done for him over the years but you've got to put yourself in his situation.

Come on Diamond. Anybody that's been around for as long as you have knows the score and for whatever reason you been comin' up short lately it's making Q look real bad and you know how important it is that daddy looks good for his public baby. That's what keeps him on top of the game. That's what keeps him a goddamn legend. He sho can't have no sheisty shit going on right here in his own family. Right now I'm thinkin' that the onliest one's that know about our situation is the three of us but if this shit gits out you know who's going to have to pay don't you sweetie?" Carrie reached across the table placing her hand on top of mine to let me know just how serious she was.

"If you are having money problems you know you can always talk to Q. I'm sure he'll let you hold something 'til you work it out. He ain't never turned you down yet, has he? You know Q feel the same way 'bout you that I do. And the onliest reason I figures he's so upset now is that we both know that you ain't on no dope or nothin' but you still comin' up short ever since you got back and that's almost three weeks now. And you ain't said nothin'—not a goddamn word to nobody. Q's like your daddy girl. And iffen you can't tell your daddy you got problems then who the fuck can you tell? Hell, even if you couldn't tell Q I thought you and I were close enough that you could confide in me. But you ain't said shit to me either. We've always been like family and you know there ain't no secrets when it comes to family. And what you don't realize is how much it hurts us when you keep secrets from us. Do you understand?"

I understood and I nodded my head to let her know that I did but what she didn't understand, what she didn't have the ability to comprehend was that I was tired. There were other things in life besides runnin the streets whorin' and bein' pimped by men. Not only that I was tired of the game and having to watch my back at all times. I was tired of men using me or at least thinking they could fuck with my mind and then my body as well. I don't know where they got the impression that I was nothin' more than a Fisher Price toy to be played with when they saw fit but those days were over and Q or no one else was going to use this sista anymore. The hell with

Q and every other dick swingin' bullshit artist out there who called himself a man. And fact of the matter was that there wasn't a goddamn thing any of them including Q could do to me that hadn't been done by some low-life motherfucker already. Not a goddamn thing. One thing was for sure though. I'd be damned if I'd sit around and grow old and be worn the fuck out like Carrie's ass. Never will you catch me chasin' around behind some two-bit hustler to do his bidding for some damn dick while he robs me blind. Might have happened in the past but I'll be damn if I ever let it happen again. Not in this lifetime.

Chapter 3

Truth of the matter was that I'd never met a man whether preacher or pimp that was interested in anything more than sexin' me. No matter how the relationship started off it all came down to the same thing. And to the man they'd all pay me to do that. Still, I really thought the good reverend with all his holier than thou talk of starting over and healing the wounds and redemption just might be different. Yet, he turned out to be the same as all the rest in the end.

At least Q made it a point to be upfront about his shit. He never pretended to love me then try to use me like the good reverend had. And not once did Q give all that lip service to loving thy neighbor and not committing adultery. Well, truth be told, the good reverend didn't know a goddamn thing about loving thy neighbor or anybody else for that matter. He didn't have a clue. The only thing he was ever concerned with was me throwing a dress on Sunday mornings to dress up that old tired congregation. And I'm supposed to know men. I should have seen it coming.

What was it Q used to say about every man wanting a sophisticated woman in the study and a hoochie and a ho behind closed doors. Well he'd certainly been right about that one. Hell, the reverend didn't love me any more than he loved that damn Escalade he spent all day waxing. And in the end he hardly ever saw me. Oh, I'd be there but he never saw   me.

Chocolate had center stage now, gyrating slowly while Usher cried about a lost love and Carrie continued singing the praises of the only man she'd known—Q. It was too bad that he hadn't the time, in all the years they'd spent together to come to know her for the person she was beneath

that hard exterior. Diamond's thoughts drifted. She wondered how she'd gotten to this place, to this point in her life. It seemed like just yesterday that she could smell the sweet aroma of her mother's homemade biscuits and bacon frying. She could still here her mother singing in the kitchen as she dragged herself out of bed and got ready for school. It all seemed just like yesterday. Where had the time gone?

Once, a few years back, she thought she'd seen her father across the subway platform and her heart soared but a train pulled into the station just as their eyes met and when the train pulled away he was gone as well. Several times, she thought about stopping by just to see how they were getting along but her foolish pride refused to let her. She missed them. Lord knows she missed them but she'd grown calloused and enjoyed knowing that if she hurt then they hurt as well.

Sitting there across the table from Carrie, Diamond reminisced, her thoughts racing as she tried desperately to put the scattered remnants of her life into some type of order.

Diamond's thoughts kept drifting back to the men that had come and gone in her life and for some reason thought of Rasheed. He'd been her first boyfriend and probably had as much to do with her being in the bind she was in than any other man she'd come into contact with before or after.

Chapter 4

I was sixteen when he first came along. He was twenty or twenty-one. We got along great and had a world of things in common except for the fact that he was sexually active and I wasn't. But aside from that everyone thought we were the perfect couple. Still, it bothered me. Oh I'd let guys touch me and I'd even let one guy rub my stuff once but I'd never even considered going all the way. For that to happen I would have had to be in love and whoever it was would surely have to be the one.

As far as Rasheed went, there's no doubt that I liked him a lot but I was still having my doubts about whether he was in reality the one for me or not. Sure, I liked him. I liked him a lot. And I really hated to think about losing him simply because I was trying to hold on to my virginity.

I knew that it was just a matter of time before he'd get around to asking. After all they all did and every time she told them no, they were gone within a matter of days. Oh, the nicer guys hung around a little longer but in the end, they left as well. I hoped that Rasheed would be different but something inside told me that he would leave too if I rejected him. Up 'til the he'd been pretty much the gentlemen when it came down to pushing me into anything. Still, I kind of knew it was coming. Then there was the fact that all my girlfriends were already kickin' it and they didn't seem to any the worst for it. But I knew that I wasn't like the rest of them. Besides daddy already had me going to Dartmouth and here I was only a junior in high school.

Hell, when I received my acceptance letter at the end of my junior year mommy and daddy lost their minds and made more to do about it than I did. To me it was no big deal. I was a good

student whose whole life centered on doing well in school. It wasn't that I was a nerd or anything but I hardly ever went anywhere beside school and the library. I was on every committee and by the time I became a senior I was named president of my senior class, was a member of the National Honor Society and the Spanish Club. I was named captain of the softball; swim teams, and spoke both Spanish and French fluently. My career goal was to be an interpreter at the

United Nations and all was well within my reach. But like I said I wasn't a nerd or some kind of bookworm or anything. I just didn't have anything better to do since my parents refused to let me hang out with the low-lifes and street people as they called 'em.

Chapter 5

Raised in Harlem's, Sugar Hill with its rich tradition Diamond's parents kept a close eye on her making sure she was in the house by nine o'clock every day, leaving her little time for boys or dating. She knew even less about the people and the goings on that made up Harlem's storied street life. Her father used to tell her there'd be plenty of time for all that later but right now all she needed to worry about was graduating.

'The streets have been in Harlem long before Black people knew there was a Harlem,' he would tell her and 'they'll be here long after most of these Black folks are dead and gone.'

All the same, to Diamond Massey the streets of Harlem held something special, something breathtaking and alive, pulsating. When she first met Rasheed, a bright but struggling artist, he seemed to epitomize the very essence of the Harlem life she wanted so badly to know and be a part of. He epitomized the very essence of Harlem and he had the unique ability of being able to capture it on canvas and bring it home to her each night. His portraits and collages of everyday people scurrying to and from work, of winos with their bottles of cheap wine in their back pockets proselytizing on street corners and junkies doing their best to hold up the crumbling walls of vacant tenements saliva drooling from parched lips only ingratiated Harlem in Diamonds eyes. Each work brought another piece of the mystery that was Harlem closer to Diamond and she could remember sitting for hours on end discussing the portraits and the motivation behind each. For in Diamonds eyes it was the playas, the hustlers, along with the musicians, the writers and the movie stars that made up a Harlem she was in the midst of but knew little or nothing about.

With each stroke of his brush, Rasheed brought the ambiguity of the streets to life for Diamond. She knew and understood Chaucer, Milton, and Langston but she had no idea why Mrs. Hamilton in 2C would chance leaving her newborn baby alone to cross Lenox to get a hit of crack. It puzzled her and intrigued her at the same time. She just didn't understand. Most of Harlem apart from her stoop was a mystery but just knowing and being with Rasheed, helped Diamond to better understand.

Even when it came to sex, she had a hard time understanding what all the hype and hoopla was about. Nowadays that was all the boys her age talked about. Well, that's all they talked about besides hip-hop and playin' ball.

And Rasheed was turning out to be no different. When he first moved into her building a few months before they started seeing each other they'd talk casually as friends. When she'd told him of her plans to attend Dartmouth the following year, despite the fact that she could barely afford it and that was with a full scholarship he was the one that told her that she shouldn't let anything dissuade her or get in the way of her dreams. Those were his words. And those words endeared him to her and made him somehow different from the rest of the boys that teased her about being a virgin and a goody two-shoes. But lately she hardly recognized him. Now he too seemed obsessed with nothing but the idea of them sleeping together. And the more she rejected

his requests the more he insisted. Every now and then when he'd become angry or offended with her refusal she'd let him fondle her breasts until she became nauseated but that was the extent of it, at least as far as she was concerned.

One night after an art showing down in the village where he had some of his portraits on exhibit, Rasheed invited Diamond back to his apartment to celebrate and immediately began his pleading in earnest. In the past week or so this was all he did. Their relationship declining rapidly Diamond wondered what had happened to the Rasheed of old.

Where was the Rasheed that told her not to let anything stand in her way? It had only been six months ago. She remembered the conversation. They'd talked about Ms. Hamilton in 2C who was only a couple of years older than Diamond. Ms. Hamilton had received a full scholarship to Columbia but was forced to defer when she got pregnant and was now not only a mother at nineteen but locked into Harlem's drug scene as well. And all for some sex. And where was the baby's father now. The only men Diamond ever saw visiting the young woman now were the dope boys from up on St. Nicholas who always made it a point to drop by on the first of the month when she got her check from the welfare people. Diamond would be damned if she'd blow her chances for a dream of a lifetime for fifteen minutes; for a feel good fantasy from a man she hardly knew.

Only last week she'd experimented with her mother's toys while showering after softball practice and thought she'd even experienced an orgasm or two but in the end it only left her

feeling guilty and then there was that nauseating feeling again. The next day she'd used her fingers after watching some porno flick she'd found in daddy's closet and had to admit that it had gone better but it wasn't good enough to give a thirty thousand dollar scholarship that was for damn sure. What's more, the way her girls talked about it sex wasn't really shit accept that it kept the brothas from hounding you all the time.

Now as she watched Rasheed move around the tiny apartment with his head stuck up his ass, his attitude growing worse by the day she wondered just how bad it could be. At least if she agreed she'd have the Rasheed of old back and she had to admit that a happy Rasheed was hard to beat.

It was the first time her parents had permitted her to date anyone and even let her stay out past nine. But Rasheed had made an impression on them that was hard to beat. They thought he was bright, talented, sincere and mannerable so unlike most of the young men that hung around the neighborhood. And he had a future that was almost as bright as her own even if he was only an artist. He was moving, making inroads, strides, and all those other things that parents see and equate with moving in the right direction. But they hadn't seen this side. They knew nothing of his manic mood swings and the pressure he was now putting on their little girl when it came to sex. It was all a bit much for a sixteen year old who knew little of boys or matters of the heart.

Tired of his constant badgering and the verbal abuse he'd only recently started to demonstrate, she finally gave in to his wishes and decided to let him have his way. But there were stipulations. This would be the first and the last time until he put a ring on her finger and said those two words. I do. After he agreed, it took her four shots of tequila and a glass of some

cheap wine he had lying around to get her to finally undress in front of him. She was still having some reservations minutes later when he carried her to his cot but after convincing herself that she loved him and he loved her in return she felt a little better.

When Rasheed finally entered her she couldn't believe the pain and despite them being on the seventh floor she was sure Ms. Hamilton in 2C heard her screams. God how it hurt. Then just as suddenly as the pain began it subsided, replaced by wave after warm wave crashing into her and she could believe how good it felt. She could feel the tide rising within her loins until she was sure she was going to explode. She was riding high now, and pictured herself a surfer trying to hang on and meet the ebb and flow of each wave that came crashing into her. She was soaring, arms reaching for something, anything to hang onto. She screamed and thrashed, tearing at his body with freshly manicured nails until he was sure he had no skin left on his shoulders or back and still she begged for more. God the shit was good. She wrapped her legs around him now, locking them and prayed that he would never stop, then cursed the gods for not letting her know it was this good sooner. The tiny beads of sweat that were there at the start turned into streams and then oceans as she parried to meet each of his thrusts. Then when she was sure that she could stand no more and was on the verge of losing herself in her first true to life orgasm Rasheed pushed her aside abruptly, stood up and walked away.

Speechless and out of breath she lay there, her pubic hair covered with the remnants of his semen. Still shuddering in the midst of an impending climax Diamond stared at the fading figure wondering what it was she'd done wrong. Unable to breathe, let alone talk she finally managed to whisper the words.

"Why'd you stop Rasheed? What about me? Did you forget about me?"

No longer self-conscious about her nakedness all that concerned her now was his departure, which left her on the very edge.

"What about you?" Rasheed asked throwing the dirty towel at her so she could wipe the semen from between her legs. "What can I tell you Diamond. It doesn't always happen at the same time. This ain't the movies, girl," he replied laughing and lighting a cigarette.

"So come back and finish, 'Sheed. I really love the way you make me feel, baby."

"Finish?" he laughed. "I am finished. You said one time and I believe that counts as one time. That's it for us, baby," he said laughing again. "I keep fuckin' around with your lil' fertile schoolgirl ass and the next thing I know is I'll be runnin' around tryin' to market my work with four or five little rugrats tagging' along behind callin' me daddy or some shit. No you said one time and that's it and I'm with you there."

"Yes, Rasheed. I said one time and you're right. Neither of us need to take any chances but you didn't finish. Now what am I supposed to do? You're not bein' fair. You came. Now what about me?"

"What about you? I don't know what to tell you, sweetie. Only thing I can say is I got mine, get yours," and with that he grabbed the towel from her hands and headed for the shower.

Diamond spent the next few minutes, dumbfounded and confused, trying to comprehend the words and refusing to get up until he'd finish the job. After all this time, she figured it would be hard for him to dismiss her nakedness but turning to his painting he did just that and began a new work, a sketch in charcoal of a woman walking away that only faintly resembled her. Was he trying to tell her something? It would be ten o'clock soon and he knew that she'd have to go soon.

When it became obvious that even naked she no longer commanded his attention she stared at his back and watched him paint and wondered how he could love her one minute and ignore her the next. It was almost as if she'd only existed for one thing and now that that had been accomplished it was time for her to move on. Knowing that her parents would be worried she tried for the last time to get him to rejoin her. When she couldn't she found herself having to be satisfied with her hand gently massaging herself until she finally got hers.

In the weeks that followed, she saw less and less of Rasheed and there were times that she sat alone in her room and read to occupy the time but for the most part she just cried. Never had she felt so alone or so abandoned. So that's what it had been all about. The sex was her drawing card and once he'd achieved that he'd bounced just like her girl's said he would. She hadn't believed it at first but then the phone stopped ringing and even her mother noticed that he'd

stopped coming around. When she did see him in the hall, or on the elevator he was always too busy doing this, or with some new exhibit he was involved in. However, he always promised to call her or stop by. He never did and a month later she was pregnant. When she knocked on his door to tell him she found the door open and the apartment vacant except for the easel and the picture of a young girl walking away. She didn't know how long she stood there staring at the portrait but never understood why he hadn't chosen to sketch a man walking out since that's exactly what he'd done.

With nowhere to turn, she borrowed the money for an abortion from her favorite aunt over in Jersey with the stipulation that she not tell her parents. Before she could arrive home that evening, her parents knew everything. Her father promptly threw her out although she wasn't sure if it was because she'd gotten pregnant or because she'd had the abortion. And despite her mother's protests he refused to talk about it or let her back in. She ended up spending the remainder of her senior year at Julliard   living with this friend and that.

There were days that winter when she had absolutely no place to go and ended up sleeping in Central Park until some overzealous red-necked cop would poke her with a billy club and tell her to move on. At other times when the cold, blustery winds rolling in off the Hudson cut through her cardboard blankets and she felt like she was going to freeze to death she'd take a chance and sneak on the subway and ride from one end to the other and then back again just to stay warm. At other times, she'd ride up to Hunt's Point in the Bronx with the hopes of finding the bridge all

the young boys in the neighborhood used to talk about where fine ass ho's sold pussy for twenty dollars a pop. She went up there a few times that winter with the idea of selling herself so she could grab a bite to eat and a cheap motel room. But each time she'd stand back and watch as the professional streetwalkers plied their trade then hop back on the train and make her way back downtown to her cardboard blanket.

Times were tough that winter but then by the grace of God she found a job as a waitress and managed to get by and even save a few pennies for books and to cover most of the things her scholarship didn't. By September she was nestled in at Dartmouth. Still, with no support whatsoever survival once again presented a problem and it wasn't long before she was forced to drop out. A couple of friends she'd met while there managed to scrape up enough to get her bus fare back to the city but the city presented the same old challenges and stark realities she'd tried so desperately to leave behind.

Not long afterwards though she couldn't exactly recall how; she'd wound up with Q. It didn't matter how. The fact was that she was in his employ and a man had placed her in this foul predicament. She'd been young, gullible and perhaps a bit immature but it was men like Rasheed and her father who claimed that they loved and cared for her so much that had her out here trickin' just trying to eat and stay alive.

When it came to men it just seemed like it was always them first and she was tired of playing second fiddle and having to always finish the job herself. Hell, if that was the case what the hell did she need a man for? And that remained her attitude until Henry Barnes came along.

By the time she met Henry the years at Dartmouth were no more than a blur, a distant memory lost in the deepest recesses of her memory. Since then the bridge at Hunt's Point had become her home. Her relationships with men all told amounted to fifteen or twenty minutes in an abandoned vehicle or a half an hour in some sleazy motel room.

During this time, all of her assessments concerning men rang true. Well they rang true up until that night at the Ritz Carlton when Diamond Massey finally met the man of her dreams.

Chapter 5

Henry Barnes turned out to be everything Diamond Massey could've ever dreamed of. He'd been oh so utterly charming their first meeting that she was almost ready to throw every stereotypical view of men right out the window. Maybe there were some good ones left after all. And he didn't just have a few good qualities he had all the qualities she desired in a man. He was tall and handsome, soft-spoken and sensitive and best of all he catered t her every whim and made her feel like a queen.

Diamond thought back to the very beginning. God how she had loved that man back then. He was the first man since Rasheed that actually stirred something in her with all his fiery talk of redemption and salvation. She could even remember that first night when he came sashaying down the circular staircase at the Ritz followed by a deacon or two and a few portly sisters filling out his entourage and close on his heels. One thing was for sure. You couldn't tell the brotha in the peach suit with the burgundy loafers nothin' that night.

And although she didn't recognize him she knew he must be someone fairly important with an entourage that large. And it just followed that if his entourage was that large then his money had to be that large as well because as she'd come to learn from Q the people were only there as long as you were on top.

To Diamond they were a motley crew and she figured they had to be from somewhere down South from the way they were dressed in their purple and orange suits looking like they just stepped off a banana boat. The women accompanying the gentleman in the peach suit donned peach and white shoes and here it was damned near January. And the dresses... Why she'd never in all her life seen such an array of colors. There were floral prints in pastel colors splashed everywhere. One thing was for sure and that was that they were definitely not from the city. That was for sure and the first thing that Diamond thought was how easy the pickings would be.

He wasn't particularly her type in that country-assed suit, with the too wide lapels and that big assed diamond stickpin. Still, he did look clean and since the new millennium and the Aids Epidemic cleanliness was definitely of the highest priority. Diamond watched the man in the peach suit closely as he leaned his head back in laughter and then patted one of the women on the back as he escorted her into the ballroom that now served as a large dining room.

Diamond couldn't figure it out. If there was a playa's ball in town she would have been one of the first to know. Q would have asked her to escort him knowing full well that she would never but he still would've asked. In any event she would've known about it. Diamond watched for awhile then followed from a distance. The ballroom now serving as a dining area was huge and packed like she'd never seen before with Black people everywhere all looking just as country as

the man in the peach suit and his party. The women were dressed just like the ones she saw with the man in the peach suit wearing pastel dresses with colorful hats.

The men, on the other hand, wore expensive designer suits covering virtually every hue in the rainbow. There were yellows and shades of reds and purples she had never seen before. Some of them doffed mahogany canes with diamond and platinum handles. Lincolns and Escalades were double parked everywhere. Seeing the array of cars and people there was no doubt in her mind now that this was a playa's ball and these niggas were definitely from outta town. Maybe even as close as South Jersey or Philly. They were the only niggas crazy enough or country enough to pull off a stunt like this right under Q's nose. Then again there was no way Q didn't know. Wasn't a thing that happened in the tri-state area that Q didn't know about. Nothing. He had connections in Jersey and Philly where he used to hang out and gamble with a few of the brothas from time to time.

He'd probably given them the okay but just didn't want any of his girls hanging around these mackin' motherfuckers.

Now that he had gotten older, Q seldom if ever went to any of their functions or anything else that would draw attention to himself or put him in the limelight. Everything was on the down low now. He'd already established himself. Now he avoided center stage at all costs. Everyone knew who Q was and knew what would happen if you crossed him so what was the point.

Q used to say that after a while everyone's number eventually came up and as much as he'd done, it was inevitable that his number was at the top of the list. It was simply the Law of Karma. What goes around comes around. Q knew it and wasn't about to rush the laws of nature. He was like the Wall Street power brokers who controlled the nation's money but did everything anonymously. Of course, he'd agreed to do an article on himself but that too would be done anonymously. Aside from that, everything he did, he did discreetly. Gone now were the flashy clothes and the cars. For all intents and purposes, Carrie ran the business. If any enforcement was needed, all he needed to do was make a phone call and Jay would take care of it. Nevertheless, Diamond was sure that if anything as grand as this Q had to know about.

Standing at the rear door of the dining area gazing through the tiny porthole Diamond couldn't make out what was being said but at once knew that she'd struck gold. Chocolate was right when she called to give her the tip. There were a hell of a lot of young, good-looking prospects and if they were staying at the Ritz there was a lot of money circulating too.

Diamond watched from the lobby where she sat, legs crossed exposing her long thick, caramel colored legs that blossomed into perfectly proportioned caramel colored thighs. Her breasts were neither too large nor too small but appeared more like small ripe honeydew melons. Though ample and inviting enough to show some cleavage, she chose to sport the very conservative Jones of New York suits instead, masking her allure, she was content to keep most men guessing about what lay beneath. The mixture of a Puerto Rican mother and West Indian father instilled in her a beauty not known to too many women.

Her chocolate mocha skin, full lips, Roman nose and Oriental eyes gave her a beauty rarely seen among the streetwalkers of New York. And there were some beautiful women walking the streets of New York.

The fact that Diamond stood apart from most of her associates did little to endear her with them. And in the beginning she'd taken her bumps and her bruises just because she was different but since Q took her under his wing and given her his stamp of approval she hadn't had a problem. And it wasn't long before she had her own steady clients. She hardly ever walked the streets anymore and only danced when business was slow at the club or she wanted some extra money.

Q took thirty percent, which was basically a finder's fee, and for protection despite the fact, she needed no one to find her anyone or anything now. Most of her clients were family men. They even more than she did not want and could not afford the idea of getting in a commotion with anyone let alone a high-class hooker. They were professionals who spurned the attention and the spotlight as much as she did. They weren't about the games and the other bullshit that came with street life.

In fact, many of the relationships she had with these men had in many instances, evolved passed the point of just having sex. Often times, they would stop by just to talk about their families,

their jobs or just to spend time with her before heading upstate, out on the island, or over to Jersey where they resided. In fact, she only had one client who she really and truly detested and that was that rich, young, white boy from Yonkers. He was a C.P.A. for some legal firm downtown and even he wasn't really a problem anymore.

He had threatened her once when she refused to adhere to one of his freakish demands then spent the next two weeks apologizing, sending her roses and cash to help cover her expenses but he still frightened her. He was a freak of sorts but she eventually took him back and he soon became content with just watching her masturbate. There were still times when he grossed her out but for the five hundred dollars and hour that he left on her nightstand once or twice a month she learned to endure his freakish fantasies. At times he still frightened her but not nearly as much as Q did.

After eighteen years, the Pretty Toney incident was the first time she'd ever actually seen him become violent. And it frightened her but she was tired. She was tired of Q taking her money, tired of stripping on stage while niggas pawed and grabbed at her. She was tired of sucking stranger's dicks 'cause that was her job. And more than anything she was just plain tired of being tired. It was time for her to get out of the hustle and flow that was the game. If it meant her holding back a little from Q here and there and moonlighting for her to get out that much sooner then she'd take her chances.

At the Ritz Carlton, Diamond made her way to the farthest part of the lobby. After the meal they just had she knew it was only a matter of time before they'd be making their exit and heading for the bathrooms. Diamond drew her lipstick from her clutch and dropped it next to her bag on the floor. It was a simple con but it was tried and proven. Clearly in the path of the bathroom it was only a matter of time before some kind gentleman would wander by on the way to relieve his bladder, notice the lipstick and the beautiful young woman. As soon as he made a move to pick it up he would be hers. And since they were staying at the Ritz already they would already have a room, which insured her that they wouldn't be causing any problems.

Not only that she wouldn't have to worry about travel time this way but with a phone call and a recommendation she could go from room to room without leaving the hotel, and do twice as many as she could running back and forth to the Budget Hotel.

The only downside was the chance that Q might find out about her being there and she really didn't need the drama that would follow. If Q found out she was moonlighting in addition to holding back from his regular take he would probably try to kill her. Seriously considering leaving, Diamond bent over and grabbed her pocketbook and the tube of lipstick. But before she could a hand beat her to it.

"Drop something ma'm?" The deep voice resonated through the lobby as the tall, stately gentleman handed her the tube of lipstick. Glancing up into the dark brown eyes of the

gentleman now standing directly in front of her, Diamond quickly recognized the tall stranger as the same man in the peach suit she'd seen earlier.

"Thank you," she muttered. "Thank you very much. Glad to know there's still some gentlemen left," she said.

"Actually there are a few left. The name's Henry Barnes. And yours?" he said extending his hand to her.

"Diamond. Diamond Massey. Very nice to meet you, Mr. Barnes. Very nice indeed. I believe I saw you earlier. Quite an entourage you have," she was in her element now, flirting, teasing as she lured him into her clutches.

They'd spent the evening together and Diamond found him so utterly attractive and endearing that she allowed him to take him to dinner forgetting her reason for being there. She soon found herself laughing at his humorous little anecdotes and damn near choked to death when he revealed the fact that he was a minister.

"Oh my God! Do you mean to tell me that I almost picked up a minister? Lord have mercy," Diamond couldn't stop laughing at the proposition. "Lord, knows I'm going to hell now," she said still chuckling to herself.

"What do you mean you almost picked up a preacher? If I recall correctly I thought I was the one that asked you out to dinner. I thought I was the one picking you up." Henry chuckled failing to get the joke.

Diamond continued to smile and almost hated to break up what had been up to that point quite an enjoyable evening but this was totally new to her. And for once she felt more than just a little uncomfortable with the situation she now found herself in.

"You don't get it do you reverend? I'm a working girl. I'm a call-girl, a prostitute, a hooker."

The good reverend who had been cool, calm and reserved in her presence up until then was stunned. The shock of Diamond's revelation etched across his brow and he had trouble finding the right words to respond. For the first time that evening there was an uncomfortable silence between the two. Diamond at first unable to find the words to break the silence suddenly felt very ashamed.

"Don't worry reverend I can pay my way if you need to leave. I didn't mean to put you in such a compromising situation. You don't know how sorry I am about the misunderstanding."

Diamond was the one stunned this time, as the good reverend seemed to regain his composure and broke into a big wide grin that Diamond had trouble deciphering. Puzzled Diamond apologized again but the smile remained.

"What are you smiling at reverend?" Diamond asked not knowing what to think now.

"I'm smiling because a few minutes ago you called me a gentleman. Now you're insisting on paying for dinner. I'm just trying to figure out what kind of a gentlemen would that make me," he said still smiling but nowhere as close to the way she grinning inside. With that resolved they continued to conversate until late in the evening when the maitre de told them in no uncertain terms that the restaurant was about to close but he would be glad to see them again tomorrow should they so be inclined.

"I'm sorry but I believe my lady friend and I will be dining in China Town tomorrow evening but perhaps the day after. Shall I make reservations now," he asked turning to Diamond.

"Are you quite sure that's what you want to do, Henry?" Diamond asked trying to feign indifference while inwardly ecstatic with the proposition.

"I'm positive. How's nine o'clock sound?" Henry asked.

"Nine o'clock sounds good to me," Diamond replied.

"I'll pencil you in for nine o'clock on Friday evening then," the waiter said turning to go. "You two have a wonderful evening and thanks again for dining at the Trio Café,"

The good reverend ignored the waiter and grabbed Diamonds hand and held it gently.

"And tomorrow?" Henry asked staring deep into Diamond's eyes.

"What about tomorrow?" Diamond replied pretending not to hear in an attempt not to seem too anxious.

"Well, I was thinking that if you weren't too busy that you might like to go see Tyler Perry's new play and afterwards we could grab a late dinner down in Little Italy or China Town. That is if you can find room in your busy schedule for me, Ms. Massey."

Diamond wondered if the good reverend truly understood what it was she attempted to tell him at dinner.

"Reverend Barnes I don't really think you understand what it is I do for a living."

"I believe I'm familiar with the terms prostitute and call-girl," he said smiling, "but I can't see what that has to do with dinner tomorrow unless tomorrow night is bad for you. If it is I believe there's a matinee showing tomorrow. I can't see why it would be hard switching the tickets and if I push I believe I can have you home by eight or say nine at the latest."

"No, no, you don't have to go through all that on my account. It's just that—well—what if someone were to see you with me. Say one of your congregation. I don't think it would go too well for you—me being a call-girl and all," Diamond commented matter-of-factly.

"Well now that's a bridge they'll have to cross when they come to it unless you would like for me to introduce you as the newest member of our flock and then hand each of them a copy of your resume. I personally have no problem with the career choice that you made as long as you are willing to pursue the broader pastures that await you. And I believe you are since you're currently in my company," he said smiling and not appearing at all condescending.

"In any case, I can't recall job status being a prerequisite to joining any church. Now that you mention it, I can't recall any of my congregation revealing their occupation when they joined us. By the time they find out they'll know like I know that you're a wonderfully warm and charismatic person and won't want to let you out of their grasp. Trust me. I know my congregation. Now is it the matinee or the late show?" he said still smiling.

"You know you're pretty awesome," Diamond heard herself say.

"And you're like a breath of fresh air," he replied.

She then turned to the good reverend and whispered in his ear. "Are you aware of the fact that you could have bought my services for the whole night for the price you paid for that dinner and the two carriage rides around Central Park," she asked trying to see where his head   was at.

"Oh no that's impossible. You're certainly worth much more than what I spent so far tonight and the night's not over yet. In fact I was thinking how cheaply I got off to have had the pleasure of your company for this long. Then again maybe I could have but I wouldn't have gotten the

same quality of conversation with you screaming in my ear telling me how utterly fabulous I was. Then you'd be blowing up my phone in the morning begging for more. And how could I be sure at that point it was me you really wanted to speak to? You might just be calling me because the sex was off the hook. But this way I think that I can get a more sincere and honest appraisal of myself and our evening together," he said still smiling.

Diamond liked that. Whether he was sincere or not and it was certainly too soon to tell the good reverend knew just what to say to make a girl feel good about herself. But he was hardly finished and though she was used to doing all the talking she was quite content listening tonight.

"Seriously though, and not to diminish in any way what it is you do or how good you are at what you do or anything like that but you'd be hard pressed to top the way you made me feel tonight Ms. Massey."

"Well, thank you Reverend Barnes. That's one of the sweetest things anyone has ever said to me. And without sounding trite I have to say that the feeling's mutual and I am not one prone to giving in too easily to matters of the heart but your company has been rather refreshing, to say the least." Diamond replied.

"Still, after all you've given me tonight I still have one last request."

The smile on Diamond's face faded. 'Oh here it comes,' she thought. She was used to men wining and dining her then coming out with some twisted fantasy at the end of the night. And she didn't know why he would be different. Another wasted night she thought to herself before the sound of his voice interrupted her thoughts.

"Are you gonna let me make my request?" the good reverend asked.

"Go ahead reverend. You haven't hesitated yet."

Henry noticed the change in attitude and wondered how someone so young and so beautiful could possibly be so bitter.

"I was just wondering if it would be too late for me to call you when you got home so we could continue our conversation. Or perhaps you'd like to take another ride around the park?"

"No," Diamond said suddenly relieved that there was nothing more before breaking into a broad smile, "No reverend. Three rides around the park at sixty dollars a pop is quite enough for one evening. You know we just passed my apartment. If you'd said something earlier we could have stopped for a nightcap and finished our conversation there," she said now regretting she hadn't said something earlier.

"How 'bout I call you when I get back to the hotel? she asked still smiling from ear-to-ear.

They were now approaching the front of the Ritz Carlton and as much as she hated to part she didn't want to seem too easy.

"Do you want he carriage to take you home or shall I summon a cab?" he asked.

"Neither. You've already been too kind. Besides I want to walk. I need to get my feet back under me. And maybe just maybe the cold air will help stop my head from spinning," Diamond replied.

"Too much to drink?"

"No, I don't think so. It's just been a long time since I let a complete stranger sweep me off my feet," she replied.

"I hope that's not just a line, Diamond because I'm feelin' the same way. But anyway, let me flag this cab for you. It's safer and I'd feel better. Besides I'm waiting for a very important phone call."

"And what does that have to do with me taking a cab, Reverend Barnes?" Diamond asked somewhat puzzled by the remark.

"It's Henry and it seems to me that it has everything to do with you. You see the sooner you get home the sooner I'll get that important call." They laughed as Henry hailed a cab, paid the driver in advance and kissed her on the cheek.

"Call me," he shouted as the cab darted off into the evening traffic.

Ten minutes later Diamond entered her penthouse apartment. Sitting down on the living room sofa, a large smile spread across her face. The fact that she was exhausted and hadn't made a dime mattered little. And all she could think of was the tall gentleman in the loud peach suit. She smiled at the thought and decided to shower and fix herself a cocktail before making that call.

"Let him sweat just a little," she heard herself mumble before smiling again as she struggled to get out of her suit jacket. Before she could the phone rang. Diamond wondered who would be calling at this time of the morning and prayed it wasn't Q wanting to know where she'd been all evening. But to her surprise it was Henry and she wondered how he'd gotten her number but it mattered little now. She grinned at his persistence.

"I was just about to call you," she lied.

"I'm sure but I couldn't take a chance of you not calling," he replied.

That morning they talked 'til almost dawn about anything and everything from her missed opportunity at Dartmouth, their shared loved of the Knicks, her returning to school and still they had more to say. When they were finished,

Henry decided to skip the afternoon seminars and the revival meeting, much to Diamond's dismay.

Instead of attending the convention he took her to lunch instead at a little deli across from Lincoln Center where they acted like two junior high schoolers on their first trip to the malt shop

sipping a single strawberry shake from the same straw and giggling so uncontrollably that several times the other patrons turned to look at the couple. Diamond even went so far as to take a napkin and write, 'do you want to be my boyfriend?' Check the box. Yes... No... Maybe... Both howled when Henry wrote, WWJD, for 'what would Jesus do?

"I was thinking more along the terms of husband," he said only half-joking.

"Oh no Mr. Barnes, it's way too soon for that one. We'll have to give that one some much needed thought. Ask me again tomorrow though and we'll see," she laughed.

Diamond had never been so happy in all her life. Henry, on the other hand, missed all of his seminars and workshops for the next two days complaining of a stomach virus and asked God to forgive him for his weakness and went right on seeing Diamond every chance he had.

Diamond continued working, shuffling appointments so she could be available when Henry was free. Their days continued like this for the next six or seven months with the two not missing a day in each other's company. And just as Henry had predicted the church accepted Diamond almost to a man although many of the women had a slightly harder time. Yet, after some thorough soul searching and a few timely sermons from the good reverend including one entitled, 'He Who Has Not Sinned', there was little or no question of her place among the congregation.

And never once in the entire time that Henry and Diamond were together did Henry ever approach her around her continuing to prostitute herself. Nevertheless, she knew the flock would never accept her entirely without a total reformation and a testimonial renouncing her sinful past. What she feared even more was that despite Henry's silence on the subject she knew that she would never have the kind of future she so desired until she changed her lifestyle completely.

The transformation though long in coming wasn't hard. After all, it wasn't a lifestyle that she'd chosen but one that had been cast upon her. For her, prostitution had been nothing more than a means of survival so there was little to give up other than the fact that she had to tell Q. But even that had gone smoother than she'd expected. And now that she had absolved herself she knew one thing. She could never prostitute herself again for any man.

Often times she had to pinch herself just to make sure she wasn't dreaming. At other times, when she thought of all the sorry, trifling men she'd come across over the last ten years or so, she'd get some paranoid feeling that Henry was also running some scam on her even though she couldn't for the life of her figure out what it was or why she continued to think like this. After all, he'd given her no reason to question his motives. It was during these times that she'd send him on some on some ol' crazy wild goose chase just to test him.

Still, she couldn't believe that he would have her in lieu of her reputation. And this alone, meant a great deal in her eyes. Often times alone, except for the soft subtle sounds of Nina Simone or Sade playing in the background, Diamond would chuckle to herself as she thought of how utterly

absurd the whole situation was. Who would have ever thought their union possible? The preacher and the prostitute. She had to laugh. It was not only ironic—it was simply too good to be true. It was at these moments that she would stop and ask herself. 'What could he possibly want with me? Here he was single, attractive, well-educated and in obvious demand. He was the pastor of one of the largest Black congregations in the city with women at his beck and call, a healthy salary, and as he liked to say, in his own corny style—the best boss in the world.

So what could he possibly want with her? A college dropout who was apt to spread her legs and perform any act a man could think of as long as he put the money on the table first. She hardly knew the answer to that one. But what was it her father used to tell her? Never look a gift horse in the mouth. Henry chided her about constantly living in the past. 'What's past is past' he would tell her. 'There's not nearly enough time ahead to be looking back'. So, Diamond left all that had been wrong with her life in the past and pushed on.

Nowadays her thoughts centered on all the wonderful things that had transpired in the last few months and realized that for the first time in her life she was happy—truly happy. For the first in years she could actually feel her life moving in a positive direction. And she had Henry Barnes and Henry Barnes alone to thank for that.

Henry restored her hope when she was hopeless, restored her pride and dignity with simple conversation. He showed her how utterly insatiable she was whether scrubbing the bathroom floor in a pair of old faded blue jeans and tattered sweatshirt or whether dressed in her favorite

suit. Fact is, he barely seemed to notice a difference. And he never looked anywhere other than into her eyes the entire time he was with her. It didn't matter if she were wearing something low cut and revealing or a mini skirt up to her tutu. There had even been a time in the beginning when she wondered if he was gay.

At first, she appreciated the fact that Henry had no interest in sleeping with her. It let her know that he was more interested in who she was as a person than what was in her pants. And that in itself separated him from most of the men she knew and made him special in her eyes. But when weeks passed and he still showed little or no interest in her physically she had to wonder. Months later, his disposition had not changed one iota and by this time she'd become so unnerved that she wondered if he had tendencies and was attracted to women at all. She certainly couldn't tell from the way he treated her. And if there was anywhere

Diamond felt she might have an advantage when it came to Henry Barnes it was in the bedroom.

Almost certain that he loved her for her; all she wanted to do now was return the love and rattle his bones behind closed doors. That was if he'd ever give her half a chance. Diamond could hardly believe she'd be the one begging for sex but here she was sitting, conniving and wondering what the hell was Henry Barnes' problem. And since he hardly if ever spoke on the subject and she feared stepping on hallowed ground Diamond Massey decided that there was only way to find out if Henry Barnes was physically attracted to her. And so on Friday she arrived late at the home of Henry Barnes clothes in her arms and promptly explained to him that

she hadn't had time to shower and wondered if it were alright if she took a quick shower there? Always, aware of the chance that this church member or that would stop by unexpectedly she knew what would happen if one of those gossipy old women got an eyeful of something they thought was improper no matter how innocent. But tonight she didn't care.

It had become almost a weekly tradition that they went out to dinner on Friday nights and although she was confident that Henry had already made reservations that was not her first priority this evening. Stepping out of the shower, Diamond cracked the bathroom door, "Henry honey," she yelled, "Would you be a sweetheart and grab me a towel?"

Diamond stood there dripping wet; waiting until she was certain she heard Henry's footsteps approaching. When she was certain that he was right outside the door she yelled again. "Henry, darling," before opening the door widely to make sure he heard.

Henry stood there shocked, mouth open, mesmerized by the sight of the woman now standing before him. And Diamond in her attempt to feign surprise stood there as well making sure he got an eyeful and enjoying every second before reaching for the towel in Henry's hand.

"Oh, sorry baby," he said mumbling   his eyes never leaving her body.

102

Grabbing the back of his head she pulled his head forward and kissed him passionately. He responded hungrily, so hungrily in fact, that Diamond had to wrestle from his grip.

"Can't forget our dinner reservations, now can we?" Diamond teased, wondering at the same time when it he last time the good reverend had been in bed with a real woman. When Henry asked for her hand in marriage that night she knew her reformation was complete. When he pulled out the largest diamond ring she'd ever seen, she also knew that the last nine years had only been a test, a stumbling block, a bad dream at best. She still had doubts concerning his motives and his sincerity—having been duped by countless guys just like Henry but he really had nothing to gain. So, before she could give it a second thought she heard herself screaming 'yes' loud enough for the entire restaurant to hear.

Embarrassed and excited she grabbed the napkin from her lap and wiped the corners of her eyes. Henry was on his knees now, placing the ring on her finger while the three-mariachi guitarists strummed a congratulatory love song. In the weeks that followed, Diamond could not ever remember being so happy.

Yet, on the following Sunday, on their way to church when Henry asked Diamond if he could announce their engagement he was surprised when she asked him to hold off on making the announcement. Here she was spending every waking hour making wedding arrangements and for some reason she was leery of letting the congregation know.

Problem was she'd endured too many heartbreaks, setbacks, and letdowns from too many empty promises and wasn't sure if she could stand another one right now. As much as she loved Henry and wanted to believe him she simply couldn't stand another misfortune and he was, after all and despite all of his positive attributes still a man. So, before there were any announcements she was going to make good and goddamn sure Henry Barnes was sincere.

Up until now she'd done everything she could possibly do to that poor man to test his sincerity and he'd risen to the challenge each and every time without so much as a whimper. But this was different. Here he was asking her to enter into a covenant and that didn't mean walking out when the road got a little rocky. She couldn't allow him to just walk out the door when the church started losing members or when a younger more attractive woman made a play for him when she was no longer up to par or on her last leg. No, this covenant, this commitment, this road, this journey he was asking her to embark on was for life. Henry Barnes needed to prove himself. Prove he was sincere and that he would be there for her until death do they part.

And despite the love he demonstrated he like all men needed to be tested and that was exactly what she intended on doing. Looking back now, as she sat watching Carrie dance on the tiny stage in front of her, Diamond's thought drifted again. She recalled the night she insisted that she too was too ill to move, explaining that her monthly was on her again. And since she'd been running errands for him she hadn't had a chance to stop by the store and pick up any Tampons.

It was two o'clock in the morning and Diamond curled up in a fetal position cursed the day she was born a woman in an effort to sound convincing. The only store open at this time of morning was the tiny Quick Stop directly across the street from the house, which was convenient except

that that's where Sister Helen moonlighted at night to supplement her day job and keep an eye on the good reverend.

Now it was common knowledge that Sister Helen was a gossip from way back and Diamond knew that if she even got an inkling that Henry Barnes was buying Tampons at two a.m. in the morning the whole damn congregation would know by Sunday. Henry mumbled obviously thinking about the trials and tribulations Diamond put him through but being the good soldier he was he stepped bravely out into the brisk January air and made his way across the street.

"I don't know why you're complainin', Henry. You should be glad it's here." Diamond replied.

They'd had sex once or twice since Henry proposed and in both instances Diamond had taken the initiative and seduced him when he was at his most vulnerable. And in both instances the good reverend had grieved for what seemed like forty days and forty nights afterwards for giving in to sins of the flesh. Diamond also prayed after the encounters. Only she prayed that Henry would never know or lose his God given talent in the bedroom.

Hearing the front door close, Diamond pulled herself up to the window, pulled the blind back just enough for her to see Henry cross the street and enter the store. There, plain as day, was Sister Helen pulling overhead rack down and filling the slots with pack after pack of cigarettes. And just as Diamond hoped there was no way Henry could avoid her.

Chapter 7

"Good evening. Up kinda late aren't you reverend?" the woman behind the counter asked.

"Not really, at least no later than usual. I've been workin' on this weeks' sermon and ran into a bit of writer's cramp. I thought the cold air and some of your freshly brewed java would wake me up."

"Well, it ain't Starbucks but it'll definitely wake you up. I just brewed a fresh pot. It's the one on the left. The other's decaf. Help yourself," she replied as she watched the reverend make his way over to the coffee dispenser.

Sister Helen was hitting forty but looked no more than thirty on her worst day. A fitness fanatic, she worked out regularly, running five to six miles a day. Attractive, well proportioned, and well on her way to being single the rest of her life Sister Helen had all intentions of winning the reverend over even if she didn't consider him exactly her type. At least that had been the plan until Diamond had stepped into the picture out of the clear blue.

At the time, she'd been more than a little annoyed, no angry, that this little tramp with the questionable past appeared so unexpectedly out of nowhere to steal her thunder and her man. At first she blamed the reverend for being so stupid and so gullible. When her anger subsided though, she had to admit that she was in large part to blame. Sure, she'd been coy, virtually unresponsive when Henry first attempted to talk to her but that's what women; well, any self-respecting God fearing woman was supposed to do.

She remembered the tears she'd cried when she learned of the reverends new romantic interest and thought of her younger sister Lucy's thoughts on the whole situation when she called Lucy to tell her that she was first interested in the new pastor.

"Sis, let me tell you the good news. First Abyssinian has a new pastor and you have to hear him preach," Helen stated.

"Okay. But is he fine?" Her sister asked.

"The brother's young, articulate, and bright as a whip," she beamed.

"But is he fine? Lucy asked.

"...and he didn't just get the calling like most of these jack-leg preachers out here today. This here brother graduated from Colgate before going to the seminary. Colgate's Ivy League isn't it?" Helen asked.

"Yeah, but is he fine?" Lucy repeated for the third time.

"Damn girl, is that all you think about? There's more to life than just good looks."

Lucy laughed.

"Guess you basically answered that. Sometimes I wonder if we're really related or if FedEx dropped your ass off. You love you some 'Bamas, don't you? What's up with you and the Ben

Wallace, Sam Cassell looking brothers? What you got a corner on ugly men? What's the dealio, girl? Is it easier to control them or is it just that you like the worship factor?"

"You've got it all wrong, baby girl. First of all, I don't date ugly men," Helen replied.

"I know. You call them intellectuals. I call them cyborgs but go ahead, continue." Lucy said teasing her older sister.

"Girl, hush. Let me finish telling you about Henry."

"Oh, y'all on a first name basis already. What you do, drop your draws when he stepped into the church vestibule?" She laughed. "Is he that fine?"

"No, little sister, I'm not you although that may be a possibility down the road if he plays his cards right."

"You still ain't answered my question," Lucy teased. "Now I know he must look like Busta Rhymes," Lucy laughed.

"You know something, Lucy, that's why you will always be single. You don't have your priorities in order. You're too worried about all the wrong things. You're too busy looking at the external bullshit instead of worrying about the content. But if it's of any consequence, Henry's very handsome, and also very single."

"Damn girl! You all serious and shit. Geez! I didn't know it was like that. I'm sorry. If it means all that much to you then go ahead tell me. How's he rate on a scale of one to ten…?" she said laughing again.

"Oh, the hell with you, Lucy, let me get off this phone. You can't even be serious for a minute. I call to have a serious conversation and share my happiness and you act like a damn two year old."

"I'm sorry. I was just trying to add a little levity to the whole situation. You know how you get Helen. First, you get all uptight, thinking you found Mr. Right. Then you place all your eggs in one basket. Then when Mr. Right makes a left and turns into Mr. Wrong and the shit doesn't pan out the way you planned it I end up having to console you. Been there done that. But seriously, what's the game plan?"

"Ain't really no game plan. I just called to share a little of my happiness with you. Hell, I haven't really even approached him yet. I'm trying to wait for him to come to his good senses and approach me. You know, ask me out to dinner or something along those lines. I am working his ass though but mostly on the subliminal tip. Shit, just last Sunday I rocked that red knit dress. You know the one I got from Macy's when we went to Atlanta last year.

Girl, let me tell you about the dress and how I worked it. That shit was so tight I could hardly cross my leg. But you know I had to. And when I did I had all the brothas sweatin'. I had the

deacons shoutin' 'Yes, Lord' and 'Help me Jesus' and that's before they even got in the church. I ain't lyin'.

The whole time he was preachin' he was glancing at these long sexy legs in the front row. It tickled me 'cause his sermon was on young people and abstinence. At one point, he glanced over at me and said it takes a strong individual not to

108

give in to the sin of fornication. I'm really gonna test his faith. I hate to say it but he may have to put Jesus on the back burner for a minute cause I plan on getting some of that. And don't you know, no sooner than service was over he came right up to me for something or another but I played him off," Helen laughed.

"What the hell did you do that for? I thought you said you liked the guy," Lucy asked.

"Because he was so obvious. Here I am just exuding sex, the shit's oozing from every pore and it's obvious that I'm enticing the hell out of him and he runs right up to me like a dog in heat. He hasn't seen me yet. All he really noticed were these thick, well-toned thighs, sexy legs and six-inch heels that he's only seen in Playboy and Hustler. I really shouldn't have worn them to church. They weren't really appropriate but the served their purpose. But seriously speaking, dogs in heat ain't me. I'm ol' school. I'm more of a cat and mouse person. I like the chase. I want the intrigue of being pursued. I'm playing hard to get right through here. That's something you wouldn't know nothing about," Helen giggled.

But it's just a ploy right now but in the end the results are more tangible. When you play hard to get you become more valuable, more alluring, more enticing because you're inaccessible. It drives your stock up. You see, being unattainable makes you all the more treasured and all the more valued as a person." Helen said rather matter-of-factly, hoping to teach her younger sister something.

"I don't know about all of that but one thing I do know, you keep playing hard to get and you may not git got. That's one thing I do know."

Both laughed at the time but it wasn't soon before Lucy's omen rang all too true. After that day in church, Henry asked her out on more than a few occasions over a period of two or three months but she'd cordially refrained. He no longer seemed solely interested in just her body. There relationship grew outside to a point where he would call now just to exchange small talk and she considered

109

him not just a friend or her pastor but a trusted confidante as well.

Now It had been months since he'd asked her out to dinner and although she had all but given up hope of making him hers and hers alone since Diamond had entered the picture. She hadn't given up on the idea of dinner or even being pillow pals and she promised herself that the next time the good reverend asked her out things would be different. The only thing was, that there wasn't any next time. What made matters worse, he stopped calling and if it was one thing she did not do, it was call a man. At church, he was his usual congenial shelf but something had changed.

The next thing she knew, Henry Barnes was spending more and more time with the new parishioner at the First Abyssinian Church of Christ, Diamond Massey.

At first, she was so hurt that she considered leaving the church altogether. But Helen Altovese Harden had never been a quitter at anything and she didn't intend to start now. If Henry Barnes was the man for her and it was meant to be then it would be.

Still, she was a firm believer that God only helped those that helped themselves and she wasn't about to let some two bit hustlin' hoochie momma step into her playpen and steal her dream.

Chapter 8

Diamond grinned devilishly as she watched Henry head for the coffee machine with Helen's eyes still fixed on him. Stirring the coffee, Henry glanced around the store.

He loved Diamond, loved her to death but on nights like these he wished she'd gone back to her own place. Here he was a single man, a pastor, preaching against the sin of fornication here buying Tampons for his live-in girlfriend with one of his own church members at the register. To make it worse the woman at the register had had her sights set on him, as well and there was no way to know how she'd react. Up until Diamond arrived, she just knew she was first in the running to be the new pastor's wife. If it wasn't bad enough she'd been brushed

110

to the side or as she liked to refer to it 'kicked to the curb'. Now here he was, in her store, shopping for Tampons for the woman who had helped eliminate her from the running. There was certainly no telling how she'd react. Would she tell the congregation? Who knew? So far she'd ignored the situation and he only hoped she would continue to do so.

There wasn't anything in the world that he wouldn't do for Diamond. She was the first woman he'd ever met that made him feel whole. Whatever emptiness, whatever deficiencies he felt, Diamond filled with her presence.

And although he'd done everything to walk in the footsteps of the Lord, he'd grown increasingly weak in her presence, seduced by his love for her and eventually given in to her sexual advances. Now since he'd tasted the forbidden fruit there was no turning back.

The good reverend understood the brothers and sisters in the rehab centers he visited every Wednesday so much better now. Diamond had him hooked-strung out-and all he wanted was more. Now look at him. Here he was buying coffee, ice cream, Pepsi and oh yeah, how could he forget, sanitary napkins, at three a.m. in the morning and Sista Helen was the cashier.

Henry knew that it was store policy not to leave a woman alone in the store at night even though the neighborhood was still relatively quiet and hoped that the other person would relieve her at the register so he could be on his way. But Sister Helen's young African counterpart was busy stocking the cooler and Henry had no earthly idea how he was supposed to get past her without her noticing the Tampons.

Meanwhile, Diamond doubled over in laughter as she watched Henry look at cans of Quaker State motor oil, then move to the cooler where he grabbed a gallon container of milk and a dozen eggs. It had been six months now and he'd passed every test with flying colors. Lord knows, he'd do anything in the world for her. If tonight didn't prove that, nothing would. God, how she loved that man.

It was now three thirty a.m. in the morning and Henry was certain that if it had been anyone other than Sister Helen working the graveyard shift they would have long since called the police. Tired, aggravated, and seeing no way out, Henry walked straight to the register, grabbed the contents from the basket and placed them on the counter. It wasn't the first time that Henry had frequented the store at this time of morning but he'd never shopped quite this long.

Helen was convinced that shopping wasn't all that the good reverend had on his mind and was absolutely positive by the time he reached the register that he had ulterior motives. She'd always noticed that he was more than a little shy and was probably after a roll in the hay with that tramp, Diamond, finally coming to his senses. Probably just working his way up to asking me out, she mused. Now she was glad she'd been running late and hadn't had time to change into that ugly uniform.

The Nike running outfit she wore left nothing to the imagination. Form fitting and hugging every inch of her well-defined body, she knew she had his attention. And for once she was glad the air conditioning was preset. It was always cold in the store and her nipples responded accordingly poking through the latex running suit like missiles ready to fire. Removing her apron she made sure the reverend got an eyeful. Glancing out of the corner of her eye as she rang him up she was glad to see that her dark brown nipples protruding through the Carolina blue top had his undivided attention. And the more he stared the more erect they became. The good reverend would truly have to be a man of the cloth to ignore the way she looked tonight.

112

Certain he was there for no other reason than to ask her out Helen stood poised. If he couldn't gather the nerve then she would. The thought of a man who could feel comfortable addressing three to four hundred people every week but couldn't garner the courage to ask her out to dinner made her smile.

She'd long since gotten over her anger and disappointment with Henry. After all, those were just wasted emotions. They wouldn't help her at all in getting what she wanted. And what she wanted was him. If it meant lowering her standards and acting like Lucy and giving him some on their first date, then she would. Hell, it wouldn't be the first time. The bottom line was she'd do whatever it took to get that man. She had long since come to the realization that she and no one else was to blame. She pushed him away after he'd made pass after pass. And no man, especially a man with Henry's charm and allure is going to sit around forever while a woman puts him on hold. Rejection was a hard thing for any man. It had to be twice as frustrating for a man of Henry's caliber.

Henry laid the last of his items on the counter. Boy was she ever sorry she'd turned him down.

Asking a man out to dinner was totally out of character for her. The hell with character. Character and strong moral fiber had no place in this equation. Character didn't add up to a hill of beans. After all, Diamond had no character, no scruples, and no dignity; in fact, she had no redeeming qualities, to speak of, other than she was young and naturally beautiful. If the truth be told, she really didn't have anything to do with that but even with no character and no moral

fiber that she could see Diamond still had one thing. She had Henry Barnes wrapped around her finger. And that was with no character.

This time she'd follow Lucy's advice and be the assertive one. As she rang up the items, she assured herself of one thing. No matter what it took the good reverend wouldn't get away from her this time. Henry smiled as he watched her ring up first the milk and then the Tampons. Helen glanced at the item and then at Henry.

Embarrassed, Henry felt obliged to say something. Before he could think twice he heard himself say. "My sister arrived in town today and I must say not under the best circumstances." Henry said, smiling nervously, as he glanced down at the worn, white linoleum curling up at his feet.

"It happens to the best of us," she commented dryly, her mind obviously on something else entirely.

The good reverend breathed a deep sigh of relief and felt foolish for having wasted so much time trying to mask his humiliation. He grabbed the plastic bag of groceries and reached for the bag but she kept hold of the bag until their eyes met and she had his attention.

"By the way, Reverend Barnes, I know you've asked me on several occasions in the past to dine with you. But you know, with managing the fitness center, and working here I hardly ever had the time. But I'm off next Friday and I'd like to make it up to you. So, if you're schedule permits

I'd like to invite you over to dinner, nothing fancy but I am a pretty good cook and like I said I am free on Friday."

"Sounds good to me Sista…" Before he could finish, she said.

"Call me Helen," and smiled. "Hold on a minute while I write down the address. Do you still have my phone number? Actually, I'm not giving you my phone number 'cause I don't want any excuses," she said as she wrote down her address. "Is seven-thirty good for you?" she asked smiling now.

"Seventy-thirty is fine. I'll see you then," said the good reverend as he thought to himself. 'Any time's fine as long as none of this gets out.'

Diamond watched as Helen folded the yellow sticky paper in half, then put it in the top left breast pocket of Henry's coat. Diamond was livid.

"Why that bastard—that dirty bastard!"

There was little she could do or say considering the fact that she shouldn't have been in the window spying on him to begin with. The plain truth of the matter was that she'd set the whole thing up because of her own insecurities. Now, she was finding fault with him because he'd allowed himself to be duped by that slimy heifer across the street. She'd gotten exactly what she'd bargained for but oh, how she hoped Henry had been the one to break the stereotype

Chapter 9

No sooner than Henry Barnes exited the tiny store, Helen let out a shout that brought Abdul running from the stock room.

"Are you okay, Ms. Helen?"

"Never better," she replied as she grabbed the broom from behind the counter. Helen rushed to the door, grinning like a Cheshire cat, pushed it open and began sweeping nonexistent trash out into the street. For appearances sake she was doing her job. To Abdul, she was watching Henry but what Helen Altovese Harden was really watching was the upstairs curtain as it fell back into place.

It was not the first time she'd seen the curtain and the blinds move when Henry came in the store. At least they would move when Diamond's car was in the vicinity. It hadn't occurred to her what was going on at first. Well, that is, until that day Diamond stopped in several months ago for a bottle of champagne, a pack of Newports and made it a point to ask for directions.

Sister Helen remembered it clearly.

"Oh, Sista Helen, I didn't know you worked here. It's so good to see you," Diamond lied. "I never did get around to telling you just how much I enjoyed the Christmas program you had the children put on. Sista May told me you coordinated the whole thing with little or no help. If that's the case then let me tell you. You are definitely in the wrong business," Diamond said smiling. "Definitely in the wrong business..." she said making light of the minimum wage job.

115

"With talent like yours you should definitely be thinking about doing something downtown even if it's off-Broadway."

"Well, thank you, Diamond. I'm just trying to do my part as much as possible and trying to provide a positive role model for our kids. Not to sound too preachy or anything but I think it's important that we provide them with another alternative to BET where all they see is rappers bling blingin' and the women in the background. What do they call 'em? Oh yeah, video ho's shakin' their butts for a fast buck," Helen said. "It's so unsettling, wouldn't you agree?"

Diamond shook her head in agreement although she wondered if Sister Helen was referring to her when she made the comment about ho's shakin' their butts but she ignored it. She had to stop being so darn sensitive. Sister Helen continued.

"Every now and then, my nieces and nephews stop by to visit and the first thing they do is turn to BET and I just cringe. I keep trying to tell them that everything that looks good ain't always good for you. But you know what Diamond? I don't turn the channel. I just bide my time quietly 'cause I know that it's only a matter of time before they come to their senses. Of course, when they do and they turn to me for some assistance, you know I'll be there for them in every possible way I can. Right now I can't compete with them lil' hooched out mama's with no clothes on so I just bide my time until they wake up and smell the coffee. You understand what I'm sayin' dont'cha sister?"

Diamond understood alright. There was no doubt that Helen was referring to her. Diamond smiled. This was her forte and if she had had the time, she'd have rocked that country-ass bitches' world. Here she was trying to be nice and this heifer wasn't even being subtle. She was so obvious, so ghetto in her ways that it stirred something in Diamond that she hadn't felt since she left the streets and even then she'd avoided the petty catfights. She hadn't thought about the streets or Q in a long time but shit like this used to go on all the time within Q's stable. Diamond reckoned it to be like two hens at a cockfight trying to see who was going to take home the prize cock. At first, she'd take the verbal abuse and walk away hurt and confused. But after watching for a while, Diamond not only knew how to play the game, she became virtually unbeatable at it.

And what was it Q used to always tell her? 'If you act like a pussy you're gonna get fucked.' And that's exactly what Helen was doing right now. Funny thing though, Helen's anger and disappointment were so obvious that it didn't make sense for her to lower herself to Helen's level. Besides, she'd attained what she wanted and she hadn't stepped on anybody's toes to do it. When she met the good reverend he'd been single and admitted that he was attracted to Helen and had even approached her on several occasions but she'd never shown an inkling of interest. It reminded her of the Carole King song her mother used to play when she was little that went, something like this, '...everything seems to go and you don't know what you've got 'til it's gone. Now they've paved paradise and put up a parking lot...' Well she had had her chance and missed the opportunity. Now there was no need to hate or cry over spilt milk. It was simply time for her to move on.

Diamond smiled cordially at the woman's insinuations, biting her lip at the same time, praying that she could stay within herself. To get into a catfight with this heifer would only bring her down to this heifer's level and she refused to lower her standards for anyone, anymore. Besides Helen Harden was little league. The years with the roughest mothafuckas in the world made Diamond not only a major leaguer but an all-star.

On the other hand, if there was anything Diamond had learned in all her years in the streets it was the fact that you just couldn't let a mothafucka walk all over you and do absolutely nothing 'cause if you allow that to happen he'll feel he has license to treat you like shit. She smiled again. She really didn't have time for any of this but her pride demanded that she leave Helen with a little something to ponder.

"You know I really hadn't thought about it before but you're absolutely right about providing proper role models for the children. But you know it's not just BET portraying negative images of women. It's right here in our own communities." Helen smiled now. So, she had gotten her point. But Diamond wasn't finished.

"Sometimes I watch some of the women who come to church on Sunday mornings, dressed in six-inch heels and dresses tighter than anything I've ever seen on BET. It makes me wonder what they're really there for. Reverend Barnes tells us all the time that God doesn't care how we look, so who are they dressing for? I've never been able to answer that but you're right it really

doesn't provide a proper image for our young adults and especially our young women to see. You are so very right, sista." Helen was speechless.

"Well, let me get outta here. Reverend Barnes asked me to run a few errands for him. I have to drop off these flyers for him. Do you know this address," she asked, rummaging through her pocket for the tiny piece of paper with the good reverends' address. Finding it amidst all the junk in her purse, she handed it to the woman at the register who was still so stunned by Diamond's ruthless put down that she could hardly respond.

"Yes, Reverend Barnes lives right across the street in apartment 17F. It's on second floor. See where the light is flickering." She said, quickly realizing she'd said way too much. "Probably has a short. That man stays so busy he probably hasn't even noticed."

"Well, since I've got some extra time on my hands before I start back to school in the fall, I guess I can try to help him out as much as possible. You don't sell light bulbs do you?" Sister Helen pointed to aisle two where Diamond promptly grabbed the bulbs and returned to the register.

"I hope it's just the bulb. I got him the one hundred watt bulbs. Do you think that's too much?" Before Sister Helen could answer she continued, "Yeah, one hundred watt is good. That way he'll be able to see everything," Diamond remarked on her way out the door. Fifteen minutes later, the phone rang at the Quick Stop.

"Sister Helen, this is Diamond. I just wanted you to know that it wasn't a short. The bulb was just loose. I replaced it anyway. And boy what a difference between the old light and the new. Can you see from your angle? Hold on; let me pull the curtains back. Looking up Helen noticed the curtains pulled back and the naked silhouette of a woman in apartment 17F.

"Why you little whorish bitch," Helen whispered to no one in particular.

"Well, let me let you go. I know you're hard at work. Thanks for the conversation. It was really enlightening. Maybe we can get together and chat some more soon. If not, I'll see you at services on Sunday." And with said she hung up the phone grinning from ear-to-ear.

She really hadn't meant to engage or get involved in any of this tit-for-tat bullshit. That was for bored housewives and old hypocritical church heifers who called themselves sister and who were always half a heartbeat away from cutting each other's throats on the daily to see who ran the committee for the next church barbecue. Of course, since it was in the name of the Lord, it was alright to rip each other's heart out today since they could repent and testify tomorrow.

Even though she hadn't planned to, she had to admit that roasting Sister Helen alive was even more gratifying than she would ever have imagined. She looked forward to the next time. But the next time hadn't been the same and Sister Helen had definitely won this round. Diamond couldn't believe that Henry could be so easy. Only a week before he'd asked her to marry him. Now this.

Diamond gathered herself. She wouldn't mention any of what she'd just seen to Henry. In his guilt, he would probably just blame her for spying on him, anyway, and then go on a tirade about trust. Well, to be perfectly frank she didn't trust Henry or any other man on God's green earth. Given the chance at some new pussy, at some strange and nine times out of ten they'd go for it if they thought they could get away with it.

Why should he be any different? Just because he donned a collar on Sundays didn't make him God. Ain't no way in hell he'd ever be able to do forty days and forty nights in the desert let alone marriage until death do they part. Hell, he couldn't even make it across the street and back without getting weak for a ho in a jogging suit two sizes too small.

Diamond was tired, more tired than she'd ever been. She was tired and angry. She was tired of trying to find happiness that seemed to be so elusive, so hard to pin down. God knows she was tired. But she was more angry than tired. Angry because once again she'd allowed herself to be duped into thinking that there was or could be a pot of gold at the end of the rainbow. She was angry that she'd allowed herself to once again be dependent on someone other than herself for her sense of happiness.

Why was it that she felt she needed a man to feel whole? She could survive on her own. In fact, she had. And not only survived, she'd thrived. She was sitting on close to a hundred grand in her savings alone and that was aside from what Q had invested in her Green Fund, a series of low yielding stocks and bonds, a kind of retirement fund that paid her tidy dividends every year. She

had all that, a beautiful apartment on the Upper East Side, a cute little Ford Focus to zip around the city in and for all intents and purposes; she really didn't have to work unless she wanted to. And she still felt like something was missing. And that something she always equated to the opposite sex.

Turning her back to Q she cursed him, then caught herself. Wasn't it her daddy that told her after she became pregnant and blamed Rasheed that noone can do anything to you unless you allow them to. How right he was. She in all honesty couldn't blame Henry for her inadequacies, for her insecurities or for her fuck ups. She could only blame herself. Yet, words of wisdom no matter how real, no matter how truthful, could do nothing to diminish the pain of a broken heart.

Diamond thought about getting dressed, heading across the street and stompin' the bitch but then Helen was no more to blame than any other single Black woman was. She was simply starvin' for a good man to share the remainder of her life. And this Diamond understood. Like it or not they were in the same boat. Hell, instead of being at each other's throats they should have been acquaintances; maybe even friends.

Too many soap operas do that to women. After awhile, you actually start to believe the shit you see. A two-car garage with an SUV and a station wagon become mandatory. Baseball games and barbeques imperative. And of course to complete the package, every woman needs a good strong man to rely on to make all of these things come true. That man is your savior. Too many Black women really believe this. And through no fault of her own she knew she'd fallen into the trap.

Diamond grew even more surly at the thought. It was all a bunch of bullshit if you asked her. If you don't have kids you're not a woman. If you don't have a man you're not a woman. This is what defines a woman. A complete woman, a successful woman has a man.

Diamond thought about all of her girlfriends. Diamond thought about her associates, many of whom claimed they hated men on a regular basis. At least, they claimed they hated them until some man, any man, proposed and then they were fit to be tied. It was there. Entrenched in the darkest recesses of their psyche, was the fact that Black women believed that they had to have a man to be a woman. And as many times as she'd felt the pain and misery of being burnt by men, here she was, right smack dab in the middle of hell's inferno.

No, in reality she had no right to blame Helen for wanting the same things out of life that she wanted. She could blame her for not having the decency or self-respect to keep her hands off her property. That wasn't to say that she owned Henry but it was obvious that they were deeply involved and trying to move forward in spite of all the gossip and bullshit they had to endure. She could blame her for being so goddamn hungry, so love sick, so starved for a man that she lost all respect for herself and lowered herself to finding a job across the street from the man's residence so she could be close enough to monitor his whereabouts. That bordered on obsession like some fatal attraction. And that was just plain sick.

She could blame her for calling three and four times a day then hanging up. She had to know full well that the caller I.D. plainly showed her number. Diamond could blame her for all that. But those reasons in themselves, though they would have been enough five years ago, just weren't good enough to make her lower her standards and approach her around some man. She'd come to the conclusion, long ago that when a man gets ready to go he's gonna go. People weren't possessions and you couldn't possess or own them. You couldn't keep them when they decide it's time for them to go. As badly as you may want to you just can't.

Chapter 9

Diamond never mentioned the piece of paper tucked in Henry's coat pocket with Helen Harden's address printed on it. And Henry never mentioned the proposed dinner date with Sister Helen that Friday night. As it turned out, he was glad he didn't after witnessing Diamond's fiery temper the following evening.

Seems there was a small misunderstanding about an insurance policy and its beneficiaries. Henry didn't get the entire gist of the conversation as he stepped in the door but he knew he'd never envisioned that Diamond could ever get this angry over anything.

Kissing her gently on the cheek, Henry made his way to the shower where he quickly showered, dressed and made his way back out the door almost as quietly as he'd come in. Diamond was off the phone by this time but it was obvious that she was still seething. When she spoke to him she did her best to play off whatever it was that had infuriated her so. It was to no avail. She was angry, no, livid and Henry sensed that it had be something more than the matter of an insurance policy and its beneficiaries. No, it was obvious that something was troubling her deeply but he dared not ask. When she was ready, she'd tell him. The problem was, she never did.

The following day was Friday. Henry spent the greater part of the morning putting some last minute touches on his sermon hoping to guarantee a rousing chorus of 'Amens' and 'Hallelujahs' that Sunday but no matter what he did he couldn't seem to concentrate on the yellow legal pad before him.

No coffee in the house, he thought about walking across the street and grabbing a cup but decided against after glancing out of his bedroom window and noticing Helen's car around the side designated for employee parking. He thought about calling Diamond who surprisingly enough he hadn't seen or heard from in days but decided against it. She'd been in rare form the last time he'd seen her. These days she was unusually irritable and short-tempered. Though she admitted to being so she gave no reason for it.

At first, he thought she might be pregnant but she laughed as if it was an impossibility. Trying to concentrate on his sermon once again it suddenly dawned on him why he couldn't concentrate. There was no writer's cramp this time. What it was instead was a simple matter of conscience. Tonight was his dinner date with Helen. He'd purposely failed to mention it to Diamond for fear that she would go off. She had so little faith in men and it had taken him so long to get her to trust him that he hated to tell her for fear that she would place some part of the blame on him. It was obvious she didn't care for Helen or the fact that she wore skin tight outfits all the time regardless of the occasion and made bones about the fact that she was trying to entice the good reverend. Diamond knew women and Helen Harden had two serious character flaws. She talked too much and she had no qualms with sleeping with another woman's man. In fact, it almost seemed that she wasn't interested unless the man belonged to someone else. Diamond had alluded to this on several occasion. When he seemed not to hear her she came flat out with it and made it a point to tell him what she thought of Helen Harden.

Henry could recall Diamond's words verbatim. "Henry we've talked about this before so I'm just going to come to the point. I want you to stay away from Helen Harden. She means you no good. She means me no good. She has no respect for you. She thinks that you're so low that you'd cheat on me. She has no respect for me because she's going to entice my man to fuck her. If you did and I were to find out then what? I'm gone. And you know that no sooner than you took your dick out of the bitch she'd be on the phone letting the world know. Your career at First Abyssinian would be history. That's just how she is. There are millions of women out there, just like Helen Harden, who seem to derive pleasure from other people's pain.

C'mon Henry. Think about it. She had her chance. She didn't want you then. Why is she so obsessed about having you now? Now that I have you, you're the best thing since sliced bread and she's just got to have a piece.

Maybe she figures that since you are sleepin' with a former call girl that you've stooped low enough to fuck her. I'm sorry Henry I know shouldn't have said that but it is what it is. And all I know is that for whatever reason and I am truly clueless, she wants our relationship to end. Maybe we appear too happy when we're together. Maybe she just envisions herself in my place. Maybe she finally realizes that she may have blown a golden opportunity. I don't know.

Like I said before and I hope you're hearing me is that she doesn't want you Henry. She may not want me to have you. It may mess up the good name of the church. I don't know. But you want to tell her the story of Mary Magdalene the way you told me.

On the other hand, she may just want to fuck you so she can put another notch in her belt or say she fucked the good reverend. That would certainly bring you down a peg or two in the church's eyes. Most of those people there have so much respect for you. The elders like Sista Gerty think you're the second coming. Yeah, that would certainly bring your ass down a peg or two.

Do you remember telling them my story? You had faith. I didn't. At first they were angry and they understood and accepted me because you believed in me and you led the way. I'm serious. I don't know if they'd be as forgiving if you messed up though. I think it would be like suicide; almost like crucifying your own self.

I really don't know what's up with ol'girl. I truly don't know. I do know that there are women out there that do things like that though. I don't understand how it elevates their status in the whole scheme of things or if they simply don't care but Helen's one of those people. Trust me, Henry. Call it women's intuition if you like but stay the hell away from Helen Harden or stay the hell away from me. She's bad news.

This may be stretching it some but Helen reminds me of those fools in jail that rape other men. Back on the block, it seems like they're all too proud to tell someone, anyone, that they raped somebody and then calling them a faggot. I heard one say, "I'll toss your salad like I did when we was upstate. You remember that don'tcha, you little faggot', and I usta wonder and ask myself, 'if you raped him what does that make you, homeboy?'

Henry hated Diamond to talk about such vile things or use such language. She'd come so far to revert back but he knew that when she did it wasn't out of anger but done purposely and as a last recourse to get his attention and to get her point across when he wasn't hearing her.

He was listening now, though. Usually quiet and unassuming despite her physical attractiveness she was so much more animated than he'd ever seen her and that included the time they spent behind closed doors. He'd listened to her and made it a point to avoid Sister Helen. That was until the night Diamond, needed those damn Tampons and put him on the spot. Now here he was trying to jot down the last few lines of his sermon and all he could think about were Diamond's words.

In less than two hours he'd promised Sister Helen he'd have dinner with her and if he knew Sister Helen the way he thought he knew Sister Helen she was already prepared and chomping at the bit as she thought about having him for dessert. He couldn't even call to cancel.

Pushing the legal pad aside and placing the pen on top, the good reverend folded his hands and put his head down on the desk. He remembered South Carolina. He remembered how he had to jump on the first thing smoking. And why? Women that's why. The situation wasn't much different than this one except for the fact that for the first time in a long time he was truly happy and in love. Sure, the temptation was there. The temptation was always there.

There was time, a while back when he would have given anything for a night, just one roll in the hay with Sister Helen. She was fine; maybe the finest woman at First Abyssinian until Diamond appeared. But it was different with Diamond. She was stunning but she put her looks on the backburner. It was her looks that put her in the situation that she was in. Have her tell it, 'if this were Greek mythology, then my looks are my Achilles heel.'

She was conscious of them. How could she not be but she wanted more. If looks were Diamond's Achilles then sex was the good reverends. Though neither spoke of their weaknesses openly to each other, they understood each other perfectly. The reverend made it a point not to sleep with Diamond unless Diamond knew that unlike most of the men she'd encountered he desired her for her.

Diamond fully conscious of the temptations that were placed before the good reverend in the form of Black women each and every day made sure that he was satisfied despite his protests. Why run out for McDonald's food when you could stay home and dine at Tavern on the Green she would tease while unbuckling his belt buckle. Henry smiled as he thought of Diamond and wondered why he hadn't heard from her before deciding that Sister Helen would just have to be disappointed. Right now, he needed to see Diamond.

Grabbing a light jacket Henry Barnes headed outside and then to his car. His only thought was of seeing Diamond. He only hoped that traffic wouldn't be too bad on the West Side Highway. He'd only been to her place once and that was when they'd first met.   He would've never

thought Diamond would bring someone to her home but as he exited the elevator that particular night some six months ago, a young White preppy, gentleman stepped out of her door. Henry had had the presence of mind to duck back into the elevator without being noticed or saying a word, with the hopes of saving both of them a good deal of embarrassment. He never mentioned that evening to her. It had taken him the better part of a week after the episode to call her and he vowed never to go back without calling first again unexpected. That was up until now

Tonight it didn't matter who was there or why. He needed to talk and he needed to talk now. He wanted to tell her that he didn't need a woman in his life to feel whole. He needed her. He wanted to tell her about the incident with Helen Harden and how right she'd been. He wanted to tell her that he'd not only become a better minister but a better man because of the person she was. He wanted to tell her just how much he'd learned from her. He wanted to tell her that couldn't wait another minute longer and that he had to marry her tomorrow if he couldn't marry her today. He had to tell her that he was nothing without her in his life. And although it had taken her leaving to make him understand this, he understood and readily admitted it. Now all he had to do was tell her.

Surprised to find traffic relatively light for this time of day, Henry made his way downtown quickly. Double-parking the SUV in front of her building, Henry made his way into the lobby where he promptly hit the intercom, buzzing

Diamond's apartment. Lord knows he had so much to tell her.

Henry smiled as he waited anxiously for Diamond to answer as the doorman stared. When there was no reply from Diamond's apartment the doorman made his way from where he's he'd been sitting reading the newspaper and headed over to Henry.

"If there's any way I can be of assistance sir, please let me know," he said the English accent apparent.

"Yes, I'm looking for Ms. Massey," Henry replied.

The doorman glanced around before speaking again, then whispered. "Do you have an appointment sir? Or are you just another friend drooping by to see Ms. Massey?"

"No, I do not have appointment to see Ms. Massey. And for your information I am not just another old friend dropping by. I happen to be Ms. Massey's fiancée," Henry responded his voice cracking in anger.

The doorman was stunned and apologized for his stupidity. So, sorry sir Ms. Massey has so many callers I just thought…"

Henry didn't let the doorman finish and headed for the door in disgust. The doorman followed the good reverend to the door still apologizing for his blunder.

"I am truly sorry sir if I misunderstood. A limousine picked Ms. Massey up about an hour ago. To the best of my knowledge, she usually returns no later than eleven—eleven thirty at the latest. Shall I tell her you called?"

As far as Henry was concerned, he'd heard quite enough and there was really nothing more to be said. He'd made a mistake going back there after he promised himself he wouldn't. Only this time he knew it was the last time. Now that he knew that she was up to her old tricks he was finished. If there was a need for any explanation she'd have to seek him out. The doorman was equally stunned and apologized.

"So sorry sir, Ms. Massey has so many callers I just thought..."

Henry didn't allow the doorman to finish and headed for the door. Aware of his blunder, the doorman followed the good reverend to the door still attempting to apologize for the error.

"I am truly sorry, sir, if I misunderstood. A car, a limousine picked her up about an hour ago. She usually returns no later than eleven or eleven thirty at the latest."

There was no more to be said. The doorman said it all. So, she was back to her old tricks. Henry vowed he would never bring up the incident with the doorman and never but never go to see Diamond again. She would have to come to him and this time she could do the explaining.

She returned later in the week but there was no mention of her sudden disappearance other than her saying that she needed some time alone to think and handle some financial matters she'd been neglecting. It was not long after that all was back to normal, the wedding announcement was made the following week and Helen Harden did not return to the First Abyssinian Church of Christ.

Chapter 10

Diamond's thoughts returned to the woman sitting across the table from her. Carrie's tired face reminded her of how far she'd regressed since she'd met the

129

good reverend and her mind drifted again. This time she became immersed and felt herself drowning in a blue, green sea of melancholy as she thought of the late Reverend Barnes, who was for all intensive purposes dead in her eyes. Dead! Dead! Dead! But as angry as she was, at being betrayed once again by a man she'd come to know and trust something stirred deep inside of her when she thought of Henry. And she knew that as calloused and hard as she'd become over the years there still remained a soft spot for Henry.

Turning to Carrie and looking at the older woman who seemed to age before her very eyes, she prayed that she would never look back on lost love with the burning regret of not knowing what could have been. Turning to Carrie, Diamond grabbed the woman's hands in her own and said, "Carrie, tell Q I'm out for good this time. I'm going to marry that man."

Carrie smiled and the tears rolled down her cheeks in a flood of emotion.

"You're doing the right thing, girl. Just promise me one thing, Diamond."

"Anything, Carrie."

"Promise me that when you walk away this time you'll just keep on walking. Promise me that you won't turn around. Promise me that you'll keep on walking and won't look back."

The two women hugged briefly. Carrie assured her that she'd take care of Q and that there wouldn't be any repercussions. Diamond thanked her before dressing quickly and heading uptown. Knocking on Henry's door, she was surprised to see how much he'd aged in so short a time. Looking gaunt and broken, his demeanor changed at once and she knew then if she had ever doubted before that he loved her dearly.

She wondered how she could have ever doubted his love and devotion and cursed herself for her own stupidity. And then for the second time that day, she did something she hadn't done in years. She cried. She cried long desperate streams of broken promises and lost dreams. She cried out for the pain and sorrow and bitterness that had become so much a part of her life. She cried for the clouds that blocked her view and refused to let the sunshine in. She cried because she had lost the trust and the innocence that made life beautiful. But mostly she cried because she was happy to be given another chance to live and to hope and to dream.

Henry cried too as he repeated, "I knew the good Lord would bring you back to me. Oh, you don't know how hard I prayed that he would. And he has certainly answered my prayers."

They talked into the wee hours of the morning about anything and everything as lovers will do who have been apart. Diamond told him how she'd faked her period that night she'd sent him to

the Quick Stop to test his loyalty. And Henry told her of Sister Helen's attempts to blackmail him into having dinner and who knows what else. Both had to laugh at how foolish they'd been and made it a point to never hold anything from the other. And then they'd made love and for the first time in her life Diamond understood what Carrie had been telling her about that so very special feeling only Q could give her. Only it wasn't Q that made Diamond tingle all over. It was Henry. Henry Barnes.

The days that followed were a hubbub of activity. Henry made the announcement that the wedding date had been changed and would take place the following week. And no Diamond wasn't pregnant, just very anxious but he hoped that she would soon be so he could keep a closer eye on her. The congregation laughed. All that was left now was the blood test and the ceremony itself. Diamond and Henry both had to admit that they had never been so happy. In Diamond's eyes, this time around was even better than the first time. But there was still so much to do so little time that she was constantly feeling tired and fatigued. Yet, she remained focused and diligent running Henry's and the church's errands during the daytime then staying up half the night working on he wedding plans. Henry joked about seeing her less now than when she was gone for those three weeks but now at least he knew where she was and what she was doing.

"Don't get it twisted Henry. You won't see me at all if I catch you looking at Helen Harden with her six inch heels and jogging suit," she joked. They both laughed. Sista Helen had returned but hardly spoke to either after hearing the announcement.

Times were good, as good as either had ever known. Now two days before the wedding Diamond made her way through the busy cross-town traffic to the travel agent where she had to pick up the tickets for their flight. Henry wanted to go to Mexico and she to Puerto Rico for the honeymoon and since they couldn't agree he'd given in to her second choice and settled on Jamaica, which Diamond insisted was halfway between the two. But as long as they were together, it hardly mattered to Henry. He was just happy to have her back, and to make her his wife. After leaving the travel agent, Diamond stopped by the doctor's office to pick up the blood tests. She was making good time. All that was left was to pick up the wedding bands from the jewelers where they were being sized and the marriage certificates from City Hall.

Diamond was surprised to find Henry at the office when she arrived and even more surprised that Henry was not in one of his better moods.

"I wish I had known you were coming Henry. You could've saved me the trip. I still have to g to the jewelers and," before she could finish Dr. Sheldon interrupted.

"Miss Massey would you mind having a seat. I have some well, rather disturbing news. Your husband called me earlier this week to tell me that you were suffering from being overly tired and fatigue at which time I suggested some over the counter supplements, as I would do for most of my patients. However, since I had your blood work here I thought, why not take a closer look at which time like I said I found some rather disturbing things Miss Massey," the doctor paused, took off his glasses and rubbed his eyes.

"What the hell are you talking about? What the hell is he talking about Henry?" Diamond shouted.

Henry turned his head to the wall to avoid Diamond's stare. For the first time since they'd met, he didn't have the strength to face her. The doctor continued. "Miss Massey, I'm afraid you've somehow contracted the HIV virus and it seems that you're in the latter stages. Now it's nothing to..."

She was gone before he could finish. Neither Henry nor the doctor could catch her to try to console her. The last glimpse he saw of Diamond was running, screaming, arms flailing in every direction, as she crossed Fifth Avenue in the direction of Central Park.

For two weeks, Henry searched every nook, cranny and every hole in the wall from Soho to Castle Hill, all to no avail.

And then when he least expected it, he received a call from Carrie who he'd seen only an hour or so earlier to let him know that Diamond was at her parents house up on Sugar Hill. Henry had felt so relieved. He would have never thought to check there.

"Thank you. Thank you so very much, Carrie. I've been so worried."

"I guess when worse comes to worse there's no place like home. "No I guess there isn't" she responded. "I'm just glad she could go home. They asked me to give you the address," Carrie said. Henry was ecstatic.

"I know it's not going to be easy," he said reaching for the pencil, "but with the help of the Lord we're going to make it. By the grace of God we're going to make it," Henry said. "Go ahead Carrie." I'm on my way as you speak. "You don't know how crazy I am about that woman."

"Henry, I'm not sure you understand."

"What's to understand? It's just another one of life's little tests."

"No Henry Diamond's parents asked me to give you the address with the sincere hope that you would somehow find the strength to perform the service.

"You see Henry, Diamond passed away this morning."

African-American?

Tucking my leggin's in to my socks,

while the ugly, cold, steel-grey of mornin'

sweeps in off the Hudson

creeping through the tear in my blinds

into my Harlem flat

I shiver.

Trying to shake the cold from my achy bones,

I swear fo' God I does my able-bodied best

just ta get dressed.

And though I know your still waitin' fer some mention of Sweet

I must confess that I has a certain tendency to digress.

Yet, come ta know me

and you'll understand that I will eventually get there.

(Ta my story that is)

Unless somethin' else is on my mind 'causin' an unnatural stress

and then I must let be known my protests.

Again, I must confess,

so much has been thrown at me

that it's been a might hard ta swallow

and digest.

For just in my lifetime

and at your behest

I've been

Colored

Negro,

Black

and a variety of other hues

you may not deem so correct.

But today

I am

an

African-American.

And yet,

just as sure as clear skies will most certainly make haste

 for the thunder clouds

and the sun will give way to the rain

I am sure my forecast will also change.

Yes

today

I am an African-American.

But most of the time

I do not have a clue

as to who I really am.

And ya know,

it's a might peculiar thing

but

tomorrow

I'm not exactly sure

who the hell I'll be.

Still,

it's a funny thing.

But you always remain you

even when I'm not always me.

Whether Irish or British

Arab or Jew

whether war or peace time

you always remain

you.

While morning after morning,

I still awake

so utterly lost and confused

that it's getting to the point

where it takes me quite some time now

ta do somethin' as simple as

ta tie my shoes.

I'm not sure that I get it

or perhaps wholly understan'

if today I'm Black

or

African-American.

I ain't rightly sure

but

I's willin' ta bet that

it's not something ta play with

or

later

have some regrets.

For an error can make you

unpatriotic

or

even

a

terrorist threat.

Now you laugh my brothas

but laugh not in jest

for the penalty can be severe

if you

don't pass the test.

May sound harsh

and a bit much to digest

but

it's important my brotha

if ya wanna progress.

That's why those

closest ta me

know how much I tend ta stress

the importance

of bein' a

strong Blackman

and knowin' the history of your

African-American –ness.

Well, by now I guess

you're sittin' there puzzled,

scratchin' your head

tryin' ta figger out what da hell it is

I jes' said.

But it's quite simple.

don't ever fergit you're a

nigga

or

you might jes' wind up

dead...

The Street Corner Philosopher

Now that you've had a chance to read my poem, I guess you've gained a new
perspective or at least some insight into the nature of racism and prejudice. I
wrote that poem because racism and prejudice have always been a pet peeve of
mine. I don't allow them to be any more than a pet peeve because I simply
don't have the time to dwell on such negative matters for long. I have also
found that those that those that allot too much time to either of these subjects
often times become overwhelmed and consumed with them which in turn can
lead to a preoccupation with the subject and a certain amount of bitterness. Still,
I must confess that in my encounters with those persons who tend to have a
certain tendency to prejudge others I have found some rather peculiar
commonalities. And being that most Americans have a tendency to prejudge
then I hardly feel any remorse about taking a few minutes of your time to

generalize about the generalizers. And so, in the truest tradition of the generalizer I would like to throw out this blanket statement that I am sure will raise the ire of many and come to rest somewhere between a significant truth and the anger of those wrapped in a shroud of blind patriotism. In any case, here is my statement.

Most Americans don't know a hill of beans about much of anything aside from their own day–to-day lives and even fewer are willing to try and find out about things they know little about. Most of 'em are content to just sit back and let someone else paint a picture and then draw a conclusion from someone else's depiction before making the effort to come to know someone firsthand.

Take me for example. They call me Willie the Wino but those that have hung that moniker around my neck don't know me. What they are referring to is the fact that a large part of my day is spent somewhere on this block between Sherman's Barbeque pit and Ortega's Bodega and Liquor Store. Here I am sometimes content to just sit and shoot the breeze and other times I like to just stand here and make scattered observations on the daily activities from afar.

I see a lot perched up here but unlike my peers, I seldom if ever allow myself to draw conclusions from a first impression. People are much too complex for me to do that. If I did that, I would be doing both of us a disservice. And not only would I be doing both of us a disservice, I would be doing a disservice to my profession. You see a good anthropologist must have the ability to stand apart from the group almost like the proverbial fly on the wall, a nonexistent entity and simply observe and record the facts before him with no opinion whatsoever. Then through the scientific process, he can cipher through the facts and come to a logical conclusion later on, somewhere down the line. Only then can he do this and only after some pretty intensive and careful deductive reasoning.

Now, did I mention the fact that I spent some time up at Columbia and followed Margaret Meade's career for a spell. In any case, whether I mentioned it or not I believe that it may be important for some to know that I spent some time up at Columbia doing some rather in depth research. Many a winter in the early sixties, you could find me in the Anthropology Department. You see I'd sit in on quite a few lectures right through there for the sake of furthering my studies and of course to keep warm. Usually the professor would have two or three hundred students in

142

one of one them great big ol' lecture halls and wouldn't even notice me there. Well, that was until I began to participate and he sought to find my name on his roster.

Most of them cats didn't know as much as I did about the field of anthropology. Only difference was they were credentialized and I wasn't. By the time, they got to the point where they really began to search in earnest to find out who I was in order to award me some extra credits for class participation I was on to my lecture. I guess you could say I was a non-matriculating student. While most of them kids were there because they needed the credits to graduate so they get a good job, I was there solely for empirical reasons. I was there primarily for the purpose of observation and acquiring knowledge for the sake of bettering myself and furthering my education. That and the fact that it was one of the coldest winters I can remember and it was too darn cold to be standing outside panhandling.

Anyway, those couple of summers there were some of the most informative I've ever experienced. It really sparked my interest in anthropology and it prepared me to take my show on the row. It also taught me how to separate myself from those I was observing as well as to be careful in drawing conclusions without some very in depth analysis and evaluation which brings me back to my starting point. And over the years I have composed a rather vast and in depth study of people and in particular Harlem Negroes. And I have done this primarily by avoiding the easy lure of drawing conclusions from first impressions.

Take ol' Sweet for example. I've known my boy, Sweet ever since he moved up to Harlem from Georgia back in the early '40's. I couldn't help but get to know the brotha because no more than

a week after he arrived we both got the call from Uncle Sam to sign up for the big one. That was close to fifty years ago. And like I said, he may be my oldest and dearest friend but I still can't say that I really know him. But let me tell you what I do know about him based on careful observations made over the years.

Being that Sweet was the onliest Negro, (We was Negroes and Colored back then), that I recognized down there at the induction center when we got our papers to report we quickly became ace boon coons; you know partners; road dogs. Now Sweet was sho'nuff geechie if there ever was such a thing. You know he was real, real country. He had that real strong Southern drawl and most of the other privates, both Colored and white used to tease him about it all the time. Like I said, he had that thick Georgia drawl and I guess they hadn't heard nothing like it before, being that most of was from right here in New York or right across the water, in Jersey. Anyway, once we got shipped out it wasn't half so bad since all almost all the boys in our unit was from the south, just like me and Sweet. And I'll tell you something else I bet you're not aware of. Despite what the history books might tell you, most of the boys that hit the beaches of Normandy on D-Day with us looked just me and Sweet. You think I'm jokin', dontcha? I'm tellin' you the God's honest truth.

When we hit those beaches it looked just like an oil slick had washed upon those crystal white beaches, it was so many of us Colored boys. Talk about a black cloud descending on something. Now every now and then you'd see a platoon or two of Marines that was all white that hit the beaches but mostly it was us Colored boys, like me and Sweet that secured those beaches over in France to end World War II. That ain't takin nothin' away from them there white boys that gave

their lives but it was so many of us Coloreds soldiers that we thought that D-Day meant darkie Day. Funny thing, but to this day I never did find out what D-Day really stood for. I heard a lot of my buddies sayin' it meant Doomsday and I swear I believed that when we first hit the beach.

Man, when we first hit that beach Coloreds boys was runnin' this a way and that screamin' and hollerin' and fallin' and cryin' and dyin'. Limbs were flyin' this way and that and I though for sure I'd fallen into Dante's Inferno or some other hell hole. Colored boys were dyin' all around me. And the Gerry's, (that's what we called the Nazi's) was relentless in their assault. They hit us with everything imaginable. Mortars, artillery. Their air force, the Luftwaffe was circling overhead dropping bombs like they was gumdrops. Machine gunfire pinned us down at first but my boy Sweet knocked him out with his first shot letting us advance a few paces. So much stuff was being thrown at that all we could was try to find some cover and dig in. By the time I got myself dug in the Gerry's

144

had me really and truly believing that they were the superior race.

Anyways, the whole time me and Sweet are making our way up onto the shoreline I'm looking around for some place to run and hide. At first I thought the hell with diggin' in. I'm lookin' to get back on ship or for some place to hide and there ain't so much as an anthill to hide behind so I started asking myself, who in the hell came up with this strategy. Then it dawned on me that the people in charge were the descendants of the same folks who in past wars sent row after row of soldiers in formation against muskets and howitzers and cannon fire. That was in the Civil War. And from what I could see from my foxhole they hadn't learned a thing about strategy

since then. I hadn't minded much when I used to watch those old Civil War reruns and would think how stupid but it hadn't really bothered me much at the time. Only now I minded since my butt was on the line. And as I lay there trying to bury myself like a horseshoe crab trying to dig a hole to China while at the same time bullets whizzed around my head I really truly began to wonder if Hitler hadn't gotten together with the Allied Forces on a coalition to eradicate us Coloreds the same way Hitler was doin' them Jews over in Germany. Lying there on the beach that day while the Gerry's kicked up sand all around me in a blistering barrage of artillery fire I thought about a lot. Being half-a-heartbeat from death will force you to think about a lot of things you wouldn't normally think of or may tend to just overlook.

I thought about the conversation I had with my drill instructor when I was back in boot camp out on the rifle range. And I thought about just how wrong he'd been. It was the first time I'd ever held a gun, as I'd never had any reason to outside of the war. Back on the block, at least back then, guns was almost unheard of. They wasn't big business like they are today. Back then the only two things you needed to protect yourself was your mouth and your hands. You had to be able to either talk yourself out of a fix or fight your way out of one. And since I was pretty good with both my mouth and my hands I had no real problems to speak of. In fact, the only time I ever saw a gun was when I went to the picture show and John Wayne or Audy Murphy was brandishin' one. And I hated them even then. Most of the time, they were either killin' bad guys or Indians. (I always sided with the bad guys and the Indians since we both had a common enemy).

In any case, I knew two things for sure anytime they took out their guns. First, that was it for my hero. And secondly, any time the Duke's gun left its holster the movie was over. So, I hated guns and everything associated with them. Not only that, I was afraid of them. No, I was more than afraid. I was petrified. Anytime that rifle was put in my hand I would start shaking. Still, I did my best to hide this fact in order to save face and keep my reputation intact. So, when the time came for me to qualify with my rifle I stepped up to the plate just like everyone else and squeezed off the required number of rounds in the general direction of the target as my drill instructor barked the order to fire.

When they reeled the targets in to see how well I'd done one thing was for sure I was no sharpshooter. My target showed no clusters, no patterns of rounds hitting the bulls eye. In fact, in more instances than not, I hadn't hit the target at all. If I had had any thoughts of a career as an army sniper it was now totally out of the question. After two weeks on the rifle range, my ineptness with the rifle was a well-known fact. As far as my reputation was concerned, it suffered irrefutable damage and there were whispers around camp about my prowess on the rifle range or better yet, lack thereof. It was all in good fun though and I always responded when chided by Sweet and my other buddies that I was a lover not a fighter. They responded, in turn, that I must surely be a double agent and they were going to make sure that I was on the front lines and not bringing up the rear behind any of them. The whole affair proved to be pretty humorous at the time providing everyone with a good laugh but I was beginning to have my druthers about heading into a combat situation not knowing how to shoot straight.

Meanwhile, my boy Sweet was receiving all kinds of praise for his expertise with the same rifle I couldn't hit the broad side of a barn with. Now I have never been one of those type of Negroes who get green with envy and I was as proud of Sweet as anyone but at the same time I was just as worried about my

146

own inability to shoot. I knew that it was only a matter of time before we would be shipped out and since I didn't speak Kraut and Joe Louis had already whipped Schmelling's ass I knew my mouth and my hands weren't going to do much good. Harlem rules didn't apply where I was going. That was for sure.

When I explained this to my drill instructor, he just laughed and said, 'believe me, boy, when them Krauts get to firing at you, you'll learn to shoot.'

Now, here I was lyin' on the beach with Sweet by my side and the Krauts running, screaming with a reckless abandon that made me wonder if the dampness I felt was from our beach landing, my own sweat or the fact that the Gerry's had scared the pee outta me. Lying there, I couldn't help but remember the last movie Sweet had taken me to see stateside called the Strange Island of Dr. Moreau and that's what this reminded me of. There were limbs maimed and disfigured all around me. The stench of death rose and fell with each swell of the ocean tide. Men with torn limbs and blind from the flash of blasts screamed in pain and agony screams that can only be associated with the agony of the battlefield. I could feel the tears of fear streaming down my cheeks. Glancing over at Sweet in the foxhole next to me, I noticed the empty glaze in his eyes. He was firing with a rhythmic regularity now and each time he fired another Gerry would fall

screaming in pain. I often wondered how many German widows Sweet made that day and knew it had to be more than twenty. I wondered if he thought he was still down in Macon County, Georgia shootin' coons so cool was he as he squeezed off round after round. I, on the other hand, fired steadily in the general direction of those advancing and although I spent five or six magazines holding twenty rounds apiece I can recall only winging one or two the entire day. I fired off so many rounds and kicked up so much sand from the dunes that first day that I can at least say that I held them at bay. Of course, they kept us pinned down as well. But on day two our fortunes changed as wave after wave after wave of air support came with our fighter pilots blasting the hell out of the German frontline until they were forced to retreat.

The days following were quiet, solemn ones for the Third Battalion as we spent the majority of our time collecting dog tags, filling body bags and tending to the sick and the wounded. Sweet and I saw a great many of our buddies with legs and arms blown clear off. One soldier had half of his face and skull burned

147

down to the bone from a mortar blast and was in such a state of shock that he continued to fire at the hilltop where the Gerry's had been with his right eyeball dangling from the socket.

No one said anything about the horrors that surrounded us. It almost seemed like any mention of the atrocities that faced us would somehow and in someway bring about our own demise. And even though it wasn't mentioned I knew that the horror and pain we faced in those first few days on the beaches of Normandy would forever affect us.

Funny thing though, my boy Sweet, who was in line for a medal for all the Gerry's he'd killed upon our landing hardly seemed affected at all but went about his duties as methodically and dutifully as he had in training. I was incredulous and the whole affair was difficult for me to even fathom. There was so much blood, so many bodies and so much to do those first few days that every time the soldiers came off one of those horrible details we'd crawl back into our foxholes and close our eyes doing our best to shut out the pain and suffering and all the other grim reminders of war. A lot of us Colored soldiers spent that time reminiscing about the good times back home wherever that might have been but for most of us these were quiet times.

Occasionally, we would hear the buzzing sound of the Luftwaffe or German air force and then the steady staccato of beats as they bombed those who now took the front. And sometimes, I really wished I was on the frontline instead of being left with the burial death. At least, when you were on the front lines in the midst of the action you'd didn't think about how any day you could be on the wrong side of the burial detail. At least when you're on the front lines in the midst of the action you're so concerned with staying alive that you can't think about anything else and especially your own impending demise. But now as I carried body bag after body bag to the U-Boats to be shipped back home, all I kept wondering was how long it would be before one of my buddies would be folding my arms across the huge gaping hole in my chest and stuffing me in one of these body bags to be shipped back across the water. The stench of death filled the warm salty air and I was never so happy as when they sent my little, narrow Black ass back up to the front.

Besides, with Sweet by my side I knew I had a pretty fair chance of surviving. Ol' Sweet and I had become fairly close by this time and I enjoyed the time he and I spent huddled together in our foxholes, with him ramblin' on about the backwoods of Decatur, Georgia where he'd spent the majority of his boyhood chasing coons, and rabbits and pretty girls. I'd glance over at him and tried to imagine this big ol' burly Black buck tryin' to hide behind a mulberry bush tryin' to get a bead on some itty bitty rabbit and the whole scenario would seem almost comical. Then out of nowhere, machinegun fire from the Gerry's would interrupt my thoughts and I'd find myself back in the middle of hell's kitchen.

This second push led by us Colored soldiers didn't last long, at least not nearly as long as our first assault and pretty soon we'd driven the Gerry's from France altogether. When we did, it was almost like we were gods or something. The French had parades and celebrations everywhere we went. Now I ain't never been whatcha might call a hero or stuffed shirt or anything like that but when us Colored soldiers stepped into town you would've sworn it was the Second Coming of Jesus Christ himself.

The old people would run out and break formation and hug and kiss us. When we were given liberty, they'd take us into their homes and feed us and bed us down as if we were long lost relatives finally returning home after a long exile. And the women, oh my God, the women. These little French gals were some of the most beautiful gals in the world and trust me I've seen

a lot of beautiful girls and a lot of the world. Not only were they beautiful, they had a certain quality about them, a certain gene se qua—you know—a sort of subtle elegance.

When we first got there, I gotta admit, I wasn't even thinkin' about lookin' at no French gals being from Mississippi and all but the French acted like we was people and a lot of us Colored boys thought we had died and gone straight to heaven. Sweet, on the other hand had a harder time adjustin' to that French hospitality than most of us and I suppose that can be attributed to his being from Decatur and all. When we first arrived on the shores of France and were hunkered down in our foxholes ol' Sweet used to recollect on how he would see a Negro swingin' from a Weeping Willow on occasion for something as petty as supposedly glancing in the direction of a white woman. So he had a harder time than most of us Colored soldiers accepting the fact that these people weren't white or French. They were just people.

Now when ol' Sweet realized he wasn't going to be lynched he just went hog wild. You would have thought that the French had liberated Sweet from Hitler instead of the other way around. And in a way I guess they had. I remember him telling me one night while we were on leave that this was the first time in his life he really, truly, felt like a man. And I had to smile since I knew how he felt but somehow all the killing took some of the luster away from the whole affair as far as I was concerned. To top it off, the French women looked at Sweet like he was some big ol' chocolate teddy bear and I guess for the first time in his life he felt like a celebrity of sorts. And every couple of weeks they'd throw us a dance at the U.S.O. and them French gals would line up

to dance with my boy Sweet like he was something good to eat. Still and all, he never appeared to take a real liking to chasin' those gals like some of the other Colored soldiers. I suppose that ol' Jim Crow mentality was just embedded too deeply. So, instead ol' Sweet kinda adopted the first family that showed him some kindness and generosity.

The family had a farm down in the southern part of France, not a stones throw from where we were stationed the better part of our first year there. Sweet's adopted family had a vineyard, which the Nazis had all but destroyed, where they made wine. I believe they referred to it as a winery but what they really made was the sweetest, bubbliest, and champagne that I have ever had the good fortune to taste. And Sweet was as much responsible for getting that winery up and running after the Gerry's left as the owner himself.

150

Now from what I understand the farmer who owned and founded the winery, along with his two sons got word of the impending invasion and made the fatal mistake of joining the French Resistance. When the Gerry's found out about their affiliation with the allied forces the Nazi's shot both their sons in front of the old man and his wife and burned the winery to the ground.

The old man also had three daughters who had been hiding with relatives in Paris since rumor of the German invasion. When they learned of their brothers murder the girls returned home and went about the task of trying to ease their parents grief and rebuild the winery which as Sweet and I were to find out was a next to near impossible task. As if that weren't enough the three sisters were on every conceivable committee to see that the Allied forces were comfortable

during their stay in France. Sweet and I just happened to meet them at a U.S.O. Appreciation Day Dance they'd arranged for us Colored soldiers. And of course all three sisters swarmed to Sweet like bees to honey.

By the end of the night when the old man came to pick up his daughter's Sweet pretty much knew the whole story of the family and the winery even though he didn't parley vu a lick of French. Still he promised to help in any way he possibly could. All the old man had to do was pick him up the next morning, which just happened to be Saturday, and one of our rare days off. Now I didn't much mind Sweet being a Good Samaritan. In fact, it was one of the things that attracted me to Sweet in the first place and a quality that endeared him to so many others as well. But when he volunteered my services it was quite another matter altogether.

In any event, the old man arrived at our barracks at somewhere around five a.m., tooting the horn of his little Renault truck like it was reveille or something. My head was still spinning from the night before so as you can probably guess, I wasn't the least bit happy about this little progression. Truth be told I was mentally and physically exhausted. I hadn't slept well since our landing— well—not regularly anyway. Instead of seeing the pitch black of night when I closed my eyes all I saw was red, blood red. It flowed everywhere. Dead, lifeless, limbless bodies, sometimes skinless bodies moving swimming in bloody lakes settled in deep pools all around me. I'd awake bathed in a cold sweat, feverish, staring at the starless skies above me afraid to close my eyes.

At other times, I'd awake screaming. Eventually, sleep would overtake me and I would somehow manage to get in an hour or two before reveille. But there was no reveille this morning, no bugle blowing and no mad scramble for the makeshift showers. There was only the ever so annoying blaring of the old man's horn. Despite the fact that I wanted to shoot myself for agreeing to accompany Sweet I knew that with my aim I'd probably end up shooting one of my sleeping comrades instead so I grabbed my clothes and proceeded to get dressed and made my way to the farmer's old beat-up pick up.

By this time I had come to view Sweet as more or less like something of a younger brother and in the end there was nothin' I wouldn't do for him. And whether I wanted to admit it or not Sweet was probably the only reason I wasn't pushin' up daisies along with a bunch of my comrades. Back when we first landed in Normandy, the Gerry's would've certainly overrun us if hadn't been for Sweet's steady rifle fire. I ain't gonna lie to you and pretend to be Audie Murphy or John Wayne now that much of the fighting's done. Like I said, at the very least, he's the reason I'm not pushin' up daisies now. So, when Sweet told me we were going to help the old man out at the winery and as much as I hated the idea of getting up on one of the first mornings we'd been awarded leave in a month of Sundays, I bit the bullet and climbed up in the back of that old man's flatbed truck.

By the time we reached the old man's winery some forty-five minutes later I was not only quite awake but so shaken from the speed and carelessness with which the old man drove that I vowed

to walk back when our task was finished. After we arrived though, I was glad I'd come. It's a mighty funny thing. But being an observer of people, the only thing that stood out up 'til that point or at least since we'd landed was that hardship, and I mean the worst kind of hardship which is probably death to a

152

loved one will make the most arrogant of human beings as humble as a cloistered monk.

Now that's not to say that the old man and his family were arrogant. Hell, I don't know them form Adam so I can't say that I know how they were before I met them. Yet, it is hard for me to believe that they could own one of the largest vineyards in southern France and be as quiet and assuming as they appeared to me on that crisp, cold, wintry morning. And I guess I'm just like Sweet in one regard. It's just hard for me to fathom a white man, a French man or any man with everything that that old man possessed being anywhere as humble and assuming as that man and his wife appeared that morning. They too acted as if we were the Second Coming. I can't remember my own mother treatin' me any better. It was almost like we were family, almost like we were the two sons the Germans had killed. And you know I wasn't useta nothin' like this even though I was comin' from the land of milk and honey. I'm telling you the truth when I tell you that those two old people was just as nice as they could be. While we was there, they offered me and Sweet the world. They simply could not do enough for us. And I simply fell in love with the French Cuisine. (That's just a lil' French word that I picked up that means food).

The old man's wife was as gracious a host as you will ever find and you could tell that she was used to preparing for seven or eight people at the very least and missed her sons dearly. The minute Sweet and I walked in that old woman took a real liking to us. And made sure we didn't want for anything. Every time we'd come in from mending a fence or repairing the torn down poles in the vineyard the old man's wife would be shoving a hot buttered croissant, a baguette or some other type of French pastry I couldn't pronounce in my direction along with a glass of her best wine.

Now Sweet was pretty much a teetotaler but I made up for his abstinence and made it a point to be as cordial and receptive a guest as you'll ever see, tasting everything and partaking of everything the old man and his wife offered. And although we fought to understand each other at times with the language barrier and all, when she handed me a glass or a carafe I understood I was to taste it and relish each and every swallow and praise every sip, which I pulled off with little or no problem whatsoever.

This required little or no translation since I'd never ever tasted anything quite so refreshing in all my life. The old man's wife seemed to enjoy my rather candid appraisal of her brew as well. And we just naturally hit it off the way two old wine connoisseurs do standing on the corner of any American city. After all winemaking is an art form just like painting and writing and since most artists need the confirmation of another artist to validate their work I was more than happy to accommodate.

Now from what I could gather from the oldest daughter who spoke just enough English to get me through the rough spots, the old man and his wife used to have an annual wine tasting celebration each fall before the German occupation. Here they would introduce their newest line of wines to the general public. And they say the festival had become such a glorious event that some folks would travel from French Provinces over a hundred miles away just to grab a snootful of the old woman's latest concoction. I'm not sure that I would have gone that far but since I was here anyway I felt almost compelled to help the old woman out. And since she and her husband had grown virtually immune to the rather subtle differences in taste and the festival interrupted by the war I would like to think that I was what you might call indispensable to the couple right through there. What they weren't aware of was the fact that they were helping me as much as I was helping them. No more did I wake up in the middle of the night bathed in a cold sweat. The nightmares ended just like that. Aside from that, I've always been a very compassionate type of fellow when it comes to aiding those in need so I did everything I could possibly do to help the old woman out by being her official taste tester which was to both our satisfactions.

The remaining work around the winery was anything but hard, at least in comparison to what Uncle Sam had us Colored boys doing during the war so I didn't mind much. In fact, I kinda took a likin' to bein away from the base and all the talk of killin' even though I knew the memories of those first few days hitting the beach would probably linger with me forever. Still, the work at the winery was a sort of a reprieve, like a religious retreat or one of those church revivals my grandmother used to take me to that I enjoyed so much when I was knee high to a grasshopper.

The work around the vineyard must have reminded Sweet a lil' of bein' back in Georgia 'cause I ain't never seen him happier than when he was out there followin' along behind the old man's plow horse and diggin' up God's green earth. He and the ol' man stayed out in the fields until long after dark. Now, I've never been a stranger to hard work but I gotta admit I ain't never seen a soul work as hard as Sweet and that ol' man. I kept up with them but every now and then I had to take a break to let nature take its course. But lookin' back I can't even remember them stopping to do that.

I guess the fact that I didn't want to offend the old woman's needs and hospitality didn't help my plight much either. You see every time I'd take a break to use the john she insisted that I have another taste of the grape. And no sooner than I'd join the old man and Sweet in the fields then I would have to use the john again at which time the old woman would be positioned at the door with another carafe awaiting my approval. Not wanting to offend her, I would embellish with gusto thus initiating the whole cycle all over again.

Looking back, I believe this is where I first acquired my affinity for the grape although I am not sure that it was the winery or the war that influenced my love for fine wine and spirits. One thing I did know. The nightmares ceased. There were no more bloody dreams of skeletons and

body bags. And I slept more soundly than I ever had before. And from that day forth I continued to imbibe.

Despite the problems with my bladder, I put in my share of work and was more exhausted following my leave than I had when I started out. I vowed never to let Sweet talk me into anything so foolish as working on my days off again. But when we received leave the following weekend, there I was once again hard at work laboring, again in the ol'man's vineyard. This went on for several weeks until I found myself forced to take a break from sheer exhaustion.

That Saturday off, I spent the entire day in my rack until summoned by one of my comrades and informed that there were two women to see me. Dressing quickly, I thought my comrades were playing some kind of joke on me but when I heard women's voices in the next room I knew it was no joke even though I had no earthly who could be possibly be calling on me on a Saturday night. Exiting the barracks, I was pleasantly surprised to find the ol' man's wife and daughter in the flatbed truck a carafe in the of the old woman's thin, spindly fingers.

"For you," she mumbled in her best-broken English.

"Come, we must go," her daughter said motioning for me to get into the tiny truck beside her as she slid over next to her mother who was in the driver's seat.

I'd grown quite fond of the old woman and her daughters over the course of the few months I'd spent with them at the winery but we wasn't at the vineyard now. We were on post, an

American Army post and despite our liberating the French from the Germans the fact remained that, I was a Colored first and foremost, and if I even thought about riding up front with these two white women, I wouldn't be a Colored soldier any more but more like one dead nigger.

So, I declined although I'm not sure they understood or saw it for what it was worth but they agreed to let me ride on the flatbed at least until we got through the gate. And even then, I covered myself with my army blanket and prayed that the MP'S at the front gate would not think to detain an old French woman and her daughter. And I guess being that it was Saturday night and there was so much traffic coming in and out of the base, they let us pass without stopping us.

In any case, I ended up despite my rather weak protestations right back at the vineyard, eating and dancing and of course, down in the wine cellar helping the old woman sample and compare the different vintages until the wee hours of the next morning. Somewhat intoxicated to say the least, I somehow managed to climb the stairs with the aid of the old woman and entered the kitchen where Sweet and the rest of the family sat. The old man's two youngest daughters sat on either side of Sweet, their heads draped on each shoulder smiling and in deep conversation.

From what I could muster and it's been close to forty years since this took place but from what I could pick up from the little French that I'd come to pick up the old man and his daughter's were making an impassioned plea that we stay on after our unit pulled out.

Now like I said, don't quote me because a good deal of time has passed since these events transpired. But if I remember correctly, the old man was not only offering us a share of the vineyard but a share of everything including his eldest daughter who had her eyes set on Sweet and was quite intent on marrying my boy. Sweet was all for it and production at the winery had already resumed, although minimally but the returns were already proving handsome from all accounts.

When the old man attempted to share, the revenues as payment for the labor Sweet and I contributed over the last few months to get the vineyard up-and-running we both declined. After all, in truth, we were as much in need of him as he was of us. In any case, the old man continued with his pleas or better yet his offer, sweetening the pot after each rejection.

Sweet, who, I guess was in love for the very first time didn't seem at all opposed to the idea of jumping ship and going A.W.O.L. To Sweet, France was a dream come true. Yet, I knew a little something about Colored boys dreamin' back then just like I know about Black men that dream now.

Dreams for a Black man are nothing more than a façade. Nothing more than fluff; kind of like cream puffs with no flavor. It's always been in our character, in our very makeup if you ask me. So then, as now I refused to let myself dream. I have over a lifetime learned not to dream. It's not safe for a Black man to

157

dream. If you don't believe me just ask yourself what happened to the last Black man who said, I Have a Dream.

I tried to infer, what I thought was some rather rational and logical rationale to Sweet but being in love is in itself irrational and feeling at home in the fields with the father he'd never known, all appealed to my buddy, Sweet. But what really appealed to him was the fact that these people looked at him as a man and respected him. They valued him as a person, as a human being, and that wasn't something I believe he ever experienced in Decatur, Georgia or even in New York for that matter.

I understood what was going through his mind but I was wary of what Uncle Sam would do to a deserter. But ol' Sweet wasn't thinkin' about none of that. He wasn't thinkin' about the repercussions and confessed to me on the way back to the base the next day that he was seriously considering turning in his card thus renouncing his club membership. As he explained it to me he was tired of being a niggra in America, saw no real room for advancement and the dues had only recently become too goddamn high.

Again, I understood but tried to explain that the penalties for renouncing his membership at this point in time and informed him that this could be harmful to his health. I was almost like a Russian defecting in America's eyes. And so after much conservation and much as he regretted it ol' Sweet remained steadfast though hardly content to be a niggra, as he would so aptly refer to himself, in Uncle Sam's employ.

Some months later, after saying goodbye to his adopted family, Sweet and I were shipped back to the good ol' US of A where we were promptly thanked for helping to restore democracy and peace to so many European nations. We were then given our discharge papers at our disembarkation point in Charleston, South Carolina and dismissed.

Feeling pretty damn good about the job we'd done overseas and glad to be back on friendly shores, Sweet and I quickly made our way to the nearest diner for one of those good ol' Southern breakfasts we used to remember so fondly and speak about regularly while hunkered down in our foxholes with German bullets whizzing all around us.

"There's a diner right there, Sweet ol' boy," I shouted out already tasting the fried porgies and croakers I planned to have over my grits and stacked high up on my plate.

"I can't wait to wrap these here lips around some fish and grits and homemade biscuits, baby." Sweet replied. "Can you believe it's been four years? Damn! I just hope the food's good."

"Anything, slightly resembling fish and grits would be good at this point." I laughed just glad to be back home.

"Ain't that the truth," Sweet replied.

"Let me ask these two gentlemen how the food is before we waste our money," I commented enthusiastically. "I want to make sure my first meal back is RIGHT ON," I declared.

As two men exited the restaurant I held the door for them excused myself and asked, "Gentlemen, how's the food in this establishment? We're just getting back from the war and ain't had no good home cookin' in close to four years."

"Well, if that's truly the case you're in for a treat" the man responded. "Patty's got some of the best southern home style cookin' you'll find anywhere," he replied "Oh, and by the way, you boys did a nice job over there against them Gerry's".

"Thanks a lot,"Sweet and I replied simultaneously, grinning from ear-to-ear.

It was sure good to be home and despite the horror, the bloodshed and the friends I had lost, maybe, we finally garnered the respect and recognition we'd given up life and limb for.   At least, it seemed so now talking to these two gentlemen. After all, here was a white man deep down in the heart of Dixie complimenting two Colored boys on a job well done.

"Yes sir, you boys did a real fine job with the Gerry's .Real fine! I was over there in the first one, myself. That one weren't no joke either. I think the hardest part about the whole thing was getting reacquainted with everything back here after you get out. Sometimes, it's not an easy adjustment after all that death and dying you've just witnessed. Sometimes you forget things. It's just hard sometimes to get accustomed—you know—acclimated to the way things is done back home. Over there everything is very lax. It took me quite some time to get adjusted to the way our system works when I got back here and I'm sure it'll be that way for you for awhile too.

It's not the big things you tend to forget. It's the little things. As I said, everything is very loose over there. Kinda laid back, that's why the Germans could roll through them European countries and take over like that. But over here we got everything structured and in proper order. Everything fits in its own place. Yes, sir we got a system over here. And I'm sure it's gonna take y'all a little time to get reacquainted but don't let it getcha in no trouble. Oh, and by the way, I hope you boys ain't forget that niggras need to use the backdoor when entering a white establishment."

Reverend Barnes

"Brothers and sisters, I'm certainly glad to see you all gathered here today in spite of the weather. This is two weeks in a row we've have to endure a bit of inclement weather but I'm not going to spend too much of your time talking about the weather since Sista Gerty reminded me just the other day that I spend far too much time talking about the weather.

Now as you all well know I'm not in the business of going door to door or asking ya'll to dig deep into your pockets in the Lord's name. No sir, brothers, and sisters I'm not in the business to ask for tithing or to make you feel guilty when you can't. That is not why the Lord put me before you. I am neither judge nor jury but leave that for the Good Lord to do. The Lord said, 'You will reap what you sow'. Only you know, brothers and sisters... Do you hear me? Only you know... Only you know what kind of harvest you will bring on that day of reckoning. Praise the Lord.

And believe me brothers and sisters I am quite aware of what the Church has asked of you from time-to-time in the Lord's name and sometimes I wish I was the only one that was forced to give just to make it a little easier on you." Reverend Barnes chuckled.

"I know that at times it gets pretty hard. You don't have to tell me. Lord knows it's hard for me as well. Just working in the Lord's name and trying to keep up with Sisters Abernathy and

Preston after they done collected for the Children's Relief Fund, the Children's Dance Choir, the annual church picnic, which by the way, seems to come two or three times a year nowadays and the various other worthwhile projects is no picnic," a soft murmur of laughter swept through the congregation.

"I kinda feel like Keith Sweat trying to follow Marvin Gaye, if you know what I am mean. It's like Houdini trying to follow the Lord's parting of the Red Sea." He chuckled. "It's just a very tough act to follow. Still and all, I must ask y'all to dig deep one more time and if all you feel is lint, then I want ya'll to reach into that other pocket and grab hold of that checkbook you all hold in reserve. I know you all know what I'm talking about. Dig deep brothers and sisters. Take hold of that same checkbook you pull out the first of the month to pay the landlord. Take hold of that same little blue checkbook that you pulled up on when you saw that cute little skirt you been eyeing' in the department window for the past two weeks. Dig deep and pull up on that same little blue city bank checkbook you used down at the ABC store to get that bottle of Alize you just had to have to go with that special dinner you fixed for that special someone last night. Can you hear me? You all know what I'm talking about.

Brothers and sisters, I want you to grab hold of that same little blue checkbook and buy some more food today. Only today, I want you to invest in some spiritual food. Today I want you to dig deep into your checking or your savings and buy some spiritual food. I want you to invest

not in food that helps maintain and helps your body to grow but spiritual food that can help you grow in the name of the Lord Jesus Christ. Shout Amen if you hear me."

There were a few scattered Amen's but no rousing thunderous response the good reverend was used to.

No, when it came time to Black folks loosing their hard- earned money; the Amen's were hardly ever as loud. The good reverend knew this and was not to be put off. He continued with all the ferocity and passion of a man late on his next car payment.

Stepping back from the pulpit, he grabbed the purple hankerchief from the top pocket of his suit jacket and dabbed liberally at his soaking brow. He'd already preached a sermon and a half that had the young people clapping and the old people leaving for water and a breath of fresh air. It had been one of his better sermons and he knew it. It had to be. Enrollment was down and the church needed both a new roof and water heater. To make matters worse he was three months late on his car note after Diamond failed to make the payment and moved out taking his money with her. He'd chalked up her leaving to the

162

devil's calling and decided to let vengeance be the Lord's, but Lincoln Mercury couldn't wait on the Lord and so here he was preaching his behind off and making this impassioned plea that came as close to desperation as he had in the eleven years he'd been pastor at the First Abyssinian Baptist Church of Christ.

"Brothers and sisters in Christ let me appeal to the goodness in all of you. I have been pastor here at the First Abyssinian Church of Christ for more than eleven years now. I have watched our tiny church of twenty-five devout parishioners grow from the humble beginnings to a flock of nearly three hundred. I have watched the ground-breaking ceremonies for our new church and the pride and exuberance in which you the faithful have shown in serving the Lord. I have been to your homes, prayed for your sick, baptized your younguns' and buried your loved ones and during this entire time, I have never asked you for anything. It is, after all, not I who asks that you give but the Lord.

I have listened to your testimonies and you have listened to mine. We are here today because we are united in a common cause, a common goal and that is to partake of the life of Jesus Christ and be better Christians and human beings because we share his blessing. Can I get an amen?

The flock was more appreciative this time and Reverend Barnes noticed the old women nodding in agreement. A loud chants of amen could be heard this time, but it was still not the response the good reverend yearned for and so he continued his impassioned cry for aid.

"Brothers and sisters we have stood the test of time. We have encountered the jaws of the lion and we have not failed in our attempts to come to know the Lord. When the city said no to the land for the church we held fast. When the contractors raised the price of the materials we held fast. When vandals broke in and stole every fixture and painting that wasn't nailed down, we held fast. We were not deterred. We could not be deterred for we know that the Lord Jesus

Christ has our backs. We held fast because we had something larger to hold on to than the Philistines and the pharaohs who opposed us. We had each other brothers and sisters. We had convictions," his voice was growing louder now as it always did when he was about to make a point and was trying to stir the crowd.

"But most of all we had faith in the Lord Jesus Christ. As we can all attest, you cannot lose with the Lord on your side. How many have really come to know the Lord and feel the Holy Spirit since you've been her at Abyssinian? I ask you again, brothers and sisters. How many have you have come to know the Lord since you've been here at Abyssinian? I don't mean how many of you have been baptized and gone through the ritual of being Born Again. Everyone here has done that. Heck, that's common practice nowadays. The Word is out and most people and most churches in the city in the country and everywhere else for that matter know that there's only one true way to heaven and that's through the Lord Jesus Christ. Some of you may even have received the Word in other churches before you even thought about joining Abyssinian. That's not what I'm asking you, brothers and sisters. What I'm asking you today is, how many of you have felt your lives change for the better since you became a member of Jesus' flock here at The First Abyssinian Church of Christ? If you have then let me see a show of hands."

The hands shot up in the crowded church in unison. He had them now and he knew it. As long as he steered clear of their pocketbooks he had nothing to fear. They enjoyed his preaching. In all they were a good congregation. They were pretty damn generous too. At least they were in

comparison to his last congregation down in that little one horse town they called Decatur, Georgia. They were good people too, pretty generous, even if took three of them together to scrape up one good nickel. But those were different times.

He'd just gotten the calling fresh out of the seminary, but he was more interested in the short skirts in the front row, the deacon's wives and spreading himself around than spreading the word. He'd been there about four years when the whole thing blew up in his face after one of the wives had come forth, and when one did they all did. He'd caught the first thing smoking out of there and really was thankful to God for giving him a second chance.

He'd been resolute in his desire to be a pillar of the community this time around and averted his gaze for the most part when a deacon's wife approached or a member of the choir would stop by with a plate on a cold winters evening. He'd been tempted, many times over, but if the Lord could spend forty days and forty nights in the desert with the devil on the prowl, he knew he could resist the intermittent forays of a handful of starving women. That was until he met Diamond. She was different than all the rest, and despite what the deacons and his parents told him she had his heart from the outset. He'd never seen her coming, and just as suddenly she was gone. She'd taken almost everything he owned. Everything he worked so hard to achieve and in the week since her disappearance, he dared not tell a soul for fear of them losing all respect for him, because he was supposed to guide them.

After all, they'd all warned him about her and he had ignored them. How could he call himself a shepherd, a leader, when his own life was in such shambles?

He told himself that it was not simply a lesson, but a test, a test of his faith. He thought of Job and took the attitude that his unwavering faith would easily stand the trial now before him. That was until the dealership called. Lincoln Mercury could care less about the situation he now found himself in. They wanted their money and they wanted it now. No if, ands or buts about it....

He was three months in arrears and they'd contacted him several times previously, but had yet to receive a payment. When he denied having any contact with them or knowing anything about being late on his payments, they promptly pulled out his folder and began quoting dates, times and the contact person.

Mr., err, excuse me Reverend Barnes, I called on the 1st, 15th, and 30th of October and spoke to a Mrs. Diamond Massey, who identified herself as your personal secretary. She assured us that your payment was in the mail. I did the

165

same in November and December and we have yet to receive a single payment.

The reverend apologized and promised that he'd have the payment first thing Monday morning. That was on Friday afternoon. At the bank that evening, he ran into a similar situation and found that not only had his accounts been emptied, but both checking and savings were overdrawn as well. His initial reaction was typical. He wanted Diamond's head on a platter. But his faith

took over and he quickly realized that despite his own personal loss he'd really lost nothing since he still had his faith in the Lord.

What bothered the good reverend more than Diamond's betrayal and departure was the fact that he had to face his congregation. They were a congregation that had encountered a similar situation some years earlier when that fool woman, Etta Mae Jones had accused him of cheating on her and physically attacked him right outside the church. If he could live that down he could live anything down. But this was different. He truly loved Diamond. She inspired him and made his life, for the first time, complete. Just seeing her sitting in the first pew, her eyes staring at him let him know that only heaven could be better. He truly believed that God had awarded him Diamond as a reward for changing his ways, despite her own troubled and sordid past.

Despite their pasts, the good reverend was truly convinced that they were both headed in the right direction now, and with the Good Lord's divine intervention there was no way they could do anything but prosper in the Lord's name. The wedding was only a month away and Diamond had been, or at least seemed to be channeling all her energies in that direction. He saw her less than usual since he'd proposed, but in a way he was glad. There would be plenty of time for them to share later on. After all, they had a lifetime to spend together.

On several occasions in the last few month's members of the congregation had stopped by his home up on Fordham Road in the Bronx and found Diamond there, shoes by the Lazy Boy in the front room, jacket thrown over the edge of the bed. The good reverend knew it didn't look good. He knew it was only a matter of time before those envious of Diamond's drop dead good looks

166

would begin to talk. And rumors were one thing he did not need. So, they announced their engagement with the hopes that that would hush the talk and for the most part, it did. But there was still a strong contingent that didn't want to see the good reverend with that woman. After all, she wasn't what they considered family. She'd appeared out of nowhere, only yesterday.

There was just something about her that made them uneasy. The good reverend tried to explain that she was no different from the rest of the Lord's scattered flock who'd been lost and finally found their way home and she should be treated accordingly, despite the skeletons in her closet.

Now, he had to admit they had been right. But how could he admit it to them. Not yet anyway. It was enough that there would be speculation since she wouldn't be in her usual spot in the first pew with the rest of the deacons' wives and girlfriends. For now, he would allow them to think she was under the weather, but he knew that this little charade could only go on so long and he'd have to tell them eventually. But right now he had more important things on his mind than Diamond, or what the congregation was thinking.

How would it look if he lost the finest woman in the congregation and had his car repossessed all in the same week? He was a preacher and what separated a shepherd from the rest of the flock was the way in which he carried himself. His was a confidence game and he always had to appear in control of not just his destiny but the destiny of all those who looked to him for guidance. He had to do better, know more, and look better. After all, he was representing the Man. He couldn't come half-stepping' and expect others to follow his lead. That's why he had

the spot directly in front of the church cordoned off and marked Reverend Barnes. That's why the Lincoln sat there for all the adoring flock to see and admire; the key being that if you believed as strongly and your faith was as resolute as the good reverends then you too would reap the reward of the Lord's goodwill.

Back in Decatur, the good reverend had preached the same sermon. The only problem was that he didn't believe it. But since Diamond had entered his life he believed it and passed in on to the congregation with such a zeal and exuberance that the church seemed to double in size every time the annual picnic came round and they were held at least three times a year. Such zeal and exuberance brought them in from miles around. They came from Queens, Brooklyn, Staten Island and even a few as far as Long Island, but he'd never preached as he had today.

"Brothers and sisters in the Lord, again I ask you in closing today to dig deep into the recesses of your mind and ask yourself this question. I want you to really dig deep before answering this question, brothers and sisters. Ask yourself if you are not better off than you were when you joined the congregation of The First Abyssinian Church of Christ. You may or may not be. I can't answer that for you. I don't know your particular situation. But I do know that I am a better minister, a better man and a better representative for the Lord Jesus Christ and his divine word and inspiration since I have been here. He has blessed me with you, a congregation intent on growing in His love and in His name. And don't think he doesn't recognize the effort and the sacrifice each of you has put forth to make His name shine brightly and his word ring out."

They were moved now and stirring in their pews. The good reverend was talking about them now. And you could hear the 'Amen's' and 'Preach Preacher', clearly now as they sang his praises.

He continued through the chorus of shouting.

"Yes the Lord not only sees but he can feel you, feel the goodness in your hearts. He can tell when you're exhausted and ready to collapse. That's when he steps in and gives you that second-wind and allows you to finish whatever it is that you've started. He's there for you when you've got nothing left. Do you hear me brothers and sisters. I said the Lord is there when you don't have anything left to give. Do you hear me.?"

Again, there were a chorus of 'Amen's' and 'Yes Lord's'. They were moved, feeling him now as the sweat dripped from his face. He was preaching now.

One of the sisters approached him with a clean white towel and wiped his face.

Thank you Sister Henderson but I need to know, he turned to the older woman dressed in all white and whispered into the microphone.

"Sister Henderson, I ask you, do you think they hear me?

She smiled, looked him in the eye, nodded her head up and down and said, "I don't think they heard you. Preach preacher preach."

Turning back to the captive audience, in front of him he knew he had them now. He sipped the glass of water slowly on the table next to the pulpit and listened. Yes he had them now. You couldn't hear a pin drop. It was time for the coup de tat; time to let the chips fall where they may.

"Now, I've told you how I've changed since I've been here as pastor and member of The First Abyssinian Church of Christ. I really feel truly blessed each day that I am allowed to step foot into this building. It is like coming into an oasis after you've left the desert. Imagine how Jesus must have felt after those forty days and forty nights in the desert. Sometimes hot, sometimes cold, temptation always lurking around the next corner. Imagine how he must have felt to finally be able to come back home to the father, to that unconditional love, to someone who will never betray you....

That's what it feels like each day that I step into the Church of Jesus Christ. I feel warmed by the unconditional love of my Lord Jesus Christ. Do you feel it brothers and sisters? If you feel it, shout his name aloud. Yes, Lord! Let me hear you say amen.... Can I get a witness? He gives us so much. Can I get an amen? He never stops giving. Can I get an amen? He never stops giving.

Look at this beautiful church he has built for us to worship him in. Look at your spouse sitting next to you, your children. Let us praise his name for he is a good God, a benevolent God. But let me ask you this and yes Sister Gerty I know I've kept you a lot longer than I usually do and most of you still got to get ready to meet the man tomorrow. But just let me ask you this brothers and sisters. With all that the Lord Jesus Christ has bestowed on us, have we dug as deeply as we can to repay him for His goodness and His blessings?

I'm going to leave you with that thought to take through the week and for those of you who already know the answer and aren't trying to nickel and dime the Lord, I want you all to stop by and see Deacon Fred and Deacon Henderson on your way out and show the Lord just how much you appreciate the blessings he's bestowed on each one of you. Miss Mamie will you please lead the choir in that old Negro spiritual. 'We Will See.'

The young minister watched before making his way towards the front door and was relieved to see the flock lined up, check books in hand, around the two deacons at the front door. Praise the Lord the good reverend murmured to himself. He'd hit payday again. At least his troubles were over for now .

Making his way towards the front door he noticed another commotion outside and excused himself from the host of well-wishers congratulating him on his upcoming wedding and those who had been clearly moved by his sermon.

"Loved your sermon reverend," mumbled Sister Gerty as she made her way past the pastor.

"Preached a mighty sermon on digging and giving. As you can see it certainly moved them. Look at the checks in the offertory," beamed Sister Townsend, the church treasurer.

"But you were absolutely right Reverend Barnes. These niggras so interested in the material things nowadays they are not thinking about the hereafter. They only are thinking about right now. Think they can buy heaven right here. You can't buy heaven here on earth. That's why I'm glad you took them to task reverend, made them part with something close to them. That's the only thing that'll make someone appreciate what they have. Else they forget that Jesus Christ makes it all possible. Lot of them get to doing pretty good, you know, materially speaking and forget where it comes from. They take it for granted. It's like that singer said in that the song. "You know the one." "They paved paradise and put up a parking lot." That's exactly what she was saying. Well, I have to go reverend. I'll call you and give you the numbers this evening. And don't forget to tell Diamond that I hope she feels better when you talk to her. Tell her I still have her down for the Youth Choir, but if she isn't feeling up to par I guess I can find somebody else to lead them. If she needs anything else you just let me know.

By the way, you want me to run this week's take to the bank in the morning, or are you going to take it?"

He kissed the old woman on the cheek as two or three other church members gathered around.

"That's okay, I don' mind taking it tomorrow, Sister Henderson. I'll stop by the house around nine in the morning if that's not too early. You can save me a couple of those biscuits too," the good reverend replied.

"And to think I thought you were coming to see me," the old woman flirted as she made her way to the door. A moment later she was back with Mr. Henderson by her side.

"On second thought, reverend I think I'll take the money to the bank in the morning. They just towed your car.

171

Anna Mae Jones

Anna Mae sat listening intently as the rain pelted her windows like the steady rhythm of a Neptunes beat. The weather channel said Hurricane Isabel was approaching rapidly from the mid-Atlantic and was due to hit in the next day or so. Her oldest son, Christopher who was seventeen and knew most everything about weather and watched the weather channel the way other children watched The Cartoon Network said it was just another ploy by the government to boost a sagging economy.

There was little doubt that Lowes and Home Depot were cashing in selling plywood and generators better than they had had since the last threat of a hurricane back in '96. Local grocery stores from all accounts were selling out rapidly as people rushed to grab bread, milk and water. But not Anna Mae. It wasn't the fact that she like her oldest doubted the media hoopla surrounding the forecast. It was just that she was broke. If she hadn't been she might have been out there with the rest of them stockpiling water and bread.

Now from the sound of the wind howling and the rain she was sure something was coming in off the Long Island Sound. And from the sound of the trees paying homage to the winds Hurricane Isabel was fast approaching if she wasn't already there.

Thinking back she only wished now that she hadn't been so quick to take that hit. But when had she ever waited. Most of the time she was pushing the nigga out of the door and throwing the chain lock on before he even left. And if she was out as she was now there always came when she'd spend her last whether she had a way home or not. Her   seventeen –year old and her baby

172

of eleven were home alone, scared out of their wits and probably wondering where in the hell she was. Then again, they were used to her stepping out without so much as a clue to where she was going or when she'd be home. It had been months since she'd taken a hit and then out of nowhere Dee had just shown up out of the clear blue. And of course, he was straight. He always was. And of course she just happened to have twenty dollars that day. It was all the money she had to her name and he was almost certain to get it. As soon as she saw him, she knew the money was spent.

The first hit was always the best. She'd never been able to describe the feeling that crack gave her but she could explain how she felt now. Gone was the twenty and so was the dope. She searched every stash she had hoping to find a crumb here or there but there was nothing. There never was. In the twenty or so, years since she'd begun smoking that shit she'd never found anything. Fact of the matter was when it was gone it was gone. And inevitably it always was. Gone. Now there was nothing but hell. She searched all her usual hiding spots but there was nothing. Damn! Nothing and man did she want another hit. She'd sold everything of value and the weather outside sure didn't lend itself to her makin' any real money. And she knew Dee wasn't going to extend her any credit.

She had always paid him when she owed him but he was deep in the game now. And where as he useta extend her credit freely, he'd grown coarse and hard like everyone else in the game. Someone has obviously beaten him and messed it up for everybody but hell she wasn't the one

that did it so she couldn't understand why he wouldn't extend her any credit but she'd be damn if she'd beg him for a twenty or sell herself like some of the other losers she'd met along the way. Hell, no she still had far too much pride for that but damn she wanted a hit.

She hated herself for putting herself in this position. It wasn't the first time and probably wouldn't be the last.

There wasn't a day that went by that Anna Mae didn't wish she could live crack free but the minute she got a little change in her pocket homeboy was the first person she called until later that night she lay twitching just like this craving another hit. Was it worth it? Hell, she'd been asking herself just that for the past twenty years and had never ever really come to any decision until it was over and a memory was left and she lay sweating and wondering how she could come up with a few more dollars to alleviate the pain.

Back in eighty-six the money didn't matter and it was nothing for her to spend a couple of hundred at a time. But times had changed.

The good jobs had gone right along with her good looks and money was scarce for everyone since the Republicans came into office. Now it was hardly ever, no ever, that she spent her all or anything more than twenty dollars at a time. All the people around her made it a point to tell her what a waste it was nickel and dimin' herself to death but that's just the way she did it now always telling herself she wasn't going to spend more than twenty.

There were too many other things she had to do, too many people she owed in one way or another and basically she was afraid that if she did more than a twenty she'd find herself strung out again. Hung out to dry with no way home... But of course after that first hit that was it and she'd watch the money dwindle twenty by lonesome twenty until there was no more and she was begging someone for a hit and a ride home. But that was the reason she refused to spend it all at one time. Sure she knew she was playing herself but that meaningless effort in their eyes was what set herself apart from the crack heads she knew who put all their money on the table up front and bought weight knowing full well that they didn't have anywhere to sleep that night. It was just like smoking cigarettes. She'd been smoking cigarettes for who knows how long, and was certainly smart enough to know that buying a carton would save her money but buying a carton seemed just so final. And even though she'd end up buying a pack of Newports every other day and spending twice what she would spend if she'd bought a carton there was the idea that she would and could stop after that pack. But if she bought a carton she was giving into the fact that she was hooked and she couldn't and wouldn't stop until that carton was gone. It was the same with cocaine except everything moved faster and was so much more expensive

174

in the long run. The money was bigger, the high more intense and once she started there had never been any turning around or quitting but still she played that game with herself. In her mind, she would never succumb to the idea that she was a crackhead although deep down inside she knew she was.

The last time she could remember spending big was that one day, less than a year ago, right after her mother died. She'd worked the local flea market, made a couple of hundred bucks selling odds and ends, and for once decided to get everything at once. She was tired of waiting on Dee to make his deliveries with her twenty always last on the list. But the truth of the matter was that she hardly cared about anyone or anything since her mother died including her kids.

So she went ahead and bought an eighty or was it a sixteenth. She always told herself it was only going to take just a couple of hits and no more than twenty dollars but not this time. The next thing she knew she was running around the house, hiding a stash here and a stash there and then when she was sure, absolutely positively sure that the cops were coming to get her she wrapped it up and buried it in the flower pot. The sweat poured from every pore but then it always did when the coke was good and she'd taken a mammoth hit. Running to get a towel to mop up some of the sweat that just wouldn't stop flowing she'd forgotten where she'd hidden her stash and when it came down to the end and her heart was pounding like it wanted to burst right through her weary flesh and her eyesight was so blurry that she couldn't make out the images on the TV. Yet, she could make out the sound of the reality show COPS and so she turned on the sound on TV down so she could hear the real ones when they came up the steps to bust her and take her away and give her twenty years for the twenty years she'd been smoking this shit and gotten away with it.

As she took another hit and held it until she thought her chest was going to burst wide open, Anna Mae thought of Deryl's twin sister now locked up in the mental institution down in Butner.

Beryl had taken one too many hits and inevitably lost her mind. It was just another horror story among the millions associated with crack. It was a story that Deryl couldn't really bear to tell and one she really didn't care to hear. Hell, it really didn't affect her anyway. She was way too strong for anything like that to happen to her. Beryl obviously wasn't. And if she did lose her mind it would be because she'd run out of dope and didn't have access to anymore but she would be damned if she'd lose her mind with a twenty in front of her and more than a thirty stashed in one of those fucking flower pots and the cops probably kneeling down outside her door waiting to pounce at any moment.

No, not her, not Anna Mae Jones... She had too many common, normal people problems like losing weight and putting food on the table and buying birthday and Christmas gifts for the kids and keeping up with their schooling and writing when she had time to and paying bills. No she didn't have the time to be no crackhead and spend all of her time out there demeaning herself and selling her body and trying to make a dollar outta fifteen cents for a three dollar hit and then sittin' up in a crack house begging somebody she really couldn't stand and losing her mind while she waited a lifetime and a half for someone to offer her a hit.

Checking the chain on the front door and then the double bolt lock she retired rather hastily to her bedroom, after checking the clock and making sure that there was still time before the kids

got home from school. She was chasing the dragon now, looking for the genie in the bottle. She was hoping, praying that the next hit she took would be as warm, beautiful and heavenly as that first one even though she knew it could never match the first. It never did. But that never stopped one from trying to get that feeling again. And after twenty years it sure wasn't going to stop Anna Mae now. So she chased the genie in the bottle and thought about running out and cringed at the thought.

Closing her bedroom door and winding the blinds shut she knelt down and slid her hand underneath the cherry wood dresser drawers and pulled out the stem she needed and took the rock from her mouth. She always kept the crack in her mouth even though she was in the confines of her own house, behind closed doors. That way when the cops came...

Breaking a tiny crumb from the rock, now on the dresser top she made sure the top of the stem was full and then held it upright and lit it pulling softly until she felt her mouth fill with smoke and then pulled harder and harder until the cool cocaine smoke filled her lungs to capacity. Feeling the rush she threw the stem back under the dresser and raced to the ashtray to light both the stem, stick of incense and the Black and Mild that lay dormant in the ashtray to cover the sweet smell she exhaled when she was sure that her lungs were about to bust. The sweat poured out again and she wondered how in the hell heaven could be sweeter.

She remembered thinking the same thing about sex when she was seventeen and met Lil Jon but this was different. Men came and went but not the pipe. The pipe and she'd remained bosom

buddies for close to twenty years now. And although it had clearly been a rather tumultuous twenty years it was still lurking around making promises and even keeping her attention for so many hours in a day and nothing else including men she'd known could attest to doing that. She'd given up everything for the pipe and there was no comparison. When the dope was good she just knew that if there was a heaven, then this is what it would be like but when it was over and the money and the dope were gone she knew that she'd met Satan first hand. No greater high or lows had she'd ever encountered. And no matter how many times she'd sworn to leave the dope alone she would always return more steadfast and earnest than ever in her quest to relieve whatever pain it was she felt. Continually, she told herself that this shit couldn't beat her. No way. Not as strong-willed as she was but each time she returned to it, it did exactly that taking a little piece of her soul each time she raised the stem to her lips.

On the days, she was straight and they were fewer and fewer now, she'd tune into the local television evangelist with the hope that they could save her from

177

this hell. And the one thing she would always take away from those shows was the fact that for the first time in her life she understood the ministers when they said they'd been called and only wondered why it had to be that her calling had to be from the devil himself. She'd prayed over it, cried over it, and been to rehab. She understood the nature of the beast but could hardly control it. When it called, she went.

Anna Mae remembered the trip her parents had taken to Africa a few years back when her mother was still alive and they were living in New York. They'd invited her to come along, all expenses paid and when she protested that she didn't have the money they'd even gone so far as to give her the forty dollars to pay for her passport.

Anna Mae remembered the day, some years ago when her father agreed to meet her in the subway station somewhere around midtown to give her the money for her passport photo. Back then all she could remember doing was waiting for her father to turn the corner and then racing like she was Marion Jones in the hundred meters to get the forty to her local street corner pharmacist. She'd missed that trip and every other trip and family reunion that were to follow and eventually missed her family altogether as they aged into the twilight of their lives and then passed on.

Several months after the passport incident, she moved to North Carolina after throwing a party at her house. There had been a lot of this and a lot of that at the party but ultimately it had come down to everyone sitting around the dining room table waiting for the pipe to be passed. The music, as loud as it was, had become a low humdrum of irritating noise that overshadowed any thought of being cautious and being able to hear the cops they should they decide to drop by. And, of course, that was always her first concern, even back then when this whole crack, free-basing thing was a novelty to her.

When the party was over and everyone was gone, there was nothing to do but cleanup and she didn't mind a bit. Spilled glasses of Hennessey and dirty ashtrays were everywhere and she cursed when she found the large roach burn in her brand new leather sofa but even that wasn't a real concern now. She was craving something awful and cleaning up just gave her an excuse to run her hands down in the crevices of the sofa and loveseat to see if anyone had stashed something of if she'd put some money aside. Of course, she hadn't but her mind was playing tricks on her now. It always did but that didn't mean she was going crazy like Deryl's sister Beryl. It just meant that the dope was good.

This would last awhile; this craving but at least she wasn't crawling around on all fours searching the floor like so many of the crack heads she'd seen.

When she first started smoking and saw her boys, Nigel and Gary crawling around on the dining room floor on all fours looking for crumbs she didn't understand. Anna Mae remembered staring incredulously as they tried to pick up anything and everything white, resembling a hit of crack including yesterday's bread crumbs, pieces of lint, bits of paper, dried toothpaste and cum stains from the previous tenant.

The smell of toast in the stem only pissed them off and when they exhausted their searches and were finally convinced that there was no more crack there they left like everyone return with something. She believed them and knew that they would eventually run into was a joke and she knew it. Her money and supply gone, she served no purpose for them now. Tomorrow they

would remember that they were friends but tonight they couldn't see her or anyone else. They were on a mission now and the only thing they could see was the next hit. She had to smile as she sat on the sofa in the living room, hugging the throw pillow tightly and rocking back and forth methodically like the retards she used to watch at the group home. Like it or not every time she smoked she rocked back and forth and searched her pockets digging and searching trying to find a crumb or a piece of rock that had fallen out of the package. Better, she find it than the cops when they   searched her, she thought.

Hell, everyone had their thing, their little idiosyncrasies when it came to this shit. Nigel would drool after he'd take a hit and search the floor while Gary would start talking and joking and become animated. Anna Mae guessed that this was his way to cover up the fact that he was high and the shit was fucking with his mind. Dancin' Mike, a graduate of Texas A & M and one of the brightest cats she'd ever met would jump up as soon as he'd taken a hit and start yelling and brushing his chest off.

"Get it off me," he would yell , standing straight up and try to brush the bugs or whatever it was that was on him. He would yell and Anna Mae just knew that the cops would be there any minute as loud as Dancin' Mike was. And that was Anna Mae's thing. Searching her pockets and hiding from the cops. Guess it was her guilt but as soon as she took a hit, she'd rush around and start hiding things just in case the cops were coming and for her the cops were coming every time she took a hit. Every single time…

Searching through the flower pot, she remembered going to work high one fall morning, in only her second year of teaching after pulling an all-nighter and began sweating profusely in front of her fourth graders who adored her. It was that day that she decided that as good a teacher as she was she was no longer a role model for her children and resigned soon after.

Teaching was the one thing she truly loved her only real passion in life and on the day she resigned, she went home and found that her tiny house in Queens had been robbed.

Everyone in the neighborhood knew that her boy Gary was the responsible party but it hardly mattered now. Crack cocaine was the responsible party but the loss of her job was more of a loss than all the household possessions Gary could steal in a lifetime. She was hurt but not so much the fact that her house had been robbed and her privacy violated but that a substance had taken control of her enough to make her give up the one thing that she loved more than anything else in this world. Teaching…

Not long after she'd received her final paycheck and then her 401K. Both had gone the same way; up in smoke. When there was no more money , no prospect of a job and no one around anymore she'd contemplated suicide. And even gone so far as to grab a steak knife and walk towards the swamp out by Kennedy Airport to do the deed. But she'd only gotten as far as a block or two when it dawned on her that she was too strong and nothing had ever beaten her and nothing could beat her now if she just decided to quit.

After all, she remembered her senior year in college and the first time she shot up. She had never felt like a rush like that before and the next day she was right back letting Kenny Wysocki, the quarterback of the football team tie her off and shoot her up again. They called it bangin' then and she had never ever experienced anything quite so titillating in her life and had bragged about it but after a week straight or so she lost interest and just walked away. This would be no different. A change of venues and she would be fine. She just needed to get the hell out of New York. Her parents had moved to North Carolina a year or two earlier to open a restaurant and on her first visit, she'd found the so-called New South invigoratingly alive. The people were so friendly and she loved the southern hospitality. She found a cute little apartment next to a Baptist church about ten minutes away from her parents and a job not long after. She immersed herself in the running of the restaurant and started a delivery service that thrived and began writing for the little Black newspaper out of Wilmington.

Everything was going as well as possible. And before she knew it she was working two full-times and a part-time, was dating frequently and then just like that she met this guy, ended up on the wrong side of town, in a crack house and was back to her same old tricks, smoking and binging and looking for the cops to finally come and get her.

Greensboro was her next move, though she fared no better there. Her mom and dad were only an hour and a half away but she had so damaged the relationship by this time that they hardly ever came to see her anymore and she couldn't blame them. They had been as supportive as any parents could ever be. But she'd abused their love. And after a while they'd grown tired of the rocky road and the constant ups and downs and although they loved her they avoided the painful reality that their oldest child was a drug addict.

In a way, she was glad they'd abandoned her. She knew they loved her. They always would but she was tired of disappointing them and they were tired of the disappointments so the phone calls grew less and less frequent, as they waited for her to finally get herself together. After all she was forty-five now and no spring chicken.

She was first-born, was supposed to have been the golden child. They'd sent her to the best schools and exposed her to all the right people, and this is what she'd chosen, and there was no excuse. Her father had explained to her over the course of time about mistakes and stupidity.

"We all make mistakes, Anna Mae. It only becomes stupidity when we repeat our mistakes over and over again."

Anna Mae knew her father was right and only had her best interest at heart but cursed him nevertheless. After all he knew nothing of a calling. And as much as she wanted to stop when the calling came she had to stop right then and there, or so it seemed and make that phone call.

When it was over and she would sit there broke, staring into space, sweaty, smelly, and blurry-eyed from crying, she'd swear that this was the absolute final time.

Then she'd ask God and Jesus Christ to show her a sign, take her into the fold, and show her the way and please do whatever it took to release her from the grips of this devil that was possessing her and devouring her very soul. Anything that was but have the police come and take her away. She lay awake, begging his forgiveness, praying, pleading for him to be her Savior. But the calling came just the same.

And although she fought the temptation as she had for the past twenty years and would rise up and rejoice when she made it more than a week or two each time she slipped back into the bowels of her own little hell, a little more of the fight within her lost. The one thing that remained that she could cling to was a tiny smattering of hope.

At the time, her mother still called to check on the kids and keep her abreast of the family goings on but Anna Mae knew that mommy was just calling to get a feel for where she was and could almost sense when things weren't exactly right. But then when was the last time things had been right. It had been that long ago.

Anna Mae had heard the stories of how twin siblings could move away from each other into different cities and states and when one would experience pain the other would also and she often times believed that she and her mother shared this rather unusual link. She would always call when things were slightly askew and Lord knows if Anna found a reason to avoid talking to her mother, she would. Her mother would always suspect something was wrong and of course there would be. And that something inevitably would be her addiction.

There was no hiding, no lying, or denying. Mommy knew. She just did. She always did. Mommy knew her better than anyone else in the world. She could almost sense when there was something wrong. That's just the way she was. And when she'd call the house and Chris and Nicky said mommy's not at home, she knew when she did arrive she had to account for her whereabouts.

The last time she'd talked to her mother it had simply been an update on the latest church function and how she'd prepared for some two hundred people for one of the priest's twenty-fifth anniversary. They hardly talked anymore about anything other than what was happening at the church and Anna Mae would listen with half an ear and even once thought to herself that they'd come to the end of the road as far as conversation. It almost seemed that everything had already been said. They'd gotten to the point where if one started a sentence the other could finish it. That's how close they were.

183

Mommy was suffering from asthma, bronchitis, and a host of other illnesses including heart disease, cancer that had already taken one breast but she had an indefatigable spirit, and despite her chronic complaining, Anna ignored her talk of ailing and ailments. Hell, she was close to seventy-two and just finished fixing dinner for two hundred people. Anna Mae didn't know too many women half her age that could pull off such a feat. And her mother used to do it on the regular when she had the restaurant.

The week her mother had gotten sick, a few years ago, and she was forced to take over the cooking duties, she realized just how strong a woman her mother was. She'd done her best but

by the end of the first week, she was thoroughly exhausted and was losing customers by the carloads.

But she was still her mother's child; the person in the world most like her, personable, outspoken, rebellious with a strong ethic and moral responsibility.

Wherever she was, Anna Mae carved out a niche with her charismatic personality. Everyone that met her either loved her or hated her. And the spirit that made her mother so well loved and so well hated and allowed her to do in spite of the illnesses was the same spirit that wouldn't allow Anna Mae to concede to this drug shit no matter how strong, manipulative and persuasive it proved to be. No, she would never concede by buying weight, sell her body, rob somebody, and admit that she was a crackhead. No, to Anna Mae it was just a substance abuse problem, just a day in the life, just a stage in an ever-evolving life that was almost certain to resurrect itself any day now.

Yet, that was then and this was now. A lot had changed since her mother died. A large part of her died also or so people who knew her well said.

The morning her mother passed away she'd been smoking, getting high, holding her breath while her mother gasped for her own breath, for her very life only an hour and a half away. She'd started smoking the night before at sometime around ten thirty or eleven the previous night and had lost all track of time and money. The dope had been flowing   with the young dope boys some as young as fourteen or fifteen flowing through Delaney's spot on Ashe Street like it was Grand Central at rush hour. They sat in the kitchen waiting for prospective customers while bedrooms and bathrooms became increasingly crowded until somewhere around one a.m. there was hardly an empty spot left.

Anna Mae had her spot and sat silently taking care of the house, which was simply cocaine etiquette. Take care of the owner of the house and then take care of yourself. And she did it as she had a thousand times before until she was bone dry and the dope boys tired of serving her had finally gone home.

Her clothes that were crisp and pressed neatly were now drenched and wrinkled, her perfume stale, she tried to move but found that her muscles had atrophied and had a mind of their own. She shook when she tried to stand and was annoyed when Delaney or some other sorry ass waiting, begging for a hit asked her if she was okay. Of course, she was okay. She stammered, stuttering, trying to respond but found that the words had become lodged somewhere deep in the recesses of her soul. Hell, this was not a social event and she never but ever sat pleading begging someone for a hit. And she hated those that sat around and waited for her to turn them on. Hours later when she sat in the living room alone broke and without anything trying to get herself together, she'd be alone and if she were alone then why wouldn't they leave her alone now. She would inevitably give one of them a hit.

Anna Mae knew how it was to sit and crave and wish and hope and be ignored. But she also knew that the very nature of the shit would never allow her, no matter how much she spent to be satisfied. It was like life and death. When it was over it was over and you couldn't take any of it with you. So, she shared and was labeled soft and a sucker and it bothered her but not enough where she would or could sit in a room with and crumb herself the whole night and ignore everyone around her as much as she   wanted to.

185

Actually, the people didn't bother her as much as the pretense. When you had, dope mothafuckas you'd never seen before were suddenly your best friends, ready to throw down their very lives for you if the case demanded. When the dope was gone so were they.

As Anna Mae sat in the kitchen that night, trying to gather her thoughts and Delaney and Yvette pulled out the stashes of dope they'd been given for simply being the house or dope they'd robbed from unsuspecting victims and closed the bedroom door to smoke in peace she searched her pockets finding nothing. Taking her stem from her pocket, Anna Mae took the wire hanger that hung on the doorknob, straightened it and then bent back and forth until it broke. She then pushed the screen to the other end as well as a nights worth of crack buildup and fished for her lighter before glancing at her watch. The last hit would be massive but it would be the last and she was already fiending and afraid to drive home.

The sun had been up for hours when Anna Mae put the stem to her lips for the final time. Glancing at the clock she was surprised to find that it was close to eight thirty in the morning. Now her only thought was where she could get some more money. After nine or ten hours of non-stop smoking her only thought was where she could get some more.

At this time of morning and could only think of the flea market where her son and daughter spent their weekends. They'd surely made twenty by this time of morning.

Anna Mae raised the stem to her lips, lit it and held the smoke in until she thought she would die and felt the 'caine rush through her bloodstream. Jumping up from the table she rushed through the house checking the blinds in the kitchen and living room to see if the ringing in her ears was the cops. But of course there was no one there.

An hour later, she felt she'd gotten it together enough to back the old beat up '86 nissan Maxima out of the driveway and drive the five or six miles to the highway. Still, paranoid, Anna Mae drove the extent of highway 29N steering in the rearview mirror. She was so tired she had trouble maintaining her speed and had to push herself to pick it up to the speed limit. After what seemed like forever and a day she finally reached the crowding park lot of the flea and soon located her kids.

Looking at her eleven year old she wondered why God or was it Jesus Christ had chosen to bless her so. Fools and babies, she'd heard them say. And at forty-five she was definitely no baby.

Something was awry and she looked for her seventeen year old. Chris was coming out of the front door of the flea and she suddenly sensed that very something that she'd felt all morning. Something was definitely amiss. Pulling the car up in front of her son, she called to him and immediately noticed the tears streaming down his brown cheeks.

"What's wrong?" she said trying to remember the last time she saw him shed a tear.

"What's wrong?"

"Grandma died he yelled and threw his arms around her." he whispered.

Taking the money this morning from her son she headed home, numb, to make the phone call that would bring her peace and then sat and waited for the cops to arrive.

Body and Soul

Who's that crossing the street? Is that Lacy? Damn sure is... Good God almighty! In and out of uniform, that girl looks good! You know, she could have very well been my daughter. She sure is somethin' else. I remember when she was no more than knee high to a grasshopper. Boy time has sure changed. That's why I tell these younguns around here not to procrastinate. No, suh. Time waits for no man or woman either for that matter.

Hell, it seems like just yesterday that Lacy was runnin' around here tugging at her mother's skirt tails and now look at her. I remember her in knickers and pigtails. Back then she reminded me of Pippi Longstockings for the world, the way her braids used to shoot straight out; almost like antlers on a deer. She was a cute little tike even then but who would have imagined she'd grow up to be as fine a woman as she's turned out to be. Never in a million dog years would I ever have expected her to turn out like this. She's the first woman I've ever seen in a police uniform that makes that old ugly blue look absolutely scrumptious. Just look at her walk. If that ain't class...

Boy, if I was twenty years younger. Hell, twenty years, I don't think I'd mind a bit if she put me in handcuffs today. In my prime there ain't no tellin' what I would have done with somethin' like that. Ain't she somethin'? That's my girl. I don't know who it was on the N.Y.P.D. that came up with the slogan New York's Finest but they must have had Lacy in mind. But then again, she can't help but be fine.

Her mother, Monica, could surely have been Miss New York State if they'd allowed Colored women to compete when she was in her prime. I'm tellin' you, her mother was one pretty sista' back in her day. Yes sir, she was one pretty Black woman. Her mother was the kind of woman that would make a man step back if he was the least bit unsure of himself. She was so pretty she was almost what you might call untouchable or   unapproachable.

188

She was black as coal; the way sisters useta be when they first come over here, before they got all mixed up and diluted. She had the prettiest, smoothest skin you'd ever wanna see. And man was she tall, just like Lacy. Did I tell Lacy was almost my daughter? Anyway, Monica, that's Lacy's mother stood about six foot two or six foot three in her stocking feet. And she wasn't ashamed of her height, no sir, not one bit. She didn't try to hide it the way some tall people do; walking all stoop shouldered and hunchbacked the way some tall people do when they're embarrassed about their height. No, siree, buddy. She useta throw on them heels in a minute and parade around these here streets with her head held so high that I wondered if she ever saw any of us little people gawkin' at her. She was like Gulliver in the land of the Lilliputians.

My buddy, Saul Greenberg who useta own the little Jewish grocery over there on 45th used to liken her to an African queen. Now I know that ol' Saul probably ain't never seen an African queen and neither had I but we both agree that if we had this is what she would probably look like. And it wasn't because she had the darkest ebony complexion I'd ever seen or because she had that long thin Roman nose or even because of those full ruby red lips. It wasn't any of those

things. It wasn't the fact that she was taller than most of the women I'd ever seen or that she had hips and breasts so firm and fine and thick. It wasn't even that she had the brightest most evenly proportioned pearly white teeth I'd ever seen or a smile to die for. It wasn't the dimples or the short-cropped hairdo that she always kept natural, long before that style became fashionable. To tell you the truth, I don't think it was any of those things that set her apart from all the beautiful women I'd encountered. It was the way she carried herself. Monica had an air of elegance and dignity reserved for royalty that seemed to engulf her and everyone in her presence. She exuded elegance. Class and refinement oozed from every pore and from the minute I saw her I knew one thing. I was in love.

Now, I've always been the type to be pretty cautious in my undertakings. When I'm not absolutely sure about something I proceed slowly; never with reckless abandon and I've found out over the years that this strategy has served me well.

When I did proceed on a course without setting my sights on a goal and without a well planned out strategy I've always found that I ended up somewhere other than where I intended to be and more often than not if you pardon the clique, I ended up crying over spilt milk. That's always been my Achilles heel, and I was fortunate enough to recognize that fatal flaw early on in my life. Monica helped me learn that the hard way. So, before I delve into anything new now I sit back and observe, plan a strategy and then proceed cautiously thus eliminating any unnecessary faux pas.

The strategy has served me fairly well in my anthropological endeavors and most other aspects of my life as well. That is until it comes to the subject of women. And Lacy's mother, Monica was no exception. The only difference with Monica and the women that followed her was that she had seen rough times too, at the expense of the opposite sex. Yet, I can't say she was bitter because of her experiences. In fact, she hardly held any animosity towards men at all. She just didn't deal with them. I mean she was cordial. She spoke when spoken to but dating and relationships were out. That was until I came along. I don't know what attracted her to me when she could have had any man she wanted but I was glad she chose me. Still, I was pretty apprehensive since I was no more than a novice myself in the game of love but she treated me with a good deal of kindness and respect. Still, whenever we were together I found myself floundering, like a fish out of water, so tickled was I just to be in her mere presence.

I had a hard time talking to her and the few times we went out to dinner I would always find a way to embarrass myself either by dropping something or spilling something. After awhile, I would grab a taste of the Rose before we went anywhere just to calm my nerves and get rid of the jitters but of this, she did not approve. At a loss as to what to do or how to handle this nervousness I felt when I was around her I thought about throwing in the towel but found that to be impossible to do as well since I was, I thought, in love. With no solution in sight, I continued my feeble attempts at courting, all the while feeling, as if I was swimming upstream in unchartered waters.

I was a pretty handsome guy, back in those days, and a lot of our peers thought we made a rather nice couple. And I had to agree. And as long as we were among friends everything would go wonderfully well but the moment we were alone I'd be overcome with fear that I wouldn't or couldn't meet her expectations. At these times, I'd always manage to somehow stick my foot in my mouth or do something utterly foolish and out of character.

I don't know what Monica's sentiments were during this whole charade but she never mentioned any of my foul ups and would go on with the evening as if nothing had happened.

After several months of dating, which included dinner and long walks in the park, I never once made a pass or sexual advance towards Monica and I think this she respected. It was my intention to let her know that I was different from my counterparts and was not interested in pursuing her for mere sexual gratification. Yet, each evening that I would leave her at the doorstep of her brownstone and head home I kicked myself and would end up grieving the night away thinking about a missed opportunity. I was always telling the kids in the neighborhood that there was nothing worse in the world than wasted potential and missed opportunities. Nothing fails but a try was my motto and yet I had neither the heart or the gumption or the heart to even consider asking this African queen for a kiss goodnight.

In my attempts to salvage some part of my self-esteem and in an effort to reconstruct my tattered ego and feel better about the whole situation, I'd make it a point to stop by Saul's grocery anytime I had a date with Monica. Saul always made me feel better since he felt the same way

about Monica that I did yet he could barely utter a word in her presence so taken aback was he by her whole countenance. We'd share a glass or two of wine at the end of the day, usually a glass of Manischevitz or some other kosher wine he'd have on hand and talk about Monica and women like her. (I think Saul was more in love with Monica than I was and though he was happy for me I'm sure he felt just a little animosity although he was never one to visibly show it).

Talking to Saul usually gave me the courage needed to venture out on another of my excursions with Monica, or perhaps it was the Manishevitz. (Saul always called it courage in a bottle). But whatever it was, I continued to see Monica going on the better part of a year. And during that whole time, I never made an advance.

At the same time, there were men of every persuasion and from all walks of life, making regular advances to what I now deemed, my woman. And at regular intervals, I had to stop and wonder if she might not be considering a few of the proposals being tossed her way since we really had no formal agreement or arrangement stating that she belonged to me or I to her.

And being that I was petrified of commitment and the idea of marriage sent cold shivers down my spine I wondered how long it was before they entered into the equation. And although Monica hadn't said a word, the pressure was mounting. And I knew it wouldn't be long before the subject arose. It was at that time that I decided that the pressure was too much for me to handle and perhaps I should bow out altogether.

I weighed this decision for the better part of a week but being that I had grown accustomed to and really looked forward to our Saturday night jaunts down to the Village and our Saturday morning walks through Central Park I truly wondered how I would survive without her in my life. And the idea that I might just by chance see her with another man ate at my very soul. I was at a loss as to what to do and knew that I couldn't ask Sweet for advice and Saul would have given me some ol' long parable from the Torah that would take me weeks to decipher and I was at my wits end. Fact of the matter was that I needed an answer and I needed it now.

I was losing sleep now and when I did sleep, I had murky visions of Monica clouding my every dream. I had not bargained for this when I first introduced myself and the fact that she was pervading my every thought began to hinder not only my thought processes but my work as well. The lack of sleep along with the wine that I was now drinking, during office hours, in increasing quantities to keep my mind off this woman were really beginning to have a detrimental affect on me.

No longer was I analytical in my observations. And my self-esteem plummeted. All I thought about during my waking hours was the next time I'd see Monica.

As if that weren't enough, I'd been celibate for the better part of a year and this hadn't occurred since I was sixteen years of age. Even when I wasn't dating anyone, it wasn't hard to recognize my physical needs when they arose.

Carefully, I observed, evaluated them at length and caught the first train smoking up to the bridge in Hunts Point. Once there I met with a longtime associate who was perfecting her career as a Customer Service Representative for men in need of relief, such as I; spent my twenty dollars and returned to Harlem where I would promptly take twice the recommended dosage of penicillin and return to my work.

However, being that I had always been monogamous out of both faith and fear I decided early on in my relationship with Monica that my monthly liaisons with my associate under the bridge in Hunt's Point were now a thing of the past. Yet, my needs were mounting and I had no idea on how to resolve them.

Several months prior to this dilemma, and after one of our Saturday evening outings I stood on the steps of Monica's brownstone at which time she informed me that Lacy was at a sleepover at her best friend Anna Mae's house and invited me in for a nightcap.

Aware that she'd had more than her usual to drink and was a bit tipsy, I declined. I'd thought about this night ever since I met Monica and wanted more than anything to take her up on her offer but as I was more intent on wooing her with my chivalrous nature and wanting her to be in full control of her faculties when I made my move I declined and kicked myself in the teeth all the way home for missing another opportunity.

Yet, because I am a keen student of nature of which human beings are apart, I knew that if she'd asked once then it was only a matter of time before I would be asked again. However, there must have been an error in my theory, as she did not ask again. I don't know if she took my declination as a rebuff. It hardly was, or if she had merely grown tired of trying to figure me out but I was never given this request again and in those days to suggest a trip to a hotel or a getaway weekend was simply out of the question with a woman of her royal stature.

So, here I was the better part of a year later consumed with passion, still unable to enunciate clearly when alone with her and incapable of continuing my work with any type of professionalism as I could do nothing but think about her. To make matters worse I was so consumed with her and distraught at the idea of losing her that I simply stopped everything. That was everything but seeing her. This I continued and began seeing her even more than I had before. In the evenings I waited at the steps of the subway where she'd appear fatigued after a long day's work and I'd wait anxiously to shoulder her bags of groceries and walk her home, at which time she would bid me farewell and enter her home. I always felt a deep sigh of anguish when that door would close in my face but I knew the type of woman she was and knew that she would never allow another man in front of her daughter unless she was married to that man.

Proud to be with the finest woman ever to grace Harlem's streets since Lena Horne and tired of that door closing in my face each evening I came to a rather hasty conclusion that I gave little or no thought to.

At this point, I knew there was only one thing for me to do and that was to ask for Monica's hand in marriage. And so I made plans as I did every week to take her to Small's that Friday. Duke Ellington was scheduled to headline the show and the word around Small's was that Billie Holliday and a few other musicians of note would be showing up for a sort of impromptu gig since it was Duke's birthday. I was going to work the first show and with the few dollars from that and a loan from Sweet coupled with a loan from my buddy Saul I'd have enough to put down on that one and a quarter carat diamond engagement ring I'd seen in Friedman's Jewelry Store down on Delancey. I'd get Duke to play, 'In My Solitude', since that was her favorite song and then have him call her up on stage where I'd proposed.

At home that night, I rehearsed my lines and ran the scenario over and over in my mind so as to make sure there were no slip-ups and I'd left nothing to chance. When I was convinced that this was my only out, my only alternative, my only chance to preserve the little sanity I had remaining I called Sweet and Saul who both agreed to aid me in my endeavors. Feeling assured of my pending success I broke open my emergency bottle of Richard's and drank heartily relishing each drop and then turned on Billie Holliday and spent the remainder of the night crooning 'Loverboy' with Billy's accompaniment.

That Friday arrived sooner than expected and everything was going pretty much according to schedule and Sweet, being the good friend that he is did me the favor of stopping off on Delancey and picking up the ring for me paying both Saul's and my shares so I would save time and wouldn't have to travel all the way back downtown and then have to get ready for work.

Saul, on the other hand had one of his suits tailored to fit me and made sure that it was cleaned and pressed before presenting it to me. And then he cried. Saul always cried. But this time I wondered if he was truly happy for me or was crying about his own loss. In any case, I was certainly grateful for having two of the best friends a man could ask for.

When I was finished my shift I talked to Duke, who was in unusually good spirits that evening and he agreed to play 'In My Solitude' midway through his set at which time he would stop and call Monica to the stage to sit next to him. As rehearsed, I would join them and make my proposal or as Duke suggested, after noticing my anxiety, perhaps just hand her the ring and let her fill in the rest.

I drank rather heavily that evening and pondered my impending actions until I could no more. It then dawned on me. From out of the clear blue, there came a revelation. I was suddenly convinced that for a woman, even a woman as beautiful as Monica to be able to get a free-spirit like me to decide to settle down was incomprehensible. And to propose to her without ever having so much as kissed her was unthinkable. No, something was wrong. Something was definitely amiss.

It then dawned on me. Monica had to be some kind of an African voodoo priestess who had cast one of those spells Margaret Meade had documented so well in her travels. I realized at that very moment that that was one of the reasons that I lost the ability to speak when around her. It was all coming to light now. The fact that I couldn't speak when she was near me had to be some kind of spell since it only happened in her presence. The fact that I couldn't bring myself to touch or even kiss her goodnight was all due to the aura surrounding her that would not allow me to enter her space.

I'd read about Haiti and New Orleans and how in the islands off of South Carolina and Georgia these African traditions were still prevalent and still practiced in secret. God, how ignorant was I? It was obviously, that's what made her stand apart from every other woman in Harlem.

Hadn't she told me when we first met how she was from somewhere down around Charleston only a generation or so removed from African ancestry? She'd never said exactly where but I was now convinced she was from those islands off the coast that had never been really incorporated into mainstream America. Those islands remained as aloof and regal as she was. It all made sense now. Even the accent, which I'd found so utterly sultry and seductive. That was her lure, her snare, her trump card, (not that she needed one with her powers and all). That's why I couldn't eat, drink or sleep without her invading my every thought. She was using mind control and as strong as my mind is she'd bent it to her will until it had taken over my goals, my ambitions, my very constitution.

I drank freely now and wondered if she'd let me continue, being that she did not particularly favor my imbibing. When I summoned the waitress and ordered a double my next round I glanced over to see if she would interfere but she said nothing. But then why would she?

She knew that she had me now. I was, if nothing else, committed. And she knew it. I'd already borrowed the money from Saul and Sweet for the ring, told everyone of note to please attend my little get together for a very special announcement and commissioned Duke to sing. She knew as well as I did that there was no turning back now without embarrassing the both of us in front of our closest friends. And I knew it too. I was petrified. I'd never been in love before so I didn't know the ins and outs nor had I ever had roots cast on me before so I had no idea of where to go or how to respond or if I had the ability to do anything at all. And so when Duke started playing, 'In My Solitude', I did what I was commissioned to do. I stood up with the bottle of champagne and glasses in my hand and headed for the stage. Passing the side door, I turned slightly to make a beeline but found that I was unable to do so. Staring into the darkest recesses of Monica's hazel eyes I felt summoned by a power I'd never felt before. Climbing the steps to the stage I felt one leg give way and wondered if perhaps I'd drunk too much and was falling. But my knee caught me and I found myself properly situated on one knee in front of this woman who now controlled my life. And for the first time since I'd known her I had no trouble speaking and letting her know exactly what it is that I wanted.

"Monica, my darling", I heard myself say as I took her hand in mine and brought the ring from my vest pocket in the same motion. "Would you be so kind as to grant me your hand in marriage?"

To which she replied in a voice that sounded as if had come from the darkest depths of hell. "Yes, William I'd be   honored to be your wife."

My heart sank but I smiled and Duke finished with a rousing rendition of 'Misty'. Leaving the stage, we were greeted with congratulations from everyone in attendance that night and in the days to follow.

In the days that were to follow, Monica seemed to be delighted by her good fortune which by now I deemed my misfortune. But deciding that I was right in my evaluation about her having some type of mystical powers I was careful to control my negative thoughts as I did not want to incur her wrath should she truly be a voodoo witch doctor or high priestess since I was sure she knew my every thought.

In the next few days, I was beside myself with grief and made it a point to seclude myself. So sincere was I in my effort that I made sure no to tell Saul or Sweet about my self imposed exile since I knew neither of them had any control when it came to keeping something from Monica. I drank heavily during those first couple of days and began regaining my sanity not long after and

wondered how as smart as I was or considered myself to be, how I could've possible let myself fall prey to a woman.

Time to sort things out is what I sorely needed and on the third day of my exile I was feeling somewhat better but no sooner had I regained my composure and decided that I would confront Monica despite the repercussions and tell her that I was having second thoughts than there was a knock at the door.

Assuming that it was the hotel manager looking for the days rent I didn't bother looking through the peephole but opened the door with haste to tell him that I would be out by eleven thirty, which was checkout time. But instead of it being the manager, it was Monica who stood before me looking as gorgeous in her finery as I'd ever seen her. I, aware of her seductive lure now bit down hard in an attempt to summon my resolve in an attempt not to let her control my mind. But seeing her standing there tall, dark and lovely, ruby red lips shimmering despite the lipstick that was fading quickly I knew this would be no easy task. Where there was once eye shadow, there were now tears and I wondered, no, I knew they were on my account and felt both embarrassed and ashamed. Despite what she'd done with the curses and the roots, I should have never have run but stood up on my own behalf and been man enough to tell her how I felt instead of causing her all of the grief and anguish that was so apparent.

Yet, I knew deep down in the bowels of my soul that I was no match for whatever it was that she held over me.

"May I come in, William?" she asked mumbling the words as the tears rolled down both cheeks.

I opened the door to the hotel room, which was a mess. Empty wine bottles were scattered everywhere, the previous day's newspapers and empty containers of leftover food stood festering and a foul odor hung in the air.

The cockroaches ran back and forth hastily ignoring Monica's interruption. And I upon opening the door wider to let her enter became, at once, fearful when I thought of the ensuing conversation and the power she held over me. I was sure the repercussions would be devastating and wondered if I would be maimed, blinded, or even killed when I told her that I'd thought long and hard about this whole marriage affair. The speech I'd prepared went something like this.

After considerable thought, some lengthy reflection and after some rather intensive research over the last three days on the whole institution of marriage it has come to me Monica that there is something inherently wrong with the institution as we know it which is why the divorce rate in America is so astronomically high.

Furthermore, marriage or better yet monogamy is a European invention designed to manipulate people into a unit, in an effort to maintain control. It was designed as such because there were so few women at the birth of this nation that there were scarcely enough women for every man to have one wife let alone two or three. However, being that I am of African descent and it is commonplace to have two or three wives, I fear that somewhere down the road this may occur, as polygamy is as inherent in my gene pool as are two eyes and two legs.

Much to your great misfortune, I would thereby be considered a cheater or a bigamist and you would be without a husband. And neither of these are humiliations which I would want someone as lovely as you to incur.

That is what I had planned to say her. Yet, when Monica entered the room that day all beautiful and teary-eyed I knew that if anything I'd once again grown weak in her presence.

Yet, I knew I had no choice. I had to tell her. The marriage was off. There was no way that I could continue to conduct my anthropological studies, (so devoted was I to my work), and be a loving father and husband at the same time. But she was insistent on speaking first and being the gentleman that I am, I let her have her way.

I held firmly to my stance and rehearsed the speech in my mind over and over during the first few minutes of her visit so she wouldn't be able to throw me off guard and somehow enter and take control of my psyche as she'd manage to do before when I'd been vulnerable to her seductive beauty and charm.

"Do you mind if I sit on the bed, William", she asked.

"Wherever you feel most comfortable," I replied still rehearsing the speech in my head.

I made it a point to have a seat next to her and realized that aside from the park on Sunday afternoons this was the first time we'd ever really been alone. Taking her hand in mine, I felt strong, in control. There was no doubt that she was beautiful and it didn't take me long to figure out what it was that first attracted me to her. Again, I repeated my speech.

"William, I've been so worried, so very worried. I haven't heard or seen from you in three days. I was so worried. I thought something might have happened to you. I spoke to Saul and Sweet and neither of them could or would tell me a thing," she was crying again and I felt terrible but had to remember the power this woman possessed over me.

Reaching over me to the box of Kleenex on the table, I was in full view of the long split that ran the length of the chiffon dress and gasped aloud when I caught a glimpse of her dark nipples as the dress fell from her breasts when she leaned over me.

Monica seldom if ever wore a bra but it hardly mattered since I'd never been in such close proximity. But as she leaned over me now I could do little else but notice her nipples and they seemed to be spreading in diameter with each sobbing sigh. I felt myself becoming weaker with each glance but could do nothing to avert my gaze. I was mumbling my lines now, almost incoherently, as if repeating a mantra but could feel myself slipping back into her clutches. The words were meaningless now and I only hoped that she would have the kindness and the decency to release me from her spell.

"I am a man of African descent", I began jumping from the bed and facing the woman but Monica grabbed me by the hand and pulled me back down next to her.

"William, don't think that I haven't noticed the way that you look at me. To your credit you have never once approached me or attempted to take advantage of me and don't think for one minute that it's gone unnoticed. I'm sure it hasn't been easy for either of us to keep up the facade. I had to, for the sake of my daughter and I'm sure now that you did it out of respect for me and I am sincerely grateful."

I repeated my speech to myself and did my best not to into past Monica's mesmerizing gaze.

"As handsome a man as you are I know you must have been quite active before you met me. I see the way all the girls look at you when we're down at Small's.

201

I'm not blind you know. And I also know that you've given up all of that just for me. I've done my homework when it comes to you, Mr. Longfellow and everything has come up smelling roses. Thanks to you, I've never been happier in my entire life."

Well all that is about to change. I thought to myself and no matter what you say I will not marry you. I repeated my lines to myself again before standing.

The perfume she was wearing was my favorite and was starting to have a debilitating effect on me so I thought standing would give me chance to breathe and clear the cobwebs from my head. I could feel the voodoo presence trying to take over again but I was quite sure of myself now and

I would not, could not stand to be married to any one woman for the rest of my days. After all, I was of African descent and from the very first or as long as anyone could remember, we had been polygamous. I would not, could not, go against such ancient customs and traditions.

"Why are you standing, William? And what is it that you keep mumbling? When we're married the first order of business will be to get you to throw away your reliance on that cheap wine. That'll be the first order of business. You told me that you loved me. Well, you never actually said you did but I knew it when you asked me to marry you in front of all those people at Small's that you loved me and if you really loved me you won't drink in front of Lace or me. That's the first order of business."

We weren't even married and she was already making demands. There was no need to rehearse anymore. No, need at all. I wasn't marrying this woman with the sweet smelling perfume, the long slender legs and the hazel eyes. The fact that her nipples were dark and pierced the sheer, white, chiffon dress like stars in the night sky mattered little. This woman who I hadn't known a year and knew nothing of my work, the gravity of it or my passion for it was attempting to change the whole analytical process by which I worked by.

There was simply no way that I was going to allow her to come in, out of nowhere and affect my life long labor. She could rant, rave, cut the heads off

202

chickens, and rattle bones all she wanted. She could stick pins in whoopee dolls that resembled me and bay at the moon for all I cared. I wasn't marrying her.

Up 'til that point I hadn't said a word and it wasn't 'cause I was in her presence and she had me tongue-tied or because she had worked her voodoo on me again. It was because she was airing her grievances and me being the cordial host that I am, decided that the proper thing to do was to let her have say first. But when she mentioned me giving up the Rose and I knew it was high time that I spoke up and cleared up a few matters even though I knew that I might be moving in harm's way. But enough was enough and I knew that I would burst at the seams if I attempted to bite my tongue any longer.

Monica must have noticed I was getting a wee bit agitated at her ramblings because she stopped cold.

"Is there something you wanted to say, darling," she asked. "You still haven't told me what you're doing here."

"I just needed time to get away and think that's all," I lied, thinking how to begin in such a way that I didn't bring the wrath of Hadee's down upon me.

"Come here, darling," Monica whispered seductively.

"I'm sorry, Monica. I just can't. There's something I need to tell you and I don't know any other way to tell you than to come flat out and just say it."

I was on a roll now and knew that despite the consequences there was no stopping me now. At which time Monica crossed her leg and leaned back on her elbows revealing more than just the split in her dress but everything I'd thought and imagined about this Black queen since I first met her.

"Are you married William? Is that it? Is that what the big secret is all about?" She asked.

"No. No, Monica, it's nothing like that." I replied staring at the ceiling so as not to gaze upon the most beautiful woman I'd ever come into contact with.

How many nights had I lain in bed frustrated, staring up at the peeling paint on the ceiling in my flat wondering what was beneath the floral prints of those flowing dresses she wore? And now just as I was about to break the whole thing off she was giving me a peek of what could have been. It didn't matter though; at this point freedom was worth more than a lifetime stroll in the park with any one woman even if it was the queen who sat before me now. I had to admit, though that Monica was even more beautiful than I had ever imagined, at least what I could see of those long chocolate thighs. And despite my protestations and dislike for the institution of marriage and the fact that I hated being in such close contact with pagan religions such as

voodoo I have to admit I was deeply moved by Monica's latest revelation. Yet, I remained strong in my beliefs, repeated my speech again, and grew stronger with each word I said.

Monica continued.

"I tried this once before, William but I got the impression that you weren't too interested in me in the condition I was in but I was going through some changes myself. You have to realize that you never ever have come out and really expressed your feelings towards me or told me if you really had any feelings towards me at all other than what I would consider platonic. And I was desperate to know where we stood. I'd never slept with a man aside from Lacy's father and vowed to never again after he left me but I saw something in you, something beautiful, something I wanted to be apart of and so I got drunk and prayed that you were the one to fill all my dreams and expectations. And you know what? You have.

The day you asked me to marry you was the happiest day of my life. I realized then that you wanted me as much as I wanted you and the only reason you didn't take me that night is because you wanted me to be sure. You wanted me to know that you weren't typical; that you weren't like the rest. You wanted me to know that you wanted me, for me, not for these long legs or thunderous thighs that God has blessed me with. You didn't want me drunk but fully conscious of our union and so you more than anyone should understand that I want you the same way."

My head was spinning now and I tried to repeat my speech but I was again at a loss for words. I remembered something about being polygamous, something about my gene pool not allowing me to be monogamous but my thoughts were random and disjointed and before I could gather them together to make sense of any of it Monica stood before me and said, "I understood you that night William and that's why I can stand before you now, sober and ask the same of you. I want you to remain sober as well. That's why I am giving myself to you now with no guilt or mixed feelings. The commitment you've given me has washed away all my fears and inhibitions and all I ask for now is that you come to me free of the wines and spirits that haunt you and keep you at arm's distance. All I'm requesting is that you take me, William. Take me body and soul and make me yours forever. Is that too much to ask?"

And with that said, Monica let the sheer chiffon dress with the floral design cascade to the floor and hard as I tried to recall my speech about monogamy being a European ploy and how African tradition was founded in polygamy, the only words that came to mind were, "Oh, Monica, my darling, how I've waited for this moment."

Mama's Friend

"What's up, yo?" The clean cut young man with the fresh fade approached his best friend a broad smile reaching across his dark brown face.

"Ain't nothin'. Same ol', same ol'. You know. What's up with you Vaughn? I know you saw your boy, A.I. last night?"

"No doubt. You know I don't ever miss Allen Iverson or the Nuggets when they're on. That's my man. Broke the Piston's off something proper-like, didn't he? He's got one helluva crossover dribble don't he? I saw him cross Chauncey and Tayshaun over in the first quarter. Made 'em look stupid—damn near ridiculous."

"For sure. They can't do nothin' with him. Just imagine if he had a better supporting cast to take some of the scoring load off of him."

"Whaddaya mean? Hell, he's got Carmelo to help him." The dark-skinned round-faced boy said to his friend, D'Jay.

The two boys had been best friends for as long as either of them could remember and it wasn't uncommon for one to start a sentence and the other to finish it, but not when it came to basketball where both knew that they were the supreme authority on the subject.

206

"Carmelo? I know you're not talking about 'Melo helpin' to shoulder the load. Man please. 'Melo's always been soft. That's why Denver ain't going nowhere."

"Man, how can you say that? You know the boy's injured. I really think he came back too soon. You know it takes more time to come back from an injury like that."

"Whatever. But I remember when he wasn't injured and he still played soft in the playoffs. That's why Denver never ever had no real chance. Instead of playing hard-nosed basketball, like a true power forward he's up there taking jumpers from the top of the key like he a point or a shooting guard or some shit. That's why I say he's soft. It's like he doesn't wanna mix it up down low with the big boys. Maybe he's scared. I don't know. But your boy Allen will mix it up with the best of 'em. Allen don't fear nobody. He'll mix it up with the best of them."

"For sure. A.I. plays a lot whole helluva lot bigger than five-ten. I'll say that for him. And it ain't like he got this enormous wingspan like Rasheed or Tayshaun. He just got heart. Hell, he ain't even as tall as you are, Vaughn. How tall are you anyway? You gotta be about six 'cause I'm five-nine. Shit, come to think of it, your ass should be dunkin' big as you are," DJ laughed, "Lose some of that weight and you probably could," DJ said runnin' from his friend.

"Fuck you, DJ!"

"Ah, man you know I was only bullshittin' but on the real if I had your height I'd be slammin' on niggas left and right," he said stealing Vaughn's dribble then spinning left before hoisting the

ball high at an imaginary hoop before catching the rebound and passing the ball back to his friend.

At close to six feet and weighing nearly three hundred pounds, Vaughn was the bigger of the two and also the quieter with an easygoing personality that made it seem like he gave less than a care about anything. Well, that was anything except for basketball and his dream of one day playing in the NBA. Neither could pass for a choirboy and both stayed in more trouble than either cared to think about and it was nothing for them to skip school to go across town to play ball. Walking along, Vaughn broke the easy silence with a thought. The thought was a recurring one and one that hardly ever left his mind.

"You know, I don't give LeBron a lot of props but Iverson's different. Did you hear what Rip Hamilton of the Piston's said about him? Said Allen had the heart of a lion. He knew that when A.I. was with Philly they didn't have a chance in hell of beating the Pistons but Allen pushed them to the limit each and every time he got the ball in his hands—even when his teammates didn't show up at all. It was almost like his teammates gave up before the series even started. They was like—'wow we're playing the World Champion Detroit Pistons. We can't beat them'. Almost like they was intimidated by all the hype and hoopla and 'cause the Pistons got all those stars. But Allen didn't care. Even when they were down three games to one, he still played like it was game one and it was anybody's series to win. That's the way I'm gonna be when I get to the NBA."

"When you get to the NBA? Hell, nigga you can't even get outta the house let alone get to the NBA. You know your momma's boyfriend got yo' ass on lockdown. You bout the only nigga I know in Harlem that don't never make parole or get no time off for good behavior. Every time I see you he's got you locked up for something or another. That's why yo' ass wanted to skip today. That's the only way you get to see what the outside world is like.

But on the real though, Vaughn, I don't see how you let this punk ass walk into your crib outta the clear blue and start tellin' you what to do. I couldn't do it but I give the boy his props. He one helluva of a playa. He screwin' both you and your moms at the same time. Two women in the same house. Now that's what I call a true playa for real. I don't even think my man, Q could pull off some shit like that and he 's the biggest hustla in Harlem," DJ said laughing and moving out of his friends' path at the same time.

"Fuck you, DJ," Vaughn said the anger obvious in his voice.

"Ahh, come on man, I was just joking he said apologetically now sorry he'd said anything after looking at his friend's face.

Vaughn smiled an uneasy smile followed by a lull. There was a silence but it was a comfortable silence, the kind that came with friends who'd known each other all their lives and could never be offended or hurt by the other regardless of what the other said or did. Still DJ's words hadn't fallen on deaf ears and Vaughn's only thoughts were of momma's boyfriend who had moved in

once again and for who knows how long this time. Each time he moved in he promised momma that this was it. This was the final time and whatever it took, they would make it this time. No matter what happened, they would make it. A month or two later, momma would be in tears all over again and Todd would be long gone. But he wasn't the only one. He was just this month's savior and hero.

Vaughn could remember the men that had passed through and he'd always been receptive, always trying to get along, hopping that this one would be the one that put a smile on momma's face and keep it there. But no matter what he did to help the situation they never stuck around long.

Todd was different though. He'd really liked Todd in the beginning. But no matter what he did or how hard he tried to get along with the man something would inevitably go wrong. As soon as things seemed to be going along smoothly he'd always managed to do something stupid and get caught red-handed like the time he stole Todd's precious cd's and DVD's and taken them to school and sold them. Or the time he'd picked up the change on momma's dresser without asking. Hell, it was bad enough that momma never had any extra money to buy him any new clothes and when she did she refused to spend it on buying him the stuff that everyone else was wearing because it was always too expensive according to her. And she sure as hell wasn't spendin' no hundred dollars on no damn tennis shoes just so he could look like every other lil' thug runnin' the streets. That's what she would tell him.

What was even worse was the fact that he had to stand in that stupid line at school for kids receiving reduced lunches. These were the lunches that were usually for the kids receiving public assistance or welfare and even when he was in this line he never had the forty cents for that. He'd thought about joinin' DJ and a couple of his partners down on the corner sellin' rock but Lord knows he wasn't sure about that but if things got much worse... Anyway, he just didn't know right through here. Hell, everybody was doing it but slingin' dope was always the beginning of the end. He'd seen too many bad things happen around drugs. And he still had a future ahead of him.

So, he didn't think there was anything wrong with taking the dollar or two in change that momma used to leave up there on top of her dresser. And she never said anything about it and she had to know he was taking it even though she never mentioned it but then Todd had come along and all of a sudden it was a big thing. Well, maybe he should have asked. But if he knew momma like he thought he knew momma she wasn't going to say anything but no if he asked her and like he said he hated being with the low-income kids when he knew momma was just too cheap to pay. But Todd said that taking the money without asking was the same as stealing and had made a fuss and then momma had made a fuss although she didn't really make a big fuss. She just kinda of supported Todd because he was the only man that really and truly acted like he loved her.

He'd never really expected anyone to find out though, until one day he picked up Todd's change instead of momma's and being that Todd was broke all the time he counted the few pennies he had. Matter-of-fact, it surprised Vaughn that Todd wasn't rich since he knew everything about being a strong Black man and every other subject that came his way.

At least he pretended to know something about everything just because he used to be a schoolteacher. He'd given up teaching to write. But after receiving rejection after rejection he'd grown tired and frustrated and now he couldn't even get his old position as a teacher back. So, now he was broke and evil most

210

of the time. And it just seemed like any ol' thing would set him off.

Vaughn remembered when Todd had first come into their lives. He was seven or eight when momma first brought him home and he seemed like a pretty cool dude at first but one thing was obvious from the git-go. Todd didn't like him. Not one bit, not even from the start when he hadn't done anything to make him dislike him. Vaughn didn't know if it was because he was fat or if it was because he was a little loud or because Todd just wanted momma all to himself. All he knew was that Todd never liked him although if he had a sip or two and wasn't screamin' and shoutin' at momma they would get along pretty good. But as the years went on and after he'd gotten caught stealing Todd's shit on a couple of occasions it just seemed like there was nothing he could do to make Todd like him, so he'd just given up and said 'fuck it'.

Besides he had no idea why he did the things he did. Fact of the matter was he never even thought about it. He didn't know why he stole stuff. He sure didn't want to be no hoodlum or go to jail or make momma be upset with him. He didn't understand it himself. He just did it. His older sister, Jasmine had done the same thing. And when momma couldn't take no more and Jasmine was sixteen momma put her out. But that was different. By the time she was sixteen, Jasmine had been arrested something like twenty-six times for larceny and been in and of jail and boot camps and even though momma had put her out she kept doing the same things over and over again. And then there was daddy. Vaughn had never met the man but from all of momma's accounts his daddy had been in jail most of his life. He'd come out fathered him then done something and gone right back in. Daddy had done everything from kidnapping, attempted murder to armed robbery and that was just to name a few. He'd even overheard momma say that, 'maybe it was something in his genes when he'd gotten in trouble the last time. So, maybe that was it. Maybe he and Jasmine got it honestly but he certainly wasn't trying to be no hoodlum or no jailbird like Jasmine and daddy.

Vaughn thought about the night he'd heard momma and Todd arguing. It wasn't hard to hear them since their bedroom was right next to his and something he'd heard made him get up to get a closer listen. Standing outside momma's bedroom door, it was soon apparent what had gotten his attention. They were talking about him. Well, at least Todd was. Recently, he'd become Todd's favorite topic of conversation and as loud as Todd was talking it was obvious that he didn't care one little bit whether he heard it or not.

"If he was my son, I'd beat his ass. And as if it's not enough that you ask me to put my own two kids on the back burner and be a part of your life and make this my home is one thing. But the fact that I can't put anything down or leave something lying around for fear of it growing wings and getting ghost is a whole 'nother thing altogether."

The large, buxom woman sat there unable to answer while Todd went on-and-on ranting and raving. Vaughn, still standing outside the door, wondered why it was that some people seemed so taken by the sound of their own voices.

"I'm not saying my kids are perfect but I sure don't have to be a prisoner in my own house or lock my shit up for fear of it being stolen. You're too damn easy on him, sweetie and he's walking all over you. This shit is ridiculous and you baby him so much and refuse to listen any advice that it's no wonder he does the things he does.

The boy can't write a goddamn sentence and he's in the ninth grade. What's worst is he's scared to go to school 'cause these little punks are runnin' 'round here threatenin' to beat his ass for some shit he got into of his own accord. And when I finally get you to go down to the board to see if you can have him transferred everyone down there knows him as a gang affiliate, whatever the hell that means.

I'm not even sure that I know what that means but whatever it means, it sure as hell ain't good. Then they go on to tell you that the boy's been selling bootleg cd's and DVD's in school which just happen to be mine and you come home in tears, looking like you just lost your best friend.

Shit! The only one that should've been crying is Vaughn. Should have worn his ass out right then and there, right on the spot. Come on baby! Wake up and smell the coffee! You keep trying to play everything off and hoping for the best, but the best only comes from putting forth the effort, baby. Hoping and praying is fine but until you put a foot in his ass you ain't really doing shit on his behalf except avoiding the problem and reinforcing his behavior. You think quiet is good but trust me there's always quiet before the storm.

You might want to seriously consider getting the boy some help. I've worked with a lot of children in the last twenty years—kids that were considered incorrigible, with every kind of problem. I've worked with children that were considered behaviorally challenged, sexual offenders, violent offenders... You name it, if there was a negative label placed on a child, I've worked with them and I'll tell you the God's honest truth I've never worked with anyone like him. Maybe, it's because I'm older now. Maybe, it's because I'm in such close proximity and maybe it's simply because I can't get up and walk out at five o'clock and leave the problems behind me. I don't know. But if there's one thing I do recognize it's the fact that the boy needs help. And you really need to concern yourself with that before the problem gets out of hand.

But go ahead. Keep sweeping shit under the rug. It's only a matter of time before you can't hide it anymore. The fact of the matter is the boy has got some pretty deep-seated problems.

And whether you know it or not baby, I'm not meaning to sound harsh but I ain't so much worried about his dumbass as I am about yours. He's not showing you any courtesy or respect. And to tell you the truth I'm not so much interested in what's wrong with him as I am with you. I just have a hard time understandin' why you don't put your foot in his John Brown ass. The nigga

213

needs a goddamn wake up call. Then as if that ain't enough, the White folks down at the school are happy to tell you that this sorry-assed, stupid motherfucka is the one responsible for your house being broken into, not once, not twice but three times in a month. In a month!

I'm sure glad I wasn't around at the time all this shit went down. I swear I am. I would've tried to kill somebody. And what's more, I can't believe you had the nerve to call and tell me. Talkin' about you came home and went to put a movie in the DVD player and there was no player and he was home all day but he doesn't know what happened to it. Please. That would have been it right there. But no, you're gonna wait 'til he decides to come clean. I'll be damned. You'll be old and gray by the time that happens. Wait 'til he comes clean. I'll be damned! But hey, he's not my son. Thank God!!

You should have been too embarrassed to let anyone know especially since you're allowing him to still live there. Trust me. Normal people don't have the problems you have with children. I mean, we all have problems with our children but no one has problems of this magnitude on a

regular basis. I mean this shit is not a once in a lifetime thing. Every week it's something. Every single week it's something and you keep telling me that you ain't wit' all the drama. But you allow the drama to come into your house. Your house! Your house which is supposed to be your safe haven from the madness of the outside world. But you've got the madness right here where you rest your head.

Damn! You went through the same thing with your daughter. I mean a bad seed is one thing and everybody knows that kids will be kids but when you start talking about criminal activities from not one but both kids then there's something definitely wrong. I've worked with kids most of my adult life and trust me there comes a time when we as adults, as parents have to step up to the plate and acknowledge that there are some serious problems."

Vaughn knew that everything Todd was saying was true but if she'd let it go then why couldn't he. Always bringing up the same old shit like it happened yesterday. Always talking about things that happened in the past.

214

The robberies were months ago but Todd just couldn't let it rest. Always walking around talking about what it takes to be a strong Black man and all of that garbage. But he wasn't doin' nothin' but livin' off of momma, eatin' her food and running up the electric bill and pretendin' to be uppity. Hell, in the seven years he'd been dating momma I can only remember him having one job and that only lasted about two weeks before he quit. And he the one always talkin'about bein' a strong Black man.

Hell, what kind of man has a wife and two kids that he don't support and goes to see whenever he gets ready and then when he gets mad over there comes and lays down with momma.

I know he's screwin' momma 'cause I'm right in the next room and I can hear her holler when he hits her sweet spot. That's what they call it when it feels real good to them and they start screamin' and moanin'like momma be doin' all the time. Sometimes I can hear him hollerin' too and momma tells him to hush but a couple of minutes later I hear him sayin' all kinds of stuff that I don't really wanna hear like him tellin' my momma what to do in the bedroom.

One time, when I was like nine or ten, his daughter came over and spent the night with us, me and her was standing by momma's door listening and heard everything. I told momma what I heard 'cause me and momma's a lot alike and we both laughed about the whole thing but when she told him later on he didn't think it was real funny. He never thinks anything I say is real funny. I guess he figures that one day I might learn somethin' I shouldn't from listenin' to them in the bedroom. Either that or he don't feel comfortable sleepin' in the bed with momma in front of me and they ain't married. That goes along with all that 'be a strong Black man' shit. Stuff like that bothers him a lot but me and momma don't really think about stuff like that. At least I don't. But then again, I guess I kind of understand because I really don't like him being in the bedroom with momma all the time like I'm sure he wouldn't want me in the bedroom with his daughter all the time.

Sometimes, I don't think he really likes the way things are with him and momma screwin' all the time with me being around to see it. I think figures that if he leaves and momma brings another man around or starts seeing other men and they go in her bedroom too much then that's not a good image for me to see 'cause I'll think that that's all women are for. At least that's what I overheard him tellin' momma one day when he thought I wasn't listenin'. But when she calls him and says, 'C'mon Todd!' he just drops his head and says—kind of embarrassed like—and then goes to see what she wants. And we both know what she wants. But like I said, I don't think he likes doing that and at the same time trying to show me what a strong Black man is s'pozed to act like. But then I know he loves her 'cause he puts up with a lot of her shit. And I guess he figures that if she don't care then why should he? After all, I ain't his son.

Most of the time though it ain't like we don't get along. Most of the time we just sit around and talk or watch the game together. Like I said we really get along pretty good 'til I do something stupid and he makes a mountain out of a molehill over it. But most of the time though he just talks to me and tell me stuff that he thinks is gonna help me when I get older. And most of the time I listen to him seems 'cause I think he really cares about what he's saying like he's passionate or sometimes, I even think he wants me to grow up and be stronger than he is and that's why he tells me stuff so I wont make the same mistakes he did. And sometimes, he even thinks it's like he just gets real mad and real angry cause I'm not getting what he's saying quick enough or he feels like momma is letting him do all the child rearin' just to 'cause she's too into her own self to do it and just wants to get me outta her hair.

Sometimes, I think that momma thinks that as long as she does her job in the bedroom and brings in the groceries that he can have the job of making me turn out alright but a lot of the times I don't think he wants the job and momma can go too if he gotta be a father to me full-time.

And since all momma does is work and after all the trouble and the problems she had with my sister I don't really think she wants the job either. But she don't mind taking care of my sister's baby cause she still a baby and she's still cute and light-skinned and all but me on the other hand I'm pretty big just like momma and everybody says we favor but she's a woman and I know that down deep she really wishes that she was skinny and pretty like them girls on the videos so men would like her more and she wouldn't have to put up with Todd's ol' evil ass. But she ain't. She's fat just like me and I think that's another reason she don't wanna be around me since I remind her so much of herself and all the things she don't like about herself.

I know that momma loves me but if it's a choice between workin' or havin' to be a parent she'd probably choose workin' nine times outta ten. And mostly that's what she did before she got laid off last week. Basically that's all she ever did. Just worked. So, I had to take care of myself everyday since I was a little kid. But that ain't really nothing new since I been takin' care of myself since I was nine or ten. But when the house got broken into and her and Todd tried to work things out for the thousandth time, it was like all of a sudden I got a new parent or something and he just came struttin' up in here expectin' me to do stuff my own mother don't ask me to do.

Then he tells me he's gonna show me how be a strong Black man and a good student and stuff like that. But maybe I don't wanna be a strong Black man or a good student. I'm not saying that I don't wanna be. I'm just sayin' that he never asked me he just sorta shoves it down my throat like that's what everyone's s'pozed to do. And I'm thinkin' things to myself the whole entire time he's talkin'. Don't strong Black men have jobs? Don't strong Black men feed themselves? Don't strong Black men have cars? Don't strong Black men take their women out every now and then? Do strong Black men live off of women?

I think that's why he hated the word 'pimp' so much. Guess it reminded him of someone he knew.

Anyway, one day I just asked him. I just said, "Todd can I ask you a question?"

And he said, "Yeah. Sure. Go ahead."

He liked it when I asked him questions. Guess it made him feel important and some people just naturally need to feel important so, I said "Todd," even though momma thought I should call him Uncle Todd caused that showed respect. Most of the time I wouldn't call him by name at all if it meant me havin' to call him Uncle Todd.

Anyway, I said, "Todd. With all your college education and all your teachin' experience and all the books you've read and all the time you spend studyin' and on the computer and in the library then how come you can't keep a job?"

I mean I was respectful and everything but I guess I must've hit a nerve 'cause when momma came home he told her what I said and that was all she wrote.

Momma went off on me like I had just killed somebody and I knew right then and there that one of us had to go. That was the final straw. First of all, I hadn't said anything that wasn't true. Second of all, I got tired of this nigga comin' in off the street anytime he got ready to and actin' like he knew every fuckin' thing like he was some goddamn genius or something. And half the time he couldn't even afford to buy himself a pack of cigarettes. Momma had to buy them for him or else he smoked all of hers and as much as she smoked she wasn't havin' that. But the thing that really got me was that she took his side against me—her own son. Right then and there was when I decided it was time for him to go.

Up 'til that point I really didn't care if she locked me out of her bedroom and spent all her time in there letting him screw her brains out like I didn't know what was going on. Most of the time I was watching T.V. or eatin' or hangin' out so I didn't really care what they did as long as they didn't bother me.

And since she seemed pretty happy with the situation I didn't care but lately he was actin' too much like he cared or wanted to be my daddy or something and I didn't need him to be my daddy since I already had one even if I ain't never seen him. But even when I lied and told her that I didn't know who stole the DVD player or who broke into our house she never really said or did anything. But when I said I insulted and disrespected him 'cause I told the truth about him

218

not being able to keep a job, she gonna tell me—her own son—that I needed to get out, 'cause she wasn't going to allow me to disrespect her man. Now picture that.

Even when he wanted to know why I packed up all of his DVD's and put them in the desk drawer next to the back door and left the back door open, momma lied and covered for me sayin' that she must have forgotten to lock it. She didn't even get upset when he asked her what happened to the bike that he gave me for my birthday and I just played it off and told it I left it at a friend's house. Actually, I didn't expect her to act any differently than she did when I got sold the bike she bought me. I just told her about that one when she asked me she didn't get too upset. She just told me that I needed to take better care of my things and by the next day everything was back to normal and cooler than a fan.

Hell, if Todd hadn't been there she would've never noticed half the shit that was missing since she don't half pay attention to what I'm doin' most of the time. And it ain't because she don't love me. It's just that with her bein' busy with tryin' to work and feed me and my niece and all she just don't have the time to be worryin' about what I was doin'. Not even when he told her that I stole some of his cd's—which I did—she really didn't get too upset. She just covered for me the same as she always did and hoped and prayed that I would stop all the dumb shit. Of course, by now I really didn't care. I was pretty much tired of him tryin' to run things and play daddy and always assignin' me chores and books for me to read. He had even gotten to the point where he thought he had to check my homework behind me. I don't know if he was tryin' to

help me or if he was tryin' to open momma's eyes and show her just how bad a parent she was but one thing was for sure neither her nor me wanted that shit rubbed in our face.

Like I said she was doing the best she could considerin'. And what he didn't understand was that as bad as things were momma always wanted to believe that things were okay even if that was the farthest thing from the truth. Here we is livin' smack dab in the middle of Harlem but if you didn't know any better and you talked to momma you would swear we lived smack dab in the middle of Beverly Hills. You see, bad as things were momma really wanted to believe that things were okay. She's what my English teacher; Miss Dunleavy calls an 'optimist'.

At the same time, he's still insisting on me being a strong Black man like his father and his son. And that I really don't need to hear and neither do momma. Ain't doin' nothin' but putting pressure on me and momma. That's all he's doin'. Just puttin' pressure on me and momma.

After all, how many Black men do you see sittin' around readin' and bein' all studious and shit? That's like a White person's dream. It's almost like he wanna be White or somethin'. I'm sorry but when I go outside I don't see nobody standin' around readin' and actin' all pretentious. Well, except the Muslims and everybody know they crazy as hell. Hell, me and momma was perfectly happy before he got here just sittin' around watchin' television and snackin' and just basically, chillin' and relaxin'.

That's why after thinkin' about the situation for awhile I decided that he definitely needed to be on his way 'cause he was never gonna be content to just stay in momma's room and fuck her. No, DJ was right. He wasn't happy just screwin' her. He wanted to screw me too and up 'til then I was pretty happy just doin' what I was doin' which was basically nothing.

Well, he must have really loved momma 'cause I put that fool through pure hell and he did his best to hang in there even though I know it was eatin' away at him. But you know for me it wasn't really hard. You see, I'm basically lazy and I just went back to doing things the way I had before he got here with all his highfalutin' and uppity ways. Anyway, like I said I went back to doin' things the way I'd always been doin' them and if he asked me to do somethin' I would but I would do it of my own accord and in my own sweet time. Then I'd do it half-assed just the way I did things before he got here.

Well, I could see that this was driving him crazy 'cause he really and truly thought he was starting to make some progress with me. But in my heart I knew it was just a matter of time because everybody says I'm a pretty hard case. And I was right. After awhile, he stopped telling me what to do or what it took for me to become a strong Black man, and a role model and a pillar of society and all that other shit I wasn't the least bit interested in becoming.

At one point, he even turned to me and said that he was here to stay and if one of us was leaving it wouldn't be him. That's when I knew I had him. That's about the time he started drinkin' heavy again and ignorin' me altogether.

Momma could see what was happenin' and so she started tryin' to pick up the pieces where Todd left off 'cause she thought I was comin' around too and changin' for the better since he'd been there. In her eyes, and if nothin' else, at least the house stayed clean when Todd was around. And I gotta admit that he did teach me how to cook a couple of new dishes. But when momma started sittin' down with me every night to help me with my homework and he stayed in the bedroom not hardly showing his face whenever I was around I started counting the days. And I knew right then and there that I wouldn't have to count too much longer.

Funny thing though, I really wanted him to go so everything could get back to normal with me and momma but I really started to miss all the talks me and Todd used to have when it came to basketball. Now, I gotta admit that as much as he got on my last nerve he did know a whole helluva lot when it came to basketball. And I mean a whole helluva lot. And that was the thing—the one thing—that I did miss.

Still, I pretty much figured on was the fact that he'd already raised his own son and I knew he really wasn't wanting to start over with a hard case like me except for the fact that he loved momma and couldn't see me doin' nothin' to hurt her. And I also knew that he was missin' his own kids somethin' awful. And to him it just didn't make any sense workin' with me and I didn't want to learn when there were other kids out there, includin' his that wanted to learn including his own. At least that's what I overheard him tellin' momma. Besides that he was always complainin' about me not doin' nothin' and not wantin' nothin' out of life. He said that was hurtin' momma too even though she didn't show it.

And all the while this stuff is taking place, momma was tryin' to explain to him that I didn't get like this overnight and I wasn't goin' to change or get to wherever the hell he thought he was taking me overnight either. Now, either he didn't believe that or maybe he just didn't understand. I don't know. But he just kept pushin' me to do better.

Todd don't seriously believe I'm ever gonna do anything earth-shattering to make momma proud of me. And to tell you he truth, I don't think momma believes I'm gonna do much either. I think she gave up on me a long time ago but as long as I don't have any kids out-of-wedlock, for her to raise like my sister did and I don't follow in my daddy's footsteps and go to jail then I guess in her eyes if I don't do none of those things, and I get a job, and graduate from high school then I'm pretty much a success. Especially if I can get a job and take care of myself and not be in and out of work and always relying on public assistance like she has to. And so far, I've been pretty good, being that I've only been arrested once and here I am almost fourteen.

That's why I say ain't nobody thinkin' about college and careers and all that 'cept for little White kids and uppity niggas like Todd and his boy. He thinks that just 'cause everybody in his family graduated from college and he got his son down at Chapel hill on a academic scholarship and he got family in another country that that makes him Big Willie and everybody's s'pozed to follow in their footsteps and go to college. But I'll tell you what, all that stuff don't mean a hill of beans

up here in Harlem. The only 'Big Willie's' up here are the ballas and shot callas. Either you make a name for yourself playin' ball or you're hustlin' and got some clout and you're the ones callin the shots. Those is the onliest ones getting' any respect 'round here. Those are the ones drivin' 'round in Escalades and Benz's with spinners and makin' the real dough. They ain't just talkin' and bullshittin'.

Besides, my momma ain't never finished college and she ain't doin' too bad. We live in a nice apartment and got a big screen television and everything. And we always had a car. And some nice one's too. And with all f Todd's education he don't even own a car. I mean he did but he don't now. But we always had a car. So why he thinks college is so important, I just don't know. That's not to say that I ruled it out altogether. I still might go but that's only if I don't go to the NBA. But like I said before, college and the future just ain't nothin' I'm feelin' right now. And if they ain't got no college right here in Harlem I don't know if I'll ever go 'cause really I ain't never tryin' to leave Harlem. Yoou can call it the ghetto if you want but I love it. I love it here.

Oh, I been other places like in the summers when I was a kid and my grandma was livin'. Momma used to always send me down to North Carolina to spend the summer vacation with her and my cousins so I wouldn' be out there in the streets 'cause she say the streets ain't nothin' but trouble. And it was okay. I mean I had fun but it wasn't nothin' like Harlem so I just don't know. I ain't really been nowhere else but if the rest of the world's like North Carolina then I'd

rather stay right on up here in Harlem. Besides everybody knows me and ain't too many people really gonna mess with you if they know you're a stand up guy. I can go right outside my building right now and somebody'll pass me a blunt or I could even go to work 'cause the older cats got a lot of respect for me and the way I carry myself but they recognize I got a future so they really don't push me to do nothin' but stay in school and keep playin' ball.

Anyway, if I do go to college, I think that I'll probably go to Duke since they got a pretty good basketball program and I like their uniforms. Still, there ain't really no rush to decide right now and I'll be damned if I'm going to let somebody tell me what I'm going to do when I've been doing pretty good on my own up 'til now. But Todd he don't see none of that. He even went so far as to

223

buy me a Duke cap and got happy when I mentioned Duke then tol' me what I needed to get in and—well—I might not go if I gotta have four years of straight A's 'cause I already messed up my freshman year but I still like their uniforms 'cause blue's my favorite color. He even got me in a better high school where there ain't no crews or gang members roamin' the halls. But I still found some cool people to hang out with and smoke a little weed before class.

In the meantime, momma was spendin' almost all her time tryin' to play peacemaker between me and Todd and I could see her nerves were pretty much shot but I didn't care. She should have never taken his side. That's where she messed up. She knows me, knows how I am, and she should have never let him just come in here givin' orders and tryin' to rehab us when there was nothing wrong with us to begin with. What Todd didn't know was that ever since I was a

little kid my teacher's used to always say the same thing. They always said that I was disrespectful or had a bad attitude but momma always ignored what they had to say. She always took my side and would usually say somethin' like. 'I used to be the same way when I was growing up'. So I don't know why she figured I was gonna change for her or anybody else. And especially for that nigga layin' the pipe to her. Please! What was she thinking?

My chore list still hung up on the refrigerator door but he stopped demanding that I do them. And now that things were pretty much back to normal I just sat back and waited and listened. Well, it got to the point where that the house was a mess since I stopped cleaning up and he refused to clean up after me. Momma ended up doing all the cleaning just like before Todd got here and he got to feeling bad that she had to come home after workin' hard all day and then clean up. Sometimes he would try to lend a hand without saying a word but I knew it was hard on him 'cause he didn't want to tell her how to run her house anymore than he already was. And he sure didn't wanna refer to his own kids and make her think hers weren't shit or worth a damn but I could see he was havin' a hard time tryin' to understand why she was cookin' and cleanin' and mowin' the grass when there was a six-foot three, three hundred and something pound man sittin' in front of the television, eatin' and droppin' crumbs on the floor while she was tryin' to vacuum around me.

I could almost see the wheels turnin' in his head and I knew he wanted to grab her ass and call her a fat, stupid, bitch for doin' the shit I should have been doin' but instead he just left.

Now I'm figurin' that I finally got rid of him and I'm ready to celebrate a job well done but in an hour or so he was back. I think he went out and got high or drunk or somethin' crazy 'cause he just couldn't understand that this is just how we was. No crazy, high falutin' ideas about college and careers or greatness or none of that shit.

All we basically do is eat and watch TV. That's it. Nothin' more and nothin' less. Just chillin' and havin' a good time. But me loungin' around was really getting' to him 'cause all he kept sayin' was, there's nothin' worse in life than wasted time and wasted potential, whatever the hell that means.

A History Lesson for Y'all

Chapter 1

Boy this is really tough to take. I can't remember times ever being much tougher than right through here and I was around back in '29 when they had that Big Crash and a whole lotta people were suffering from depression. A lot of folks felt the crunch back then, both Black and White but I ain't never seen Black folks like they are now. It's like they still starvin' but it's not like there ain't no food or nothin' like it was back then. It's a different kind of hunger altogether. It's like Bob Marley said in one of his songs, 'dem belly full but dem hungry'. He sho'nuff hit the nail on the head when he wrote that one and I'm gonna tell ya, I ain't never been no real big Bob Marley fan.

When the stock market crashed back in '29, a whole lot of folks—and I'm talkin' White folks thought their worlds was over. They started jumpin' outta windows, committin' suicide and all kinds of ol' crazy shit. Everybody was starvin' an not just White folks. But Black folks wasn't nearly as worried about that so much as White folks was. The difference was that Black folks was used to bein' hungry and not havin' much of nothin'. Shit, back in the day Black

225

folks used to eat all kinds of things nobody else wanted. Hell, they ate pig intestines, made 'em a delicacy

and called 'em chitlins. They ate ox-tails, pig's feet, neck bones. You name it, we ate it. Anything the mas'r threw out we ate.

Hell, it was hard back then but we made the best of it. And even though we didn't have much of anything we ain't act like no fools neither. It got to the point that most of us just accepted this as our fate and it won't really no big deal. It was just anotha day in the life of a niggra. That's all. We took what they gave us and made the best of it. And you'd best believe it weren't easy either. You know man has the unique ability to not only adapt but to flourish in even the most hostile and horrendous of conditions.

Nowadays they call it adversity but I like to keep it real much as possible so I'm gonna tell you as eloquently as I can and be real at the same time. As a people we has truly been through some shit. We've suffered every kind of misfortune known to man ever since we got here. We done gone from the auction block to the cellblock. Talk about' sufferin'. If we wasn't in Mississippi runnin' from the slave catcher's dogs then we was in Birmingham runnin' from the police dogs. We was fightin' for freedom back then and we still fightin' for that same freedom today. Ain't no difference. And trust me, I been around. I know. But if there's one thing I can say for us as a people, it's that we stayed true to ourselves and remained focused. We kept our eye on the prize and it made me awfully proud to be a member of the Niggra race.

I mean as a people, if we wasn't nothin' else we was focused. We knew where we wanted to go, who we wanted to be, and what we expected from ourselves and our government. We was strivin for the betterment of ourselves as individuals and collectively as a nation of Black folks. If you think about it—I mean if you really think about it—we should've been the ones jumpin' out of windows and committin' suicide back in '29 during that there Depression. Matter-of-fact, Black folks should've been jumpin' a long time before the stock market went belly up. And to tell you the truth, we should still be jumpin'. But we just took it all in stride and I'm proud to say that we stayed the course and persevered. And for persevering we even got a few concessions here and there along the way. And this year we got Obama.

You know a lot of negative things has been said about us as a people. And they still bein' said. Somebody, and you know as well as I do who I'm referrin' to, is always depictin' us as no-good, or as criminals in orange colored jumpsuits, doin' a snatch and grab, here and there, or committin' grand larceny—whatever the hell that is—and breakin' and enterin' or some other penny ante bullshit where a brotha steals a few dollars, gets his picture on television and a lifetime behind bars.

And there's no doubt that there's a few of us out there that are doing those things. And let me say that I don't condone any of those things. But by the same token, let's call a spade a spade. You got some folks out here tryin' to steal the whole goddamn world. And like I said, I ain't gonna mention no names but you know goddamn well who I'm referrin' to. Yesterday it was Afghanistan. Today it's Iraq. Who the hell knows what tomorrow may bring? And yet you up here portrayin' a brotha on national TV who ain't done no more than try to make a dolla' outta

fifteen cents. When he gets caught it's news. Meanwhile, you is robbin' the world blind and tryin' to shift the focus to him.

Now you done vilified, victimized, dehumanized and every other '—ized' him and every other Black man out here and portrayed him as so sinister that all Black folks look like public enemy number one. And bein' that we all look alike, you got everybody—even Black folks themselves—scared of me too and I ain't neva robbed shit.

227

You got good decent folks lockin' they doors and puttin' bars on they windows of there little two bedroom, two bath, Tudor homes way out in Massapequa and Sheepshead Bay like I'm goin' to take my Visa or MasterCard down to Hertz or Avis to rent a U-Haul truck to ride an hour and a half to rob their asses. Please! My time is too goddamn valuable. Besides why in the hell would I ride way out there to rob them when I know the schedule of every one of my neighbors, can rob them, hit the pawn shop and be home by dark and not worry about New York's Finest lookin' into it. They ain't worried about what happens to my neighbors or me long as we stay up here in Harlem locked away from the rest of the world. For me it would be all about accessibility but to them it's all about fear.

Personally, I ain't robbin' or stealin' from nobody. Sorry, I can't fit the stereotype—even though somebody's robbin' from me every time I go to the store, to buy gas and pay my rent. Still, I sure as hell ain't the one doin' it. Even though you see me the same way you see every other Black man that commits a crime that just ain't my m.o. You see, unlike you, I, am aware of our

history as Black folks in America. I've read it, studied it and had the good fortune to be on the front lines when a part of our history was being made.

You see, there was a time, not too long ago that I thought it my civic duty to take an active role in The Movement with the hope that I could do my part to help promote change and ideally make this a better place to live. I'm talkin' about America. Hell, I wasn't tryin' to do nothin' great. Like I said, I was just pitchin' in and tryin' to do my fair share the best way I knows how. And to tell you the truth, and without boastin' I think I did more than most.

Still and all, I still feel a little guilty 'cause I took some time off, tryin' to lose myself while my folks was still out there strugglin' and sufferin' and tryin' to defy the odds. You see I got caught up. And maybe I started consumin' more wine than I should have trying to disassociate myself but I had to get away. Leastways I thought I did.

I don't know if you're aware of it or not but you've got to be real careful when it comes to racism. It's like a terminal disease. If you're not careful it can infect you, overwhelm you, and leave yo' ass strung out and incapacitated. That's one of the things that you've got to be real careful of when you're fighting for the cause.

You see, this here struggle ain't like joining the Peace Corps where you do two or three years in some Third World country where the natives are starvin' and you come flyin' to the rescue like some long-haired caped crusader and then you're out. Your mission is pretty much complete.

Six months later, and after a long vacation in the Bahamas you're off on your next assignment. This time it's South America to preserve the rainforest. The following winter you're glad that they've assigned you to Hawaii where you're supposed to help save the whales. Your seat in heaven is now solely reserved for you thanks to your global goodwill and humanitarian efforts.

Add that to you're resume before joining corporate America where you are now a welcome member of the round table intent on finding the best and cheapest way to corner the urban market with a new and more powerful brand of malt liquor designed for inner city youth and promising more bang for the buck. So what if it's got a formaldehyde base. That's the bang. What do you want for a buck? Throw a warning sign on the bottle which let's the buyer know that this item may cause temporary blindness, seizures, sterility, diarrhea and should not be taken in conjunction with heart disease, high blood pressure or pregnancy and you're covered. At least you're not a pharmaceutical company you say to yourself on the long ride home to Massapequa.

Any regrets, qualms, or misgivings followed by anxiety attacks from you conscience about your input into the marketing of a product that may be detrimental to Black will be addressed at your weekly retreat on Friday evening, down at the local Blarney Stone on West 4th during happy hour.

All drinks are half-price and should help quench any misgivings about the nature of your latest endeavor. However, if this is not enough, there's a note attached to your paycheck that states that commission checks will be dispensed the following Monday and post genocidal counseling will

229

be provided each and every Thursday. The counseling is free of charge for all marketing employees.

I'll tell you one thing though; it's certainly not like that out here on 145th and Lenox. No, siree! Our fight is not over corporate politics or which ad will has the best success rate when it comes to reaching our target group. We ain't got no time to save the whales or the rainforests or play missionary when we get to feelin' a little guilty about how other folks is sufferin' around the world. We're too busy tryin' to eat and stay alive and look after each other and save ourselves from some more of your charitable good deeds in the name of the Almighty.

In fact, I would venture to bet that most of us would rather wait for the Second Coming than have y'all interpret any more of the good Lord's words for us. This reminds me of a poem I read some time ago where someone said 'they told me God was coming and I went and got myself a gun.'

Although that's neither here nor there. Anyway, that's part of the reason why I feel somewhat ashamed. I feel ashamed because I turned in my membership card. Sometimes it just gets too damn hard being African American and Negro and Colored and Black all at the same time with no set rules. Yesterday an Afro hairstyle signified militancy. Today it's the mandatory look for Blacks expecting to be employed in corporate America.

Yesterday, braids were the latest fashion. A couple of years ago I went down to the islands and every White girl down there was cornrowing their hair. Even Bo Derek got hers braided and it made her a 10. Allen Iverson did the same a few years back and every lil Black boy in America took heed and braided their hair the same way. Now it's considered a contentious, confrontational, radical hairstyle and you better not show up and think corporate America or any other

America's gonna hire you with them there braids in your hair. You militant, leftist, rabble-rouser.

I don't exactly know what makes it militant but militant it is although I've never in my seventy-six years had the opportunity to see one single solitary braid of hair stand up and shout 'Power to the People, Mao Tse Tung or Karl Marx forever' and then proceed to jump on someone and beat the livin' shit out of them in the name of equal rights or socialism or Black nationalism but then it's still early I suppose.

Chapter 2

Anyway, I turned in my membership card to the movement. Turned in my membership in the fight against racism, inequality and injustice for several reasons but mainly 'cause and for no other reason than I just got tired of being a nigga. You see there are no predetermined set of rules by which to play by. Like I said, the rules are constantly changing and you can be sure the winner in this game does not appear to be me or anyone that looks like me. And losing can be very costly and often times extremely painful. Anyway, to make a long story short the dues, got so damn high I just decided to quit being a nigga for awhile.

While I was, though, I'd like to think that I made a qualitative difference in some folk's lives. In fact, I know I did. But the bottom line is I dropped out. I have no excuse other than I just got tired and quit. And I'm ashamed because most Black folks ain't quitters. Our history attests to that fact. If we were, there wouldn't be a single skin darkie in America today. No, siree. What did Malcolm say? 'We've been hoodwinked, we've been bamboozled', and through all the shenanigans not only did we thrive, we multiplied. And do you know why? Because we had to. We were bred to survive. That's what the Middle Passage and the slave breeding thing was all about. It was a conscious effort to make us stronger, more resilient than those slaves that came before us.

You didn't know there were slaves here before us, did you? You didn't know because you've been severed from your own history and don't have the brains or the intelligence or the motivation or the insight to find out who you really are. That's another reason why I turned in

my membership. Ya got Black folks runnin' round here not bit more interested in where they're going or where they're comin' from than a man on the moon. And what makes it worse is it seems like they just don't care. And I'm sayin' how can you not care when Malcolm and Martin and Nat and ol' John Brown gave their lives for you. But I don't blame you because you didn't know that and it's no surprise that you don't know these things because the slavemaster forbid you to read then and makes sure with his control of the educational system that you can't read now. So how would you know?

Anyways like I was sayin'. There were slaves here in America prior to Black folk. In fact, we weren't even the second choice for manumission. (That's just another word for slavery in case ya'll ain't know). In all actuality, we were the third choice.

Hold on just a second Youngblood, while I run in here and grab me a pint of the grape and I'll break it down for you proper like, 'cause I can see it. Yes siree! I can see the hunger in your eye, for this here bit of knowledge I'm about to bestow on you. I can see you're hungry for the straight, uncut, unabashed, unadulterated truth that most street corner philosophers just don't have the overall knowledge to bring to you.

Most of 'em is runnin' around these here streets spewin' out all kinds of crazy rhetoric about the Black man bein' the original man and how he's god and all that but that ain't helping you in your daily plight. Then they throw a tablespoon or two of some numerology in the mix and you s'pozed to go home and be able to provide for your family when your minimum wage ain't quite

232

makin' the trip even though you done put in your forty plus hours. And that's why I like Obama so much.

Obama says that a man who works forty hours in America should not be poor but there's plenty of 'em that's po' as dirt. At least he sees and recognizes and brings some hope to the hopeless. He's asking America the tough questions. He's asking what happens to that man that's out there scufflin' and tryna put food on the table for hisself and his kids and can't seem to make end meet? I don't know if answered that but I'll tell you what happens 'cause it done happened to me on mo' than one occasion.

You go home and you done lost all your respect from your wife and your kids 'cause you ain't providing for them like you used to or you's supposed to as a man. You start to get down on yourself for the very same reasons. You start to lose all respect for yourself even though you still doin' your best to make it and hold your head up high. Hard as you try, you ain't feedin' your younguns no more, the rent is due—hell, the rent is always due—and your woman is now making more than you and has taken over just about all of the financial responsibilities. To make matters worse, when you go to file taxes, she's the one filing as head of household.

If that ain't bad enough, when you turn to go to put your arm around her and try to be a man in the only manner left for you, she turns and breaks it all down to you in four easy words as she puts another spoonful of that whole kernel corn you hate so much on your plate with the rice and gravy. You wonderin' where the meat is but you afraid to ask 'cause you sure as hell can't buy

none. And you can't even get it on credit now that ol' Saul is dead. Anyways, you go to put your arm around her and she let's you know that she ain't feelin' you no more; at least like that. And you figger it's probably cause you ain't makin' enough and can't provide for her and the kids like you used to. Or maybe it's the fact that she's tired from working two full-time jobs and frustrated 'cause there ain't never enough to go around.

You try to tell yourself that at least you out there workin' but by this time you done spoiled her good. She's use to better and let's you know that—in no uncertain terms—when she turns to yo' ass looks you square in yo' eye and tells you in no uncertain terms that 'dick don't pay bills…' That's what she tells you right in front of yo' younguns. Yep, those are her words. And she ain't stutter a bit. She just come right out and says, 'Dick don't pay bills'. Now how you feel, my brotha?

Well, the way I figure it, you probably slams the door and walks the fuck out hopin' there's somethin' out here in these here streets to ease that pain. You know that whatever it is that gonna set you right and ease the pain, ol' lady Harlem's got it so you walk a half a block and the dope man's waitin' for you like sweet pussy after a six month stretch upstate.

You know you still got that twenty folded up in the corner of your wallet tighter than a witches tit just savin' it for a rainy day and things ain't never looked drearier than they do right through here. You also know that that dope ain't nothin' but a two minute high and you only gonna feel worse when you come down. Plus when you git home she gonna know right away that you been

gittin' high and that ain't gonna do nothin' but make shit worser than it already is 'cause that twenty you just spent with the dope man coulda been a piece of meat.

The liquor stores open. Hell, the liquor stores always open up here in Harlem and you know liquor's quicker but what you feelin' tonight ain't even gonna be close to what you gonna feel tomorrow when it's time to go see the man in the mornin'. And minimum wage or no minimum wage, one thing's fo' sho'. Minimum beats a blank by a long shot. Besides after lookin' at me and them other winos standin' out there drinkin' and in my present condition you probably sayin' to yourself. Hell, things can't possibly be that bad.

So, you wind up talkin' to these street corner philosophers as if they can fulfill your needs and alleviate the stress you feelin' right through here when in reality my brother the only person that can alleviate the stress and anguish you're feelin' is you and the way you do that is by gainin' knowledge of self. That

234

will in turn give you some insight as to why you're in the predicament you're in.

You see my brother, when you find out where you come from then you can find out who you are, why you're in the particular situation you're in and where you need to be headin'. Once you find out from whence you come then you can figure out where yo' ass is going. That's what I had to do, my brother. Then and only then can you plot a course as to what steps need to be taken to get you where you want to go.

When I was your age I didn't understand why shit seemed to keep happening to me all the time. Didn't seem to be no rhyme or reason. At least I didn't believe there was. And shit just kept

happenin' to me but at the same time I had this insatiable thirst. I was thirsty. And it wasn't for no wine at the time. I was thirsty for knowledge. And speaking of thirsty, if I'm gonna impart some more wisdom on you I'd better wet my pallet before I get started. Can you spare a buck or so? 'Preciate that my brotha.

Aah yes, now where was I? Oh, yeah! The bottom line is you have to know where you are and why you're here. You have to first ask yourself, why am I in the situation I'm in. That's essential. Let's forget the fact that we are the original man and all that other good shit the Five Per Centers are preachin'. I been there. Done that. Nothin' personal. They reachin' some of the young bloods and they're positive. So, I guess that's good. What more can I say? But the fact that we were or were not here on this here earth first holds little relevance as to why we're here right now and why we're in the position we're in.

We are here in America today and at this time for one reason and one reason only and that is because the slaves that preceded us were not capable of doing the hard labor. Period. Point blank. No need to beat around the bush about that shit. We are here only because the Native American formerly known as Indians could not do the work expected of them. They wilted and died. And even though they were quite numerous—at least at first they were—the bottom line was that they just couldn't cut the mustard. They suffered from every kind of disease and

235

malady known to man when they were relocated and put to work in that torturous, southern sun.

Indentured servants were then brought in to replace the Indians, and fared somewhat better, and were supposed to work the land for a period of as long as seven years before they were given some land and their freedom but there was a scarcity of people ready to give up seven years of their lives and their departure, after fulfilling their obligation did not help the labor shortage. So, that system was short-lived.

Wanna hear somethin' hard to believe, Young blood? At one point the labor shortage got so bad that Great Britain promised freedom and land for criminals locked up in English jails if they'd put in the time and effort to farm Georgia. Didn't know that did you, Youngblood?

I got family down there in Georgia but I make it a point not to go nowhere south of the Mason Dixon Line. If you ask me their all a bunch a criminals is what they are. Always have been, always will be. If England got rid of 'em for disruptin' shit and preying on their own fellow Englishmen then just imagine how they gonna treat a nigga. I love my family but they gots to be coming this way they expects for me to see 'em. I don't nowhere's near Georgia no matter what they say 'bout it bein' the New South. I still remember the ol' South and ain't too many fond recollections. Anyway, my family—what's left of 'em down there—they know that. I tells 'em every time they ask. I ain't never comin' back but they can feel free to reach out and touch, but that's about as far as I go.

In any case, by this time, the Europeans were quite familiar with the African and had observed us in a lot of different venues. (That means places or settings, in case you ain't know).

For instance a pretty substantial number of us came over with the Dutch and Henry Hudson and I'm not sure if they were indentured servants or what made him tote them along initially but one thing I do know; they won't no slaves. In fact, several of them became rather large landowners out on Long Island and down in Lower Manhattan. I just read an article pertainin' to this area recently in the Anthropological Digest. They was tellin' how the Indians of Manhattan Island got swindled out of Manhattan. And since it seemed pretty interesting I found myself somewhat compelled to read it.

Anyway, it seems that after trading the island away they became extremely upset after they took them there trinkets and gold beads, given as payment for Manhattan, to the local pawn shop and found out that that shit won't nothin' but some costume jewelry.

Now, from what I understand or better yet inferred from my own research what they basically wanted was a full refund which was only fair if you ask me. But when the Dutch refused and wouldn't return Manhattan to them, which would have been the correct thing to do under the circumstances the natives pitched a bitch and began attacking the Dutch settlement like there was no tomorrow. And since they were so relentless, (that means persistent just in case you ain't know), the Dutch granted the Africans they'd brought along their own area. This turned out to be a rather large parcel of land around Wall Street and acted as buffer between them and the Indians since the Indians and Blacks had no real beef to speak of. This way they killed two birds with

one stone. By granting the Africans their own parcel of land they segregated themselves from the Africans and put a buffer between themselves and the Indians who were now out for Dutch blood as retribution, (that's payback, in case you didn't know). But do you believe that? Everything I'm telling you is the God's honest truth. I swear to you. I read it just the other night and believe you me I sat there with my mouth wide open, just like you are now, the whole time too.

Just listenin' to myself rehash what happened again is giving me goose bumps. Our history does that to me you know. And this dampness in the air ain't helpin'

237

much either. Sometimes my joints get to achin' so bad with the arthritis and all. The only thing that really offsets it is a little red wine every now and then. Pardon me for interruptin' but I really could use a little somethin' to take the chill outta my bones. Do you think you could see fit to spare me another buck or so so I can grab a pint? That's only if you can spare it though. I hate to ask anyone to support my bad habits. It's just that it's been a rather rough day with what happened wit' my boy Sweet and all.

You know me. You know I don't usually let myself get strung out like this 'specially in public. It's just not professional. And if you ask anyone in Harlem they'll tell you that William Longfellow III is the consummate professional.

Anyway, Black folks were given homes down there on Wall Street to act as a buffer between the Indians and the Dutch. And this is a most interesting fact. There was no wall there at all. Black folks built a wall to keep the Indians at bay, which it did to some extent. And that's how the

center of the world's financial district came into being and known as Wall Street. That's just a little trivia for you but the fact of the matter is that we weren't brought here initially as slaves.

However, the English were viewing these free Blacks and others that were dispersed pretty liberally throughout all the colonies and noticed that when subjected to the same conditions as both indentured servants and Indians, Blacks seemed to respond better to the conditions. Truth of the matter was that we were immune to the hardships that befell the other two groups of forced laborers in part because the climactic conditions in the South were similar to those in Africa and this is the very reason why slavery had its inception and we are here today.

I said all that to say that we arrived here free and in relatively small numbers at first but when the English eventually pushed the Dutch, French and the Spanish from the continent they found that with all this rich, barren land they were in dire need of a labor force if the colonies were going to flourish monetarily and be a boon to the mother country.

When they discovered that Africa boasted an almost infinite labor source the African slave trade began in earnest. This, in turn, caused the rights of free Blacks already here to be infringed upon. In layman's terms the English saw the possibilities of a free labor source, equated that into dollar signs and lost their fuckin' minds. Wasn't long after that that the selection process began in earnest. To say the whole process was extremely discriminatory, (that means choosy or selective, just in case you ain't know), would be an understatement.

Now don't get me wrong, I'm not trying to be demeaning so don't be offended but sometimes I get so carried away when I see a receptive mind that I get to marchin' ahead and playin' my flute like I'm the pied piper and every now and then I forget to look back to see if anyone's followin'. I just want you to understand what I'm sayin' Youngblood.

Anyway, the English were ruthless as hell and when they found out they could profit off the backs of the African they jumped in with both feet. They knew exactly what they were looking for. They wanted the best Africa had to offer. They wanted the biggest, strongest and the brightest. That was their goal and they pretty much achieved it and in turn, depleted the African continent of its most important resource. Us. But the selection process didn't stop there so I won't stop there.

The process of elimination or Darwinism really came into play after the selection process ended. Those Africans that were slight of heart or not supremely fit physically died or were killed off during the Middle Passage. And it didn't get any easier during slavery.

In fact, conditions worsened. But the Darwinist ideology continued and we were bred like Kentucky thoroughbreds to achieve the perfect physical specimen. What Hitler wished for is what we were, a superior race of human beings. And if you want proof just take a look at any major league sport. There is not one that we don't dominate. And they know this. That's why they feel so threatened and try to keep us down or locked up or spaced out. They know in their hearts that anytime we are given an equal opportunity we'll excel and end up beating them at their own game; no matter what it is.

But hold on. Let me just digress for just a moment so I can elaborate. Look at baseball. How long was the game of baseball around before Jackie Robinson hit the big leagues?

You say you don't know. Well let me tell you. I just came across an article the other day that said Abner Doubleday didn't invent the game of baseball as was originally thought. They claim that baseball has been around since the 1850's or 60's. That's close to a hundred years before they brought Jackie up to the majors and in the last fifty years alone we've broken every major league record that's stood for a century and a half. And we didn't just break the records. We shattered them. What did Babe Ruth hit, sixty or so homeruns in one season? Then that ol' chocolate boy from somewhere down south of the border, Sammy Sosa went hog wild and I think either he or Barry Bonds obliterated the Babes record. I'm not real sure but one of 'em hit close to eighty dingers in one season alone. Some players don't hit eighty homeruns in a career and this man did it in one season. Bonds is so good that they come up with an allegation a day trying to discredit him. Talkin' bout he's on drugs. Hell, our last two presidents were on drugs. I ain't heard no allegations there.

Then there's tennis. Do I have to name the names? Right now, you got two sisters with basically no formal training to speak of dominating the sport. One year one takes the number one position. The next year the other one takes it. It got so bad that for a while that they ended up just playing

each other in the finals 'cause there was no other competition to speak of. And that's with no formal training in another all-white sport. Put 'em in the Olympics, as doubles partners, playing against the best in the world and all their opponents do at the end of the match is walk away shaking their heads. Any questions?

Is there a need to bring up professional basketball? What more is there to be said? In the 1996 Olympics, the Dream Team was composed of eight African-Americans, one brother from the Caribbean, another from Africa and two White boys, neither of whom should have even been awarded a spot except that whoever was on the selection committee thought that the coffee was too strong and decided to add some milk for good measure. Of course they dominated, beating the world by an average of thirty or forty points a night.

Let's skip to the country club scene, which is still a bastion of white faces and where golf is the main event. Now here comes half-a- nigga who sneaked in under the fence talking about he Afri-Asian, Amerasian or some other shit he done thought up to disassociate himself from the plague of racism. Nothin but a confused brother but he's a tiger on that golf course that's one thing that was clear from day one. Well, he certainly rocked their world. What was the Iraq offensive called? Shock and awe? Well, that's exactly what m'boy Tiger did to the world of golf.

Stepping in from out of the shadows not quite sure about his ethnicity, Tiger took the world of golf by storm and if he had any question about his ancestry when he started he certainly didn't have any when he finished. You can best believe they let him know who he was and where he

stood with them before he finished the eighteenth and final hole. 'Say boy, where you headed after you win the Masters, Disney World or KFC?"

Another niggra, by the name of Jesse Owens let Hitler and his so-called superior Aryan nation know about true world domination in the 1936 Olympics when he won about four hundred gold medals in track and field under Hitler's watchful eye. They say Owens was so overwhelmingly dominant in those Olympics that Hitler went up to his retreat in the mountains, to rework Mein Kampf to include Blacks in his Final Solution.

Boxin's no different. As soon as they let us into the game it was over. But White folks should've seen that one comin'. After kicking Black folk's ass for four hundred years you know niggas was just waitin' for some git back. The brothas was waitin' in line to step into the ring. They didn't care who they were fighting.

All they wanted to know was 'where the cracker at'? Once in the ring, it was the same ol' story.

Heard one niggra say, 'remember my great grandfather? You know, ol' Uncle Remus the nigga y'all kept lightin' fire to down at the mill. Here's a left hook. Pow! I know you felt that right down to yo' toes. That's for Uncle Remus. And remember that little girl; the one you used to grab and feel on everyday on her way to school and toss into the woods and have your way with. That was my cousin Merley Sue. This one here's for her.' A chopping uppercut would soon follow; lifting Joe 'White' Boy clear off the canvas and into the first row of seats. But before he could land good there was another flurry of lefts and rights, a jab or two, another straight right followed by another uppercut and then a chopping overhand right and a thunderous left hook that sent shivers through the crowd right behind it. All was silent and the decision rendered as the fallen boxer finally regained consciousness and was escorted to his corner. Both boxers met at the center of the ring and hugged in the name of good sportsmanship as Joe 'White' Boy wiped the blood from the bridge of his nose, his lip and the deep gash over his right eye, which was closing quickly, then leaned over and whispered, 'good fight, boy'.

The brotha hugged him back then leaned over and whispered back as the crowd cheered the good sportsmanship, "Yeah, you too peckerwood. That little ass whoopin' there was for all my relatives on my momma's side of the family."

To which the White boy replied, "Ain't none of y'all niggas got daddies?"

"Yeah, I got a daddy but my brother Lucius' scheduled to fight yo' ass next week and he representin' all the atrocities y'all committed to my daddy's side of the family. And from what I hear, they far worse than what y'all did to my mother's side so expect a thorough ass whoopin' next week as well.

Jack Johnson, Joe Louis, Muhammad Ali, were just a few of those that were waiting in line to complete the total domination of the sport. There are other sports and other athletes. Far too many for me to name but I'm sure you get my drift. And that's all thanks to the English that landed on Plymouth Rock. After selecting what they considered the best stock available, then trimming the herd on the way over, and breeding us once we arrived, what are we left with? We're left with the best and the brightest of the species.

Chapter 3

In my estimation, no other group of people, aside from the Jews, in recent history has been subjected to such inhumane treatment and survived. But not only did we survive, we thrived. And not only did we thrive we multiplied. This reality, this tiny piece of our history, in and of itself, was for a long time enough to make me feel proud to be an African-American.

And the simple fact remains. Despite everything, we persevered and triumphed as a people. We fought and scratched and maintained until we were in a position to afford ourselves a change for the better. More often than not, when we were given the opportunity to rise from the ashes we did, winning the right to vote, the right to equal education and housing and a number of other significant gains in the name of civil rights.

Martin and Malcolm and a host of others too numerous to name fought the good fight and gave their lives so our children and our children's children would have the opportunities afforded to us. Hell, I remember me, myself, getting thrown in the back of a paddy wagon for picketing just so's Negroes could vote and make a difference in their own lives, just so they could control their own destinies.

At that particular time I was workin' as a personal attaché to Dr. King. That's right, I knew the good doctor personally. Worked with him for years on a number of projects... He and I was doin' that non-violent thing and although I wasn't really feelin' it all that much I liked Martin

and since he insisted on this being the strategy for the movement I went along 'cause out of all the strategies I thought this was the most viable, (that means workable or doable, in case you ain't know). Me personally, I had seen enough of death and dying during the war and being that I had gotten out of that one alive I wasn't too much with taking any more chances. And bein' that I still couldn't shoot worth a tinkers damn I wasn't really feelin' that particular vibe all that much. So, for me, a violent revolution was pretty much out of the question.

Most of the militant brothas was angry with the direction me and Martin wanted to go. They was pretty adamant 'bout wantin' to go to war but they ain't really know nothin' 'bout no war. Besides, war just didn't seem feasible. We didn't own a damn thing. I mean think about it. How you gonna go to war against the number one arms maker in the world. What you gonna' say? Sir, I just ran outta bullets shootin' at you. Could you please see fit to give me anotha magazine full of bullets, a few hand grenades and a half a dozen mortars so I can shoot at you some more?

Now just because I liked the man personally, that's not to say that there wasn't some chinks in the armor with Dr. King's strategy. I didn't say that. Can't say that. They was still whoopin' the hell out of us and we was non-violent. But by the same token I had the common sense to realize that we wasn't dead which meant that we could rise up and fight again another day. But let me tell you something you might not know. This wasn't no new, original theory that Dr. King come up with. But see most Black folks ain't studied history the way I has and they ain't aware of the fact that Dr. King was simply using tactics developed by Gandhi when he was leading his people

against the English in the early part of the last century. Truth of the matter is there was plenty of examples of non-violence in action long before Gandhi's movement in India.

Remember that little Jew boy from Bethlehem. He was probably the first ever to be documented as the leader of a pacifist movement. He was non-violent, practiced civil-disobedience and would have probably lived a full life had he just listened to some of his boys that had his back and his well being at heart. But they said he heard voices and when he did no one could talk to him. Nevertheless, there were still quite a few people who warned him but he overstepped his limit when he started messin' with them Jews tryin' to prohibit them from gamblin' in the temple. They pretty much told him how he could be non-violent all he wanted but don't go down there fuckin' aroun' wit' 'dem Jews wit' they money if he wanted to live. But he wouldn't listen to nobody but 'dem voices. And of course we all know what happened. They killed him dead, dead, dead. Dead as he gonna die. Strung him up to a pole, they did. Else he might have seen his legacy come to fruition during his lifetime.

There were other examples of non-violence in action like Frederick Douglass who repeatedly chanted to no one in particular and always behind closed doors, 'Agitate! Agitate! Agitate!', and that was during slavery but he wasn't no fool. It was always behind closed doors or over in Europe during one of his speeches. But he ain't never ever considered no armed resistance. He'd been a slave so he knew what the master was capable of. He had first hand experience. He might have supported John Brown's effort for overthrow of the government on paper but he let him

know in no uncertain terms that he wouldn't be able to meet him for lunch, brunch or anything else he had planned that day at Harper's Ferry.

So, you see Martin wasn't the first to choose non-violent resistance and Martin being a learned man, studied the plight of Jesus, Gandhi and Thoreau, the forerunners of civil disobedience and knew deep down in his heart, that this was the only possible choice that Black folks had if they was going to overcome someday.

Anyway, Black folks was gainin' ground through Martin's strategy of non-violence and forcin' them to make a few concessions here and there and every time they busted the head of some niggra refusing to fight back they showed it on ABC and CBS and the public outcry was one of utter and complete outrage.

You see, Youngblood, there ain't too many people, Black or white who ain't gonna feel some compassion when they see a little girl beaten with a billy club and dragged down the street by a cop in full riot gear or a little boy reachin' for his momma who's being dragged by her hair and thrown into the back of a paddy wagon while German Shepherds rip and tear at his pants leg. I said all that to say that although I thought Dr. King's strategy had some serious flaws it was better than the rest. At least for me it was. Still, there were times when I had a hard time conformin' to his non-violent tactics.

I'll never forget joinin' Reverend Abernathy down in Selma. I believe Dr. King was s'pozed to join us. He'd just delivered a beautiful speech on how we were winning the war on poverty and gainin' tremendous ground but we had to remain strong and steadfast while maintainin' our self-control in the face of the enemy who was literally proddin' and provokin' us at every turn to stoop to his level.

During this time, Dr. King made it perfectly clear that we must stay true to the movement, committed to achieving our goals through self-discipline and self-restraint in the face of the enemy no matter what they did to induce us into acts of violence. As always he was eloquent and I gotta admit I was truly moved by his words. But then he could do that. He had that power. He had that ability that few men have to move you and inspire you with a simple sermon. And whether I believed him or not the next thing I knew I found myself up and cheering with the rest of the congregation.

We were scheduled to march in a day or two and everyone was prepared and I'm sure—although no one showed it—we were more than a little apprehensive and a bit scared. You see we had televisions too and we saw the way they was manhandlin' niggras, and whoopin' heads straight across the South. And we knew that Selma wouldn't be no different.

By the time the march came 'round, we was petrified. I think most of us just wanted to do the damn thing and get it over with but something happened in the interim and they jailed Dr. King with the hopes of squelching the march. And to tell the truth I was sorta relieved by this latest

development. But people were coming in from all over the country. And not one to be deterred, Dr. King got the word out that we were to proceed with or without him and so me, Reverend Abernathy, Bayard Rustin and a few other notables stood in for Dr. King and the march began peaceably enough. But somewhere along the parade root the Selma police began showing up in large numbers. Still, we had our directive and the procession continued without incident. Well, almost without incident. I'd bought into Dr. King's philosophy one hundred per cent and vowed that if anything kicked off I would by no means be the weakest link.

In any case, the Selma police marched alongside of us uttering all kinds of obscenities and innuendos in an attempt to make us lose our composure and demean us to the point where we would do something stupid so they'd have a reason for dragging us off to join Dr. King in one of those rat infested urinals they call a jail.

Now, I've met a few law enforcement officers in my time but those Selma, Alabama police were some of the nastiest, most vile excuses for civil servants I've ever had the occasion to meet. And it angered them that they could not provoke us. They seemed to care little that the television cameras were on them and continued to hurl obscenities in our direction.

By the same token, I was quite enamored by the exposure and was glad I'd spent the little extra money I'd saved on my marching attire. I had just purchased a black turtleneck, some black double knit polyester trousers and a new pair of black patent leather kicks from Florsheim's down on 34th Street and you couldn't tell me I wasn't looking good. I'd seen those shoes in the

store window on my way home from work one day and had been planning on buying them when my ends got right. I'd been saving for the past three months and was glad that I'd put in the overtime at work now. You see, I knew there would be honeys from all over the country coming in for the march and I certainly wanted to look my best just in case the opportunity arose and one of those honeys caught my eye. And by the time Selma rolled around, I was right sharp just like I planned.

Anyway, I'm marchin' along with what seemed like a hundred thousand, (even though the press claims there were only thirty thousand of us), loyal King supporters and this White cop is shadowing me the whole way tellin' me how he couldn't see my face with all that black on and askin' me to smile so there's a contrast between me and my outfit so he can keep an eye on me. Then he starts tellin' me how he slept wit' my momma last night and how good she was and starts askin' me if I'm absolutely sure that he's not my daddy. All of which, I ignored in the name of non-violence and the good Dr. King. Then he starts tellin' me how big my mama is down there and how she still cried when he stuck it to her. And all the while I'm smilin' and he's smilin' and this fine young sista who I'd met the night before grabs my hand and tells me to ignore this ignorant fool which is hardly a problem 'cause she and I had spent a pretty good amount of time together the night before and were planning to have dinner together in my suite when the march was over. So, you know I wasn't takin' this fool cop seriously. He wasn't even a minor distraction. Hell, I'd grown up playin' the dozens with some of the meanest niggas you'll ever find. I mean these niggas would sit home and do research and dig deep into your family tree

like they was Alex Haley or somebody until they found something or someone that they knew would strike a nerve or push a button.

So, I knew in the back of my mind that there was no way in hell that I was going to let this little southern, red-necked, toy cop rain on my parade and jeopardize my evening wit' this fine ass sista. Not knowing me she grabbed my hand and squeezed it tightly to distract me and I was almost glad that ol' red necked, hillbilly was there acting as a catalyst for ol' girl to hold my hand.

He continued his onslaught and I continued to smile and the more he talked the louder I sang,

We shall, we shall not be moved,

We shall, we shall not be moved.

Just like a bridge that's standing by the w-a-t-e-r

We shall not be moved.

And I wasn't either. No matter what he   said I could not be moved.

248

I was following Dr. King's strategy of non-violence to the letter. And any time he'd say something particularly malicious I'd start singin' again, each time getting a little bit louder with

the hope of drowning him out. But I really couldn't drown him out 'cause he was one persistent motherfucker.

I wasn't the only one suffering this abuse and I was glad to see my brethren exhibiting the same self-restraint in the face of adversity and I, in turn found a renewed since of resolve from observing their behavior.

At about this point, the street narrowed and we headed into the main street of some little hick southern town and the officer who had been chiding me, (that means fucking with my head, in case you ain't know). Anyway, this cop who by now has gotten on my last non-violent nerve is pressing up against me now. His jokes and cruel insinuations spent, he resorts to simply callin' me nigger at regular intervals. Realizing that he's exhausted his barrage of slurs and insults and has got to be as tired as I am from all that there walking and he even more so with all that shit on around his waist, I smiled, knowing that Dr. King was right in his assertion when he said that bigotry and hatred can never flourish in the face of love and righteousness.

I wanted to laugh at him now but realized that that was not the Christian way and was content to simply finish the march and proceed with my evening as planned, when we passed an alley way and this simple ass, southern red-neck cop, not watching where he's going trips and steps right smack dab on my new patent leather slip-on loafers that I'd just purchased for one hundred and twenty-nine dollars and ninety-nine cents, on sale, from Florsheim's, especially for this occasion.

To top that off he stepped on my foot, the one with the bunion on my pinky toe. Lord have mercy. Talk about some excruciating pain.

Before I could think about restraint and non-violence and the tactics Dr. King employed; before I could think about the strategy of self-restraint and the good and righteous Dr. King. Before I could think about doing my part for the upliftment of my people or the quiet resolve needed to help make this act of civil disobedience a success. Before I could contemplate that tight little ass of that fine little fox next to me and the surprises I hoped the night would bring if I just played my cards right. Before I could think of any of those things I'd grabbed that red-necked son-of-a-bitch into the alley by the nape of his neck and beat the ever lovin', livin' hell, out of him before you could say Jackie Robinson.

I kicked him so many times with that sore foot with the bunion that it was pulsating like the second hand of a Delancey Street watch. I had to limp the rest of the way which was another good ten or twelve miles. When I left him, he was curled up in a fetal position unable to move. So, I dragged him behind one of those big ol' industrial waste containers, threw his gun and nightstick in the container so he couldn't beat no more niggas heads that he figgered looked like me. And then, just as if nothing had transpired, I left. I don't mean I left the march. I stayed with the march 'til the very end. I ain't stupid. That was my cover. But when the march was over, I left. I mean I got the hell up outta Alabama. I didn't even go back to my hotel suite to pick up my belongings. No siree, Bob. I went straight to the Greyhound and got on the first thing smokin'. Blew my date with that sweet little honey with the tight lil' round ass and left praying every minute 'til I got back to Harlem.

A year or so later, they assassinated Dr. King and it was one of the saddest days of my life. I still 'til this day feel fortunate to have been able to have been in the presence of such greatness though it truly saddens me that there seems no connection or correlation from the Civil Rights Movement to our children. Parents want to blame the children and the school systems but ultimately I am in agreement with Bill Cosby, (although I am of the belief that he is at this point in his life where he is, as I am, extremely frustrated with the stagnation among Black folks in general). And after the struggle that we've endured it's a shame, a downright disgrace that we have for the most part forsaken the struggle in lieu of some pocket change and a new pair of sneakers.

I swear it don't make me wanna do nothin' but turn in my membership card again. But I recollect I'll feel better tomorrow when I ain't quite so drunk and see if Obama needs some help wit' his campaign. After all, and for some of us the struggle don't neva stop.

SAUL GREENBERG

Chapter 1

It hadn't seemed so long ago since she'd graduated from the University of Pittsburgh as a criminal justice major. It seemed like only yesterday that, she envisioned herself in a crowded courtroom, reporters mulling around her, microphones jammed in her face prosecuting the biggest case of the year. She could see it as clear as the day Mama had gotten sick not long after graduation and postponed those dreams.

Lacy smiled as she walked the now, all too familiar beat, nine millimeter rubbing against her right thigh abrasively. She adjusted the standard issue, and continued walking the last stretch of Eighth Avenue down past Sherman's Barbeque until she reached Greenberg's little Jewish grocery store.

Saul Greenberg and his little grocery was a permanent fixture sitting inconspicuously between the liquor store and The First Abyssinian Church of Christ. Greenberg's grocery had been a part of the Harlem scenery as long as she could remember, with its empty shelves and over time evolved into nothing more than a meat market. Greenberg's had been a part of the Harlem landscape as long as she could remember. She remembered her mother pulling her from the street games she loved so much like jacks and double-dutch to have her walk her down

to pick up a piece of fatback or a ham hock to go with the greens she ate each and everyday. Lacy hated every minute of the five minute jaunt knowing that Mr. Saul was going to go into one of his long tirades on the detriments of pork. It all seemed so ludicrous since he sold it nonetheless.

The neighborhood had changed since then. Now drugs had garnered a permanent residence in Harlem right alongside the storefront churches, liquor stores, and off-track betting parlors. It wasn't housed in any particular building but it was there, making its presence felt. More than anything else dope changed the Harlem landscape making Lacy's job just that much harder.

It made fixtures like Mr. Saul's grocery a prime target but as of yet he hadn't been touched and where other Jewish businesses headed for the suburbs, Mr. Saul had remained, and believe it or not unscathed.

Still, he like everyone else nowadays was leery. He'd seen the nicest sweetest people kids grow up and get hooked on that shit until he hardly recognized them anymore. Their souls gone, they were like animals, prowling the streets in search of their prey and no one was off-limits. Anybody was vulnerable now. Anybody thought to have more than a few dollars in their pockets could be robbed, beaten and even murdered at almost any time. Saul was an obvious target but up until now, Jehovah has blessed him. First of all, he was White and

secondly he was making his money off of the community and Black people who didn't know Saul didn't like the politics. Saul never worried arriving at work each morning at six a.m. Dawn was a quiet time in Harlem. The streets were quiet by that time and the dope fiends were exhausted from hustling all night were usually fast asleep by that time. And the only one's awake were the hardworking. But on a Friday night, or a payday weekend Saul Greenberg was a prime target and he knew it. Lacy knew it too. She worried about him constantly. Fact of the matter was she worried about everyone on her beat even the porters, maids, and busboys heading downtown to work. She worried but that didn't mean she wouldn't throw their asses in jail if they crossed the line.

Stepping into the store, she smiled at the old man.

"Good day, Mr. Greenberg?" she questioned matter-of-factly.

"Everyday, I'm able to get out of bed and stand upright is a good day, Lacy. You probably didn't know it from my good looks but I'm no spring chicken anymore," he chuckled.

"Boy, between you and mama I've never seen two people talk about age as much as you two do. You'll probably both end up living another forty or fifty

years and looking down at me." Saul Greenberg smiled at the thought of living another forty years.

"I'll tell you the truth Lacy, if I pass away today, God has granted me a pretty good life for a little Jew boy that came to this country with nothing but the shirt on his back." The old man smiled as he pulled the arm down on the meat slicer and wiped the remaining cuts of meat from the blade.

"Yes sir, he's granted me a pretty good life, if I must say so myself. By the way, how's your mother doing, Lacy?" he asked. Still as beautiful as ever, I'm sure. You know I used to have quite an eye for the ladies back in the day I was kinda handsome and a young whippersnapper. Used to have my fair share of ladies, too. But your mother... Well, that woman was a different story. She had the looks of an African goddess. I'll never forget the first time she came in here. She was in an entirely different league. It was a Friday. And you know how Friday's can be around here. The war had just ended and the Depression

253

wasn't too far behind us. People were just starting to get back on their feet. I had a line of customers a mile long when she stepped in. I'll never forget that day. The neighborhood was still about fifty per cent Jewish and this old Jewish woman... Oh what was her name?" Lacy interrupted.

"Ms. Weinstein," she added hoping to quicken the process.

"Yes, Ms. Weinstein."

The old man glanced up from the sink where he was rinsing the washrag of all the remnants of meat from the meat slicer before folding it neatly and draping it over the faucet. "Are you trying to say you've heard this story before?" the old man asked incredulously. "Oh, maybe once or twice," Lacy lied, smiling and avoiding his gaze. But it hardly stopped the butcher from reminiscing.

"Yes, sir! She reminded me of an Egyptian princess—maybe Nefertiti. Not that I've ever seen an Egyptian goddess, but I'm sure if I had she would resemble your mother on that day.

Anyway, I was waiting on this ol' Jewish woman, Mrs. Weinstein. She was a pretty good customer, a regular, you know, but I'll ell you the truth Lacy I used to hate to see her coming. At the time, everything was relatively cheap but she was ridiculous. She used to complain about everything—I mean everything. She'd come in and order fifteen cents of this and ten of that and every time she'd order.

I'd have to clean the blade. Didn't really bother me but she'd come in everyday and do the same thing and I used to ask myself why in the hell doesn't this woman save her pennies like the rest of us do and do all of her shopping on Friday at one time. I never had the gall to ask her but I wondered. Still do. Never did figure that one out but anyway..."Lacy smiled.

"Maybe she was sweet on you, Mr. Greenberg."

The old man ignored her remarks and continued.

"Anyway your mother steps through the door and I damn near cut my hand off when I saw her. I have no idea what I gave to Mrs. Weinstein that day but I botched her order pretty well because the next day she came in ranting and raving about how she was going to take her business down to Palmer's Meats if I couldn't get her order right," Mr. Greenberg chuckled. "Her order right? Nobody's order was right that day including your mother's. Heck, everything she asked me for I doubled just so she'd come back and I could see her again. That was the last time my business was in the black, the last time Greenberg's Meats ever showed a profit was the day before your mother came in. I've been given her my profit ever since just trying to get her to look my way... But she never did. And it wasn't up until a couple of years ago that I got the nerve to talk to her. She's been coming in here for close to twenty-five years and it's only been in the last two that I've gotten up the nerve to talk to her and I still couldn't tell her how I felt. He was closing up his briefcase now and lacy knew that today for the first time there was not only sincerity but some regret in the old man's tone. He looked down as he fastened the clasps on his attached and sighed heavily.

For the first time in a long time, he felt the wear and tear of the years and they seemed to have suddenly exploded all at once like fireworks at a July Fourth Celebration.   Lacy glanced at the old man who was now staring blankly. Lacy spoke softly breaking the uncomfortable silence she now felt and releasing from his thoughts.

Just as quickly, Saul Greenberg returned to her world, to his playful old self that Lacy had come to know and so admire ever since she could remember.

"Are you ready to go, Mr. Greenberg?" she asked rather nonchalantly.

The old man groaned then sighed as he rose from the tiny desk at the back of the shop.

"I guess I'm as ready as I'll ever be," he said turning the Open sign to Closed and drawing the blind on both windows before stepping outside to roll up the frayed green canopy.

They went through the same ritual every day as she took the pole from him hooked it in the circle and began to roll in the green canopy with the words Greenberg's Grocery on it. When she finished she placed the pole in the back room and joined the old man, key on hand, as he lock the door.

Several years ago, he'd had a hard time accepting the fact that he was growing older, and was now fair game for the criminals that now roamed the streets of Harlem. Back then he would tell her that he didn't need anyone to walk him to the '61 Rambler parked only a block or so away but his humiliation grew more and more futile as time went on and his attempts at feigning anger and disgust became muted and less frequent as she ignored his pleas.

After awhile he not only accepted her walking him to his car but welcomed it. Now it was routine. Even on her day off, she made sure that there was always someone there to walk him the block or so to his car. When she had a premonition, she would call and remind the officer of the day to have someone to stop by and check on the old man.

Lacy was not the only one fond of Saul Greenberg and after her father left the house, she would hear her mother ranting and raving and carrying on about how men weren't shit. The only good man she'd ever knowed was her daddy and oh yeah, Saul Greenberg. At times, her mother would get to going on about how if Saul wasn't White she mighta considered marryin' him. Leastways he ain't gonna run off fo' some high yalla bitch knowin' full well he's got a wife at home and a baby girl who ain't off her mama's tit yet. Sorry ass nigger.

256

Lacy used to cringe when her mama would go on like this. She didn't know if mama was serious or not. And Lord knows the kids at school would tease her about not havin' no daddy but hecks that was better than havin' a White man as a daddy and especially a Jew. Hell, they wasn't but a half step above a nigger themselves.

The mere sight of Saul Greenberg used to give her the willies back then. But she had gradually come to warm to the man. And in the summers when all the other kids stood for blocks waiting for the city to bestow a job on them she could count on sweeping up and helping Mr. Saul out for three to four hours everyday.

When her loan for her final year at Pittsburgh University was denied, she'd cried rivers, deep long tears, enough to fill an ocean. She knew mama loved her but mama was in no position to help and was struggling each and every month just to keep a roof overhead and pay the bills. How often had she called home just to say hello and check on mama since she'd gotten diabetes and found the phone had been disconnected. When this happened who was the only person to get mama a message but Mr. Saul. Now that she was in her final year at college and struggling to finish, she kind of wished mama had been serious about marryin' Mr. Saul, no matter what those little heathens at school had said.

Lacy never did tell mama the real reason why she took her sophomore year off. Her mother had been livid when she found out but she had enough on her just to keep a roof overhead and she sure didn't need this to worry about as well; especially since she couldn't do a damn thing about it.

When school was over that May and she returned to the block all she could see were the dregs she had fought so hard to separate herself from. Sure, there were still those good hard working people that she'd known all her life. They were still there, still struggling and making do but not even they wanted to see someone return to the neighborhood a failure and that's exactly how she had felt. Once you left, you had to make good. The only ones who could return; returned successes because they chose to not because they had to. Friends and associates smiled and were cordial but in her eyes and theirs, she was a failure. She was a failure to everyone except   Saul.

257

"Why aren't you back in school, Lacy," he asked as he prepared her mother's order for the week.

"Everyone else has gone back, already."

She tried to lie but after years of working together he'd come to know her too well. When she eventually broke down in tears and told him of her plight to which he replied.

"Have you ever considered being a butcher?"

"A butcher?" What the hell was on his mind? Who the hell would want to stand for ten to twelve hours a day covered in blood and sawdust for the next thirty or forty years waiting on some poor niggas who couldn't even afford the regular grocery store. If it weren't for Saul's rock bottom prices most of them wouldn't know what meat even tasted like. Half the time he gave away more than he sold

Hurt, dejected and angry for having shared her feelings with this cold, callous little Jewish man whose best reply was, "have you ever considered being a butcher," Lacy made it a point to avoid Greenberg's Meats for weeks until her mother forced her to go down there one Friday afternoon to pick up their order. The fact that she hadn't been to work and hadn't called in seemed to bother the man a little. As she approached the counter to pay for the order, she lowered her eyes so as not to meet his.

"Lacy it is good to see you. You are certainly a sight for sore eyes."

Now she really felt bad. The old man continued. "I thought for sure you'd worked out your little problem and headed back to school. It didn't seem right you not saying goodbye but I figured you probably had so much to do that you'd probably just run out of time and didn't get a chance to stop by and say goodbye."

Lacy felt worse than ever. Sliding her foot back and forth, impatiently, nervously, piling up a mound of sawdust between her feet the same way she used to do when she was a little girl waiting for mama wishing she were back on the block playing jacks or double-dutch with her Anna Mae. Those days were long gone and only the nervous impatience remained. Now nineteen, she felt just like she had back then. No, worse and Saul Greenberg seemed to be enjoying her discomfort as she did everything to avoid his gaze. She wanted to curse him and tell him to hurry up with the fuckin' order but she knew she could never do that; not to Mr. Saul. Besides Mama would beat her silly. Just a few short years ago when she was in junior high and senior high school and mama was running a little short of money at the beginning of the school year and she mentioned the other kids going back to school with brand new outfits it was Mr. Saul, who took a little away from each check without letting her mama know it when she came to get Lacy's paycheck every Friday. He held it 'til the beginning of the school year so Lacy could buy a new outfit or two. When school started and her best friend

Anna Mae and the other girls at school talked about the jobs they'd held this summer and how this employer or that that had made advances bordering on rape Lacy could never join in

So, being disrespectful to Mr. Saul was out of the question although Lacy sure wanted to curse somebody for her plight. But it could never be Mr. Saul. Hell, he was more of a father than any man she had ever known including her own so-called father. He'd even gotten to the point, when she was a junior and senior in high school and the neighborhood had started to change for the worse that t he'd walk her home, even if it had been an especially busy day at the store and they had to work late. Oh how she hated that. Lacy sometimes wondered if Mr. Saul knew he was white. Outside the social workers and the police he was the only white face bold enough to walk Harlem's mean streets. When Mr. Saul walked her home at night all the kids would tease her about getting her good hair from her daddy, Mr. Saul, 'the butcher.' Saul acted like he didn't or couldn't hear

them when the little kids in the streets would line up and hold their noses when they saw the two of them and shout things like "Phew, phew, smells like a Jew."

Lacy remembered those times and thought I'd be so embarrassed both for myself and him but mostly for him. He just acted like he was deaf, dumb and stupid. Mr. Saul would and start tellin' me that this was nothing compared to what the Germans called him at Auschwitz. At the time, I had no idea what he was rambling on about, so I just ignored him wondering why he would endure this grief every Friday and Saturday after waiting on evil Black folks all day long. Some whom hated him for just being white and owning a store in Harlem.

Everyone knew except Mr. Saul that Friday and Saturday nights were the absolute worst nights to walk the streets if you didn't have some melanin.

In fact among the tenants, Friday and Saturday nights are known as Harlem Hospital night cause Black people working downtown all week for little or no money finally get to come home, relax and grab a sip or a hit of something before they have to head back downtown to kiss Mr. Charlie's ass again on Monday morning. And since there ain't no White people or bosses to take their frustrations out on up in Harlem after dark. So on the weekend when they'd get all high and liquored up they take them out on each other. And boy, does Harlem

Hospital do a booming business. There were so many stabbings and shootings that you can't even get a room on the weekend.

Walking home with Mr. Saul I'm thinking to myself, if that's what Black people do to other Black people out of frustration, just imagine what they'd do if they found a White man like Mr. Saul uptown after the sun goes down. I never told Mr. Saul any of this because it wouldn't have made any difference anyway. He was a stubborn man and I'd have to hear more long drawn out stories about Jehovah from the Torah and about Germany back in the day, so I just kept my mouth shut, dropped my head and trudged along. But I'll tell you that would be the longest walk and it really wasn't that far from the store to my house. I mean I must have walked it a thousand times and it really ain't nowhere but walking with Mr. Saul under all that fire was the longest walk.

Soon as I'd get home I'd run past mama and up to my bedroom window to watch as Mr. Saul would make his way back down the block taking the same abuse he'd taken coming. I'd close my eyes before he got to the end of the block, and wonder why people had to be that mean, and why he had to be so stupid So you see, even when he asked me again that day why I wasn't back in school and if I was ready to learn how to be a butcher, I still couldn't lash out at him. Even though I thought it was the dumbest question he'd ever asked. It was so

insensitive, so unlike him. Still, he was Mr. Saul so I did my best to listen intently while he told me one of those old long drawn out stories from the Torah about patience. The story or parable as he liked to call them had nothing to do with nothing , so I thought at the time. Then he made me promise that I'd be there for work the next day at six a.m. in the morning. I was shocked that he'd offered me my job back after I walked out on him, but I was glad for the Torah's teachings then. Mama was struggling to make ends meet and her health wasn't the best, so I jumped at the chance to go back to work for the old man since I wasn't doing nothing else anyway. That way I'd at least lessen the load on mama some.

I was there bright and early the next morning and began my apprenticeship as a butcher much to my distaste and a few months later I'd like to say I'd could cut meat almost as well as Mr. Saul.

My next-door neighbor and best friend Anna Mae was the only person I saw during those days. She would be the only one I'd seen from school. The only reason she'd stop by was to borrow a few dollars here and there. Things had changed between us and the years since high school had not served her well. There were rumors that she was prostituting herself to buy dope. I knew Anna Mae was too smart for that and dismissed the rumors because she was and had

been my best friend for as long as I could remember. Every now and then, I'd meet a pretty nice guy and they'd ask me out, but I never went. I was always too tired after work to go anywhere. Those first few months of my apprenticeship I couldn't do anything but walk in the house, take a quick shower and dive into bed. More often than not I'd get no further than lying across my bed with my bloody apron before mama would wake me and force me to take a shower. Half the time I didn't even eat. If I did eat, I didn't eat anything with meat. Butchering was no easy task and after twelve long hard hours a day, six days a week working side-by-side with Mr. Saul, my respect grew for the old man.

By the time Christmas rolled around that year I had a nice little nest egg saved. It wasn't nearly enough to get me back in school but it was enough to give me some hope.

By the end of May, I'd save enough for the fall semester but I wasn't really thinking about school now. I was making good money and despite the long hours I was really starting to enjoy my new trade.

Funny thing is, when Mr. Saul saw this instead of asking me if I wanted to be a butcher, he started asking me if I was ready to go back to school. When I told him that butchering was fine for now he just turned and walked away.

That Saul Greenberg is a funny man. When all my thoughts were on returning to school for my final year all he wanted to know if I wanted to be a butcher. Now that I was firmly entrenched as a butcher, he wanted to know if I was ready to return to school. I guess I'll never understand White people, I thought to myself, as he looked away and headed down the aisle to wait on a customer. Mr. Saul said little the remainder of the day. For the life of me, I couldn't understand what I'd done to upset him. The thought was still on my mind as I closed my eyes to go to sleep that night and after being unable, to come up with any answers I thought that the best way to address the situation would simply be to ask him.

Arriving the next morning a little earlier than my usual time, I greeted him with his usual cup of coffee, a bagel with lox and cream cheese that he so loved, but decided to wait until our first few customers arrived so I wouldn't be subjected to a long parable from the Torah. But before I could approach him on the subject of his disdain, Mr. Saul approached me with an envelope.

"Lacy some of us are teachers, some of us are rabbis, and some of us are butchers. Jehovah gives us all a purpose in life. I am to be a butcher. I am not sure what Jehovah has planned for you but you are not to be a butcher. That is

not to say that you have not learned your craft well and would not make a fine one, but I am convinced that he has other plans for you."

With that said Saul Greenberg handed Lacy the envelope and in it was a bus ticket and enough money to complete her senior year of college.

"You were much cheaper when you were a little girl and just needed an outfit or two for the beginning of school but this is an investment that I am sure will pay off." They both cried that morning. The hugs and tears of joy interrupting many a customer's order but neither seemed to mind so ecstatic were they.

263

Now twelve years later here was Lacy a New York City Police officer in the same streets she grew up in escorting the man who'd made it all possible discussing her mother's health and her returning to law school.

"You know Lacy, I still think your mother's the most beautiful woman I have ever laid eyes on. I truly believe she was the reason I never married. I always thought she'd come to her senses one day and seek my hand in marriage," he chuckled lightly as they walked to the old green Rambler.

"You know a lot of people think I'm crazy for keeping my business here in Harlem. I don't know how many times I've heard my friends from the old days

tell me about how good life is out on the island or over in Jersey. They wanna know why I stay here with the coloreds and endanger my life."

Lacy cringed at the word, coloreds.

"They tell me I'm endangering my life. They say even the coloreds don't wanna be in Harlem no more with the crackheads and the dopers. They all look at me like I'm crazy. They say Saul, why don't you take a wife and come on out to Sheepshead Bay or Forest Hills with the rest of us but if I did that I would never see your mother again.

I'll tell you honestly, even though in the last twenty-five years, I never have had the nerve to say more to her than hello and double her order, I believe I'm ready now.

It's been more than two weeks now since I've seen her and that's too long. The last time that I went without seeing her was back in, oh, I believe it was '62. Yeah, right after I bought the Rambler and parked in front of the store to impress her. I went to Israel for a month to see the homeland and realized that Harlem was my real home and came back after only two weeks so worried about the store and my customers and missing the sight of your mother's face that I came rushing back two weeks early."

"Does she know any of this Mr. Saul?" Lacy asked as they leaned against the old green Rambler that shone as if it had only been purchased yesterday.

"I've never had the nerve to tell her," he mumbled quietly, underneath his breath yet loud enough for Lacy to hear.

Lacy smiled. She was in a world of her own.

"You're grinning like a Cheshire cat, Lacy. What do you find so funny?"

"Well, well, well!" Lacy continued grinning from ear-to-ear. "I'll tell you if you promise not speak a word to mama. She'd have my head."

"Tell me child."

When the conversations became serious, Saul always referred to Lacy as if she were still a child, the child he had grown so fond so many years before and who he still adored as if she were his very own.

"Well, when I was growing up and papa and mama would argue, and papa would leave, mama would always say how she wished you had been the one. And the few times she dated after papa she would always come home angry with whomever, no matter how nice they tried to be. Now I understand. No one could or would have ever been good enough because the whole time she had her sights

set on you. It all makes sense now." She paused. "So why didn't you ever approach her?"

Saul, who had been listening intently, dropped his head.

"I never approached your mother because I was afraid. She was beautiful and men were always trying to woo her. Strong, handsome, powerful men. Men with money and influence, men with position right here in Harlem. Who was I?

265

I was the little round-shouldered little Jew immigrant who cut meat for a living. I was the butcher and she was an African queen. I was afraid that if she said no my life would have no purpose. I would have no reason for living."

"Oh, you can't be serious. You two are a trip. Look, I can't listen to any more of this." Mr. Saul, the man who taught me everything that I know, that read the Torah to me on the daily. The tiny little man who has the strength to weather Harlem his entire adult life is afraid to let a woman know that he loves her. That's just too much for me to fathom." Lacy chuckled.

"Don't berate an old man. I thought I taught you better than that child. You never kick a man when he's down. Besides, I've grown tired of the game myself and have decided to ask her out. At seventy-four I believe I can outrun, outwork, and out hustle most of the young men out there half my age. I'm sure

she's still got a few suitors out there but I don't believe any of them are of any real consequence. After all, I'm just coming into my prime. How old is your mother anyway? Seventy-one, seventy-two? Still a young woman. Do me a favor call her and ask her if she'll have dinner with me tomorrow night."

"I'll do you one better, Mr. Saul. I'll call and you can ask her if she'll have dinner with you tomorrow night."

Lacy pulled out her cell, dialed the number, and handed the old man the phone.

Saul Greenberg's face turned a shade of crimson red that Lacy had never seen in all of her years around the butcher.

"Saul Greenberg, of Greenberg's Meats here, your daughter suggested that I call you. Yes, yes, I'm doing fine. And yourself? Lacy just informed me that you'd been a little under the weather."

It was obvious that he was nervous and hedging but Lacy wouldn't allow him to retract and egged him on.

"In any case, I've been meaning to ask you for sometime now if you'd like to have dinner with me?"

There! Finally, it was out. There was a long pause and Lacy stood there, hardly breathing awaiting the outcome almost as if it were her fate on the line. She knew her mother. She knew how outspoken and abrasive she could be at times and held on waiting...

Saul clicked the tiny cell phone shut.

"Well?" Lacy asked.

Saul stared down at the ground as a huge, gray rat scurried into the gutter only a few feet away. Both looked but neither seemed to notice.

"She said no, she wouldn't like to go out to dinner because she's not really feeling up to par." Saul glanced at the girl her navy blue uniform drenched in the warm August heat.

Her body suddenly going limp Lacy reminded him of the rag doll he'd seen in the store window of F.A.O.Schwartz. He could tell she was hurt. And he knew that she felt for him. She'd never meant to hurt him and she knew this hurt.

Gazing up at the old man she hardly knew what to say when she noticed a broad smile creeping across his worn and wrinkled face as he gazed at the rat who was still only a few feet away and by this time had gotten himself wedged quite

nicely in the corner of the sewer with a tenement cat fast approaching. She glanced as the cat pawed, talons extended ripping, and tearing at the rat's hind quarters, the rat unable to move or fend off his foes attack.

God, she felt bad and here he was smiling. Saul Greenberg, she knew, was one hell of a man but this was too much. She wanted to grab him, hold him and console him in his time of grief but she couldn't.

"Anyway, your mother said that she wasn't feeling particularly up to par and wasn't sure she would be able to make it out to dinner tonight but wouldn't mind if I came over for dinner."

Lacy jumped for joy, grabbing the butcher and hugging him as tightly as she could, the teas running down her face, the nine millimeter jabbing him continuously in the midsection.

The last time she'd been this happy was when he'd given her the envelope with her tuition for her senior year at Pitt. It seemed like all of the best things in life revolved around this little man so out of place here in Harlem. Saul Greenberg was elated too and it showed as the color returned to his olive brown complexion.

"Do you know what she asked me, Lacy? She asked me what took me so long. God, what a fool I've been."

And with that said he jumped in the old green Rambler that looked like new and headed down Eighth Avenue for the Lower east Side.

An hour or so later, Lacy stepped into the foyer of the spacious brownstone and was surprised to hear Moody's Blues playing softly on the old Victorola in the living room. It had been quite sometime since she had heard that and that usually meant a party or some other good tidings. Recently it lay dormant, silent, collecting cobwebs and dust as the months and then the years passed on.

Chapter 2

At first, she was sure that it would only be only a couple of months before she'd be back in school and working on her law degree. The doctors were sure her mother's diabetes could be stabilized just by changing her diet but mama was mama and after a couple of weeks she was back to her old tricks of eating what she wanted when she wanted and before she knew it they were talking insulin by injection. Now Lacy knew that law school in the near future was out of the question.

For a while mama had really tried giving up so many of the delicacies that she had come to love but after awhile it just grew too much for her and she was back in the hospital again only this time in a diabetic coma and on the verge of death. She was still a very attractive woman but her face was now drawn from the medications and somehow she'd contracted asthma and bronchitis.

The illnesses bothered Lacy. But mama was strong. She'd never before let anything beat her. That's not what bothered Lacy. What really bothered Lacy was that mama had seemingly lost the will to live. She would often sit for hours without so much as muttering a word. The doctors blamed it on the numerous

medications that she was on for this illness or that. Lacy blamed it on life's unfulfilled dreams.

Resigning herself to caring for her mother Lacy found herself back in the place she had so desperately tried to escape. And even though she had finally, after six and a half years of taking a class here and a class there been able to finish law school and pass the bar there wasn't even a remote chance of her practicing law with mama in the condition she was in. And with mama's social security and her own paltry civil servant's salary she could hardly afford a caregiver or

Cna to come in and look after the old woman.

When her mother first grew ill, Lacy wanted to curse her but as the years trudged by she resigned herself to taking care of her mother, her only regret being that mama hardly seemed to care about herself or her declining health anymore. She seemed tired of battling and unbelievable as it appeared if you knew mama she'd somehow lost her reason for living.

That's why it startled Lacy to find mama up at eleven thirty traipsing around the house as if she were nineteen or twenty singing and humming and dusting and sweeping like it was Christmas and she was preparing for Santa. The last time Lacy could remember mama this active was when she heard papa's all

too familiar whistle coming up the walkway. Oh, how bubbly and effervescent she would become.

Now here it was again. Lord if she'd known that hunchbacked, old stoop shouldered, Saul Greenberg, the butcher could have had that much effect on mama she would have moved him in here the day daddy left. She had been hesitant to tell Saul about her mother's melancholy and now thank goodness she wouldn't have to. But with the new split shift, she would certainly tell Saul about this when she saw him in the morning.

Several times during the night, she heard dishes clanging and smelled aromas from her childhood like fresh rolls baking and world famous sweet potato soufflé and the music was still a bit to loud but she could give up a night's rest for her mother's happiness. God, it was good to have her back.

Lacy awoke the next morning, more tired than the night before. Showering quickly she grabbed one of the rolls her mother had baked from the night before threw a pat of butter on it, threw it in the micro, kissed her mother who was finally sleeping on the cheek and headed out the door and down to the precinct.

She thought about stopping by to see Mr. Saul first. It was six a.m. and he would just be arriving to open but she was running late and so she turned abruptly and headed for the precinct instead. Besides, she'd see him in an hour or so for breakfast when she brought him his coffee and bagel with lox and cream cheese the way she had for the past twelve years or so.

The 44th Precinct was even more chaotic than usual and she could only attribute it to the fact that she wasn't as well rested as she usually was but still there was something different almost as if there were a full moon. She hated to admit she believed in such nonsense until two plainclothes officers with a large somewhat irate gentlemen between them almost knocked her down trying to get the burly subject to go willingly into the holding pen.

"Sorry, Lace," one of the two officers shouted in passing as they attempted to throw the unwilling suspect into the holding pen.

Yes, there was something definitely askew this morning and she only hoped that her first sergeant wouldn't keep them too long in muster.

Hell, it was the same every day. Be careful, watch your back; don't attempt a collar without backup. The last one was always meant for her as she was the only female on the street and she had one of the worst beats uptown or so they said. She took it all in stride. That was for them   Hell, she'd grown up here

and knew 'em all. Those she didn't know she'd gained the respect of through the course of a run in here or there.

She hated all the unnecessary paperwork and so she didn't make collars just for the sake of making a collar. When she saw a kid smoking a blunt and she only hoped they had enough respect to put it out when they saw her approach.

Crack was a different story. It was eating Harlem up like a cancer with no cure. She ventured to say in muster one morning that crack was responsible for ninety per cent of the violent crimes in Harlem. Few of her fellow officers disagreed.

She hated that shit. And she hated it even more when it was finally confirmed

271

that Anna Mae, who happened to be her best friend since she was knee high t a grasshopper and also her next door neighbor ever since she could remember had fallen victim to the plague. Since their high school days, Anna Mae had gone from a straight A student with a free ride to both Columbia and Vassar to a five dollar ho up on Sugarhill.

Lacy cried when she first found out and extended a helping hand on more than one occasion but after sliding back into the throes of the devil, time and time again, Lacy, like everyone else in the neighborhood threw in the towel.

Still, Lacy remembered the pajama parties and weekend outings so when they crossed paths all Lacy could do was ask Anna not to work Eighth Avenue and Anna Mae agreed.

The rest of the neighborhood was fine except for a few domestic squabbles here and there and an occasional break in or arson by an absentee landlord for insurance purposes. After awhile Lacy had come to actually enjoy the streets and the people that made them up and they welcomed her. So when muster commenced she left the Saturn parked in front of the 44th and walked slowly up Eighth past Sherman's Barbeque Joint, inhaling the day old ribs, mixed with spaghetti and coleslaw mingled with the smell of urine that rose from the overturned garbage cans that littered the sidewalk. It stunk. Sure. Further up Eighth, the fresh sweet aroma of Jamaican meat patties and coconut bread and rolti greeted Lacy. She wanted to run in and grab a meat patty but somehow one led to two and went straight from her lips to her hips and no matter how much she walked it was easier putting the pounds on than taking them off.

God how she loved the diversity that was Harlem.

Roll call had been quick this morning and she was grateful for that. It was six thirty now and she knew, Mr. Saul's coffee and bagels were ready and waiting. Grabbing them she headed back out into the warm August air. It was

272

early and already the temperature was in the mid-nineties. You could already see the rainbow of heat waves rising from the pavement but she hardly felt the warm sun beaming down on her visor.

In another minute or so, she'd be having breakfast with her good friend Mr. Saul. She couldn't wait to tell him about the sudden metamorphosis in mama. Turning the corner and approaching the store that had been her home away from home for the past twenty years, she saw a small crowd milling around. Her co-workers had already cordoned off a huge patch of sidewalk in front of the butcher's shop.

Dropping the bagels and coffee, Officer Lacy rushed forward pushing her way through the sea of familiar faces. Lying on the ground, not five feet in front of her, a pool of blood streaming from his temple, lay Saul Greenberg, the butcher, pole in hand the familiar green canopy rolled half way up before someone had obviously walked up and bludgeoned him to death with a blunt instrument.

Turning away abruptly, Lacy screamed, one long incessant spine-chilling wail that comes only with the death of a loved one. She screamed until there was nothing left and then turning again, she walked to the closest police car to brace

herself as her fellow officers assisted, only to see Anna Mae her former classmate and best friend slumped over in the back seat, eyes glassy and distant.

The Second Sermon

"Brothers and sisters, I certainly am glad to see you all gathered here today in the Lord's name in spite of all that afflicts us. When you look at the weather, our ailments, and all the adversities that plague us on a daily basis it's a wonder that there's a soul in attendance this morning. I guess that's the difference between looking at the glass as being half-empty or half-full. I guess those that see the glass as half-empty chose to stay home and those that see the glass as half full are here today. You see if we look at all the Lord has bestowed on us, then it's obvious that you and I are truly, truly blessed.

It's a funny thing though... Despite all the blessings the good Lord has bestowed upon me; when I woke up this morning and heard the rain and hail banging against my windowpane I wanted to turn over and go right on back to sleep. Despite all of the blessings he has bestowed upon me I really thought seriously about taking a day off and calling in sick to the Lord.

Cold weather has a way of making people want to call in. All I really wanted to do this morning was pull that big ol' warm fluffy afghan over my head, curl up in a ball, and go right on sleeping. I tried to hide the feeling from Him but He knows that deep down in my heart that's what I wanted to do."

The congregation of The First Abyssinian Church of Jesus Christ chuckled loudly.

"In any case, I'm here and since I am I'd like to share an interesting set of circumstances with you in lieu of the sermon I prepared for you this week. As most of you know, I volunteer any extra time I may have in the evenings, down at the midtown Crisis Intervention Center, answering the phones and doing what I can to help out those in need. Now usually and in most businesses that we consider thriving and prosperous the proprietors define good business by the amount of customers. That however is not the case with the Crisis Intervention Center. Usually the more calls and the more customers we receive the worse things are.

You see at the center when people call us it's usually because they're in dire

274

straights so you see good business in this case is bad business. And I'm sorry to say, that for some reason, last night, was a particularly busy night which is not good. I don't know if it was a full moon or the devil just stepped up his game. I'm really not sure but it wasn't a good night at all.

In any case, I had one phone call in particular that stood out from the rest and disturbed me more than all the rest put together. That's not to say that any one call is any more or any less important than another. They are all important when someone is in trouble and in need.

When people call that number, there are some things that you can be pretty doggone sure of. You can be sure that they're desperate, that they're in trouble, and that they're on the edge. You can also be sure that somewhere along the way, they've lost their faith in the Lord Jesus Christ as their Savior.

As I was saying though, one phone call, in particular, stands out from all the rest. And let me repeat myself so you don't get the wrong idea. It wasn't that this conversation was any more or less important than any of the other phone calls I received last night but this particular phone call made me sit back and think for a minute. It was from a brother, who I would gather, from his conversation, was about my age. For some reason this phone call really disturbed me although I didn't know why at the time.

The call came in when I first arrived at the center, somewhere around nine or nine-thirty last night. And this brotha and I talked for about thirty minutes. I can't tell you the content or the gist of the call because of confidentiality but I will say this. The brotha was deeply troubled about certain things going on in his life and was or seemed to be in a great deal of pain. What's more important though is that he was at a crucial juncture and uncertain of to how to alleviate the pain caused by his troubles. He was tired of doing drugs and admitted that he'd accidentally overdosed twice in the last month alone and was tired of taking chances with his life. He knew they were they were killing him, was determined to quit. He talso told me that drugs weren't the problem in of themselves but simply a way of dealing with a deeper seated problem. By the time he broke down to call me he was at the end of his rope and considering taking himself out.

When I asked him if he had considered letting Jesus in his life I was met with some of the foulest language I've heard since... Well, in all honesty I can't recall. And trust me I was no choirboy growing up in Brooklyn. Back in the day on the streets of Brooklyn, I used to be holdin' it down yo."

Everyone laughed.

"That was long before the Lord called me to his ministry and shortly after my father found out I was out there trying to be a thug and started wearin' out my hind parts. You see my father was a big man. He stood about six-four and weighed somewhere around two hundred and eighty pounds. Trust me, brothas and sistas, I wasn't holdin' it down for long. Believe me there is something to say for corporal punishment. At any rate, the brotha calls to tell me what's troubling him and I'm sitting there feeling so inept, so helpless. I think of all the years I spent in the seminary studying, learning and gathering information on how to serve the Lord in the best way I possibly can. I thought of all the hours I'd spent laboring over the good book seeking answers that would help my fellow brethren in times just such as these. And last night when the game's on the line, all I can ask him in the end is if he has considered taking Jesus into his life.

Then it dawned on me that if the brotha knew how to bring Jesus into his life he wouldn't be calling the Crisis Intervention Hotline and talking to a complete stranger at nine-thirty on a Saturday night, now would he? Anyway, he calls back to apologize for cursing me out but I was on another line and asked him if he would hold. When I got back he'd either hung up out of frustration or been disconnected. I ended up getting off at around two in the morning. I don't know it might have been

later. But the whole evening I'm thinking about that one phone call and praying to God that he made it.

Now usually when I'm driving home, alone, at this time of the morning it gives me a chance to unwind. I have a little ritual I go through that helps me put all that happened at the Crisis Intervention Center behind me. The first thing I do is I run through the next day's sermon; then I run through my calendar and think about things I should've done during the day that I somehow wasn't able to get around to. But last night was different. All I could think about was the phone call from that brother, who like I said, had to be about my age and was in some serious trouble. For some unknown reason I kept asking myself, why out of all the people I spoke to last night did this one caller stand out? And I couldn't sleep for worrying about it.

By the time, I did fall asleep; this morning, I still had no clue. So, I did what I do when I've expended too much energy on something and keep coming up empty. I turned to the Lord and asked Him to please help me understand why this phone call bothered me so. I guess I fell asleep before he could reply and before I knew it, I heard my alarm ringing in my ear and saw the raindrops against my window.

Now I'm gonna tell you something brothas and sistas, and please don't judge me too harshly but both last night and this morning I found myself asking why I ever wanted or even considered wanting to be in the ministry of the Lord Jesus Christ. It dawned on me that if this was a typical nine to five, I wouldn't have only been in bed last night at a decent hour but chances are I wouldn't have had to work at all this being Sunday. Aside from that, I would have never received that disturbing phone call that bothered me so much then and still bothers me now. And even if my worrying kept me up for half the night, I could've called in sick today. That's right. I could have curled right on back up in my bed with that big ol' soft poly-posturepedic mattress and slept right on through the afternoon. Even now that sounds kinda nice?"

Reverend Barnes looked out over the ever-growing population and paused before wiping his brow.

"Before I continue, let me ask you a question my brothas and sistas. How many of you were considerin' curlin' up in your big ol' comfy beds this mornin' when you heard the rain this mornin'? How many of y'all said, 'Ol'Reverend Barnes won't miss me just this one Sunday. Besides, I can't remember the last time I missed a Sunday service. How many of you said that when you saw it raining out there this morning? Let me see a show of hands. C'mon now, I want y'all to be honest. Remember, you're in the Lord's house."

Everyone laughed.

"I know somebody said that 'cause we ain't hardly as full as we have been in the past few weeks when the sun was shining. Look around you at all the empty seats. I ain't gonna mention no names but appears to me that quite a few people

277

must have said that this mornin'.

It's a funny thing. Sister Helen was complaining last Sunday about having to leave home earlier and earlier to get a front row seat. You didn't have to leave home early this week did you Sister Helen?

C'mon now, once again, If you didn't want to brave the rain and the cold this mornin', let me see a show of hands."

Almost every hand in the congregation shot up except for Ol' Sista Gerty's, who was close to ninety and hadn't missed a Sunday service in umpteen years, or at least as far as anyone in attendance could remember. Fact of the matter is, Sister Gerty would have hitched a ride with Noah before she'd let a little rain stop her from missing Sunday services.

"Well at least I know I'm not alone in my imperfections. And don't worry Sista Gerty I'll be getting to the sermon soon. For those of you that don't know, sometimes Sista Gerty gets a little agitated if I ramble on and take to long getting to the point. I try to explain to her that I'm like a performer workin' the crowd in the good Lord's name. Sometimes she doesn't realize that it's my job to get you to a fever pitch, so I can bring y'all to a climactic ending so you'll remember the message. But..."

"Go on so you can git to the sermon boy, I ain't got no time to be messin' around talkin' 'bout who not here 'cause a da rain. They'll just have to answer to da Lord fo' dat demselves. Meanwhile, I got a ham in the oven 'bout to burn waitin' for you to finish. So, git on wit' it reverend. And don't be talkin' dirty in the Lord's house. Talkin' abut that climactic stuff. Just git on wit' da preachin' at hand," Sista Gerty shouted out.

"Yes m'am. Thank you Sister Gerty," Reverend Barnes replied.

Everyone laughed.

"Yes, the Lord knows it would have been so much easier to sleep-in than to confront the rain and the cold. It has to be below freezing out there today. Does anybody know what the temperature is today?" Reverend Barnes asked as he took a gulp of water.

Sister Helen a rather attractive woman in the first pew wearing a tight red dress and six-inch heels raised her hand immediately.

"Sister Helen says its twenty-eight degrees out there. I'd say that's a wee bit nippy. Anybody disagree? But you're here; despite the cold and sleet. You're here in the House of the Lord. You, His loyal followers, who call your selves Christians are here this morning to hear the Word of God through his ambassador so that you can take the Word out into the streets and spread the Word amongst those that are truly in need.

You know, brothas and sistas, as cold as it was this morning; once I got up and out this morning I felt a sort of warmth come over me. And that warmth didn't come over me because of the heater in the car. That warmth came over me because I knew that on this cold, rainy morning the Lord had blessed me with His presence. That warmth came over me because I knew that the good Lord, praise his name, had called me to be His ambassador. He called me in the same way he called Moses to the mountaintop. He called me in the same way he called Martin and Malcolm to lead their people out of bondage.

And this morning it dawned on me as I drove here to see you that he called me last night too, in the form of that troubled young man. And now I know that the reason that particular phone call bothered me so much last night was that the Good Lord, praise His name was letting me know that that young man who seemed so troubled and so lost was no one other than me without the blessing which he's bestowed on me. Can you hear me out there? Do ya feel me?"

Reverend Barnes paused as a loud chorus of 'Amens' and 'Preach brother preach' rose from the congregation.

Reverends Barnes continued.

"The only difference between that man and me is that the Lord has seen fit to take me into the fold and granted me His blessing. All praises be to the Lord Jesus Christ. Can I get an Amen? So, when you see the homeless and the disenfranchised, when you see the crackhead and the prostitute trying to find a dollar to pay the devil, when you see little Iraqi boys and girls dying under heavy artillery fire, when you see prison inmates screaming at the top of heir

279

lungs, when you see Aids victims and cancer patients withering away before your eyes, when you see all of the atrocities that man bestows on his fellow man do me one favor brothas and sistas. Whatever you do, don't look away. As followers of Christ remember this if you don't remember anything else. Remember that our Lord and savior Jesus Christ never looked away. Jesus confronted the problem and found a way to make a difference. And we as Christians, as followers of Christ must do the same. We must find a way to confront the problem and make a difference.

Whatever you do brothas and sistas, do not make the same mistake I did last night, I forgot my role. I was what you might call, arrogant in my ignorance.

Harlem Blues

Lord, I sure as hell don't know what's happening out there in these here streets. Yesterday Black folks was walking around here like we were kings. Their heads was held so high we couldn't see for the clouds. We were proud of where we came from and proud of where we was going. I'm talking P-R-O-U-D. Proud! Pride flowed through these Harlem streets like water through the Nile.

But that was then. Now the only thing that seems to flow through these streets is drugs and violence. And if you don't think it's having an effect on all of us hard-working Black folks, all you gotta do is check out the shit that's happened this week alone.

Let's see. I started off telling you about Sweet but something always came up

280

and I suppose I just never got around to it but I guess now's as good a time as any.

As I told you earlier, Sweet and I grew up together, here in Harlem. I mean we was both southern boys at heart. He was from somewhere around Decatur, Georgia and me I from way down in 'Don't Wanna Remember', Mississippi.

Anyways, we both arrived in New York a week or so apart from each other, was inducted into the army on the same day, served two years in the same unit fightin' Gerry's in France and come right back to Harlem together.

Long as I can recollect me and Sweet's been inseparable, like brothers. We even came back and went to work on the docks together for a couple of years after the war was over up 'til that fool Presley ran over my goddamn leg with the damn fork lift with his drunk ass.

Lord knows, I'll never forget that day. Hell, I'll never forget that pain. I remember Presley talkin' about callin' an ambulance. Sweet was like, hell no! Back in them day's ambulances and Black folks was like oil and water. We just didn't mix. And ol' Sweet knew that, so he just scooped me up like I was a little ol' rag doll, my leg dangling, crazily off to one side and ran the seventeen blocks to St. Mary's. You think I'm jokin', don't you. My boy lifted me up like I wasn't nothin' but a bag of cotton

balls and ran eighteen or nineteen blocks to the hospital. I swear fo' God I ain't lyin'.

And I'll tell you somethin' else. I ain't never in all my life felt no pain like I did that day. Never before and never has since... I ended up spendin' about three months in that there hospital. Altogether, I had somethin' like six or seven operations and two pins inserted in my hip, but aside from when it gets real cold, or it gets to rainin', it don't hardly bother me.

The doctors said that Sweet's quick thinkin' is probably the only thing that

281

saved me though. Him splittin' my leg and rushing me headlong to the hospital else I coulda lost my leg and maybe even my life. Least ways that's what the doctors said.

Afterwards, I sued the dockin' company we worked for and I've been on easy street ever since. They wanted to give me one lump sum but I had the payments broken up into monthly installments 'til I reach seventy-five. I get somewhere around 'leven hundred a month and then a few hundred more from my pension, social security, and workmen's comp. It adds up to a

pretty penny and far more than I need to live on being a single man and all.

The workmen's comp is a funny thing, though. You see I've got this lil ol' gal that I met down there when I first got hurt that's been makin' sure that I get a check right up until now. I been getting' a check for the last thirty-five to forty years and you know those benefits don't extend for no more than a year at best. She's head supervisor and pretty much runs the place so I guess ain't nobody checkin' behind her too much.

Anyways, me and her, we used to have a thing, we did. And I guess that's why she extended my benefits. When I broke off our romantic ties we still stayed in touch and met practically every week for a glass of wine or dinner and I noticed that my checks were still comin' rather regular like even though my benefits was supposed to have expired a long time ago. But since she didn't say nothin' I saw no need for me to bring it up. My grand pappy used to always tell me to never look a gift horse in the mouth and I saw no need to start now. Besides, I think that was just her way, a kind of insurance clause, to make sure we always stayed in touch.

Anyway, ol' Sweet was the one really responsible for my financial security and I guess in large part for me being able to collect it at all so I made sure I offered him a sizeable chunk just as soon as my lawyer settled which was about a year and a half later. And because of the settlement my lawyer refused to let me work and in the entire year and a half that I was out of work before the settlement, Saul made sure I had food on the table and Sweet made sure all my bills were covered. To tell you the truth, I don't think I was livin' that well

282

before the accident.

I'd hobble on down to Saul's in the afternoon and he'd always have some type of meat and a vegetable, ready for me. Sometimes he'd even cook it himself if he thought I wouldn't do his choice meats justice. And Sweet would come up on payday and just bust in always ready to show me the suit or pair of slacks he'd picked up for me so we could hang out that weekend. And I think that year was the first year that my rent wasn't late one time. Not once.

So, when I got my settlement, I settled up with Saul first and then went on a shopping spree like never before. But I didn't buy a damn thing for myself. I didn't need to. Sweet had been hooking me at up his own expense and his appearance didn't look as good as mine a lot of the times so worried was he about me being straight. There was also another reason that Sweet was so intent on hooking me up. There was a young girl working down at Feinstein's named Wilomena that he had his eye on.

In any case, the day I received my settlement, I went straight to Feinstein's and had Wilomena pick out everything that Sweet had been eyeing for the past couple of months. She knew precisely as she'd been the only person he allowed to wait on him so I ended up getting just about everything he could possibly want except for that yellow and brown pinstriped zoot suit that he insisted on having and that Wilomena and I both agreed made him look like a bona fide fool. But everything else he'd even mentioned in passing was in one of the seven or eight shopping bags now clustered around me. To top that off I invited Wilomena who was getting off to join me and Sweet at dinner at Small's Paradise later that evening which she gladly accepted. And even

went so far as to volunteer to help me carry my bags home so I wouldn't have to pay the cab fare.

Puzzled about our relationship yet knowing that I was all the way, one hundred

283

per cent USDA, Grade A, man her curiosity getting the better of her she was inquisitive as to why I would be purchasing close to seven hundred dollars of clothes for another man without buying anything; not one single stitch for myself. I guess it did appear a little odd, so I told her how Sweet had saved my life and carried me for a year and a half without so much as a whimper about the burden it was imposing on him. I found out later that this one of the biggest mistakes I'd ever made.

In any case, my boy, Sweet was tickled to death and even happier when he found Wilomena sitting there waiting for him at Small's that night in all of her finery and a bottle of Dom Perignon on the table. I think it even made up for the zoot suit. I'd like to say I saw a tear in the corner of his eye but he brushed it away so quickly and got on with the courting part of his evening that it was hard to tell.

The next day I offered Sweet a portion of each month's settlement checks but he wasn't havin' it. I told him he could take a quarter of each and every month's check and then find a job that wasn't quite so strenuous and demanding 'cause I knew from experience that dock work was by far the hardest and most dangerous work there was. But he seemed not to mind so much so I let it go. Still, I knew there'd come a day, down the road when, like me, he'd either get injured on the job or grow tired of it and want to retire early and that there pension and social security wasn't enough to keep up his current lifestyle. So, I just set aside some money in Sweet's name for a rainy day and well, 'cause I could afford to and 'cause I wasn't no dummy. I made sure when I signed my first lease that that would be the first and last lease I ever signed. And right now because of rent control and with all my utilities included it only comes to one hundred and twenty-five dollars a month which leaves me close to fifteen hundred dollars a month free to do with as I please. Well, that is 'cept for food which I still get for little or nothing or at least at cost from Saul.

Sweet wasn't always so wise, financially that is, so I had to look out for him, too. I made sure he signed a lease that had rent

control also. You see he respected my opinion and usually took my advice except that is when it came to women. Where womens was concerned I don't think nobody, includin' his mama, could tell him what to do. And even though he tended to be pretty slow and deliberate and methodical about doing most everything when it came to women Sweet would run headlong off the side of a cliff with a sign indicating 'Danger Cliff Ahead', if the right woman came along and told him to do so.

And that's where Wilomena came in. Talkin' about a woman taking over a man's life and havin' his nose wide open. Well, that was Wilomena's m.o. She was an attractive woman, more attractive than most of the women Sweet found himself with, and she was boisterous to a fault.

In all my years, I've never seen a woman with more of nothing to say than Wilomena. But whatever it was that she happened to speak on she said not only adamantly but loudly as well. It didn't matter how loud the band happened to be playing or how loud the crowd was at Small's on a particular night one thing was for sure; if there was one voice that could be heard above all the rest it was Wilomena Williams.

Me, myself, despite her helping me carrying the bags on the train that first day I met her, never liked her from the git go. I just never did. I can't pinpoint any one thing. It was just something about her. Maybe it was because she claimed to be from Sugar Hill and had these uppity ways about her. She useta talk real pretentious like, too. Like tellin' everyone how Miles had invited her to attend Julliard with him but because music was her second love she decided to go to City College instead. That don't even sound right. Anybody can go to City College but how many people pass on an opportunity to go to Julliard. I'm thinkin' she probably went to City College like I went to Columbia and you know how I went to Columbia. And up 'til this day I don't believe anyone's ever seen her degree. And Sweet was so damn pussywhipped, that he believed everything that that heifer told him.

It was obvious to almost everyone what had really caught Sweet's attention besides her constant goings on about how she was a close friend of Miles and Dizzy and Duke. She even told a group of us, one night, how Miles had personally sent for her to visit when he was performin' in Montreal and I said to myself, sure he did; you lil' lyin' bitch but I never let on that I knew she was lyin' or that I didn't much care for her since Sweet was my buddy and probably wouldn't have heard me anyway.

And since he and I had never said an ill word in our entire friendship and since

285

he had saved my ass in France during the war and done the same that day on the docks I sure wasn't going to be the one to rain on his parade. If my boy, Sweet, was happy then I was happy too although in the back of my mind I was sorry I'd talked him out of going A.W.O.L back in France. There was no doubt in my mind that that little French gal, the farmer's daughter would have suited him better, having his best interest at heart. But then who was I to say?

Nowadays, any time I saw Sweet, he was asking either me or Saul for a few bucks, here and there, and this was a man I'd known for close to I don't know how many years and in all that time he'd never even consider borrowing a dime from anyone.

That was just the way he was. Strong. Proud. Independent. But now when I did see him and that wasn't all that frequent anymore, since he'd had to pick up a second gig to support Wilomena who had moved in with him.

Anyway, when I did see him, it was usually down around 34th Street. Both hands would be filled with shopping bags and hatboxes. Wilomena would be there clutching his arm and pointing in some store window or high priced boutique over on 5th Avenue and grinning like a Cheshire cat.

I'd usually see them on Saturday afternoons when Monica and I would take our afternoon picnics in Central park then go window-shopping along 5th. We'd stop, exchange pleasantries and agree to meet that night at Small's before continuing our journey. Monica, like Saul, would look at Sweet, arms overflowing with bundles of packages and Wilomena crooning over this or that and just shake her head in amazement or perhaps bewilderment, yet she never spoke a word. She didn't have to. I understood.

Like I said, my boy, Sweet was working two gigs now, both of them full-time and the little extra time he had, he spent hanging on to Wilomena's apron strings so I began to see him even less than before. When I did see him, it was at Small's on the weekends he didn't have to work but he was so fixated on Wilomena that often times he never saw me.

Within, less than a year they were married. Of course I served as his best man and when the preacher said does anyone know a reason why this couple should not be wed in holy matrimony, I started to move forward and say, 'Yes, sir, Mr. Preacher man. I have a whole lotta reasons that these two should not be wed in holy matrimony. For one, sir this woman that stands before you and who claims to be born and raised in Sugar Hill attended City College and is a close friend of Miles Davis, Dizzy Gillespie and Duke Ellington and who claims to speak fluent French and Portuguese after living abroad for six months is in my opinion no more than a no-good, low-down, lyin', ghetto gold digger who has latched on to Sweet because he's a slow plodding, hard workin' fool who can't see the forest for the goddamn trees and she plans to milk him for every dime he's got. And right now the poor wretched fool can't see past nothin' but them big ol' chocolate thunder thighs and that plump ass she be cartin' around. I wanted to say Mr. Preacher Man can't you see that the poor man's gone virtually blind from her high falutin' pretentious talk. He can't see nothin' no more. He done plum lost sight of everything 'cause for the first time in his life he been pussy whipped. It happens to the best of us reverend but we can't let one of our own just bite the dust because of it, now can we?

It was at that precise moment when I began to move forward that I knew along with half the congregation that Sweet was in desperate straits. In fact, thinking back, I think everyone in the congregation was aware of the fact, save Sweet and the preacher that my boy was being taken for a ride. And it was then and there, like I said, at that very moment that I decided if I was any friend at all I needed to step up and say something on Sweet's behalf despite the repercussions and even if Sweet ended up hating me for the rest of my natural born days.

Moving forward, I felt a firm tug at the small of my back. Saul must have been reading my mind, as the strong arm of my friend the little Jewish butcher would not allow me to move.

Turning to face him, he sneered, shaking his head, ever so slowly indicating that he understood fully but that now was neither the time nor the place to make a scene. And because of respect for my good friend, Saul Greenberg, I relented.

Later, at the reception, I must admit, I was glad I had, as I'd never seen Sweet happier. Yet, I still had my druthers and relayed them to Saul. Normally, I could have discussed them with the good Reverend Barnes, whom I considered a close friend as well but just having lost his fiancée, Diamond, to AIDS he would hardly have understood my standing in the way of a seemingly loving couples chance at wedded bliss and happiness.

Walking out the door rapidly after making a very brief appearance, GQ handed the couple an envelope and made his way over to me. I knew Q, knew him for what he was but passed no judgment on him. He did what he did and I did what

I did and though our paths collided from time-to-time over the years and we talked at length on such occasions it was never about his business or mine but the business we had in common, which was the plight of Black folks in America. I found him to have a good sense of history and our history in particular as well as being very astute politically and to have a keen eye out here in the streets. Of course, he had to since his very life depended on the latter and his longevity was a testament to his being able to size up a situation quickly and thereupon to act on it.

Anytime there was a political upheaval of any sort, say an upcoming election or some other political travesty about to unfold I could count on him pulling up in that ol beat up Chevy, (or whatever the hell it is he used to drive), and tell me to get in, then head downtown where he was inconspicuous and we'd grab a quick drink or a bite to eat to get my views on the subject. That's just how me and Q rolled.

I figured him to be a bright sensitive cat with loads of intuition. You just didn't go in there shuckin' and jivin' and bullshittin' 'cause Q could see right through a nigga. You see Q was as literate as they come and could have very well been teaching up at Harvard as leechin' down in Harlem but the cards just didn't fall that way for the brotha.

But I'll tell you this. I know quite a few professors right up on the hill at Columbia that couldn't hold a candle to Q when it comes to poly-sci. Sometimes his theories seemed a bit radical even to me and his insight a bit skewed but I attribute this to his always seeing the seamier side of life, I suppose, but the brotha knows his field like he knows these streets. Ain't too many fools able to stay out here as long as Q has. It takes an innately wise man to stay and maintain himself and have some longevity out here in these mean streets of Harlem. What was it Richard Pryor used to say? Richard said, 'I listen to ol' people 'cause ol' people is wise. You don't get to be old bein' no fool. I seen a lotta young fools runnin' round here thinkin' they was wise that's deader than a mothafucka'.

And for that reason, if for no other I respected Q, even if I didn't like his career choice. So when he came up to me as the reception was getting under way, looked down at the ground, shook his head, before shaking my hand and leaving, I was immediately suspicious.

First of all, it was very rare for Q to show up in public anywhere and if he did it was almost certainly by invite and then and only then when the person doing the inviting was an employee or former employee. Either that or they had to be very close to him and in all my years knowing Q I knew no one who he held very close to him.

Aside from that there was little doubt that Q seemed deeply troubled about something though in his line of work it could be a myriad of things. Still, no matter what was going on in his personal or business dealings the one thing I liked about him was that he always maintained the same decorum when we met. Always some conversation and always but always with more than just a nod of the head a handshake. But not today which in turn, let me know that somehow whatever was botherin' him was somehow connected to me and the only thing here connected to me in some way or another was Sweet. It was obvious that Q knew somethin' but was or did not feel as though he were not at liberty to tell me so instead of facing me he just moved on. That was the final piece of the puzzle.

Now all I had to do was fit the pieces together correctly so that everything fit but before I could do that Saul approached an inquiring or better yet with a troubled look on his face as well. Everyone in the neighborhood knew GQ, or knew of him and never at a loss for words, Saul asked, "And who invited our friend Mr. Q?"

Now it wasn't unusual for Saul and I to be on the same page and when it looked like our best friend was no more than an asterisk, a footnote at his own wedding reception, I had to believe there was something amiss. There were just too many question marks. Too many questions.

Saul must have noticed my bewilderment because before I could answer his query or even give him my opinion on the subject he made the comment to no one in particular, "Every man must make his own decisions and then either live or die with the consequences of his decision. I'm afraid if I had allowed you to interfere in our friend Sweet's decision he would have harbored ill feelings for you one way or the other for the rest of your life. Let's just say that you could have stopped him from going through with the marriage. He would have blamed you, if not hated you for standing in the way of his happiness even though you and I both know from experience that our friend Sweet has not made a wise decision. I do not know or even like your friend Q but I know that he is a pretty smart fellow and from his gestures and from his body language alone I gather that he does not agree with Sweet's decision either but it is not our decision to make or to live with".

After Saul's chat I realized how wise my little friend, the butcher was and managed to put aside my feelings and simply hope for the best for Sweet.

Surprisingly enough, the marriage endured longer than any of us would have imagined. The time Sweet and I spent together diminished accordingly, as you can probably imagine, almost to the point where I hardly saw him at all. Of course, he was a married man and husbandry has a way of constraining or so they say. I, however will never know.

I continued my work and watched as the neighborhood around 145th deteriorated with each passing year and there were often times when I wondered what happened to the Langstons, the Dukes, and the Dizzies, that made Harlem the place to be.

Now there was even talk of Small's going out of business and a McDonald's taking its place. My best buddy, aside from Sweet, Saul had been bludgeoned to death in front of his shop after serving Black folk for close to fifty years. It was all beginning to be a bit much to take.

When all the other Jewish merchants were fleeing Harlem for greener pastures, Saul had remained, catering to his faithful clientele for close to nothing in comparison to what he could have been making out in Bay Shore or even over in Tom's River where his only surviving sister had a home. But having a good heart, Saul refused and I really believed that somewhere deep inside the old man he truly believed that Harlem was his home.

I remember him grimacing when Lacy and I would tease him telling him that he'd be much safer somewhere else. After all, home is where the hatred is but he'd just brush us off like a fly on a hot dog at a summer barbeque. Cynical is what he'd call us with a scowl that would have scared Mother Theresa, then grin ecstatically when those old buzzards, the ladies auxiliary of the First Abyssinian Church would ask him to cater their latest church event. And it seemed like they had one every week.

Then he'd frown and scowl and grimace all at the same time when I'd inquire somewhat facetiously as to how much he'd made from the ladies latest event. I knew good and well that he'd probably catered the whole thing at below cost and probably had to come out of his own pocket for a portion and I know he

290

threw in some choice cuts of meat to boot. That's just the way Saul was. I couldn't fault him for his generosity. That was just the way he was. Of course, I wouldn't have given them old buzzards nothin'.

In all the years I've known him, I'd never seen him happier than when the good Reverend Barnes and the First Abyssinian Church of Christ threw a Saul Greenberg Appreciation Day Celebration and Dinner to commemorate his fifty years of quality service to the Harlem community. It was quite a hoe down. I can't remember the last time I'd seen so many people of color come out to pay homage to someone of the opposite race but then Saul Greenberg transcended color and race and all that b.s.

The celebration went on for what seemed like hours, no days, and I ended up having to cancel my date with Donna but I guess Saul was a worthy enough cause even though I had all intentions of heading back down to her loft after dinner too release some tension. Seemed like a whole lot more fun than sittin' in the midst of a bunch of ol' hens just a cluckin' away about who was doin' who around the neighborhood. But anyway Saul asked me to stay and as he was my friend I couldn't say no, bad as I wanted to.

The celebration ended with reverend Barnes sayin' some ol' long drawn out speech about what a good man Saul Greenberg was. Thank God Sister Gerty was there to curtail that epic reading or else we might very well still be there. The good reverend's speech was followed by Officer Lacy and myself awarding Saul an achievement award and plaque for '50 Years of Outstanding Service to the Harlem Community' and a check for one thousand dollars. On accepting the check, Sweet shouted out, "Hey Saul, that ain't nothin' but the money Willie owes you for carrying him all these years".

Everyone fell out, knowing full well that a check for that amount was no more than a token of appreciation. We'd all fallen on hard times at one time or another but he'd never once seen fit to turn some down he deemed hungry and in need. And we were there for him as well, like the time he got that call one Friday night some years ago alerting him that his mother was in Jerusalem on her deathbed, her only wish to see her youngest and only surviving son before she passed on. Being that it was a Friday evening, the banks long since closed, Saul panicked not knowing whether his dear mother was going to last the weekend or not.

Well, Sweet and I reassured that we'd have him on the next plane available to

Jerusalem. But in the meantime, he needed to stop worrying, close up shop early and since he was having qualms about leaving his regular Friday customers in a lurch with no food for the weekend I had to grab his coattail this time and explain to him that he wouldn't have been able to serve anyone if his dear mother hadn't labored to bring him into this God-awful world. It took some time for him to finally get the message. Even then he had some reservations, so I sent Sweet to get Lacy who agreed to take some vacation days and man the store until Saul returned. Then Sweet and I went right outside to the subway station where we let everyone know Saul's dilemma and within an hour and a half we had Saul's ticket to Jerusalem.

Now here he was standing here holding a plaque, tears in his eyes, trying to thank everyone in Harlem for something or another and I'm hoping the damn thing's over with enough time to pick up some Chinese food and still get down to see Donna before it gets too late. But Saul wasn't having any of that and insisted that I escort him while he attempted to say thank you to everyone in attendance. Then when he was certain that it was too late for me to escape and had screwed up my plans completely he disappeared into the kitchen to help the women's auxiliary slice the meat into what he referred to as, 'tender, servable portions'.

So utterly touched was he by their efforts that instead of going directly home afterwards he insisted on stopping by the store to hang up his newly awarded plaque. It took Saul close to two hours to hang his plaque thus negating any plans I may have had but being that it meant so much to him I was glad to be able to spend this time. Two days later I was even more grateful that I'd had that opportunity.

Two days later, here was Sweet banging on my door at six o'clock in the morning, shoulders rolling in a great thunderous motion, rising and falling under the enormous burden he was carrying. Unable to make out what he was saying through his muffled sobs it dawned on me that this was the first time I'd ever seen Sweet shed a tear. That in itself let me know that whatever had taken place had to be worse than devastating because France and the war were more devastating than anything I'd ever experienced and he hadn't dropped so much as a tear.

No, whatever had just occurred had to be far worse than anything I'd ever known. Either that or something had happened to Wilomena. Yet, when he grabbed my arm and began leading me in the direction of 8th Avenue I knew he was far too composed for it to have been Wilomena. And then I saw the red and blue flashing lights in front of Saul's and Lacy's figure between two patrolmen. I couldn't gather what it was they were attempting to do. One officer seemed like he was trying to console her while the other seemed as if he were trying to restrain her.

With one arm extended, Sweet cleared a path and I wondered if it were Monica. We made some headway and ended up in front of Saul's before making our way over to Lacy who for reasons I could not discern was screaming at the top of her lungs.

"Why, Anna Mae? Just tell me, why?"

"Why, Anna Mae? It just ain't fair. Just please, tell me why? He never did anything to anybody. Never did nothin' but try to help you and this is how you choose to repay him?"

Still at a loss as to what had transpired I went to seek out my good friend Saul who always seemed to have a rather good perspective on Harlem's latest tragedy, was always in control and on an evil keel especially at times like these no matter what tragedy had just befallen us. I found the entrance to the tiny grocery packed with people and even with Sweet's help I had a hard time advancing any further.

It was at this point that I began to hear the whispers and the chattering.

"They said that ol' crackhead bitch killed the ol'man."

"He was a good man, too."

"He certainly was."

"Wasn't like the rest of them Jews."

"How you gonna say some shit like that. You don't know no more 'bout Jews than you do 'bout any other race."

"I might not know 'bout Jews like you say but I know that Saul Greenberg was a good man. I know that much"

"I don't blame the girl though. She's just a victim of those allowing that poison to enter our communities. I feel sorry for the old man don't get me wrong but there's a greater problem than one dead Jew. Our children are runnin' around here strung out and we don't own one goddamn ship or plane to fly that shit in here. That's the real problem if you ask me. That girl they got locked up is only a victim of the greater problem. Who's going to address that? Where that ol' sanctified preacher that's always runnin' 'round here talkin' about Jesus this and Jesus that? Here we are losin' our next generation right here in front of our faces and y'all worried about one dead Jew."

"Shut up, nigga! All that shit may be well and good. And I ain't sayin that you ain't abso- fuckin'- lutely right but Saul was a good man and this is neither the time nor the place to bring up global goddamn problems. Now git the fuck on outta here, nigga. A nigga got a right to mourn don't he?"

More people were arriving on the scene; the crowd swelled and the conversation began anew.

"What happened?"

"Crazy bitch, strung out on that shit killed Saul."

"Damn!"

"Didn't they just have some kind of awards ceremony for him over there at First Abyssinian?"

"Sho' did. Crazy crackhead must have heard he got that check."

"Ho, Bitch!"

"You ain't lyin'. Someone ought to string the heifer up by her toes. Can you castrate a woman?"

"Anybody know for sure why she did it?"

"What you mean why? There ain't never no good reason for one person to take another person's life. It's that simple."

"Damn that ho."

294

"And for what? The old man ain't never had no money. He was so busy givin' niggas a fair shake that he never made no money hisself. Always tryin' to help somebody. And see what it gets ya."

"Nothin' but dead, dead, dead!"

"And what she get? Nine dollars and some goddamn change."

"Oh, trust me, she gonna get a whole lot more than that. I got family on the inside. Anywhere she goes, I got family, and soon as I find out where they sendin' her ass, all I gotta do is make a phone call. I'm gonna make sure they go to that ass. First place they gonna send her after central booking is the Tombs and both my sistas, Jamesha and Janita are there. I'm gonna make sho they go to that ass. Hell, Saul done help feed two generations of us Jones. She gonna have to pay for this shit."

"Hell even durin' the riots, no one touched Greenberg's Meats. Everybody knowed who ol' Saul was."

"I swear, it's this younger generation, runnnin' round here half high and half crazy. Mothafuckas just ain't got no respect for nobody, nowadays."

"I'm surprised Lacy didn't whip that ass. Saul was like a daddy to her. Put her through school and everything. Lacy need to get medieval on her ass."

"I think she's tryin' to. I don't know why they just don't let her go on and do the bitch and save us taxpayer's some dollars."

"Nigga what you talkin' about. Your corrupt ass ain't paid taxes long as I've known you and that's been damn near twenty years. You ain't never held a job long enough to pay taxes."

"Mother, fuck you!"

"I'm surprised them white cops ain't do a Rodney King on her ass. Don't worry. They get her ass behind closed doors she gonna wish she was Rodney King."

"What they ought to do is wait 'til tonight and drop her ass off in Bensonhurst or better yet drop her ass off over there in Crown Heights and let them Hassidics know what she done did. That's what they ought to do."

"For nine dollars and forty-three cents."

"What is the world coming to?"

I was numb. Physically and emotionally I was numb, frozen, unable to move. I'd heard it all but could not comprehend. The impact had been too great, too overwhelming. It left me standing there, synapses running short on enough electrical charges to meet the other and make sense of it all. But maybe that was the problem. No sense could be constructed, because there was nothing but fragments lying around, nothing but disjointed fragments of madness and here I was trying to collect the data, the random pieces in an attempt to find an answer when none existed.

And then it dawned on me that it was all just some sort of silly dream, or better yet, a nightmare. Yeah, that was it. It was a nightmare; it just had to be. I only wished that someone would pinch me so I could wake the hell up and make sense of this hellish dream.

It could've been the mixture of Jamaican meat patties, the Richard's and all that curry I kept sprinklin' on my food the other night at that little Turkish restaurant with Donna. I told her that I didn't want to eat there but she'd insisted and now look at me. Exotic foods often gave me spine-chilling nightmares of the worst sort causing me to scream out in my sleep. Somethin' about how the chemicals in the food interacted with the chemicals in your brain. I don't know the medical terminology but that had to be what was happening now.

The only problem was, was that I wasn't havin' the least bit of luck pulling out of it. When Sweet and Lacy found me much of the crowd had dispersed and I was still standing there staring at the chalk outlines where Saul's body had been.

I don't know how long I stood there with Lacy and Sweet on either side of me but I know I was still standing there when I heard Reverend Barnes whisper in my ear as he placed his hand firmly on my shoulder and said, "The Lord has taken him to a far better place than this, William."

I wanted to tell him to kiss my Black ass and show me the ticket stub that verifies the flight and destination time of Saul's arrival in a far better place but Monica approached me her eyes brimming over with tears and I forgot my anonymosity towards a God that would do this to such a fine man or the good reverend. Oh, the pain he must have felt. The questions he must have asked his God and mine as Anna Mae hit him over the head repeatedly with that metal bat.

My face must have bared my contempt because Monica took my head in her hands looked me straight in the eye and said, "William, often times we can not understand the Lord's ways. It is especially difficult in times of adversity. But then isn't adversity the only true test of our faith?"

And at that moment I wanted to hate her for being right when I felt so wronged but I could hardly move and so I followed her lead and when she told Lacy to take Sweet home and that I should follow her, I did as I was told.

After walking for what seemed like forever, lost in a multitude of thoughts that ranged from hatred to sorrow and then back to hatred Monica interrupted my senseless musings making an attempt to make light of the situation.

"It's a funny thing but Saul finally got up the nerve to ask me out to dinner after all these years."

"Better late than never I said not really in step with her musings."

"They say, he who waits is lost. That's what Saul used to tell me. And yet, for one reason or another, he chose to wait. But after this, it's pretty clear to me that there's no time to lose. So you, Mr. Longfellow will have to do. Besides you have some unfinished business to take care of and this time I refuse to take no for an answer. Now please do me a favor and go home and shower while I throw on something absolutely mouth watering for our picnic in the park. How's twelve thirty sound to you? Good! Twelve-thirty it is then. Oh, I'm sorry, I should have inquired. Did you have a previous engagement by any chance? Gosh I hope not. I would hate for you to have to break it. See you shortly, love."

One thing was for sure. Monica had not changed a bit. Oh there was a little pudginess where the love handles used to be. And now she was more like Quasi Moto in the Hunchback of Notre Dame than the tall stately African queen we all thought of her as long ago. The years have a way of doin' that to you. But on the day that Saul died she was never more beautiful. And I realized right then and there, as we walked hand in hand down 8th Avenue just as we had thirty years before that I wouldn't have traded in all of Monica's wisdom and elegance

297

in for a woman half her age and twice her beauty. She taught me something that day and it reminded me of something a friend had only recently told me.

He'd commented that, 'Just when I'm close to getting this thing called life down, just when I get to the point where I understand it's nuances, it's over'.

After showering for a good hour trying to wash away the filth and grime that was creeping into my Harlem playground, into my very life, into the pores of my soul, I realized that I could not and toweled off quickly, Saul's murder still quite fresh, still unbearably painful.

I wondered how Sweet was holding up and decided to stop by and check on him on my way to meet Monica. But after calling around trying to contact Saul's sister in Tom's River to see where the funeral arrangements were being held I was pleasantly surprised to find that he'd already prepared for this day and at his request his final service was to be held at the First Abyssinian Church of Jesus Christ. He had obviously been expecting this day for some time. However, his sister informed me that she had only just received the information following the appreciation day program on his behalf.

Seems Saul had spent the better part of the night talking to her about it and she had to admit that although she was one of the ones trying to persuade him to leave Harlem because of something just as this she doubted that he could have or would have met with the same joy he experienced there in Tom's River or anywhere else for that matter that he did in Harlem.

Hearing this warmed me through and through and suddenly I wasn't quite so angry anymore. When she ended by telling me that he'd left me a letter and forwarded a copy to his lawyer I was somewhat apprehensive and a little reluctant to say the least but my curiosity got the best of me so I asked her if she'd open it and read it to me which she promptly did. It was in the form of a will and I was quite surprised that he left me as custodian and executor of his will instead of his sister. However, it soon became evident why when he referred to me as being more than a bit frugal and bordering on the line of being tight.

I had to laugh at this but Saul knew the truth. Saul knew that I knew the value of a dollar and he respected this. But as she read it I had to laugh when he made certain references. For example, all meat should be herewith given to the ladies' auxiliary of the First Abyssinian Couch of Jesus Christ that is except for the prime cuts of the leg of lamb which should be given to my good friend Monica

298

since she so adored that particular cut of meat. Again I had to laugh out loud and I'm sure his sister must have thought I was crazy but I knew that Saul even in death hadn't given up on tryin' to woo Monica. He was probably just softening her up for his power move in the afterlife.

The store itself was to be given to Lacy who as he put it would probably do a better job of running it than he had. To Sweet he left the rather tidy sum of five thousand dollars, his entire life savings, when and only when Sweet came to his senses in the whole Wilomena matter. If, however, Sweet did not come to the realization of the error of his ways within the next five years the moneys were then to be donated in an equal split with half going to his favorite charity, the ladies' auxiliary, and the other dispersed by Reverend Barnes where he deemed it was most needed in the community. To me he left his most current bill of seven hundred and ninety-four dollars and sixty-three cents for his meat order and every other bill to follow until Lacy had the store in the black and could afford to foot the bill herself. This he did, the letter stated since I was always bragging about how I could have been Lacy's father. And these he commented were just some of the responsibilities of fatherhood which I had up until now neglected.

The letter brought a warm chill through me and erased the cold eerie feeling that I'd begun associating with my home, my harem, my Harlem and as I hung up the phone to step out into the cold, brisk fall air trapped between the tenement buildings I realized that Harlem hadn't really changed all that much. I had.

Saul was gone but Sweet was still there as well as Monica and Lacy. Every community had its Anna Mae's waiting in the cut, preying on some unsuspecting innocent. But she didn't define my home no more than the rats and the roaches did or the politicians that we never saw that claimed they represented us. Anna Mae was no more my Harlem than the hookers who roamed the streets while decent folk slept. They were all a part of what Harlem was but they didn't define us.

We, the good hard working folks who struggled everyday against the odds, we were what Harlem was all about. People like the good Reverend Barnes and Sweet and Lacy and Saul and Monica, and all the good, common decent folk. That was Harlem. My Harlem. My home.

The funeral services were held as Saul requested, with a Jewish rabbi speaking of the kinship in our plights as people and then Reverend Barnes put on one of

299

his more stirring sermons heralding the brotherhood of man in spite of our human frailties and the adversities which we face everyday of our lives.

He was so moving that for a brief moment I found myself thinking of Dr. King's infamous, I Have A Dream speech. Okay, maybe he didn't quite reach that mark but for once even ol' Sister Gerty looked like she was ready to drop a tear or two. Well, maybe not but not once did she interrupt while the good reverend was speaking. That in itself speaks volumes. Knowing Saul, he'd probably sent Sister Gerty a letter too, asking her to please refrain from any outbursts demanding that the reverend cease preaching, after all 'this is my final, my last best chance to get into the kingdom of heaven and from what I hear the lines are not only long but I hear it's overbooked too.'

The funeral had standing room only and there were even such notables in attendance as the deputy mayor, a city councilman and the borough president. Since none of them knew Saul personally, I'm assuring they were only there for political reasons like crying out against senseless inner-city violence and to quell any potential reprisals that might make it difficult to retain office since it was an election year. Still, it was quite a moving service and reminded me of a New Orleans funeral, though I've never been to one. Overall, it was a happy occasion in spite of our loss.

Even more surprising was how subdued the congregation was. There was no hollerin' and cryin' and carrying on. Well, that is except for Sweet who was really having a difficult time coming to grips with the untimely death of our good friend. And of course, Wilomena who screamed loud enough for them to hear her in all five boroughs and probably Jersey too. Saul would have enjoyed the show she put on for Sweet. She was certainly intent on letting someone know that her man's pain was hers as well. Either that or she was working on that new fur I'd seen her eyeing earlier in the week in Bloomingdale's.

To be honest, Saul and I had both been amazed that Sweet and Wilomena's marriage had lasted this long. But there was no time; even after twenty some odd years did we think that it would last beyond whatever particular day it was at the time. Not that I've ever parlayed in rumors but they'd surfaced rather regularly since day one.

From time-to-time, I would see Wilomena during the day out on the street, (although I made sure that she didn't see me), when Sweet was at work. She'd be flirting with this guy or that, though it was mostly with the young thugs that hung around the entrance to her building. I thought nothin' of it since they were plying their trade and trying to recruit potential customers they could get hooked on that crack. I always knew Wilomena was way too smart for that so I ignored it and as had become my custom, I paid her no mind whatsoever. But I still kept an eye on her 'cause I always felt there was somethin' about a woman who saw nothing wrong with her husband working not one but two jobs while she sat at home doing nothin' but watching court TV all day.

And although I saw less and less of Sweet during that time, he would, on occasion stop in to Saul's to say hello and pick up some chicken wings or maybe a pound of ground beef for that night's dinner. And me and Saul would both be wonderin' why Wilomena, with all the time she had on her hands couldn't have picked it up and prepared his dinner for him before he got home. This is before Saul died, mind you. Anyway, that just made sense to us. It made more sense than for him to have to come home, prepare dinner, shower, change his clothes and rush right back out the door to his second gig where he worked as a night-time security guard up in the Bronx somewhere around Yankee Stadium.

Half the time, he'd be in such a rush that he'd call Saul and leave a message for me to pick up his uniform from the cleaners so that he wouldn't have to wait in line and be late for his second job. After awhile, I just took it upon myself to pick it up automatically. And every time I did I would ask myself why in the hell Wilomena couldn't see fit to take time out of her busy schedule and cross the damn street and pick up Sweet's uniform herself.

One day I was running a bit late myself and was supposed to meet my friend, Donna, (you know, the one from Workmen's Comp), for dinner when it dawned on me that tonight being Friday and payday and all, the cleaners would be jam packed with Black folks tryin' to get their party clothes and they're goin' to meetin' clothes out and the line would be a mile long. And I knew that Sweet would be dependin' on me as always to pick up his uniform and rushin' so he wouldn't be late for work.

Of course, Saul would have his dinner order ready. Fridays were usually T-bone steak night in the Sweet household and Sweet would always invite us over but as Saul couldn't stomach red meat and I couldn't stomach Wilomena we always deferred.

Anyway, on this particular night, I was running quite late myself when it dawned on me that I hadn't picked up Sweet's uniform. Luckily, Mr. Lee, in anticipation had it hanging up and ready to go when I got there and knowing that I was in a rush told me to pay him on Monday and let it go at that. I was truly glad since the line was out the door and spilling over onto the sidewalk. Still and all, I have this thing about punctuality and just felt that this little sidestep had thrown me way behind and I certainly didn't want to mess up my chances with Donna the way I had been feeling lately. The subway being on the opposite side of the street and right in front of Sweet's building was a blessing in disguise so being that I was in a hurry I decided it best to drop his uniform off with that no-account Wilomena.

Now I've made it a point, all my life, never to go to a married couple's house when the man of the house is not at home whether he be a close friend or not. More often than not it's innocent, but why take the chance of a jealous husband or boyfriend misconstruing something and causing a whole lot of unnecessary drama about nothing. That's why I don't go. I don't want nobody to ever get the wrong impression about my intentions. After all, there's too many hungry, starvin' women in search of a good man for me to be pushin' up on somebody else's woman.

However, this particular evening was different. I think I've mentioned it before but anytime I make a decision without giving it some considerable thought no matter how insignificant the situation may seem at the time, it has always caused me an inexorbitant amount of grief in the long run. And of course, this time proved no different.

I'd seen Wilomena entering the vestibule to her building no more than an half an hour before so I knew she was home. In any event, and for some unknown reason, I didn't think to use the intercom and call before entering the building and forewarning her of my arrival. Instead I squeezed in behind ol' lady Biggs who held the door for me. I then hit the stairs running at such a pace that by the time I hit the sixth floor landing I was so out of breath that I had to pause not once but twice to catch my breath. First at the porthole in the door that led to the long hallway of identical steel doors and then after entering the hallway I paused again gasping for a few more deep swallows of air and who should I see but Wilomena locked up with some long rangy fella that looked like he could have very well played for the New York Knickerbockers.

All the while, I'm standing there, mouth open, transfixed on the couple, unable to move, avert my gaze or clear my throat to let them be aware of my presence before anything else should or could transpire. Dumbfounded, I watched as she tried to push him away with a playful shove that said, 'please don't stop, I love the attention.'

In the meantime, he groped at her breasts, lightheartedly with one hand while he wrapped the other tightly around her and drew her nearer to him before kissing her both deeply and passionately. Again, she pushed him away but this time she was much more adamant in her denial though she still flashed a deep, earthly smile that begged for more.

"Stop it now!" Wilomena screamed, loud enough for the whole damn floor to hear pushing the large sinewy man towards the elevator where ol' Lady Biggs was just now getting off. Ignoring the old woman, she said, "You know Sweet's due in anytime. Shall we say the same time Monday?"

"Sounds good to me," the playa stated. "If anything comes up, just holla. You've got my cell number, don't you?" he questioned never even glancing back towards her or me who was still standing there amazed at the utter gall of this two bit 'ho.

Turning to go back into her apartment Wilomena's mouth dropped when she saw me standing there at the far end of the hall. You could see that her women's intuition let her know that I'd seen it all, the panic so clearly obvious in her face. Eons passed before either of us could bring ourselves to put an end to the uncomfortable silence that had suddenly enveloped the long hallway. Finally, I made my way towards her remembering the reason I was here and handed her the suit of clothing. Only then did she speak.

"You won't mention any of this will you William?" she asked pleading.

I shook my head indicating that I wouldn't although I can't to this day recollect where the words came from. And then as if out of dense fog in the early hours of morning I heard a voice say almost apologetically.

"Trust me, Wilomena, I would never ever do anything to hurt Sweet."

And with that said, I turned briskly and walked away, leaving her standing there in the hallway, in front of Apartment 6-B, wondering. It was the last time I saw Wilomena.

Now according to Saul, most women caught in such a compromising situation or

303

position would run as far away as possible if no other reason than to hide their shame. But if there was an area where Saul had some rather blatant deficiencies it had to be women and in particular Black women. And not just Black women, for Saul came across many good, strong, hard-working Black women doing their able-bodied best to strive to maintain and feed their kids and often times their grandchildren as well. No, where Saul's deficiencies came was not with Black women in general but the low-down, no good, lazy shiftless exploitative sistas who seemed to be always schemin' on new ways to lay around until they found just the right prey, just the right sugar-daddy to take care of their every whim, their every mindless, miniscule fantasy; prostitutin' themselves, using sex like a promissory note to entice men to purchase whatever it was they fancied on that particular day. We called them gold diggers and Saul knew nothing about these back alley vermin that preyed upon good Black men. Still, I wasn't so much angry with Wilomena as I was at Sweet for not recognizing what we all did, so long ago.

But I believe I truly believe Saul's death changed all that and Sweet seemed almost morose in the days following the funeral. I'd seen him only once or twice since then as I was once again firmly under Monica's spell and spent many a day taking long unabbreviated walks in the park and finding excuses to meet her at odd hours of the day to bring her chocolates and flowers and anything else that I thought would please her senses.

I even went so far as to have a phone installed so I could talk to her until the wee hours of the morning like adolescents that have just come to the realization that there is an opposite sex. I even thought about getting hitched once or twice but quickly dispelled that notion when I recalled the trauma I went through the last time I'd asked her to marry me. But, on the whole, it was still nice to be in Monica's company even though at times she could be somewhat overbearing. But with Saul's untimely demise she more than made up for the void with her rather poignant chatter. And I guess with Lacy out of the house I suppose I filled a space in her life as well.

Spending most of my days at Monica's now or she at mine, (that is when she got to feeling the urge), which I must say was becoming more and more frequent, I noticed that my attitude towards life and things in general weren't the only ones that changed. And Lacy, who was quite observant and certainly no dummy, surprised both of us one day by my making the comment about her mother's rapidly improving health and how I must be prescribing just the right kind of medicine because she hadn't seen her mother that spry or that chipper in a month of Sundays. The remark caught us both off guard but I had to agree. Well, that is, I don't know exactly how Monica was feeling but I was certainly having a rebirth of sorts. Anyhow, we both fell out laughing at the remark.

By this time, I'd pretty much given up my office, opting at this juncture in my life for a sort of semi-retirement, if there is such a thing in my line of work.

You see being a street corner anthropologist has a tendency, (I don't know if I've mentioned this), to spill over into other dominions such as philosophy and sociology if you get my drift so although I was not necessarily practicing in my area of expertise at the time of Saul's death, I was still a very needed and very valuable commodity in Harlem's growth or at least I would like to think I was.

You see a street corner anthropologist is in a rather unique position since the science of anthropology is not what you would refer to as an exact science and more often than not it may share boundaries with sociological aspects of man's being and many times I am, (because of my expertise), lured into this very vague, very gray area to shed some light on other aspects of Harlem life as well because the community respects my rather learned opinion.

In any case, because of that fact I don't know that I'll ever really enjoy a full retirement but for now I am pretty much out of the loop, thanks in large part to Saul's death and to a lesser degree Monica's timely intervention. Saul's death had the profound effect of letting me know that the more I knew the less I understood which is in itself a topic for a rather lengthy dissertation. Don't know if I tol' you this and I suppose I have but I think it bears repeating and especially at my age. In any case, he said that now that he's gotten this thing called life down to a point where he almost understands what it's all about, it's almost over. Well, in response to his comments I would have to say that my life has been the converse. You see the older I get and the more information I receive the less I know that I know and understand. Right now with Saul's death I'm at a loss. What seemed so logical before hardly makes sense anymore and so I almost feel compelled to take a break.

Now don't get me wrong, I'm not quitting or bowing out if that's what you think I'm suggestin'. No siree, buddy. I'm just takin'a break is all. Monica says I'm takin' a break every time I lift the bottle of Rose to my lips but then she's never understood our relationship and never will. Actually, I think she's always been just a lil' bit jealous of our relationship, me and Rose that is but I never let it get in the way of us or anything I do for   that matter.

305

But, anyways getting' back to the point I was tryin' to make. I gave up my office space between Ortega's Bodega and Saul's Meat market simply because I feel no real compulsion to go out there into the blinding chaos anymore unless it's to grab a half pint. All the senseless violence is just too far beyond my comprehension. And I suppose the proximity to Saul's doesn't help any either but in all actuality my research was all but completed before Saul was killed and I'd been contemplating retirement long before Saul's death. In reality, I saw no real need to continue to accumulate any more data until I could process and disseminate the countless volumes already cluttering up my mainframe.

Besides, the streets weren't really changing. They were as they had always been, cold and hard. That was Harlem. And with winter coming, people were already beginning to hunker down searching for a warm fire or a heated flat or some young gal to keep 'em warm until the chill broke. So, as you can see this was my slow season and there wasn't nothin' much going on anyway. Well, almost nothin'...

The word on the street was that the good Reverend Barnes, finally gave in to that little red floozy that useta always be sweatin' him. You know the one that useta sit in the front row with that dress up to her tutu like she had just come in from Club Candlelight or somethin'. I can't recall her name and don't really know her real well but I see her around from time-to-time.

When I first noticed her she had me attending' church and wishin' I had chosen the ministry or at least been a deacon so I could be somewhere near the pulpit for no other reason than I could get a decent view of those thighs. I'm tellin' you the gal was hot, red-hot, blazin' and I don't know 'bout the rest of them ol' church goin', do-right men but she kept somethin' stirred up in this ol' heathen soul.

Anyway, the way I hear it tol' a month or so after the good Reverend Barnes had lost Diamond, his fiancée, to some illness here comes this heifer to comfort the good reverend in his time of mourning. They tell me she had plans for him long before that though and that was the reason she useta wear those dresses like that was to entice the reverend into leavin' Diamond for her skank ass. But from what I hear, she didn't stand a chance. You see Diamond wasn't just beautiful. She was bright and sophisticated too. Kinda like my Monica. You know with an air about her that just separated her from the rest of the crowd.

Besides that the reverend and Diamond was truly in love like no two people

306

you'd ever wanna meet. So, anyway, to make a long short story, she come strollin' by like all the good church ladies did to see the reverend in his time of need, he grievin' over the sudden loss of his loved one and she brings him dinner once or twice and he bein' pretty innocent and a man of the cloth and all he don't see nothin' wrong with the gesture. But when the other ladies leave that night she made it a point to hang around the reverend's apartment to help him clean up and wash all that Tupperware and bring it to the ladies on the following Sunday. And Lord did she ever clean up. They say the reverend had been sippin' more than a little wine that evenin' you know tryin' to compensate for his loss and all and before you know it he was asleep in his easy chair. And bein' the Good Samaritan that she was she just naturally undressed him and helped tuck him in. Now why those ol' buzzards from the ladies auxiliary left him with this hyena I'll never know unless they was just short of some gossip for the week. But from what they tell me, ol' girl did more than just tuck the good reverend in—and well—man of the cloth or no man of the cloth, the fact remains that the good reverend is still a man and knowing this, ol' girl took advantage of his grief and his weakness.

Now the rumor is she's got one in the oven as we speak. No one knows for sure if it's the good reverend's or not but if it is, (and in all likelihood it is if since the Lord Jesus himself would have a hard resistin' all that temptation), anyway, like I was sayin', if it is and he don't marry her quick and in a hurry, (which is what she wanted all along), the good reverend's career at the First Abyssinian Church of Christ is all but history. It's a cryin' shame too.

I've known Reverend Barnes for years and the reverend's a good man. I mean he's like all of us. He's got his human frailties but the people hold him in such high esteem that when he falters, when he acts human and makes a mistake, that's it for him. He's signed his own death warrant. After all, most of them old sisters look at him like he's the Second Coming. I think sometimes they forget that he's a man just like the rest of us. But then I guess when you assume the position of the Almighty's spokesperson then that comes with the territory. That's why when I was younger and considerin' career choices I pushed that one to the side early on. Though I think I would have made a pretty good preacha' I knew I could never overcome my fondness for the ladies. Hell, I probably wouldn't have lasted the month. Well, anyway all the gossip is just that, gossip, mindless chatter provided as usual commercial free, non-stop and uninterrupted by the ladies auxiliary.

Moments later, Lacy burst through the door of the old brick, brownstone, her shoulders heaving convulsively. So vivid and distraught her image that I can remember it almost as if it were yesterday. Monica and I were sitting there in the parlor on either side of that old Sear's Victrola, comfortable, simply content to be in each other's presence listening to Ella scat away about a 'tisket and a tasket' and I was thinking that maybe I was wrong after all. That maybe this was the way life was supposed to be after all.

Monica was sitting there knitting an afghan to replace my ol' torn bedspread and I was sitting there once again a victim of one of her spells holding a ball of yellow yarn between two outstretched hands when, like I said, Lacy stormed into the house screaming.

"Oh, mama! Oh God, mama! I can't take it, mama! Lord knows I just can't take no more of this!

Monica, as was her way, rose from the chair slowly, wrapped her arms around her daughter and whispered gently.

"Talk to me. Tell me Lacy. What's wrong girl? What's happened now?"

Lacy looked at me and then lowered her eyes, letting her teardrops fall to the faded pink carpet below.

"It's Sweet," she mumbled faintly, her voice always so strong and vibrant was now distant and muffled.

I was on my feet now, wondering what in God's name could possibly go wrong now. It had been one tough week with Saul's passing and all and I had to ask myself what else could go wrong now. I thought about myself. Thought about those that surrounded me. I thought about the Harlem that I called my home.

Oh, vibrant Harlem that I loved more than any woman. I thought about the Harlem of my youth. It seemed like it was all but gone now, crumbling before my very eyes. Sure, there still remained some of the beautiful people, the hardworking stiffs like Saul and Sweet that made Harlem go round. But even their lives had become chock full of tragedy and misery through no apparent fault of their own. And whatever it is that plagued us was now befalling us as well.

"What about Sweet?" I heard myself yell, panicking and losing any remnant of composure.

"What about him?"

No more could I stand back, apart, aloof, content to just sit and observe the goings on from a distant that made Harlem so distinct and foreign and yet so close that it was now as much apart of me as my very soul. Like it or not I could no longer stand back and choose to be objective as the world spun crazily out of control. I could no longer see a world through Rose tinted glasses and pretend that I was omniscient observing from afar. Somehow, I'd been dragged in to the melee kicking and screaming against my will. Despite my screaming fits and protests I was being drawn into the madness I had fought so hard to keep myself apart from. And now, and only because I'd somehow allowed my guard to drop I was feeling the same pitiful anguish, the same desperation Harlem had been feeling for years.

First Saul and now…

"What's happened to Sweet, Lacy?" I repeated.

The comfort Monica provided her daughter at this time of need was if nothing else inspiring and I took some comfort in it as well. If nothing else it allowed her to work through her grief enough o at least let me know what had happened to my boy.

Lacy sensing my anxiety, took my hand in hers just as her mother had done and led me back to the Queen Anne chair in the corner of the tiny parlor and had me sit before kneeling before me. I knew it was bad then as I watched the tears flow freely down her golden brown cheeks.

"Whatever it is Lacy darlin', it can't be half as bad as you're letting on," I said hoping that my attempts at consoling her would at least comfort her and me as well. I'd long ago come to understand that no matter how bad things seemed they could always be worse.

"William," Lacy started almost apologetically, "Sweet came home from work today and…"

It then dawned on me that I'd forgotten o pick up his uniform and it was then that I became apologetic but before I could venture to say anything she continued.

"They laid him off from the docks today. After thirty-three years, they laid him off."

Damn! So that was it. I emitted a long deep sigh of relief and wondered why in the hell I let women affect me so. They were an emotional lot to say the least, who cried over the drop of a hat. Yet, I expected more from Lacy who dealt with the seamier side of life on a daily basis and I was sure that if anyone was immune to the hardships of life it would be her and then I looked again and was forced to laugh. When it came down to it she was still a woman.

Hell, people were being laid off everyday. With the shape of the economy that was almost a given nowadays. And you had to be a fool in this day and age if you didn't have a couple of IRA's or some stock invested somewhere for just such an occasion. And any Negro that had gone through and survived the Depression as Sweet and I had was well prepared or at least should have been prepared for hard times. You can bet your hard earned money on that. Of course, Sweet had Wilomena and Wilomena had Sweet's nose wide open so if he did have any savings chances are it was damn well near gone with her unconscionable weekly shopping sprees. But with the money I put aside for him over the years he had absolutely nothing to worry about and I was even kind of glad in a way that I could now give something back to the man who had saved my neck on more than one occasion. Besides with Sweet just working one job again we could hang out again like we did back in the old days. So, I hardly understood what all the crying was about. And I was certain that Wilomena would leave once she found out Sweet couldn't give her anything and everything her little greedy eyes came across. And I still had Saul's money to ease the pain of her leaving which if my prediction held true had probably already occurred. Boy, how I wish Saul could have been alive to witness this little twist of fate.

My smile must have thrown Lacy for a loop as she took a long pause before continuing. But it didn't matter. I was almost ready to jump from the chair and bust out the door when Lacy grabbed my hand quite firmly and said, "No! William don't go. There's more. You see William, Sweet was laid off at lunchtime today so he came home early and found Wilomena in bed with not one but two men. After losing his job and all and then coming home to something like that I guess he just lost   it.

310

I wasn't the first one on the scene but from what I gathered he beat Wilomena senseless and then threw her off the balcony. That's six floors and she's still alive. From what I understand from the EMS workers, she's in critical condition but somehow she's still managing to hang on. They say both of her legs were broken as well as her collarbone and right arm. That's all they could tell at a glance before they drove off but a fall from six stories up and you know she's got multiple fractures as well as some internal bleeding. They say her chances are slim at best. I'm pretty sure they rushed her to St. Luke's Trauma Center but I haven't gotten any word updating her condition as of yet. God, I hope nothin' happens to that poor misguided chile," Lacy mumbled the last part the tears flowing freely once again.

"And Sweet? Tell me about Sweet, Lacy."

She was stammerin, doing her best to get the broken words out between the sobs.

"Sweet beat both men within an inch of their lives then tied them both up in the kitchen and shot them at point blank range killing both of 'em."

"And Sweet. How is Sweet, Lacy? Have they booked him yet? As soon as they book him and he has his arraignment you let me know and I'll post his bail. What time is it anyway? And see if you can get an idea of what kind of bail we're looking at? My God! I knew I should have stopped the whole sh-bang before it ever got started. I knew that girl was no-good from day one. I always said she was no damn good. Damn! I don't know why I let Saul talk me out of it. I should have never listened to Saul. What the hell does he know about women? And Sweet, Sweet needs his ass kicked for fuckin' with her dumb ass in the first place. Damn! Wasn't nothin' ever there but a big butt and a smile. How the hell could he be so stupid? Good Lord what have they done to my boy?" I asked no one in particular.

"Love does funny things to some people," Monica whispered.

I was at the front door when Lacy grabbed my hand and led me back to the parlor. I followed though not really cognizant of where I was and found myself being once again being seated in the same chair as before. 'My God! Why were they doing this to me?' There was nothing I could possibly do to help Sweet by sitting there and yet I was unable to move. I hardly knew what to d or what course I should take but I had to do something. Anything. Right then and there,

311

I felt like everything was just welling up inside of me and my chest wanted to give to the pressure ballooning inside. And I was pretty sure that if I sat there another minute I was going to explode. Taking a deep breath with the hopes of calming myself I had this feeling that I was drowning in a sea of tragedy and only now wished that I had taken those swimming lessons they'd offered me during my time in the army but this was a different kind of drowning. Or was it?

I was so confused, so utterly lost and I knew that at that moment that if the tables were turned then that Negro with the slow southern drawl from somewhere deep down in Georgia would have known exactly what to do under the circumstances.

I took another deep breath hoping it would clear my head so I could gather my thoughts and try to act appropriately in the face of all the drama. But again Lacy pushed me back. I explained to her that a breath of cold air was what I sorely needed in order to sort this whole thing out and proceed logically. Looking into Monica's eyes and then Lacy's was like looking into a mirror and I could see my own pain in her eyes as clear as day. For my pain was theirs and because they loved me they shared my grief willingly.

I was thinking now. I was using the tools of my trade, the scientific method that has always aided me in all my years in the streets. It was actually all very simple and came down to no more than a little deductive reasoning once the initial shock had passed and I'd regained my composure a bit and began the slow methodical process of sorting things out logically before directing a slew of questions for the police officer and law student in front of me.

"The judge should be a little lenient considering the circumstances shouldn't he?" I asked Lacy.

"I mean a man loses his job one minute and returns home the next to find his wife of twenty years in bed with not just one as you put it Lace but two men. The way I see it the judge can't be anything but understanding. The way I see it it's simply a case of temporary insanity any way you look at it."

Everything was coming into focus now and although I realized that tying up two men and executing was cold and calculated, making the shootings premeditated, was there a man in the world aside from the good Lord Jesus that might not have done the same thing and acted the same way under similar circumstances? It was plain as day but before I had everything in proper perspective there was Lacy again taking my hands in hers again.

"William," Lacy interrupted. I refused to let her continue. After all she was talking about what was. And all that was in the past. I was moving forward to what needed to happen. My only thoughts were of freeing my friend, my brother. My God, how much happier he would have been plowing row after row in that old torn-down, beat up vineyard over in France but it was I that had talked him out of it t come back here to this. At least as he put it he had for the first time in his life felt 'free'. Now despite all my efforts he was certainly going to lose the little freedom he had for some years to come. And for what?

My thoughts still scattered I calculated the time now that Sweet faced. The best lawyers in the world wouldn't be able to get him off Scott-free, not with a triple homicide regardless of the motives. But then again Sweet was a war hero. He'd received the Purple Heart and the Silver Star or something or another for valor that praised him for all the good killing he'd done and he'd never had even a minor brush with the law. I was sure a good lawyer could plea the charges against him down to a few years, maybe three or four maybe even two on the grounds of temporary insanity. That was the best case scenario and in the end it didn't look half bad considering all so I had a hard time understanding Lacy's tears since I knew she had a much better analytical mind than I would ever have and to top it off she knew the law. Was there something that I was overlooking?

It was then that it occurred to me that there was no one better to represent Sweet than Lacy. It hadn't been too long ago that she'd passed the bar and of course she would have Sweet's best interest at heart more so than some counsel who didn't know him at all. But when I asked and she rejected the idea without so much as giving it a second thought.

I was more than a little hurt to say the least. She was saying something but so dismayed was I by her dismissal that I simply grabbed my hat and coat and headed for the door. It was obvious that she knew I was disgusted with the way she'd responded.

"William, you don't understand. You must know that there's nothing in the world that I wouldn't do for you or Sweet but unfortunately there is nothing that I can do in this situation. Don't you see William? After Sweet shot those two men he turned the gun on himself and took his own life."

313

Never in a million years would I have believed something like this and I didn't believe it when she told me but the look in her eyes and the pain that flowed with each tear told me that the Lacy I watched grow from a toddler to a strong young, tender caring woman would never, could never have played such a cruel joke on an old man such as I. As much as I wanted to believe that there was more to the story there wasn't.

Over and over I repeated, "Not Sweet. Please tell me you're lyin'. Please tell me that Sweet didn't do that. Not Sweet!"

Not Sweet who cherished each second of each minute of each passing day the way a single ray of sun cherishes the rose petal and finds its way despite the clouds and rain that attempt to hinder its way.

Not my boy, Sweet who worked hard every day not just to insure his own happiness but the happiness of everyone around him. No, the Sweet I know would never have done such a thing, something so goddamn selfish. Not the Sweet who was so content to be the butt of a joke if it made those around him laugh.

No, I did not know this man they were now describing to me but then come to think of it I didn't know the Sweet who mowed down those Germans so methodically, so systematically, day in and day out for the better part of a year just outside of Paris and was so good at it that they awarded him medals for going over and beyond the call of duty. And he never, not once spoke a word of it or ever showed that it affected him in anyway.

I didn't know that man and I didn't know this man that left me today to fend for myself and carry Harlem's burdens alone. And so it is with Sweet's death that I have become so full of grief and horror and pain that not even Rose can numb the sadness.

And so it with Sweet's death that I've decided to abandon my research with massive amounts of data collected on a subject that I must confess I can hardly decipher or understand. I feel that it is beyond me to come to any reasonable conclusions. In fact, I would even go so far as to venture to say that in all honesty that I know less about my people than I did when I first started my study fifty years ago. And since I am growing both old and weary trying to make sense of it all I guess it's time for someone a bit younger and a bit wiser to pick up the baton and run the last leg of this race in my stead. That is the decision that I have ultimately come to.

In the meantime, I've just purchased a lil' three bedroom home out on the island not far from Montauk Point where I can sit back and watch the waves break against the uneven shoreline and play dominoes and dream of the Harlem of Jackie and Duke and Billie and Miles and Sweet and Saul. And when I get bored with that, I can take a walk along the same uneven shoreline and maybe if the coast is clear then just maybe I can sneak a sip or two since Monica has forbidden me from imbibing even though she knows how I love my Rose.

Oh, I didn't tell you. Monica must have increased the potency on one of her voodoo spells 'cause through some chicanery she convinced me to take her hand in marriage just last month.

APR - - 2013

CPSIA information can be obtained at www.ICGtesting.com
Printed in the USA
LVOW081640260313

326142LV00003B/411/P

9 781482 359336